Alison Roberts has been  South of France for severa... back in her home country ... lucky enough to write for th... line. A primary school teacher in a former ... later became a qualified paramedic. She loves to travel and dance, drink champagne and spend time with her daughter and her friends. Alison Roberts is the author of over 100 books!

Cursed with a poor sense of direction and a propensity to read, **Annie Claydon** spent much of her childhood lost in books. A degree in English Literature followed by a career in computing didn't lead directly to her perfect job—writing romance for Mills & Boon—but she has no regrets in taking the scenic route. She lives in London: a city where getting lost can be a joy.

THE DOCTOR'S CHRISTMAS HOMECOMING

ALISON ROBERTS

SNOWBOUND WITH HER OFF-LIMITS GP

ANNIE CLAYDON

MILLS & BOON

First published in Great Britain 2022
by Mills & Boon, an imprint of HarperCollins*Publishers* Ltd,
1 London Bridge Street, London, SE1 9GF

www.harpercollins.co.uk

HarperCollins*Publishers*
1st Floor, Watermarque Building,
Ringsend Road, Dublin 4, Ireland

The Doctor's Christmas Homecoming © 2022 Alison Roberts

Snowbound with Her Off-Limits GP © 2022 Annie Claydon

ISBN: 978-0-263-30141-0

10/22

MIX
Paper from
responsible sources
FSC C007454

This book is produced from independently certified FSC™ paper
to ensure responsible forest management.
For more information visit www.harpercollins.co.uk/green.

Printed and Bound in Spain using 100% Renewable Electricity
at CPI Black Print, Barcelona

THE DOCTOR'S
CHRISTMAS
HOMECOMING

ALISON ROBERTS

MILLS & BOON

CHAPTER ONE

'THAT SHOULDN'T HAVE HAPPENED. It was so unprofessional. I'm really sorry…'

Big blue eyes were filling with tears and Dr Matilda Dawson felt her heart sink another notch as she pulled a handful of tissues from the box and held them out. Night shift in a busy big city emergency department could be a challenge at any time. In the final run-up to Christmas, at the peak of silly season, it could be absolute chaos.

Everything had been under control until now—apart from having been unable to return a second missed call from her father, which was enough to make Tilly wonder if something had gone wrong with the plan for her to spend Christmas Day with her only family member. An opportunity to make a quick call had been ambushed, however, when Tilly had observed a junior nurse struggling to cope with the relatively simple task of taking an ECG on a patient who'd come in with chest pain.

Tilly had had no choice but to divert another nurse to do the ECG and whisk a clearly very unhappy young staff member into this office space to find out what the problem was. They couldn't afford to have people on the front line who were distracted enough to be unable to function efficiently.

'I'll pull myself together.' The nurse, Charlotte, blew her nose and then sniffed decisively. 'Honestly, this is stupid. I'm twenty-one. It's not as if I haven't been dumped before but...'

Oh, no... Tilly could see someone over Charlotte's shoulder, walking past the open door of this office. Someone who was smiling at her. The someone who'd apparently just broken Charlotte's heart.

'Merry almost Christmas,' he said, in that adorable Irish accent that would have captured any woman's attention if, inexplicably, the smile hadn't already done the trick.

Tilly glared at him. This is *your* fault, was the silent message. You should be ashamed of yourself, Harry Doyle.

'This is entirely *my* fault,' Charlotte said, as if Tilly had spoken aloud. Her voice was wobbling as she turned her head to see Harry's back. 'He told me, right from the start. He said he'd go to the concert I had an extra ticket for but it would only be as a friend. It wasn't a date or anything. But it *felt* like a date... And I really thought he might be the *one*...you know?'

'Yeah...' Tilly's tone was a little grim. She knew. 'Why did it feel like a date?' she asked cautiously. 'He didn't try and—'

'Oh, no,' Charlotte said hurriedly, shaking her head. 'Not at all. He didn't even try to kiss me goodnight afterwards.'

She sounded deeply disappointed and Tilly felt suddenly weary. Was Charlotte so innocent she didn't realise that making herself so available could have had a very different outcome? One that could haunt her for years to come?

'You must have been aware that he's been out with almost every single woman in this hospital, and that's quite an achievement when he's only been here for a few months.'

Okay, so that was a bit of an exaggeration, but Tilly had had him pegged from the moment she'd been introduced to him and had been the recipient of *that* smile, along with a gleam that could only be described as flirtatious in those distinctive, smoky grey-blue eyes. Harry Doyle might have come with very good professional references but, on a personal level, he was a player. A good-looking Irish rogue who could use his not inconsiderable charm to rule the world and everyone in it.

Apart from Tilly, of course.

'I know. But then you think that it might be different this time. That you might be the one *they've* been looking for all along.' Charlotte took a deep breath. 'Sorry,' she said again. 'I'm fine, really. It won't be a problem. I need to get back to my patients.'

Tilly could see her scanning the department as they walked towards the central hub. Bright red and green cardboard letters stuck to the front of the desk welcomed patients with the seasonal Maori greeting of *Meri Kirihimete* and there was a tiny, unobtrusive Christmas tree on one end of the counter, wrapped in silver tinsel with a star on top. There were two ambulance crews waiting for the triage nurse to decide where the new patients could go and some junior doctors and medical students were focused on computer screens to check past medical records or look for X-ray or laboratory results.

A cleaner, wearing a cheerful Santa hat, was mopping the floor nearby and a technician was humming a Christmas carol as he pushed a trolley past. Tilly could see that Harry was standing beside the patient who'd required the detailed ECG as part of the process of investigating whether his chest pain might be a symptom of a heart attack.

Charlotte had seen Harry as well and Tilly could almost feel her brushing off her earlier despair. She was smiling now. Almost beaming, in fact, as she caught Tilly's gaze.

'It's Christmas,' she said, as if she realised her dramatic mood change might need an explanation. 'And you never know… Miracles *can* happen.'

Harry could see Charlotte coming towards him from the corner of his eye but he didn't look away from his patient.

'Can you describe this pain for me?'

'It was like being kicked by a horse. Right here.' The man put his hand over the left side of his chest.

'So it came on suddenly? What were you doing?'

'I had a crate of beer in the basement. Couple of dozen. I was bringing them in to put in the fridge because we've got a barbecue tomorrow, but I had to stop when I was only halfway up the steps. I couldn't breathe, Doc, and then it hit me. *Wham*… My missus had to call an ambulance because I couldn't move, the pain was so bad I felt sick and I got all sweaty, but they got there really fast.'

Harry nodded. Telling the emergency services that a middle-aged man had severe chest pain, nausea and sweating *would* get an ambulance on the way very quickly. The paramedics had taken an ECG that was normal, however, and a repeat one done when he'd arrived in the department didn't show any abnormalities. The patient report form the paramedic team had completed stated no medical history of any cardiac or other major health problems either.

Charlotte came into the cubicle with an apologetic smile. 'I'm so sorry I had to dash off like that, Gerald,' she said. 'But I'm back now and I'm going to take very good care of you.'

'Thanks, darlin'.' Gerald was grinning at the pretty blonde nurse. 'I'm feeling better already.'

His smile vanished, however, when Harry put his hands on his chest wall to examine him. 'Ouch...that really hurts.'

Harry could feel Charlotte's gaze on him. She was poised to follow any direction he might give to administer painkillers. Or to deal with a cardiac arrest? She was so young and eager. And it was disconcertingly obvious that she had a bit of a crush on him.

'Can you take a deep breath?' he asked Gerald.

The intake of breath was interrupted by a sharp groan.

'Too painful?'

Gerald nodded, his face still crumpled in agony. Charlotte put her hand on his shoulder. 'It's okay,' she told him. 'We're going to look after you.'

'It might not feel like it, but it's good news that the pain gets worse with a deep breath,' Harry said. 'Along with your normal test results, we can be confident that you're not having the heart attack you thought you were having. You've pulled one of your intercostal muscles—the ones that go between your ribs and make up the chest wall. It'll be sore for a few days so you'll need to avoid any strenuous activity. I'll write you a script for some anti-inflammatories.'

He could feel Charlotte's gaze following him as he went to print out a prescription and sign a discharge summary. 'You were lucky enough to get the best doctor we've got,' he heard her tell Gerald. 'Isn't he wonderful?'

Tilly Dawson didn't think so. She was glaring at him as he paused by the central desk to deal with his paperwork. She hadn't been that thrilled to see him when he'd greeted her earlier, come to think of it. Was it because he was filling in for a friend and she hadn't expected to have to work with him? Or was it just that, for some reason, she really didn't like him? He'd long since given up trying to charm this colleague and, given her cool, controlled demeanour, he hadn't been surprised to discover she had the nickname of being the 'Ice Queen'. They had managed to avoid working closely together so far but he'd been in this department at the same time often enough and he couldn't remember ever seeing Matilda Dawson smile with any real warmth. Or hearing her laugh, come to think of it.

Somehow, her lack of friendliness seemed more undeserved tonight. It was only a couple of days until Christmas, for heaven's sake—the universal time for goodwill and kindness—and they had the rest of a night shift to get through together. It was after midnight already and he could hear a very inebriated patient shouting from one end of the department, a small child shrieking from another corner and there was more than one phone ringing. A flashing light was a signal that a radio call needed to be answered from an incoming ambulance, which usually meant that a serious case was on the way. It was shaping up to be a long night and Harry did not need any extra tension from feeling like he'd done something wrong.

So he smiled at Tilly. One of his best smiles. 'How's it going?'

She didn't smile back. 'It's fine,' she said. 'Or it will be, if you don't upset any more of our nurses.'

Harry's smile evaporated. 'I have no idea what you're talking about.'

Except…she'd been talking to Charlotte when he'd walked past earlier and the young nurse had been clutching a handful of tissues. He'd wondered at the time if Charlotte had been upset by a patient death or that perhaps she was being reprimanded for a failure to follow a strict protocol that he could be sure Tilly would have spotted instantly, but maybe he'd been miles off the mark.

And maybe it had been a bad idea to go to that concert the other evening, but Charlotte had told him it was a departmental group outing that she just happened to have an extra ticket for. He'd thought it was odd they hadn't come across anyone they knew in the mosh pit, but the music and dancing had been great fun and he'd made it crystal clear before he'd accepted that invitation and again at the end of the evening that it hadn't been any kind of a date. Hadn't he?

If Tilly could see his silent question, she wasn't about to answer it. She simply turned away to speak to the nurse who had picked up the ambulance call.

'Post cardiac arrest case en route,' he heard the nurse say. 'ETA three minutes. Fifty-six-year-old male who's in sinus bradycardia but still being ventilated. I'll get the catheter lab on standby.'

Harry looked at the growing list of patients that had been allocated to him. The sore throat in one of the curtained cubicles had been waiting a while now. He picked up the patient file from the desk as Tilly moved swiftly away towards a resuscitation area where she would be continuing treatment for someone lucky enough to have beaten the odds and survived a cardiac arrest. So far. Way more exciting than a sore throat, that was for sure.

Not that he was going to waste any mental energy feeling envious of others having a more interesting challenge. Or feeling hard done by because someone disliked him for no obvious reason. It reminded him of some of the more miserable moments of his childhood, when he'd had to change schools as his mother moved them yet again in search of a cheaper rental or a better job. He might have learned that making people laugh or feel good was a quick way to make friends but he'd also learned that there were some people who weren't going to like you no matter how hard you tried and it didn't really matter because you could just move on and make a fresh start.

Harry Doyle was thirty-six and he'd lost count of the number of fresh starts he'd made in his life so far. He'd been in New Zealand for a good three months now but, as much as he loved the country and its people, it felt increasingly as if there was something missing from his life. It might already be time to think about moving on again.

Somewhere a bit closer to home, he decided as he introduced himself to an eighteen-year-old who had come to the city to spend Christmas with friends. It looked as if Talia had come from a summer beach party with the shorts she was wearing along with an oversized singlet over a bikini top. Harry added a condition to that decision to move on before he pushed it aside to focus on his patient. His next destination needed to be back in the northern hemisphere. Celebrating Christmas in the middle of summer felt so wrong it might be a big part of the reason he was feeling as if something needed fixing in his life.

Something was also clearly wrong with the throat he found himself peering at moments later. The ominous spots on the red and swollen tissue of the throat and tonsils, combined with the fever and painfully enlarged lymph nodes of his patient suggested a strep infection and, with a young Pasifika patient, he knew the risk was greater of it becoming something more serious like rheumatic fever. Starting antibiotics had to be a priority.

'We'll do a rapid antigen test for strep throat, Talia. If it's positive we'll start you on a ten-day course of antibiotics. Are you allergic to any medications, like penicillin?'

Talia shook her head. 'Don't think so.'

'Have you got a nurse looking after you?'

She nodded this time. 'She went to find me an ice block. She said it might help make it easier to swallow.'

It was Charlotte who arrived with the fruit-flavoured frozen snack. Her face lit up when she saw Harry.

'I was just looking for you,' she exclaimed. 'Gerald's waiting for his discharge form so he can go home. Someone else was asking where you were too.' She smiled at him. 'You're popular tonight.'

Popularity wasn't Harry's goal. He would be happy to settle for being able to keep all the balls he was juggling up in the air without dropping any of them. He had a patient with severe abdominal pain that could be appendicitis. Or a kidney stone. Or possibly a urinary tract infection, but she'd been unable to provide a sample for analysis. She was due back from a CT scan but Harry needed to find the swab for Talia's rapid antigen test and check on the diabetic patient from earlier in the night who was being observed as he recovered from a hypoglycaemic episode. When Talia's test result was positive for strep throat, he went back to let her know.

'You can have a one-off injection of penicillin,' he told her. 'If that's preferable to taking a ten-day course of pills twice a day. It's very important that you don't miss any doses with the pills or stop them in a few days because you're feeling better. This bug can come back or hang around and cause other problems down the track. It can even damage the valves in your heart, which can be very serious.'

'I'm going camping for Christmas with my friends.' Talia bit her lip. 'So it might be difficult to remember to take pills. Is the injection really painful?'

'It's got local anaesthetic in with it, so it's not too bad,' Harry promised. 'Then you just need to wait here for twenty minutes or so to make sure you don't have any kind of allergic reaction.'

Harry was thinking about Talia's planned trip as he headed for the drug room to prepare her medication. It was another weird thing about this side of the world, wasn't it? He'd heard that some New Zealand camping grounds were magnets to celebrate Christmas or see in the New Year in the sun, preferably beside a beach or a lake, but he could remember how excited he'd been as a kid when it started snowing in time for the big day.

He still had a photograph somewhere of him and his mother standing beside the best snowman in the world that they'd created.

'Are your friends going to take you home?' he asked Talia.

'Yes. They got sick of waiting so they went to get hamburgers.'

'I'd like to talk to them before you go. About being careful with sharing food and drinks while you're camping and that they'll need to see a doctor if they get any symptoms themselves.'

When Harry came out of Talia's cubicle having administered the injection, he saw a patient being wheeled out of Resus with a medical team surrounding the bed that included the senior consultant on duty. If it was the same one who'd been rushed in, the change was astonishing. He wasn't being ventilated any longer. He wasn't unconscious. Propped up on pillows, the middle-aged man was awake. Smiling, even.

Harry veered towards Resus as Tilly emerged. 'Is that the post-cardiac arrest guy?'

Tilly nodded. 'He's finally stable enough to be on his way to the cath lab for angioplasty.'

Managing the critically ill patient had obviously been a challenge. Tilly's cheeks were pink and there was a strand of long dark hair that had managed to work itself loose from the tight braid she always wore. He could sense her satisfaction in the case and he knew what that felt like. He could feel a corner of his mouth lift in a wry smile. Dr Matilda might not like him very much but they had something quite significant in common, didn't they?

'Well done,' he said quietly. 'He's a lucky man.'

'He's had a massive left anterior STEMI so he's not out of the woods yet.' Tilly was scanning the department as if she was trying to decide where she might be most needed next. An ambulance stretcher was being rushed into the second resuscitation area beside them, where the trauma team being led by the HOD was waiting. That could mean there were other patients who'd been temporarily abandoned so that the incoming emergency could be dealt with. The whole department was on a knife-edge that could tip them into chaos at any moment.

And Tilly was frowning. 'Oh, no...' she muttered. 'What's wrong *this* time?'

Harry followed her line of sight to see Charlotte rushing out of the cubicle he'd been in only minutes ago, to administer Talia's injection. And something *was* very clearly wrong. Charlotte looked absolutely terrified.

'*Help!*' she called. 'Someone? I need help...'

Tilly followed Harry.

She'd been about to confirm she wasn't needed by the trauma team before focusing on whatever priority was deemed most urgent elsewhere in the department but Harry's reaction to spotting Charlotte trumped any other option. He *knew* something bad was happening—she could feel it by the sudden tension in his body language. No, it was more than tension. It felt like fear...

Any opinion that his reaction was a bit over the top vanished as Tilly stepped into the cubicle. A young girl was sitting bolt upright on the bed looking even more frightened than Charlotte. Her eyes were puffy and a rash was making the skin on her arms look oddly lumpy. More alarmingly, the high-pitched sound she was making as she sucked in each breath told them that there was a potentially life-threatening problem with her airway.

'Talia had intramuscular penicillin about five minutes ago,' Harry said tersely. He stomped on the brake at the end of the bed and started pushing it. Charlotte leapt out of the way, pulling the curtain open at the same time. 'Resus One's clear, isn't it?'

Harry didn't wait for Tilly's affirmative response. The area might not have been cleaned yet, with the last critically ill patient having only just been transferred, but it would have everything they could need in the way of equipment and drugs available for a respiratory emergency.

Everything except perhaps assistance at the level of skill that could be required. Tilly could see more staff rushing into Resus Two and caught a glimpse of what looked like a traumatic cardiac arrest being managed in there. The bedside space was already crowded so it was a no-brainer for Tilly to stay with Harry. She might have heard good things about his professional abilities, but she'd never worked closely with him personally and there could be a young girl's life hanging in the balance with what appeared to be an anaphylactic reaction to antibiotics unfolding in front of them.

Harry went straight to the drug cupboard in Resus One to draw up adrenaline.

'Can you get some high-flow oxygen on, please, Charlotte?' he directed. 'And we'll need the IV trolley. Tilly, could you get some ECG dots on and a set of vital signs?'

Tilly worked fast, sticking electrodes onto Talia's shoulders and abdomen so that they could monitor her heart rate and rhythm. She wrapped a blood pressure cuff around her upper arm to enable automatic measurements and clipped a pulse oximeter to her finger. She could feel her own heart rate increasing as the figures started appearing on the screen of the monitoring equipment.

'Heart rate's one thirty-two,' she relayed to Harry. 'Blood pressure's eighty-six on fifty, respirations twenty-eight and pulse ox ninety-four percent.'

In other words, her heart rate was too high, the blood pressure was too low and, despite rapid breathing, there was not enough oxygen circulating in Talia's blood, but Harry's words to their patient were as calm and reassuring as if this was nothing to be overly concerned about.

'I'm going to give you an injection in your leg,' he told her. 'It should start to help your breathing very soon. I know this is scary, Talia, but hang in there. We've got this, okay?'

Talia nodded. Charlotte, her hands shaking, was trying to fit an oxygen mask over Talia's face at the same time Harry was injecting the adrenaline into the muscle of her thigh.

'Let's find a non-rebreather mask instead of this one,' Tilly said calmly, taking the mask from Charlotte's hands. 'And we need to turn the rate up as high as possible.' She caught Harry's glance and the flash of appreciation that she was here and he wasn't having to deal with an emergency with an inexperienced and extremely nervous young nurse.

'Could you set up for a fluid challenge?' he asked. 'I'll get some IV access.'

Tilly found and checked a bag of IV fluid, hung

it up and then opened a set of tubing and flow control to get it ready to attach to both the bag and an IV cannula. There was also a pressure infusion cuff that needed to be wrapped around the bag to enable rapid delivery to counteract the hypovolaemia that anaphylactic shock could cause. She was watching what Harry was doing from the corner of her eye at the same time. The combination of urticaria, dark skin and low blood pressure would make it a challenge to find a vein, let alone slip a wide-bore plastic cannula into place but, again, Harry gave the impression of being calm and confident, so Tilly wasn't surprised that he completed the procedure within seconds. She was, however, impressed enough to nod at him.

'Well done,' she murmured.

The few minutes it took to accomplish these first steps meant that it was time for a second dose of adrenaline. Judging by how little response there had been to the first dose, Tilly wondered if Harry was thinking of starting an IV infusion of the drug. He was certainly on top of his plan of action.

'I'll draw up an antihistamine and steroids too,' he told Tilly. 'We'll get a twelve lead ECG, chest X-ray, an arterial blood gas and some bloods off to check her urea and electrolyte levels. Could you set up a racemic adrenaline nebuliser, please?' His gaze slid sideways. 'Talia?' He was focused on her face beneath the oxygen mask. 'How's your breathing feeling now? Is it getting any easier?'

But Talia didn't nod. Or shake her head. Her mouth was opening and closing beneath the mask and her eyes were wide and terrified. Then her eyelids fluttered and closed.

'Talia?' Harry was at the end of the bed in a single step. He lowered the end of the bed, pushed the pillows off and tilted her head to open her airway.

'She crashing,' Tilly said quietly. 'Blood pressure and heart rate are dropping.' She turned to pull the airway trolley closer. 'SPO2s under ninety.'

Talia's level of consciousness was also dropping fast and she was clearly struggling to breathe.

'We're losing the airway.' Harry's words were quiet but he was dropping a verbal bombshell.

Charlotte made a distressed sound and stepped back, her fingers pressed to her mouth. This time Harry's gaze caught and held Tilly's for a heartbeat. And then another. The decisions they had to make in this space of time were huge but could mean the difference between life and death for a young woman. A normal intubation via the mouth or even the nose was highly unlikely to be possible due to the swelling of the tissues at the back of the tongue and in the larynx, which left only one alternative to secure an airway in time—to go in through the front of the neck.

There was no time to summon extra help, like the anaesthetist who was currently busy anyway in Resus Two, dealing with the major trauma case. Charlotte was too overwhelmed to be useful, so this was down to Harry and Tilly and part of their swift, silent communication was deciding who was going to perform this invasive procedure. In the end, that decision was as much of a no-brainer as having come to assist Harry in the first place because Tilly thought she saw Harry's confidence falter. Just for a nanosecond, but it was enough.

'I'll do it,' she said.

* * *

Oh, *man*…

Tilly couldn't possibly know what was going through Harry's mind in that instant—a flashback to a scene that had started in an almost identical fashion to this and ended in catastrophe—but she saw enough to take the lead and…and it felt like a lifeline. He could—and would—have stepped up to this challenge with every expectation of success but, for this young girl's sake, it was much better for it to be done by someone who didn't have a demon to fight.

He could step back. Not as far as Charlotte had, of course. He could provide the skilled assistance that Tilly needed with drawing up drugs needed and having all the equipment available. He arranged the scalpel, artery forceps, bougie and the endotracheal tube on the sterile drape and made sure he had an ambu bag with an end tidal CO_2 detector attached. He helped position Talia by hyperextending her neck when the drugs took effect but he didn't have the responsibility of identifying exactly where to make that incision through the cricothyroid membrane and then open it, insert a guidewire and then slide the hollow tube over the top to create a patent airway.

He just needed to hold his breath and hope like hell that Tilly really knew what she was doing.

She certainly seemed to. Her focus was intense enough to suggest that failure wasn't allowed to be an option, the movements of her hands suggested that this wasn't the first time she'd performed this procedure and within a commendably short space of time the bag mask was attached to the tube and oxygen was flowing to where it needed to go. There was still a lot to do to ensure this patient's condition was stable but, as Tilly's gaze snagged on Harry's as she looked up to check the readings on the monitor, it was an acknowledgment that they were already well on track to a successful outcome in an unexpected crisis. And that they'd done it together, as a team.

He could see something else in her eyes he'd never seen before.

Respect? He knew she'd been impressed at the speed with which he'd managed that tricky IV cannulation but there was an edge of something else in that brush of eye contact and it looked like curiosity. Had she guessed that when a surgical airway had to be done he'd been facing a personal challenge of a scenario he'd never wanted to see repeated? If so, she wasn't judging him for it but rather wondering what it had been about. Maybe he'd tell her about that case at a more appropriate time.

For now, it was enough to know that that ghost had been laid, so he was unlikely to feel that frisson of doubt that could potentially affect his performance if he was ever faced with this situation again.

Which meant that he was most definitely in Dr Matilda Dawson's debt.

Big-time.

CHAPTER TWO

THERE WERE TEARS in those big blue eyes.

'It's okay.' Harry handed Charlotte some tissues. 'It was a pretty confronting situation. You did the right thing by calling for help as fast as you did.'

'I thought she was going to die. And when you had to cut into her throat like that, I thought I was going to faint…'

'Getting her airway secured is what saved her life. And she's doing very well now. She'll need to be kept under observation for a while but she'll be absolutely fine and she knows about her allergy now so she'll be able to wear a medic alert bracelet and it's very unlikely to happen again.'

Charlotte blew her nose. 'I'm not sure I'm cut out for nursing.'

'Give it time,' Harry advised. 'It might just be that Emergency isn't the right fit for you.' He checked his watch. 'It's time for you to go home now, so have a rest and don't make any big decisions in too much of a hurry.'

Charlotte nodded. 'Thanks ever so much for this talk. I feel a lot better now.'

Harry got to his feet. 'Happy to help.'

'I'd like to say thanks properly.'

'No need.' He opened the door of the office but Charlotte didn't take the hint.

'What are you doing for Christmas?' she asked. 'If you don't have something planned you'd be very welcome at our place for Christmas dinner. My family would love to meet you.'

'Ah… I do have something planned,' Harry lied. 'I'm heading out of town, in fact. With a…a friend.'

'Oh…'

Harry saw the moment that this young nurse gave up any hope of catching his interest. He could almost see her catching hold of a new level of maturity instead.

'I hope you have a wonderful day.' She was smiling now. 'I can't wait. It's my favourite time of the year.'

Harry headed for the staffroom. A cup of coffee before navigating rush-hour traffic to get home might be a good idea. Traffic that would be far worse than usual on one of the last shopping days before Christmas. It certainly wasn't his favourite time of the year. When you didn't have family, the celebration lost any real significance. And when you were somewhere where it was in totally the wrong season it was just…downright unappealing. Frankly, he couldn't wait until it was over.

With the handover of patients complete, the night shift heading home and the day shift getting into gear, the staffroom was almost empty. The only person there was Tilly, who was holding her phone up to her face as she spoke to someone on a video call.

'So there's nothing wrong?' There was still an anxious note in her voice. 'You had me so worried when I saw I'd missed those calls.'

With the room being so quiet, it was easy to hear a

male voice. 'No, no, sweetheart. Not at all. I just wanted to know what time to pick you up from the airport tomorrow, that's all.'

Sweetheart? The Ice Queen had someone in her life who called her sweetheart? Harry was almost shaking his head in disbelief as he headed towards the bench, where a glass jug of filter coffee was staying hot on its element. He was about to walk behind Tilly as she told the man what time her flight was due.

'Are you sure Harry can't come too? He'd be more than welcome, you know. He does know how keen I am to meet him, doesn't he?'

Hearing his name was startling enough to make Harry stop in his tracks and turn his head. He could see a much older man on the screen of Tilly's phone. A man who seemed to be staring back at him. Grinning.

'Is this a case of speaking of the devil? Are *you* Harry?'

'I am indeed,' he said. He could feel Tilly flinch. What on earth had she been saying about him to this person?

'This is my father.' Tilly sounded as if she was speaking with her jaw muscles tightly clenched. 'Jim Dawson. Dad…this is Harry Doyle.'

'Delighted to meet you,' the man said. 'And it's about time.'

'Oh?' Harry could feel the tension emanating from Tilly's body. He thought he heard her swear under her breath, in fact, saying a word he wouldn't have expected Dr Dawson to have ever uttered in her life.

Jim hadn't stopped grinning yet. He was looking positively overjoyed. 'Well, you have been going out with my daughter for quite some time now.'

Harry blinked, taking a moment to realise he'd stumbled into something so bizarre he felt like Alice falling down the rabbit hole. Why on earth would Tilly be lying to her father about him being her boyfriend?

Was it possibly because it was making him look this happy?

But why him of all people, when she didn't even *like* him? When sometimes he'd catch a glance that suggested she would prefer it if he didn't actually exist?

He wasn't upset about the deception but, dammit, he was as curious as Alice.

'As I was saying,' Jim continued. 'You'd be more than welcome here for Christmas. Tilly's coming tomorrow so that we've got a bit of time before the big day. We have a lot of fun in these parts. You won't have been to Central Otago before, I'm guessing? Queenstown? Arrowtown?'

'No.' Harry could at least sound genuine about his response. 'And it's a part of the country I'd love to see.'

It was also out of town. A long way out of town. And hadn't he just told Charlotte that was where he was heading?

No... Spending Christmas with Matilda Dawson? Not going to happen...

'That's settled then.' Jim was looking misty-eyed as he focused on Tilly again. 'I can't tell you how happy I am, sweetheart.'

'Um...' Tilly cleared her throat. 'I've got to go, Dad. I'll call you again later, yeah?'

She ended the call and then got to her feet, turning to glare directly at Harry.

'How *could* you do that?' she demanded, her tone appalled. 'You've just made everything so much *worse*.'

* * *

It was the combination that had pushed her over the edge.

Physical fatigue, after a night shift that had included moments of extreme tension, was the base layer, but there were other flavours swirled through the mix. Like that worry about why her father had been so anxious to talk to her and the annoyance that someone like Harry Doyle could get away with doing whatever he wanted in his sex life with total disregard for the damaging effect it could have on other people. On top of that was the real kicker. The sheer, toe-curling, cringe-making embarrassment of having been found out that she was pretending Harry was her boyfriend.

It was a stroke of luck that they were alone in the staffroom but, even if they hadn't been, Tilly might have still lashed out because there was, apparently, quite a fine line between embarrassment and anger. Who knew?

'Whoa...' It seemed that anger might be contagious, judging by Harry's tone. 'I was helping you out there. What did you want me to say? That the likelihood of me being your boyfriend is on a par with the survival of those snowballs in hell?'

'The feeling's mutual, I can assure you,' Tilly snapped.

The expression on Harry's face was one of utter incredulity. 'So why?' he demanded. 'Why would you tell your father a lie like that?'

'I wasn't lying.' Tilly's statement was vehement. Then she heard her own words and her gaze slid away from his as she cringed inwardly. Anger was rapidly crossing the line to become purely embarrassment. 'It had nothing to do with you,' she muttered. 'I just...

borrowed your name because it popped into my head. You'd started work here that day.'

'So you have a boyfriend that has another name?' Harry sounded bewildered now.

'No.' Tilly gritted her teeth. 'I don't *have* a boyfriend. That's the whole point. My father was having a bad day. He'd lost a patient.' Tilly shook her head. Why on earth was she telling Harry any of this? To try and justify being found out telling a huge fib? To try and shift that embarrassment back to what had felt like perfectly justifiable anger? 'Okay...maybe it was a white lie. And I might have used some stuff that was true—like you being Irish and...'

And absolutely gorgeous, with the most amazing blue eyes she'd ever seen...?

She'd certainly said something along those lines but Tilly stomped on that confession before it could emerge.

'And...it doesn't matter what I said. If you want something to be believable, it's got to have at least an element of truth, doesn't it? And I knew how much it would cheer him up to think I'd met someone. He... um...worries about me.'

Those extraordinary blue eyes were resting on her face. Looking unconvinced. He wasn't buying any of this, was he? Tilly felt anxiety start to compete with the embarrassment she was feeling. What if he started thinking that she was indulging in some kind of fantasy about him? What if he shared that thought with someone else? Hospital grapevines loved nothing more than a bit of gossip like that.

Tilly had to make sure that didn't happen. Maybe the only way out of the corner she felt she'd just trapped herself in was to give her explanation more than simply a brush with the truth.

'I worry about him too,' she added quietly. 'He had a bit of a health scare a while back. A transient ischaemic attack that was the first sign he had alarmingly high blood pressure. It's under treatment now and he's fine but...' she couldn't look at Harry as she was revealing the kind of personal information she never told anyone '...but it made me think about what it would have been like if he'd died, you know? If his last thoughts had been to be still worrying about *me*... That's why I told him what he wanted to hear more than anything else. That I'd met somebody. That I was—*am*—happier than I've ever been.'

The long moment of silence made her finally raise her gaze to find that Harry was still staring at her and, weirdly, for just a heartbeat, it felt as if they were not simply looking at each other but they were *seeing* each other for the first time ever. But he looked away the instant her gaze touched his and that feeling of connection was broken.

'I'm sorry if I've made things difficult for you.' His voice was slightly distant, as if he was actually thinking about something else. 'But I *was* trying to help. I owed you a favour and I thought that going along with your game might be a way to repay you.'

Curiosity was enough to distract Tilly from trying to decide if she'd rescued herself. 'Repay me for what?'

'It's kind of a long story.'

'I'm listening.' Her tone could probably have been interpreted as a demand for an explanation but this was a great way of shifting attention away from herself. It was definitely the way to stop thinking about that odd moment of connection and possibly a means to end this awkward conversation altogether.

Harry shrugged. 'Short version, then. The last time I had a patient who needed a surgical airway was for a child with a traumatic facial injury. It was about ten years ago on one of my first shifts ever in an ED. I was in a small rural hospital on a night shift with only another junior doctor who thought he knew what he was doing, but he didn't. He walked out when he knew he'd stuffed up and I had to try and carry on but…it was too late.'

Tilly swallowed. She could imagine the carnage. The horror. The heartbreak. She could feel an unexpected and distinct empathy with a newly qualified Harry.

'I've done controlled cricothyroidotomies since then but it was something I never wanted to have to face again in an emergency situation.'

He caught Tilly's gaze again as he spoke and she found she couldn't look away. For once, there was no flirtatious gleam in that grey-blue of a moody sea. She was more aware of what she could feel than see in them, anyway. And it was something totally honest.

'I've lost that fear now,' he added quietly. 'Thanks to being a part of the way you handled that situation.'

'You would have handled it just as well as I did,' Tilly said. She meant it too. She'd seen the way he worked. She'd recognised an impressive level of skill.

His single nod wasn't arrogant in any way. It was an acknowledgement of a fact. 'But, if there's ever a next time, I'll remember tonight and it will make a difference.'

Tilly caught her bottom lip between her teeth. The

thought that Harry might be thinking about her at some point in the future was providing another frisson of an unexpected connection. Purely a professional one, of course, which was far more acceptable.

'So that's why I didn't tell your father I had no idea what you were talking about,' Harry said. 'It was my way of saying thanks. And, to be fair, I was being just as dishonest as you were. I'm guessing that you had a reason for lying.'

Tilly let her breath out in a sigh. 'Haven't you ever told a white lie? To try and make someone feel better?'

Harry made a sound like a huff of laughter. 'About two minutes ago,' he admitted. 'I said I was going out of town for Christmas. I needed an excuse for not accepting an invitation but I didn't want to hurt her feelings.'

Tilly's breath escaped in an unamused huff. 'So Charlotte hasn't given up, then?'

The expression on Harry's face made Tilly think she might have to reconsider her opinion that he toyed with the women who threw themselves at him with no regard for their feelings. She also remembered Charlotte telling her that she'd known the interest she felt was not reciprocated. Perhaps Harry's mistake had been being so careful not to hurt her feelings in the first place?

His rueful expression was fading. 'Hey… I *could* be out of town for Christmas, which would mean it wasn't any kind of a lie. Your dad just invited me. And he lives in Queenstown? That's, like, way up there on any tourist's list of "must see" places in New Zealand.'

'Don't be ridiculous.' Tilly's tone was sharper than merited but she was trying—and failing—to ignore that smile. 'You're not coming home with me.'

'But I've got a few days off. And it would make your dad so happy.' Harry's tone was teasing. 'Did you see the way he couldn't stop smiling? I think he approves of your choice already.'

Tilly was shaking her head as she turned to reach for her shoulder bag, hooked over the back of a chair, but she couldn't stop her brain conjuring up a fleeting image. Of her. With Harry beside her and her father confidently waiting for the signs of a deep, romantic connection between them. Signs that she would have as much chance of producing as those snowballs Harry had mentioned. She couldn't stop the frisson of something unpleasant skating over her skin either. An echo from the past?

'There's a word for women like you... Frigid, that's what...like something straight from the freezer that nobody wants to touch...'

Tilly also knew what her nickname was around here. She could assume that Harry had also heard it so that just made his suggestion of keeping up the deception in real life even more ridiculous.

But, yeah...she *had* seen how happy her father had looked when he thought he was meeting the man she'd been seeing for a couple of months now. She hadn't seen him look that happy since...well, she couldn't remember when.

And the desire to make him happy had been there for as long as Tilly could remember. The pride and love in that smile touched a part of her heart that was so tender it always made tears only a blink away.

But she shook her head again, more decisively this time.

'As you pointed out so charmingly,' she said, her

back still to Harry, 'a snowball would have to stay frozen in hell for us to be in a relationship. My father is a very intelligent man. He'd see through you in a heartbeat.'

'Are you sure?' Harry sounded curious. 'Because I missed my vocation really. I could have been an actor.'

Tilly heard raw emotion in the growling sound Harry suddenly made and then froze as she felt his hands on her shoulders. She could feel his breath on the back of her neck.

'It was love at first sight,' Harry murmured, his Irish accent more pronounced than ever. 'And now... well... I just can't imagine the rest of my life without you in it, Tilly...'

Dear Lord... She might be frozen to the spot but there was a heat surrounding her that felt as if it could melt her bones. A heat like nothing she'd ever felt. A heat that she would never have believed she was even capable of feeling because, well...because frigid women couldn't feel that kind of heat, could they? But she *had* felt it and it must have been enough to fry her brain cells because, while Harry had been uttering them, she had believed every word. And she desperately wanted to hang on to that feeling, but Harry lifted his hands and the spell was broken instantly.

'See what I did there?'

Tilly was taking her time to turn and face Harry directly as she let any effects he'd had on her evaporate, but she could hear the grin in his voice.

'That could get nominated for an Oscar, so it could.' There was satisfaction in Harry's tone. 'Don't you think? How happy would that make your dad? It might be his best Christmas ever.'

'But it would be a lie.'

'A white lie,' Harry corrected her. 'Like the one I told. And maybe *two* white lies will cancel each other out and neither of us would need to feel guilty about anything.' He lifted his eyebrows. 'It's a win-win situation. I get to escape town and get to see a place every visitor should see. You get to make your father a happy, happy man. If you tell him down the track that things didn't work out and I've gone back to Ireland, well… that's nobody's fault, is it? It's just life…'

'You can*not* be serious.' Tilly was incredulous. 'You're actually offering to come home with me for Christmas and pretend to be my boyfriend?'

The smile on Harry's face evaporated in the sudden silence that fell between them. A silence that was stretching into something significant. Tilly could see the muscles in his throat contract as he swallowed and, when he spoke, his voice sounded a little raw, even.

'We've got more in common than you might think,' he said quietly. 'I wish it had occurred to me to try and give my mother the hope that everything she might have wished for me to have in life was just around the corner but… I never got the chance.' He gave his head a small shake. 'I get that this thing with your father is nothing to do with me, but I've kind of got involved now and…'

His voice trailed off but Tilly could imagine the words that weren't being uttered. And if he helped her, could it perhaps go some way towards making up for not having been able to do it for his own mother?

She was lost for words herself, with this glimpse of an emotional depth she would never have associated with this man, but the suspicion that he might be simply giving her another demonstration of his acting skills emerged as he smiled at her again.

'We could make it work,' he said. 'It might even be kind of fun. What do you say?'

Harry's smile stretched into a grin that could only be described as cheeky. It made Tilly imagine what this man had been like as a kid. His mother must have loved him to bits. A happy, mischievous little boy who probably got away with almost anything because he'd been born with the ability to charm those around him and make the world feel like a better place.

Her father deserved to feel like that. Especially at Christmastime.

A tiny shiver ran down Tilly's spine as she thought of that heat Harry had conjured up from nowhere with just the touch of his hands and the tone of his voice. It hadn't been real—he'd only been acting—but, just for a heartbeat, it had made Tilly remember a time when she'd believed that dreams could come true.

That the world was indeed a much better place than it had turned out to be.

And…maybe it would be nice to feel like that again. Even if it was just a pretence. Even if it was only for Christmas.

'I'll think about it,' she said.

CHAPTER THREE

'SO...WHAT MADE you say yes in the end?'

'I rang my dad back after I'd caught up on some sleep. He'd had a really busy day and looked beyond tired, but he was so excited about my visit and meeting you and...' Tilly leaned her head back, shifting her gaze to look out of the small, oval aircraft window.

And she couldn't possibly tell Harry about how it had made her feel as her father had talked about him being there with her. How appealing the idea of spending more time in his company had become. The internal tussle that the memory of the heat his touch had created had kept her awake long after that phone call because, deep down, Tilly realised it might actually be possible to pull off that deception for a couple of days and there might be a reason she wanted to do it that had nothing to do with making her father happy.

A purely selfish reason. Because she couldn't deny that part of her wanted to know if it was possible to feel that heat again.

Did she want to feel it?

Yes, of course she did. It was clearly something as desirable as finding shelter when you'd been out in the cold for far too long.

But no. She didn't want to feel it because it was terrifying. It couldn't be trusted. It could lead to getting very, very badly burnt. Even if it was only a pretence, Tilly was, quite literally, playing with fire.

Not that Harry had the slightest clue what was flashing through her mind in that instant, and that had been the real reason that Tilly had ended up saying yes. Because she knew she could control how she felt enough for no one else to guess the truth. Even her father.

Or, thank goodness, Harry.

Keeping her feelings hidden was a skill she'd perfected over many years. She could turn on the 'Ice Queen' persona with no more than a mental flick of a switch.

She could feel Harry's gaze on the back of her head. He was still waiting for her to finish explaining what had led to him sitting in the seat beside her, wasn't he?

'And…' Tilly let her breath out as she found something plausible to say. 'I couldn't bring myself to tell him you couldn't come after all and disappoint him again.'

'Again?' Harry sounded astonished. 'I would have thought having a daughter like you would be something he's very proud of.'

Oh… Tilly let herself absorb what sounded like a compliment. An unexpected one, given that they hadn't yet started their role play for her father's benefit.

'My dad's dream was that I would become a doctor and then take over his family practice.'

'And it's not your dream?'

'It was when I was a kid. Before I knew any better.' She threw Harry a wry smile. 'Along with the dream of getting married and raising half a dozen kids in the old family homestead.'

'Not going to happen, then?' Harry suggested.

'Not in this lifetime. But I suspect Dad's been waiting every year for the announcement that I'm coming home for good for at least the last five or six years. That's probably more than enough disappointment, wouldn't you say?'

'So…where is it you used to live? I've forgotten.'

'The practice is in Craig's Gully, which is about halfway between Arrowtown and Cutler's Creek. Family homestead's out of town a bit on a remnant of the original sheep station.'

'And that's not somewhere you'd want to live again?'

Tilly stopped herself rolling her eyes. 'Did you grow up in a small country town? The kind where absolutely everybody knows absolutely everybody else's business?'

'I grew up in Dublin. Big city.' Harry lifted an eyebrow. 'You should probably know that about your Irish boyfriend.'

Tilly stifled a sigh. He was right. How on earth had she convinced herself that this was a good idea? She might be an expert in hiding her feelings but she had to admit she was beginning to feel very uncharacteristically nervous. She hadn't really thought this through properly, had she?

She cleared her throat. 'So…do you still have family there? Your dad? Any siblings?'

'No.'

There was something in that single quiet word that made Tilly catch her breath as she remembered that glimpse of a part of Harry she hadn't realised existed.

Someone who had had a mother he'd cared enough about to have wished he could make her happy before she died. She would have caught Harry's gaze as well, but he was looking down at his hands.

'That's why I left Ireland, to be fair. There was nothing left to keep me there.'

Something in Harry's tone suggested that he wouldn't be keen on answering any more personal questions and that was fine by Tilly. If they both had things they'd rather keep private it would be easier to keep a safe distance.

Harry leaned in front of Tilly, so that he could see out of the window properly, and he let his breath out in a silent whistle seconds later.

'There's nothing but mountains down there. You wouldn't want to be having a crash landing, would you?'

Tilly laughed. 'Is now the time to tell you that Queenstown is one of more challenging airports in the world to land at because of all the surrounding mountains?'

As if to back up her statement, the plane tilted as it began a turn. There would be a few more of them before they landed but Tilly was used to the complicated approach. She hoped they would be coming in over the lake and then looping to land in the opposite direction, which gave the best view of Queenstown and this stunning part of the country. She might have no intention of coming back here to live but this was her home. Part of her DNA.

Weirdly, she was starting to feel excited by the idea of showing it off to Harry. It shouldn't matter at all but she wanted him to love it as much as she did.

* * *

Harry Doyle had done a few impulsive things in his time.

Okay, more than a few, but it only dawned on him as he heard Tilly laugh that he might have bitten off a bit more than he could comfortably chew this time—when it was far too late to even think of changing his mind.

Despite the engine noise, the sound of Tilly's laughter was hanging in the air between them and, from what Harry could see through the window, it seemed as if they might be on track to fly straight into a mountain that looked disconcertingly close to the aircraft. Thank goodness the pilot was starting another turn but there were some patchy lumps of cloud that were dense enough to cut visibility to nothing as they continued their descent and Harry could feel a knot of tension forming in his gut.

Maybe it was better not to watch. He sat back in his seat and closed his eyes for a moment. It wasn't as if worrying about the safety of this flight path was going to change anything.

It would also be a complete waste of time to wonder if he should have backed out of this impulsive offer to go home with Tilly for Christmas when he'd had the chance. Because he'd never really had that chance in the first place, had he?

Not when Tilly had told him why she'd lied to her father. When he'd known exactly how she must have felt when she'd got that call to tell her that he was potentially very ill. Maybe she'd got the news before they'd been able to diagnose a TIA and she might have thought he was being rushed to hospital with a stroke that could have been fatal. Listening to her had been a bit of a shock, in fact, because it had taken him straight back to when he'd got the news about his mother and how terrible that journey had been to try and get back to her in time.

How devastating it had been to fail.

He'd also caught a glimpse of a completely different person beneath that cool, reserved exterior that was the only side he'd ever seen of Dr Matilda Dawson. Some-one who could get angry—passionate, even—when she was trying to protect a person she cared about. Someone who had lied to her father about having a significant relationship in her life because she knew it would make him happy. Was it simply that her father would want to know her future was secure or had Jim Dawson been worried that his daughter was lonely in her current life?

Was she lonely?

Not that that was any of his business either, but the idea that Tilly was vulnerable beneath that icy shell would have made it difficult to back out. That slightly shocking sense of connection he'd felt listening to her fear that she might have caused her father any worry on his deathbed had made it completely impossible.

And Harry hadn't been kidding when he told her he was an expert actor. How could he not be when he'd honed that skill as a child, learning not only how to make friends and entertain his peers by being the class clown with every new school he attended but to hide his own emotions to avoid being bullied and… yeah…to hide the fear, even from himself, that came from being lonely.

It might have been in his imagination but it felt as if the connection that had come from nowhere was on both sides. A very different kind of connection to the one they'd created earlier yesterday by dealing with a professional crisis together.

And it had been fun to give her that demonstration of his talents, hadn't it?

He hadn't really expected Tilly to say yes when she'd phoned him last night, but he hadn't had the time or inclination to unpick the reason why there seemed to be a solid barrier to backing away from that offer. Besides, it was only for a day or two and…well…it was Christmas, wasn't it? A time of peace and kindness to all.

But Harry had never heard Tilly laugh before and he found he was hanging onto the echo of that sound. Because he liked it.

He liked it a lot.

The touch on his arm made his eyes fly open again.

'Look…' Tilly was still smiling. 'You're missing something special.'

She wasn't wrong. The view from the window was spectacular. Below the clouds now, the plane was banking steeply. He could see a wall of mountains. A river. Sheep that seemed close enough to count and barren hilltops that felt near enough for the wingtips to brush. Harry could see the vast blue stretch of water that was still enough to be reflecting the surrounding peaks as they sank towards a runway at the end of the lake.

Harry was soaking it in, his head close to Tilly's as they shared the window. He didn't turn his head but he could sense that she was still smiling. And he thought he could hear another soft echo of her laughter.

That was something unexpectedly special too, wasn't it?

* * *

'He's not here.' Tilly's gaze raked over Queenstown Airport's small arrivals area.

'We might be a bit earlier than expected. He's not to know that we only had carry-on luggage.'

'More likely that he's been caught up in some kind of emergency. We might be waiting for a while.'

An announcement came through the loudspeaker system as she finished speaking.

'Dr Matilda Dawson, please report to the main information desk.'

Tilly threw an 'I told you so' glance at Harry. 'Come on. We'd better go and find out what's going on.'

The message waiting at the desk was that Dr Jim Dawson was in the emergency department of Queenstown Hospital.

'Did he say how long he might be?' Tilly queried.

'No, sorry. But the message came through a couple of hours ago, so maybe it won't be too much longer?'

'Let me buy you lunch while we're waiting,' Harry suggested. 'It looked like quite a nice café we just walked past.'

'The hospital's very close to the airport. Let's wander over and see what's happening. A couple of hours is a long time to be waiting to transfer a patient.' Now that she was standing on home ground, waiting to start the grand deception, that nervousness was becoming more pronounced and her father's absence was only making it worse. What else might be lying in wait to provide unexpected challenges that could instantly expose the deception?

The heat of the midday sun hit them as they walked

out of the air-conditioned airport and Tilly wished she hadn't worn her jeans.

'I might take you down to the river this afternoon,' she told Harry. 'We'll need a swim if it stays this warm. Did you bring your togs?'

'My *what*?'

'Togs.' Tilly turned her head to catch Harry's expression. Did he not understand New Zealand slang? 'A bathing costume? Swim-shorts? Budgie smugglers?'

Harry made a slightly strangled sound and Tilly realised that she might have misinterpreted his expression. Maybe it was the idea of being semi-clothed with someone who was pretty much a total stranger that had startled him. Her throwaway suggestion had suddenly become a big deal.

A big, awkward deal that was definitely a new challenge. This was way worse than not knowing that the man who was supposed to be her boyfriend had grown up in Dublin. This was about not even being comfortable in each other's company.

Except that she'd forgotten about Harry's acting skills. And perhaps he'd seen a flash of something like panic in her face that the plan was going to fall over before it could even begin. Because he was grinning now. He was back in control.

'Didn't think of bringing my togs,' he said lightly. 'I might have to go skinny-dipping.'

Oh, *help*…

Any relief that she'd only need to follow Harry's lead in this pretence to make it work faded as Tilly felt her cheeks heating up faster than could be attributed purely to the strength of the direct sunshine they were walking in. If the thought of Harry Doyle swimming naked could make her this flustered, could even Harry's acting skills convince her father that they were more than simply colleagues? He'd see straight through this farce the moment he clapped eyes on them, wouldn't he?

Or maybe he wouldn't. Tilly found her father in a very unexpected place within the emergency department of the district hospital. And in a very unexpected condition. One that made it unlikely that he would notice anything odd about his daughter's relationship with her boyfriend.

'I'm as high as a kite, love,' he told his daughter. 'Needed a bit of jungle juice while they got my bones back into the right place.' He beamed at Harry. 'Gidday, mate. Sorry I wasn't at the airport to meet you.'

'Not a problem, Dr Dawson.' Harry eyed the heavy-duty moon boot on the older man's lower leg and foot. 'Looks like you've been in the wars.'

'Call me Jim, son. You're practically part of the family.'

'Dad...' Tilly's tone was a warning. 'Don't go starting any rumours. Or scaring Harry off.'

But, again, Harry was laughing. He draped his arm around Tilly's shoulders. 'I don't scare that easily,' he told Jim. 'Or I wouldn't be here at all, would I?'

Jim was nodding sagely. 'We'd better do what we're told. Tilly's the boss.'

Both men laughed as if sharing a private joke and Tilly found herself scowling as she shrugged off the weight of Harry's arm. 'What happened, exactly?' she demanded.

'Your dad fell off a ladder.' The nurse who came into

the room made a tutting sound. 'He should know better at his age, but there you go…'

'You're making me sound decrepit, Liz,' Jim complained. 'I'm not that old.'

'You're over seventy,' Tilly reminded her father. 'What on earth were you doing up a ladder, anyway?'

'Putting up the Christmas lights. And those Santa legs that stick out of the chimney. The ones that made you laugh so much when you were a little girl?'

Tilly shook her head. 'I'm not five years old now, Dad. What's the damage?'

'Fracture dislocation of the ankle,' the nurse said. 'He wanted to avoid surgery. The fracture's not displaced and the dislocation seems to have been successfully reduced, but it'll need careful monitoring for the next few days. We were going to admit him to keep him out of trouble.'

'No need.' Jim Dawson was shaking his head firmly. 'Why would I need to stay in hospital when I've got two doctors to look after me in my own home?'

Liz gave Tilly a long-suffering glance. 'Would you believe he drove himself in here?'

Tilly closed her eyes. 'I would.'

'The truck's automatic,' Jim Dawson said. 'It was only my left foot that wasn't working.'

'His car's still parked in the ambulance bay,' Liz said. 'But there is a bed here if you think it's in his best interests to stay.'

It might be in her own best interests to have her father safely tucked up in a hospital bed for the next day or two because it would make this game with Harry so much easier, but it was already very clear that Jim

Dawson was not about to give in without a fight. He was already starting to climb off the bed.

'There's no way I'm going to miss having a proper Christmas with my daughter,' he announced. 'Life's too short not to make the most of this kind of precious time together.'

Tilly closed her eyes for a heartbeat. The reminder that life could, indeed, be shorter than expected was precisely why she'd started this in the first place.

'And this is her boyfriend, Liz.' Jim's tone was a mix of pride and delight. 'He's an Irish lad.'

'So I noticed.'

Tilly opened her eyes in time to see Harry smile at the middle-aged nurse, who smiled back without hesitation. She stifled a sigh. Dr Harry Doyle could charm the birds out of the trees if he wanted to, couldn't he? But there was a silver lining in the cloud of her father's unfortunate accident in that it would provide a distraction that could excuse anything that might not fit with the glow of the happy couple she and Harry were supposed to be. Her nervousness was starting to evaporate now that introductions had been taken care of and Harry seemed perfectly at ease.

'Stay there for a tick, Jim.' Harry stepped forward, his arm out to prevent an attempt to stand unaided. 'You don't want to be putting any weight on that foot.' He turned to his new friend. 'Lizzie, would you possibly have a wheelchair we could borrow?'

It wasn't only a collapsible wheelchair that was made available to one of the district's longest serving general practitioners. Everybody wanted to contribute. Pillows were provided to cushion the leg on the raised footrest. Elbow crutches appeared and medications, including some potent painkillers, were dispensed, along with a warning from the consultant.

'I'm well aware you're qualified enough to be teaching me a thing or two, Tilly,' he said, 'but I remember patching you up more than once when you fell off your pony and that doesn't seem that long ago. Plus, I wouldn't be doing my job if I didn't tell you to bring him straight back in if you notice any changes, like increased pain or swelling.'

Tilly nodded. 'Compartment syndrome will be at the top of my list for possible complications. Don't worry, I'll be keeping a very close watch.'

'And don't let him put any weight whatsoever on that foot until we've seen him again.'

'I'll do my best.' Tilly gave her father a stern glance. 'Did you hear that, Dad? If you don't behave you'll be back in here like a shot.'

Harry was holding the handles on the back of the wheelchair. He leaned down to speak in a stage whisper. 'Tilly's the boss, remember? We both have to do what we're told.'

'I've made an outpatient appointment for Boxing Day for you, Jim.' The consultant lifted an eyebrow. 'That's only three days away. You can behave that long, can't you?'

Tilly looked at the way her father was smiling as he nodded. She had her doubts about just how well he was going to behave. Then she lifted her gaze to catch Harry's and...yeah...she had her doubts about *him* too.

But that *smile*...

It was doing odd things to her. Like making her very thankful he was here, now that her nervousness was almost gone. Like making her feel he was on her side and that she wasn't dealing with this unexpected personal event alone. A feeling that was enough to create a very strange melting sensation somewhere deep in her gut that took a firm mental shove to dismiss.

Harry's being here was only because he'd agreed to take part in a performance that was intended to give her father a Christmas to remember. And, although it felt as if the wheels were already falling off any plans she might have had for the next couple of days, it was far too late to back out of this by telling her father the truth. She only had to think about that look on his face when he'd told Harry he was practically part of the family and the proud note in his voice when he'd told Liz that Harry was her boyfriend to know how much it would hurt him to find out it wasn't true. The physical pain he was in at the moment was quite enough to be a shadow on any Christmas celebrations without her throwing another major blow on top of it.

Tilly knew what she had to do. For the sake of everybody involved in this pretence.

'Let's get this show on the road,' she said.

CHAPTER FOUR

THE OLD, SLIGHTLY BATTERED double-cab utility vehicle felt like a small bus to Harry as he sat in the front passenger seat, but Tilly was handling it as if it was no more difficult to drive than a small hatchback car. She was driving fast but competently, taking the curves of the road carefully to minimise any discomfort to her father, who was propped up sideways on the back seat to keep his broken ankle elevated.

Harry would have been impressed with this unexpected splinter skill Tilly was demonstrating but, to be honest, there was too much else competing for that head space. He wasn't even paying much attention to the conversation about local people and events that Tilly was having with her father until he dozed off. He was feeling very happy that he'd decided to come on this rather unusual break from the city. No wonder this area of the country was one of the top tourist destinations in the world. It felt as if Tilly was the one doing him a favour now, not the other way around.

The countryside they were driving through was extraordinary. It wasn't just the towering mountains all around them, there were stretches of sparkling blue water in more than one lake and a huge, fast-flowing river between dramatic cliffs when the road cut through a gorge. The barren dryness of rock-studded hills with clumps of golden tussock but not a blade of green grass to be seen was more than balanced by vineyards that stretched as far as the eye could see with lush foliage.

They went through a small township with stone-built cottages, a picturesque church and an outdoor produce market that could have been a summer destination in Europe, past another small lake and more vineyards before turning into a long, tree-lined driveway that led up the slope of a hill.

'Home sweet home,' Tilly announced as the house came into view.

It was another surprise for Harry, this graceful old wooden house with a slate roof that sat tucked into the hill with wide verandas, bay windows and an elegant turret on one corner. It was hugged by terraced gardens and trees, lawns and small paddocks. Tilly slowed the vehicle as they drove past a shaggy pony with its head over a gate.

'That's Spud,' she told Harry. 'He's the same age as me.'

'No way,' Harry said. He couldn't resist teasing her a little. 'Surely ponies don't live that long, do they?'

'Some get past forty years old.' Tilly's glance suggested she couldn't decide whether or not he was joking. 'But thirty-four *is* getting on a bit for a pony.'

She peered up at the roof of the house as she stopped the car. Harry followed her gaze to see the inflatable red legs with black boots visible above an old clay chimney pot.

'I'm definitely too old to find Santa legs in the chimney the funniest thing ever.' Tilly sounded exasperated. 'I can't believe you thought that was a good idea, Dad.'

'It's been a while since you were home, sweetheart,' Jim Dawson said quietly. 'I wanted it to be special.'

Tilly's gaze caught Harry's, just for a heartbeat, as she turned towards the back seat. He was already sensing undercurrents of things that weren't being said and he couldn't miss the flash of something in Tilly's eyes that made it suddenly difficult to catch his breath.

Sadness?

No…it was more like a brush of helplessness. Something deeper than vulnerability, even. An admission of failure to fix something because it was simply impossible?

'It *is* special, Dad.'

Her tone had a note in it that Harry had never heard before and he could feel a pull towards something else that was as unexpected as everything else he was discovering since he'd got himself entangled with Matilda Dawson's personal life. A bit disturbing, in fact. It was almost as if he was getting a glimpse of the shattered remains of the dream that both Tilly and her father had once shared of her future.

Jim might have told him he was practically a part of the family, but that was the last thing Harry wanted to be. He was here as a favour to Tilly. If pretending to be her boyfriend was going to be as much fun as he'd hoped—for everybody involved—he needed to take control of these twists and turns as competently as Tilly had done when she'd been driving that vehicle through the gorge. He needed to lighten up.

He opened the door of the ute. 'I'll get the wheelchair out of the back.'

* * *

The walk-in pantry attached to the large kitchen in Tilly's childhood home had been stocked with enough food to feed a small army for any Christmas celebrations.

She made ham sandwiches for their lunch, with thick slices of juicy ham on the bone, wholegrain mustard and tomatoes and crisp lettuce fresh from the garden between soft wedges of sourdough bread. They could have eaten at the comfortable everyday table in the kitchen or the formal mahogany table that could seat twelve people in the dining room, but she ended up serving the meal like a picnic on a coffee table in the living room.

Her father was now ensconced on the huge old sofa with its comfortable feather-stuffed cushions that was positioned in front of a wide bay window offering a view that stretched across vineyards to the craggy rocks of what had always felt like a private mountain range to Tilly. He had pillows behind his back and under his leg but, instead of resting, he was leaning sideways, opening the flaps of a cardboard box that she could see was full of Christmas decorations. There were more boxes stacked up at the end of the couch that Harry must have ferried in while she'd been preparing lunch and he came in with a very long box that Tilly knew contained an ancient artificial Christmas tree as she set the tray down on the coffee table.

'I did tell Jim he needed to be resting,' he said. 'We can do the tree later.' He eyed the sandwiches on the tray. 'Those look good.'

'Christmas ham,' Tilly told him. 'You'll be sick of

it by halfway through January, but you can't beat the first taste of it.'

'Glazed gammon's a taste of home.' Harry nodded as he took a plate and helped himself to a sandwich. 'It was a favourite of my mam's.'

'What else is traditional for Christmas dinner in Ireland?' Jim asked. 'I got everything I could think of yesterday, so you'd feel right at home. There's a turkey, of course, and I'm sure Tilly can look up a recipe for bread sauce. And there's Brussels sprouts and we can pick fresh peas from my garden. And potatoes. You'll be able to fill your boots with potatoes. I've even got duck fat to roast them in.'

Harry laughed. 'You're lucky you Kiwis get associated with a bird. The first thing anyone thinks of when they hear an Irish accent is a potato, which is far less interesting.' He shook his head. 'Don't get me wrong, though. I love potatoes. And I guess it's an Irish tradition to have more than one sort on the table at Christmas. Roast potatoes, mashed potatoes and my favourite—when they're sliced and baked with cheese and onions and they go all brown and crispy on top.'

'Potato gratin,' Tilly said. 'Not something I've ever had with Christmas dinner.'

'There's a first time for everything,' Jim said.

'Don't go to any trouble on my account.' Harry's wave was dismissing his favourite potato dish. 'It does seem strange that you eat a hot dinner in the middle of a summer's day, but turkey and roast potatoes sounds like the perfect Christmas dinner to me.'

'Hopefully I'll feel hungry by then.' Jim shook his head as Tilly offered him a plate. 'I'll just have a cup of tea, thanks, love.'

Tilly looked at the lines of pain she could see on her father's face. 'I'll get you a dose of your painkillers too. Maybe you can sleep for a bit this afternoon.'

But Jim shook his head. 'I can't do that. What if I'm needed?'

'Surely you're not on call? The clinic's closed for the next few days, isn't it?'

'Yes...but you know I'm always on call. Some of my patients have been coming to me for their whole lives and they know I'm always on call for them. And I've got Maggie Grimshaw, who's home from the hospice to have a last Christmas with her family on the farm. She's got a syringe driver for her pain meds that I need to refill every day. And I promised I'd be available to help in any way I can.'

'Oh, no...' Tilly could see that Harry had abandoned his sandwich as he listened to their conversation. 'Dad went to school with Maggie,' she told him. 'They've known each other their entire lives. She's been battling cancer for a long time but...' She let her breath out in a sigh. 'It makes it so much harder, doesn't it, dealing with something like this at Christmastime.' She turned back to Jim. 'I'd be more than happy to cover that for you, Dad. Maggie was like another mum to me.' Tilly swallowed hard. 'The only one, sometimes, when Mum was away so often.'

'I could help too,' Harry said, his tone sombre. 'With any calls that you want to respond to. I've worked as a general practitioner in rural areas, Jim. In Canada and England. I've also done stints in developing countries, so I've had enough experience to be ready to tackle anything.' He was smiling now. 'And Tilly and I work very well together. We make the best team.'

Tilly found herself smiling as well, a warm glow curling through her body at the praise of how good a team they made. It was true. It might have only been the first time they'd worked together in dealing with that anaphylactic shock but it had been seamless. Smooth. As if they had worked together for a very long time.

Jim's smile was suspiciously misty as he looked from Harry to Tilly and then back again. 'You couldn't have said anything to make me happier, son,' he said quietly. 'I'll have a word with Maggie soon and let her know what's going on.'

'We could drop in this afternoon, perhaps,' Tilly said briskly, shutting down that glow before the warmth became an uncomfortable heat. 'When I take Harry for a bit of a tiki tour.'

'A tiki tour?'

'It means having a good look around.' Tilly handed her father the cup of tea she'd poured. 'Harry's still learning Kiwi,' she told him. 'He didn't know what togs were either.'

'I am learning a lot,' Harry agreed. He waved his hand towards a section of wall beside where the Christmas tree was standing, that was covered in framed photographs. 'Why didn't you tell me that your mother was an international model? Or that you're half Italian?'

Jim didn't seem to notice the brief awkward silence between them. 'Chiara pretty much gave up the modelling not long after she married me,' he said. 'Her merino wool fashion business took off and she wanted to spend more time with her horses. Oh…that reminds me. I'm supposed to be judging the dress-ups at the pony club Christmas do later today. I can't let them down.'

'I'm sure they won't mind if I step in to help with that,' Tilly assured him. 'It was only because of me that you got involved with the pony club in the first place, after all.'

'But what about tomorrow?' Jim was frowning deeply. 'I'm always Father Christmas at the village barbecue. I've done that for fifty years. I'm not about to let someone else do it.'

'You might have to,' Tilly warned.

'There's nobody that could do it like I do,' Jim muttered. 'And the kids think I'm the real thing. They'll stop believing there's a Santa Claus.'

'It might be a bit of a giveaway that Santa's wearing the same big boot on his foot and using crutches just like their family doctor.' Tilly picked up her sandwich. 'They're not going to guess it's not you if someone's wearing the full outfit with that padded stomach and the bushy fake beard.'

'It's not just what I look like. It's how I talk to the kiddies. And what I say.'

'You've got time to pass on all your Santa wisdom,' Tilly told him. 'So all you really need is a good actor to take on the role. It's a good thing I happened to bring one with me, isn't it?'

From nowhere, Tilly could suddenly hear an echo of Harry's voice.

'I missed my vocation, really. I could have been an actor...'

And it wasn't only his voice that she was remembering. She could almost feel the touch of his hands on her shoulders and that heat that had been generated in her entire body. The heat that she'd both wanted, but been so scared, to feel again was hovering just out of reach, like a fragment of a dream that was playing hard to catch.

Tilly took a big bite of her sandwich. Because she didn't dare catch Harry's gaze. He might guess the turmoil that was going on as the reactions of her body and brain vied for emotional supremacy. That a part of her wanted nothing more than for him to touch her again.

But an even bigger part wanted nothing more than to run as fast and as far away from him as possible.

No... Harry couldn't believe what he was hearing. A dress-up competition? A village party? Dressing up in a full Father Christmas outfit with its long sleeves and fur trim and probably an itchy fake beard and moustache and then cooking in blazing summer sunshine?

It was more than weird.

It was...

Perfect, that was what it was. Utterly foreign, which meant there was no danger of it reminding him of any Christmas from his childhood or stirring up the sadness of losing his only family, which had been the main reason he'd left his home country in the first place.

In fact, the more he threw himself into whatever bizarre traditions that were followed in this part of the world, the easier this was going to be. It really would be acting, and he hadn't been lying when he'd told Tilly he was good at it. He was so good at it, in fact, that it was automatic. Often, he didn't even need to make a conscious effort.

Like now, as he let his smile widen until he looked like he was being offered an opportunity he'd always wanted.

'Sounds like this is going to be a Christmas to remember,' he said. 'Bring it on.'

'They don't really dress up the ponies, do they?'

'Of course. I won the first prize when I was eight. Spud had a unicorn horn on his bridle, a pink mane and tail and glitter all over and I had the most beautiful princess dress and a cone hat with a long veil.'

Tilly was driving her own vehicle—a rugged old Jeep that had as many scrapes and dents as her father's ute—as she took Harry for his 'tiki tour' that would eventually see them attend the finale of the local pony club's Christmas event.

Currently, they were on an unsealed private road that was part of the Grimshaws' high country sheep station, winding through hills that were providing an increasingly impressive view. The drop off the side of the road was slightly hair-raising at times, however. Like when they came around a tight down sloping bend to find a small mob of sheep in the middle of the road. Tilly braked instantly and then turned the vehicle into the direction of a skid that could have sent them sideways into a fence, with all the skill of a rally driver, before bringing the Jeep to a halt. It was seriously impressive.

'Where on earth did you learn to drive like this?'

'Right here.' Tilly's gesture took in the countryside stretched out below them before being cut off by distant mountains. 'Dad taught me to drive by making me his chauffeur on all his weekend call-outs. Shingle roads, four-wheel driving off road, unexpected encounters with livestock, black ice and dealing with snowstorms was all part of the training.' She threw Harry a wry smile as she drove slowly towards the sheep, who were now standing completely still, staring at the vehicle. 'It was a different story trying to deal with rush hour traffic in a big city, mind you. I hated it for a long time.' She tooted the horn and the sheep finally began moving out of their way.

'Do we need to get them off the road and back into the field?'

Tilly shook her head. 'They're grazing the long acre.'

Harry snorted. 'You really do talk a different language around here.'

'It's the grass verge on either side of the road. Easier to let the sheep out to eat it down than use a tractor to mow it. You'll see farmers using electric fences on public roads, but this is private land. There'll be another gate you can open soon, and we'll make sure it's shut behind us so the sheep don't go anywhere they're not supposed to, like the homestead gardens.'

Harry watched a few sheep that were trotting in front of them. 'They're very dirty sheep.'

'They're merinos. They always look a bit grubby on the outside, but they've got beautiful white wool underneath. New Zealand produces the best merino wool in the world and this station's famous for their micron count. Under eleven is about as low as it gets.'

'There you go again. Foreign language.'

'Micron count is how fine the wool is. A human hair is about sixty to seventy microns, so that gives you an idea of how fine the wool around here is.'

This time it wasn't a physical skill that impressed Harry. It was her breadth of knowledge. Tilly must have caught what he was thinking as she glanced at his face because she shrugged off any compliment.

'I only know this because my mother started a business in creating high-end merino fabric. And by high end, I mean the best. With her contacts in the fashion industry, she ended up being in huge demand to supply the kind of quality that you see in Armani suits or a Dior coat.'

'That sounds like a high-pressure career.'

'She was always away,' Tilly told him. 'For fashion weeks or photo shoots all over the world. Taking suitcases full of samples and meeting with designers and tailors. She took me to Italy with her on one trip but I hated it. I missed her when she was away, but I missed my pony and my dad too much when I went with her.'

'Your dad didn't go too?'

'No. He adored my mother but he was just as passionate about his work. He's always had a huge sense of responsibility to his patients and community. He still does.'

Harry nodded. 'I can see that. He's going to hate being out of action for as long as it takes for his ankle to heal.'

'I might have to take some more time off and help out until a locum can be found. It's the least I should do after he practically brought me up by himself, even before Mum died.'

'How old were you when you lost your mum?'

'Nine.'

'What happened? Was it sudden?'

Tilly nodded. 'Instant. She had a cerebral aneurysm—at a fashion show in Paris. They said she wouldn't have known anything about it.'

Harry could remember being nine years old. When his mother was by far the most important person in his world and her love had been as sought after as sunshine. Losing her mother like that—not even being anywhere near her when it happened—must have been an incredibly traumatic part of her childhood, but Harry wasn't about to step onto such personal ground by asking any more questions.

'You'd be the perfect locum,' he suggested instead. 'You probably know all his patients as well as he does.'

'Hardly. I left to go to university and I've never been back for more than a few days at a time since then.'

Harry regretted his suggestion as Tilly turned away. He could almost feel shutters coming down and the way she leaned on the horn to scatter the final sheep from the road was the kind of warning signal you might expect from an Ice Queen. This wasn't something she wanted to talk about, was it? And it wasn't any of his business anyway.

So why was he becoming increasingly curious?

Tilly might have had a closer relationship with her father, but had she been hurt by her mother's absence in her early years? Left feeling abandoned at times? Was that part of why her father worried about her being lonely as an adult? And, if she and Jim had such a close bond, why had she been avoiding spending time back here?

Harry could almost see the curling corners of layers to Matilda Dawson, and it was tempting to try peeling them off to discover what was underneath but he knew that wasn't a good idea. Getting too involved with anything—or any*one*—was never a good idea because it inevitably led to tears and even if they weren't his own tears, or if they were symbolic rather than real, Harry had learned it was better to avoid them as much as possible. You kept your distance and, as an insurance policy, you moved on and made a fresh start as often as possible.

It was a relief to distract himself as well as Tilly as they rounded the next bend and then pulled to a halt. He jumped out to open and then close the wide wire gate that would keep the sheep safely enclosed in the 'long acre'. And minutes later they had arrived at their destination.

The sprawling old homestead they arrived at was a hive of activity. A tent was being put up on the front lawn. Several small children, wearing bathing suits, were playing in the spray of a garden sprinkler, shrieking with delight. A man about Harry's age was on a ladder on the veranda, winding long strips of tinsel through the wrought iron lacework.

'Hey... Tilly... I heard you were going to drop in.' He climbed down off the ladder. 'Long time, no see.'

'Hi, Doug. How's it going?'

'Oh...you know.' He was rubbing the back of his neck. 'Kind of crazy, but wonderful. Biggest gathering of the clan we've ever had for Christmas, but knowing it's the last one for Mum is...well...' He cleared his throat. 'We're under instructions to make it the best one ever and apparently that means putting up every Christmas decoration that five generations of Grimshaws have accumulated.'

Doug was giving Harry a curious glance and he wondered how Tilly was going to introduce him, but it seemed that wasn't necessary.

'You must be the boyfriend we've heard about.

You're very welcome, mate. I went to school with Tilly, and we all knew she was going to end up being a doctor like her dad.' Doug was smiling as he held out his hand to shake Harry's. 'Knows her own mind, this one. Bit bossy, even...'

Wow...news travelled fast in these parts. Harry caught Tilly's gaze and could read what felt like a confirmation that information was not only widely shared around here but would be a subject of great interest. That there could be repercussions for anything that was seen or heard by others and that Tilly was nervous about an upset that could spoil the next few days. Mainly for her father, he suspected, but also for herself. She might be choosing not to live where she grew up, or even visit very much, but this place—and its people—were important to her.

It didn't even feel as if Harry was acting as he gave her the kind of reassuring, *loving* smile that a couple might share before returning Doug's firm handshake.

'Sometimes bossy can be a very good thing,' he said. 'Tilly's the one you want to be in charge if you're badly injured or sick, that's for sure.'

It was Doug who was smiling at Tilly now. 'I've heard that. You probably don't realise how proud your dad is of you. Come inside. Mum's looking forward to seeing you.' His smile widened. 'And the first man you've ever brought home.'

The interior of the old homestead had been renovated over the years to create a huge open area of a kitchen and living area—a welcoming space that was full of light. It was also very full of Christmas decorations at the moment. The tip of a real pine tree in one corner touched the high ceiling and was smothered with fairy lights and decorations. The bucket it was anchored into was invisible behind a mountain of brightly wrapped parcels. Tinsel and paper streamers were looped over the rest of the ceiling, numerous stockings were attached to a wide mantelpiece over the fireplace and every available flat surface had some kind of seasonal ornament on it.

The most notable feature of the room, however, was a hospital bed that was positioned so that its occupant had a clear view of the living area, the kitchen and the views of the gardens and mountains from the windows. The bed had silver tinsel wound around the metal framework, a cheerful red blanket and two small children sitting quietly on the end of the bed playing with toys. As Tilly and Harry approached, two teenagers moved closer to gather up the children and Doug scooped up a toddler from the floor nearby.

'Let's all go outside for a few minutes,' he said, 'and let Dr Tilly talk to Nana.'

Harry had seen Tilly approach all sorts of people in her work environment, patients and colleagues, in all sorts of situations. Even in an emergency—okay, maybe *especially* in an emergency—she always gave the impression of being perfectly calm and in total control. Just the way you'd expect an Ice Queen to behave.

He'd never seen her like this. With tears in her eyes and a wobble in her voice as she reached to hug the woman propped up amongst a cloud of pillows.

'Oh, *Maggie*…'

'If it can't be Jim looking after me, I'm so glad it's you, darling.' Maggie's skin was almost as pale as the white pillows she was resting against but her eyes were bright as she shifted her gaze. 'And you must be Harry. It's another gift for me this Christmas, to know that she's found someone special enough to bring home.'

Oh…*help*…

Suddenly, this game of pretending to be Matilda Dawson's boyfriend for a day or two had become something very different. Something that really mattered to people that Tilly cared about. Something significant.

'It's a privilege to meet you, so it is, Maggie,' Harry said.

'Oh…' Maggie's face lit up with a smile that was directed at Tilly. 'That *accent*… I can see why you fell for him.' She looked back at Harry. 'I had such a crush on Tilly's father when I was at school,' she told him. 'I still had my eye on him after he came back as a newly qualified doctor, but then he met Chiara when she was here for a fashion shoot in the mountains and that was that. Mind you, I could hardly blame him. She was the most beautiful woman I'd ever seen and then she became my best friend…' Maggie paused for breath and then patted Tilly's hand. 'I've got a photo of us in the box over there. I was just sorting them. Can you find it to show Harry?'

It was an old photo. Black and white. It was only Maggie's smile that made her recognisable as one of the young women sitting on a rock beside a lake, but Harry could have sworn that her companion was Tilly. Chiara's dark hair was long and loose, being lifted by a gust of wind, and she seemed to be laughing as she tried to keep it out of her eyes.

And Maggie was right. She was the most beautiful woman *he'd* ever seen as well.

He raised his gaze to Tilly and realised that he'd only ever seen her like this, with her hair scraped back so hard it almost looked like glossy black paint on her skull. If she let it escape from that tight style she could look like her mother's twin. A vibrant, dark angel with no hint of ice anywhere.

Harry listened quietly as Tilly got on with what needed to be done on this visit. She topped up the syringe driver that was delivering a steady dose of narcotics beneath Maggie's skin and she changed the transcutaneous patch that was also part of her pain relief. They talked about how effective the medications for nausea and other symptoms were and whether there was anything else that was needed medically at the moment.

And he kept sneaking more glances at Tilly's face. Imagining her with her hair loose. Taking notice of more than simply her hair. He'd noticed the difference this morning, when he'd seen Tilly wearing clothes other than the baggy scrubs she wore at work, but she'd chosen jeans and a designer sweatshirt to travel in. She'd changed almost as soon as they'd arrived home, and now she was wearing a pair of light cargo pants that ended below the knee and she had a white singlet top beneath a shirt that was mostly unbuttoned. How had he not noticed the generous curve of her breasts on that slim frame? That subtle hint of cleavage, even?

He was seeing the shape of her body in a whole new light as he realised how attractive Tilly actually was.

No... Harry could feel his heart sink as he corrected himself. As he realised how attracted *he* actually was *to* Tilly.

This was definitely not a part of the plan.

Neither was getting emotionally involved. With a family determined to make the most of a last Christmas with a beloved mother and grandmother, or with someone who had ties with this family that were linked to her own, possibly complicated, past.

He could see the tight grip of Maggie and Tilly's hands. He could *feel* the emotion and bond between them.

'I'll be back around the same time tomorrow but don't hesitate to call before then if there's anything bothering you.'

'I'll be fine.'

They all knew that Maggie was not going to be fine but Harry saw the way Tilly followed the older woman's courageous lead. She even found a smile.

'We're off to the pony club party now. I'm filling in for Dad to help judge the fancy-dress competition.'

'I've got two of my grandies there. Look out for Sammy and George. They're twins. Do you remember Doug's older brother, John?'

Tilly nodded. 'Of course. He's got a farm just outside Arrowtown, hasn't he?'

'Yes. But the twins brought their ponies here to get dressed up for the party so I could see them.' Maggie's smile was overly bright. 'They're being Christmas elves and the ponies are reindeer. Nice and easy this time. Do you remember when you won? With your princess costume?'

'You took me,' Tilly said, nodding. 'Mum was away and Dad got called to an accident at the last minute and I was so upset because I thought I wasn't going to be able to go to the party. I remember him ringing you in a panic.'

'He'll be so happy to have you home for Christmas,' Maggie said. 'Are you staying around a bit longer this time?'

Harry could sense that Tilly was trying to put those shutters up again, the way she had when he'd suggested she could work here as her father's locum. It was obviously harder for her to try and shut Maggie out, however.

'Ah, well...' Maggie reached up to touch Tilly's cheek. 'You'll be back when you're ready, darling. It's your home.' She lay back against her pillows, letting her gaze drift around the room with all its decorations and the smell of Christmas baking. 'We all need to be home in the end,' she said softly.

Both Harry and Tilly were quiet as they drove back through the mob of sheep on the farm's private road. Maybe Tilly was already feeling the grief of losing someone special in her life and he could understand that. All too well. He might be trying to stay uninvolved but maybe it was already too late. And maybe he could offer Tilly a small amount of comfort?

'It's very sad,' he said finally. 'But how lucky is Maggie to be at home with her whole family gathering around her? I was the only family my mam had, and I was too far away when she died.' Harry found himself swallowing hard. 'It's something I'll have to live with but it's made it too hard to go home ever since.'

Tilly didn't speak but her wide-eyed glance said it all. Harry could see surprise that he'd shared something so personal and a connection in that they'd both lost their mothers too soon. It was a glance that only lasted a heartbeat but it gave Harry a glimpse behind the shutters and he could see a child who had lost something she'd never been able to replace. That perhaps she'd never had enough of in the first place? He could feel that vulnerability he'd sensed when he'd wondered if she was lonely and that sense of connection that had hit him like a brick when she'd explained why she had decided to pretend to her father that she was in a serious relationship. After his own revelation when he'd seen that photograph of her mother, there was physical attraction adding a powerful new element to the mix.

Had he really thought he could stay uninvolved?

That ship had already sailed, hadn't it?

And the mix of emotion he was wading through was suddenly enough to make something else seem crystal clear.

'I think Maggie was right,' he added. 'We do all need to be home in the end. I keep going to new places thinking I'm going to find whatever it is I'm looking for and I never do. I think it might be time for me to go home. Perhaps whatever it is, is waiting for me back in Ireland.'

All he could see in Tilly's glance this time was curiosity. 'What is it that you're looking for?'

'I don't know exactly,' Harry admitted. 'I just know there's something missing.'

'Have you ever thought that you might have already found it, but you kept going because you didn't recognise it?'

Harry shook his head. 'I'd know.'

'How?'

Harry shrugged. Then he shook his head to signal

an end to a conversation that was getting far too philosophical. 'How are *you* going to know,' he countered, 'who the best dressed-up pony is?'

Tilly threw him a smile. 'I'll know,' she said. 'Because it'll feel right.'

CHAPTER FIVE

THE CRAIG'S GULLY DOMAIN, a ten-acre paddock near the lake, bordered by trees that were at least a hundred years old, with its clubrooms, children's playground, tennis courts and a barbecue picnic area was as familiar to Matilda Dawson as the gardens surrounding the home she'd grown up in. Arriving there straight after the visit to Maggie made it feel as if her entire childhood was beginning to fold itself around her like a cloak.

One that felt too heavy. Too hot on this summer's day. Too...suffocating?

She could hear the peal of a child's laughter in the distance, the barking of a dog and the whinny of an overexcited pony. She could see colour everywhere, as both children and their ponies were getting ready for the grand parade and the judging of the fancy-dress costumes. As she and Harry got closer to the picnic area she could even smell the last sausage being taken from the grill to get wrapped in soft bread with a generous splodge of tomato sauce on top.

Good grief...she could almost taste how delicious it was going to be to that hungry child who'd come looking for more food.

The area around the clubrooms was a hive of activity. There were parents tidying up equipment that had been used for games, older riders stacking jumping poles onto a trailer and rolling barrels into the storage space behind the building and other adults who were gathered near one of the big wooden tables that held an urn of hot water, a huge enamel teapot and plates of homemade biscuits and slices.

A chorus of greetings began as soon as they were within earshot.

'Tilly... Merry Christmas! It's so good you could come...'

'How's your dad? We've all heard the news...'

Judging by the looks Harry was receiving, everybody had also heard the news that she'd brought a man home for the first time, which meant that everybody was talking about her. That weighty cloak Tilly had been aware of carrying on her shoulders got a little bit heavier.

'What terrible timing to break his leg right before Christmas...'

'Tilly! It must be ten years since I saw you... You haven't changed a bit.'

That had to be the understatement of the year, Tilly thought, but she recognised an old school and pony club friend just as easily, although Shelley had cut her hair short and had a baby in her arms.

'Would you like a cup of tea? Something to eat?'

'Mrs Patterson.' Tilly turned to the older woman, who really hadn't changed a bit in more than the last decade. 'Are you still the president of the club?'

'Call me Helen, dear. You're all grown up now.' Helen was smiling. 'And no, I haven't been president for a long time, but I'd never miss the Christmas party. I'm always on the judging panel with Jim.'

Tilly was about to introduce Harry to Helen but, as she turned, she could see—and hear—a parent coming towards them, carrying a child who was cradling his arm and sobbing loudly.

'Thank goodness you're here, Tilly,' Helen said. 'We've been missing having Jim as our first aid officer. Looks like Max is our first injury of the day.'

But it wasn't Tilly who got to the child first. It was Harry. She could hear his voice over the miserable crying.

'Is it a plane? Is it a bird? No…it has to be *Superman*…'

The boy was, indeed, wearing a Superman outfit but the excited announcement of his arrival was enough of a surprise to make his cries fade as he stared at Harry instead.

'Max fell off Toby.' His mother sounded worried. 'He's hurt his arm.'

'Are you sure he wasn't flying?' Harry asked. 'Like this?' He held his arms straight in front of him, his head lowered, but he was peeping up at Max.

Tilly saw him wiggle his eyebrows. Max not only stopped crying completely, he giggled.

'Can I see your arm?' Harry asked. 'I know all about flying injuries. Batman came into my hospital once. He'd fallen out of the sky too.'

Max's mother was staring at Harry with an expression very similar to her son's, but there was less tension in her body language. 'Max is upset in case it means he's going to miss the parade.'

'Let's see about that,' Harry said. 'How 'bout we fly you over to the picnic table, Max?'

The small boy seemed happy to be lifted and swooped away to sit on the edge of the picnic table.

'Can you do the secret Superman wave?' Harry had his arms in the air again, this time moving his hands and fingers in gentle spirals.

He could.

'And can I feel those super muscles in your arm?'

Tilly could see how gentle Harry was being as he examined Max's arm and how thorough he was being, despite the unusual approach to an orthopaedic assessment. She could also see the way Max's mother melted under a smile from Harry as he finished, and she could feel herself frowning at the reminder of why she'd never wanted to have anything to do with this good-looking Irishman. Why she'd kept herself safe from falling under that charming spell.

'I don't have my X-ray vision working today, but I'm happy this isn't an obvious fracture,' he said to Max's mother. 'If we put a nice firm bandage on it, I think Max will be good to go for the parade, but if you notice any swelling or increased pain later on he'll need to be seen again.'

Helen found the first aid box and provided a bandage. She even found a tissue for Max to blow his nose on.

'You go and get ready now,' she told him. 'Maybe Mum can lead Toby in the parade for you so there's no chance of any more bumps.' She turned to Tilly. 'Head out to the middle of the domain and we'll get organised to ride in a big circle around you.' She beamed at Harry. 'And take this gorgeous young man with you. He's clearly an expert on superheroes and probably dragons and elves as well.' She turned away. 'I'll be there in a minute. I've just got to find the box of rosettes and ribbons.'

Harry was nodding but he raised an eyebrow at Tilly as Helen sped off. 'Dragons?'

Tilly pointed as she started walking towards the middle of the large grassy area. 'Over there.'

The pony had a green blanket draped over its body, and there were soft fabric spikes attached to its mane and tail. The rider was wearing a brightly coloured dress and some butterfly wings. There was a unicorn behind her and then a small Shetland pony that was covered in a fluffy white costume to look like a sheep, with her rider dressed as Little Bo Peep.

'There's Maggie's grandies.' Tilly pointed again. 'The matching reindeer and elves.'

The twins' ponies had reindeer antlers attached to their bridles and sleigh bells and tinsel on the reins. Five-year-old Sammy and George had green elf costumes with stripy red and white socks and hats with large plastic ears attached and their father walked between the ponies holding the lead ropes.

'I assumed they were identical twins,' Tilly said. 'I didn't expect one of them to be a girl. Is Sammy a Samantha or George a Georgia?'

'Could be either,' Harry said. 'But it doesn't matter—they're both adorable. Will you look at those smiles?'

But Tilly was looking at Harry. 'You really like kids, don't you?'

'I do.'

'Have you got any of your own?'

He looked startled. 'I'm single,' he told her. 'I thought you knew that.'

'Being single and being a father are not mutually exclusive,' Tilly said. 'And...well...you must know the kind of reputation you have with women.'

For a heartbeat it felt as if Tilly was looking at someone she'd never seen before. Someone who was not only hurt by what she'd said but was somehow deeply disappointed? The impression was gone as instantly as a switch being flicked, however, and the Harry Doyle she was more familiar with was back again as he shrugged.

'What can I do?' he murmured. 'For some inexplicable reason, women seem to fall in love with me with no encouragement.'

Tilly wasn't about to tell him that the reason was actually quite obvious. Or that no more encouragement than one of those smiles was probably needed. Instead, she looked away to where the line of ponies and children was getting rapidly longer.

'Have you never fallen in love back, then?' she asked lightly.

'Why would I do that?' Harry's tone was just as light. 'It might just give me another place I wouldn't want to go back to.'

Like he hadn't wanted to go back to his homeland? Because he didn't want to be reminded of losing his mother? What was that saying about many a true word being spoken in jest? Tilly stole another sideways glance. Somehow the idea of him having been so devastated by losing his mum didn't fit at all with the image of a man who wasn't bothered by any broken hearts he was leaving in his wake.

Helen arrived with the box of ribbons and rosettes and a megaphone and the parade began as ponies and riders began walking in a big circle around the judges.

'They all deserve a prize,' Harry declared.

'Well, we've got enough ribbons,' Helen said. 'We'd just need to come up with enough categories.' With a smile, she handed Harry the megaphone.

Again, here was the Harry that Tilly thought she knew. The confident charmer who could walk into any space and become the centre of attention. The man that every woman wanted to be noticed by. And the fact that he had the ability to dry a child's tears with a performance like the one she'd witnessed when he'd looked after Max would only make him that much more attractive to anyone who was seeking a father for her future children.

It was just as well she wasn't planning on having a family herself, wasn't it?

Harry quickly got into announcing categories and winners. Helen and Tilly attached the ribbons and rosettes to the ponies and congratulated the riders. By the time the adults in the audience realised that every single child was going to be awarded a prize, Harry had won their wholehearted support and the clapping and cheers got more enthusiastic.

'And the prize for the best retro costume—not to mention a reminder that we should all take the time to smell the flowers—are our hippies.'

The pony had peace signs painted on its flanks and a garland of flowers around its neck to match the wreath its rider was wearing along with her fringed vest and flared jeans.

The best nursery rhyme character went to the sheep and Bo Peep and there was an 'African animal' category for the white horse with black zebra stripes and the brown one that had been painted to look like a giraffe. Maggie's grandchildren were awarded a 'best matching' prize.

Helen made a brief speech thanking all the parents for their support and wishing them all a happy holiday period. She finished by thanking Tilly and Harry for their help with the judging.

'And please tell Jim that the whole club is wishing him a very speedy recovery from his injury,' she finished.

'Yeah...' someone shouted. 'I'm not putting my hand up to clean those barbecues again.'

Tilly was shaking her head as they drove away from the domain a short time later. 'I can't believe Dad still fronts up and cleans those barbecues,' she said. 'I haven't been to a pony club picnic in nearly twenty years. Guess it's one of those small-town things you can never escape if you still live here.'

'Why would you want to?' Harry asked. 'That was one of the best parties I've ever been to. You've already got the pony,' he added. 'You just need a few kids to go with it.'

'Spud's retired.' Tilly didn't want to continue this conversation. 'And I'm no more interested in having kids than you are.'

'I didn't say I wasn't interested,' Harry protested. 'Just that I don't have any. Yet.'

'How many are you thinking of having?'

'Six.' Harry's tone was decisive. 'That way none of them would ever get lonely.'

Tilly laughed out loud but a part of her was imagining Harry with a whole tribe of children and it was making her feel...what...shut out of something important? Like the feeling of coming home she'd had arriving back at the old house tucked into the hills or feeling the warmth of the greetings today from people she hadn't seen for so many years. Like when she'd felt Maggie hugging her back or when she'd seen Shelley with her baby and the man who'd been doing her father's job of cleaning the barbecue.

And there was something else nagging at the back of her mind. Harry had been an only child too. Had he wished for a whole tribe of siblings because of how lonely he'd been himself?

It was tempting to ask but Tilly stopped herself because she had a feeling that she might get another glimpse of the man hiding behind what Harry preferred the world to see. Like seeing the person who'd looked disappointed or hurt, even, by the suggestion he had a reputation that was less than desirable when it came to his relationships with women. Maybe she didn't want to know any more about who the real Harry Doyle might be because there was something here that went far beyond any charm or good looks. Something compelling enough to be disturbing. Something that would draw her too close for comfort.

Fortunately, Harry didn't seem to want to reveal anything else.

'It might never happen,' he said. 'I'm happy the way I am. I love my work.'

'Me too,' Tilly said. 'My career is everything I could have dreamed of, and you can't have that and have kids as well.'

'Some people do.'

'Well, it's not fair on the kids.' Tilly knew she sounded too vehement. Angry, even, so she took a breath and tried to sound like a reasonable adult and not like an unhappy child. 'I'm not going to be the kind of mother who's never there when she's needed. To have kids who know they're not as important as her damn career.'

Harry might be looking out of his side window but she could feel that he was listening to every word.

'My father pretty much brought me up on his own.'

'Looks like he did a good job,' Harry said. 'And he managed to have a career of his own at the same time. I got the impression that he's a much-loved member of this community.'

Tilly blew out a frustrated breath this time. 'I have no desire to end up as a rural GP. Can you imagine how boring that would be after years in a big city emergency department? Treating the same chronic health problems or minor injuries day after day? Anything really interesting or challenging and you'd be referring them to someone else or calling a helicopter to take them away.'

But Harry didn't seem to be listening to her any longer. He was even more focused on the view from his window. 'They work hard around here, these farmers. Will you look at all that hay?'

Huge round bales were dotted over the paddocks they were passing and there were teams of people busy with tractors and other large pieces of machinery.

'It's probably baleage rather than hay.' Tilly was more than happy to move away from discussing anything personal—like Harry's plans to go back to Ireland and create a big happy family—and go back to her role as a tour guide. 'They look like they're getting ready to wrap the bales in plastic. It's quicker to make because you don't have to leave it to dry so long and it's easier to store. But you're right. They'll be working hard to get it all in while the weather holds. And hoping to get the day off to have Christmas with their families, I expect.'

Yep. This was working well. That disturbing sensation of getting too close to the real Harry was fading fast.

'They'll be making the most of the long summer evenings. It's light enough to work until about ten o'clock at night at the moment.'

It was still more than light, and warm, enough to have dinner outside in the courtyard at the back of the old Dawson villa. Recycled bricks for paving and a lush grapevine growing over a pergola to create a green ceiling gave the area a European vibe, even without the rustic furniture, citrus trees like lemons and mandarins growing in half wine barrels and a generous scattering of candle-holders. A long table and chairs took up one part of the courtyard and there was a seating area around an enormous fire pit on the other side, near a barbecue set up that was more like an outdoor kitchen.

Jim Dawson was sitting in the wheelchair, his moon-boot supported by a cushion on the solid wooden bench running the length of the outdoor table, supervising Harry, who was cooking vegetables on a solid grill and about to add some thick slices of fillet steak to the grill over open flames.

'Put Tilly's on first,' Jim directed. 'She likes it incinerated, don't you, love?'

'It's called "well done", Dad.' Tilly put a bowl of fresh green salad on the table beside a basket of bread and smiled at her father as she began arranging cutlery and plates. 'It's good to see you looking a bit brighter.'

'The painkillers are doing a good job.' Jim nodded. 'Plus, I slept most of the afternoon while you were out. I couldn't do much else after I found that all the needles were falling off that old fake tree. I'll test out my crutches when I go and find a real one to chop down in the back paddock after dinner, but I might need some help getting it back to the house.'

'You'll do no such thing,' Tilly said. 'You're allowed to test out your crutches to get around the house when it's absolutely necessary, but that's it. If we see you even trying to put any weight on that leg you'll lose that privilege as well. I'm sure there must be a bedpan amongst that medical museum you've collected out in the barn.'

Harry was grinning broadly. 'I think she's serious, Jim. Don't worry, I'll go and cut down a tree for you.' He was using tongs to turn fried potatoes and mushrooms. 'Let's enjoy dinner first, though. This smells so good.'

'Thanks, lad.' But Jim had caught Tilly's gaze. 'Now, tell me more about how Maggie seemed and how the rest of the family is holding up. And I want to know all about the pony club parade too. It's the first time I've missed it in more than twenty-five years.'

It was Harry who added considerably to Tilly's reports on their afternoon. He wasn't simply a born entertainer, she thought, he was a born storyteller as well. He had them all laughing as he described his terror at seeing a wall of sheep ahead when he had a sheer cliff on his side and again as he role-played the response that people in Ireland might have to ponies and riders dressed up like dragons or elves.

'Sounds more like leprechauns.' His accent was

stronger than Tilly had ever heard before. 'Were they as short as our tricksy little fairies? Did you get your three wishes?'

And then he had them all almost in tears as he talked to Jim about Maggie.

'She's in the best place she could possibly be,' he said quietly. 'In the very heart of her family. And in what has to be the most beautiful part of this world I think I've ever seen.'

Jim didn't have any hesitation to ask about things that Tilly was avoiding.

'You must be missing your family, lad,' he said. 'Especially at this time of year.'

'There was only ever my mam,' Harry told him. 'And she died not long after I graduated from medical school. When I was working too many hours to be able to get home for Christmas. But I had it all planned for the next year. I was going to buy the apartment she was living in for her so she'd never have to move again.'

Tilly could see all those years of experience in hearing people's stories etched in the lines of empathy in her father's face but it wasn't hard to feel beneath Harry's words herself. She could hear the loneliness of a small boy and, if she hadn't already been aware of how hard the loss of his only parent had been, she would have heard how much love there had been between them in that desire to protect his mother and keep her safe for the rest of her life. To make her happy, which was pretty much what her motivation had been when she'd lied to her father about Harry.

'So you had to move a lot?' Jim asked.

'We had to go to where Mam could find a new job.

Or cheaper rent. I think I went to about fifteen different schools.'

'Not easy,' Jim murmured. 'Being the new kid at school is always scary.'

Harry laughed off what had probably been only a part of a tough childhood. 'Especially when you're the new kid with sticky-out ears. I looked like a wee leprechaun myself, so I did. If I hadn't figured out I could use it to make people laugh, I would have been the most picked-on kid ever.'

So his ability to put on a performance and such a convincing act had come from learning to survive? How much had he been bullied before he'd figured out a way to deflect any attacks? Tilly found herself staring at the tousled waves of dark hair on Harry's head. Did he wear his hair that little bit longer than could be considered neat because he'd learned that it could hide his ears?

Yeah…now that she was looking for it, she could see the outline of Harry's ears quite clearly and the squeeze on her heart was so hard she could feel a part of it cracking. There was something that he must have learned long before he was in control of how long his hair was and that would have been how to protect himself from being picked on by hiding any feelings that would make him seem weaker—like being scared or lonely.

Oh, man…she knew how hard it was to hide feelings like that. And how you had to do it all by yourself because telling someone who you loved the most—like your only parent—would have caused even more pain.

Sometimes, being pulled closer to someone was impossible to predict or resist. The unexpected feeling of a connection with Harry on a level this deep was like something sharp widening that crack in her heart, opening up a place that hadn't seen the light of day for a very long time.

It was so bright it was blinding.

Painful, even. And, weirdly, given that the light was only imaginary, it seemed to be bright enough to be making her eyes water.

Good grief...

What on earth had possessed him to talk about his childhood like that? To confess the curse of ears that he'd learned to disguise well enough as a teenager by keeping the waves of his hair long enough. He suspected that Tilly's father had seen through his joking about being shifted from pillar to post and bullied at every new school, but maybe it didn't matter that Jim—or Tilly, for that matter—knew more about him than anyone else.

It felt as if it wouldn't make any difference. Not simply because he was only here for a couple of days but because he felt welcome enough to feel at home, both in this wonderful old house but amongst the community the Dawsons were a part of. He hadn't been lying when he'd told Tilly that the pony club picnic had been one of the best parties he'd ever been to. He liked these people. He liked Tilly's father. He wasn't going to think about whether or not he really liked Tilly, however, because that would inevitably remind him of that unsettling physical attraction he'd experienced earlier that afternoon.

Helpfully, Jim was providing a distraction as he

reached for the crutches he'd propped against the end of the table.

'Where are you off to, Dad?' Tilly's tone suggested she was about to order him to sit down again.

'I'm about ready to hit the sack.' he responded. 'It's been quite a day and those pills have knocked me a bit.'

'Don't you want any dessert? I could make a quick fruit salad to have with some ice cream.'

Jim shook his head, but he was smiling. 'Not for me, thanks, love.' He was pushing himself to his feet, with one hand on the edge of the table for balance.

Harry started to get to his feet to help but Jim shook his head again. 'Stay there, son. You've done enough to help for one day. I can manage.'

Tilly followed her father back into the house, watching carefully that he didn't put any weight on his injured leg, but she came back to the courtyard only a short time later.

'It's a good thing the house is all on one level. He's determined to be independent, but I don't think he'll get himself into too much trouble between the bathroom and his bedroom.' She put a bowl onto the table. 'Cheat's dessert,' she admitted. 'But you can't leave Central Otago without tasting some of the stone fruit we're famous for. And it's not Christmastime without cherries.'

Harry reached for a cluster of the plump, bright red cherries as Tilly sat down, but she had the same idea and his fingers touched hers before they found the fruit. That sharp tingle of awareness as his skin touched hers should have been more than enough of a warning but it didn't stop him lifting his gaze as Tilly put a cherry to her mouth moments later and bit into it. Seeing dark red juice staining her lips made that tingle morph into a shaft of a much more intense sensation that came from deep in his belly. This was a warning he couldn't afford to ignore. There was no way he could sit here and watch her eat cherries.

Harry avoided meeting Tilly's gaze so she couldn't know the direction his thoughts were trying to go. He stood up as well, perhaps for the reassurance that he was still in complete control of his body.

'It'll be dark soon,' he said. 'Is there enough time for me to go and cut down that tree your dad wants?'

'Oh... I'd forgotten about that. Yes...' Tilly got back to her feet. 'We'd better do that, or he might head out with a saw first thing in the morning. I'll just take these plates inside and give them a quick rinse.'

'I'll help.'

Harry picked up Jim's empty plate and then stepped close enough to reach for Tilly's, only she was already reaching to pick up her own plate and, again, their hands touched. This time, it seemed that both of them were shocked by that electric tingle. Plates clattered down onto the table and cutlery jangled onto the bricks below. Harry stooped to gather up the knives and forks and, as he straightened, he noticed two things.

One was that Jim Dawson was standing in the window of a nearby room on the corner of the house, leaning on his crutches as he looked out, probably to enjoy the sight of the fairy lights and candles in this courtyard as the daylight faded. The other was that he'd somehow got a lot closer to Tilly, who had stacked up the plates on the table. She held her hand out for the cutlery.

'I can see your dad at a window,' he said. 'In the room under the turret.'

'That's his bedroom. That's where he's supposed to be.'

Tilly had wrapped her fingers around the cutlery handles, but Harry didn't let go. 'If I can see him, he can see us.'

Tilly wasn't letting go of the cutlery either. And now her gaze was holding his just as tightly. He saw the tip of her tongue emerge to touch her lips.

'So...?'

'So maybe we should give him something more interesting to see...?'

He could see the instant that Tilly understood what he was suggesting. And, despite the fading light and the dark brown colour of her eyes, he was sure he could see her pupils dilating enough to signal that she not only understood, she was up for it.

And maybe it had nothing to do with trying to put on a convincing performance of being a loved-up couple for her father.

Maybe Tilly wanted it as much as he suddenly did?

They were both still holding that damned cutlery as he bent his head to touch her lips with his own, but Harry found himself letting go as the astonishment of that first contact hit home. He needed a hand to cup the back of Tilly's head and make sure it didn't move while he took a moment to find out whether a kiss could really feel so totally different to anything he'd ever experienced before.

He discovered that it could about the same time he heard that cutlery hitting the paving again.

He could feel Tilly melting in his arms, which suggested she was under the power of the same spell he was experiencing, so then he needed his other hand to trace the line of her spine, feeling each little bump until he reached the roundness of her buttocks. Now he could support her whole body. He could also pull it a little closer to his own as he fell further into that extraordinary kiss and let his tongue explore the delicious taste of her more thoroughly.

It was when the tip of his tongue touched Tilly's that it happened.

A change as sudden as a physical blow that came from nowhere as every muscle in Tilly's body tensed so fast it felt as if someone had waved a wand and turned her to stone.

Instinctively Harry jerked back and that was when he could see an expression in her eyes that sent a chill rippling down his spine.

Tilly looked…

Dear Lord…was she frightened? Of *him*?

It was a moment of utter confusion. What on earth had made her react to a kiss like this? Or should the question be *who*, not what?

Harry didn't get time to process the implications of that thought because he could hear Tilly's name being called. Urgently. As if her father was aware of her reaction even though he'd been too far away to see it, and that was beyond strange as well.

Tilly was turning to the window her father must have just opened.

'What's wrong?'

Harry could see that Jim had a phone in his hand. 'It's not me. There's been an accident. Down on the Marshalls' farm, near the domain. They need help. Fast.'

Tilly was already moving quickly, and Harry was right behind her. 'Do you know what's happened?' he called back to Jim.

'It sounds bad.' Jim sounded upset. 'Take my truck—it's got all the gear locked in the back tray and you're going to need it. There's an ambulance on the way from Queenstown but you'll get there first.' His voice cracked. 'And they're not likely to have a field amputation kit if it's needed. Someone's got themselves caught in a hay baler.'

CHAPTER SIX

Flight.

Fight.

Or freeze.

Tilly was perfectly well aware of the physiological reaction the body had to an acutely stressful event, like the imminent threat of an attack that could involve personal harm or possible death.

She'd never experienced all three responses in such close proximity, however.

She had almost felt the initial flood of hormones being released as her body had frozen the instant she'd felt the touch of Harry's tongue against her own. She'd been aware of her heart rate increasing so suddenly and she'd known she was probably as white as a sheet by the time Harry had pulled back to stare at her because she'd actually felt the blood draining from her face.

He couldn't have missed the fact that something was wrong but, in the space of only a heartbeat, Tilly had the horrible impression that Harry knew *what* was wrong. The last thing she wanted was to discover that he had guessed a truth she'd been successfully hiding for years so she'd gone from being frozen to being ready to take flight.

Maybe she wouldn't have actually run away from him but there were other ways of creating a safe distance. Like putting up barriers. Refusing to discuss something. Making absolutely sure that he couldn't touch her again—even though, moments ago—it had been the thing she'd wanted more than anything else imaginable.

But she didn't have to do any of those things because of her father's interruption and the call to an emergency that meant she was needed to join the fight for someone's life. If they *were* still alive by the time they got to the scene. Tilly had heard of horrific accidents involving farm machinery like hay balers and she knew there was a real chance that, no matter how fast Harry was driving, they might be too late. She was still ready for a fight, with her heart rate and breathing a lot faster than normal and her muscles tense, but Tilly was relieved that the trembling of her hands was receding.

Harry had noticed that when she'd unlocked the hard cover of the back of the ute to check that all her father's emergency medical supplies were in there. She'd been fumbling with the keys and had offered no resistance when he took them from her hand and told her he'd drive.

And here they were, speeding along the open road with the magnetic light on the roof of the vehicle flashing red against an increasingly deep twilight. The levels of catecholamines like adrenaline that Tilly still had circulating had to be responsible for her astonishingly heightened awareness of every one of her senses. She could see the flash of red light catching the lamp-posts as they sped past, feel every bump in the road and hear the pounding of her own heart in her ears. She could smell freshly cut hay through the open window and she could…oh, dammit…she could still taste Harry's kiss, couldn't she?

She should have known it would have ended like that.

That it was impossible to go any further… No matter how desperately she had wanted it to. It was the first time she'd felt like that since…since…

No…she couldn't think about that. The memory might be trying to surface but it couldn't be allowed. Especially not right now…

'Talk to me.' To Tilly's relief, Harry's voice cut off her train of thought with the precision of a guillotine. 'What relevant gear have we got?'

'Intubation and surgical airway kit. Combat tourniquet. IV gear and fluids. Amputation kit with scalpels, a Gigli saw and sutures.'

'Drugs?'

'Ketamine, fentanyl, midazolam, morphine…' Tilly rattled off a list of drugs she knew her father would have available as a first responder. 'The drug kit's a locked toolbox and the key's on the same key ring as the rest. From memory, it's got a blob of red paint on it.'

'Defibrillator?' Harry wasn't taking his eyes off the road as he steered around a curve, retracing the route they'd taken not that long ago on their way home from the pony club event. 'Portable ventilator? Handheld ultrasound device?'

'Only a defib. I'm not sure that the ambulance carries a portable ventilator or ultrasound either, but I know air rescue does and there may already be a helicopter on the way.' Tilly leaned forward as if it would help her see further. 'We're almost there. I can see a fire truck in the paddock, so our local volunteers are on scene.'

'Good. I don't know much about hay balers, but if someone's trapped in a machine we're likely to need some extrication expertise.' Harry was slowing the ute to turn into the gate and Tilly heard him swear under his breath.

'He's alive,' he said grimly. 'I can hear him screaming from here.'

The sound of someone in extreme pain was unnerving and there were several distressed-looking people, who weren't part of the fire service crew, around the tractor and trailer unit. One man had his arms around the waist of a person who seemed to be leaning right inside the hay baling machine, his feet just off ground level, which made it more difficult for Harry and Tilly to get close enough to assess the scene.

'I can't let go,' he told them. 'If I do, and Jase falls backwards, he might rip his whole arm off.'

'Get me *out*...' There was another shriek of pain from the man they couldn't see.

'How did this happen?' Harry's tone was clipped.

'I didn't see it. I just found him like this. He said something was wrong with the net that gets fed out to wrap the bale, so he opened the flap to have a look. He knew not to lean in too close, but he got his hand tangled and it just sucked him in.'

'Is everything turned off?'

'Yep.' The affirmation came from one of the volunteer fire officers. 'And, as far as we can tell, Jase's arm has somehow gone down past the cutters and he's been spiked with the pick-up rake. We're getting some gear ready to see if we can cut in from the front. The ambulance isn't far away and there's a chopper on the way from Dunedin that's just taken off.'

Harry climbed onto a wheel. 'Hey Jase? My name's Harry. I'm a doctor. I've got another doctor with me and there's an ambulance on the way. We're going to get you out of here, okay?' He looked over his shoulder. 'Has someone got a torch?'

Tilly heard another heartrending groan from the victim. 'It hurts, man,' he said to Harry. 'It hurts so bad...'

'I know, mate. We're going to give you something to help with that. I'm just trying to see what's going on. It's your left arm that's trapped, yes?'

'It's got spiked...right up to my elbow.' Jase's voice was shaking. 'Oh, God...you're going to cut my arm off, aren't you?'

'I'm only holding a torch, mate.' Harry's tone was one of reassurance. 'Just having a look. Your right arm's not injured, is it?'

'I can't feel my fingers now. I've been hanging on hard to something in there, so I didn't fall. I don't feel good, man... I'm kinda dizzy...'

Tilly had the drug kit open on the back of the ute, pulling out the ampoules of the heavy-duty painkillers they were going to need. The problem was going to be not only getting the access to administer them but keeping their patient safe if he lost consciousness which would become more of a risk after administering medications like these.

But a quick sideways glance showed Tilly the vicious metal spikes attached to the rake mechanism. If this farmer's arm was impaled by them right up to his elbow and his own weight was putting pressure on the limb, it was no wonder he was in so much pain and making this even a little more bearable was a top priority. She knew Harry would be trying to assess vital signs, to record how well Jase was breathing and to estimate his blood pressure and how well oxygen was being circulated.

Wait… *Jase?*

Tilly turned to the nearest fire officer. 'Is this Jason Marshall?' she asked. 'About thirty-four years old?'

'Sure is. You know him?'

'I went to school with him.'

Harry had climbed down in time to hear her, and his gaze focused sharply on her face. 'You okay?'

She nodded as a response. It might be a rare thing to be personally acquainted with a patient who turned up in an urban emergency department, but it was something that happened all the time in a rural situation. 'How's he looking?'

'His airway's clear but he's tachypnoeic at thirty breaths a minute and tachycardic at well over a hundred beats a minute. I can't reach in far enough to assess injuries or the degree of entrapment but his left arm's pulled so far in, the shoulder's almost dislocating, which will only be adding to his pain levels. I couldn't try to get a radial pulse on his uninjured arm to get an idea of blood pressure because he's too scared to let go of whatever he's holding to support himself.'

'We need to get IV access to give him some pain relief. Or intraosseus if we can only reach his leg? I want to get fluids running. Oxygen on. And a cardiac monitor as soon as we can.'

'We need a better platform to support him. If he crashes, we could well be looking at having to do an amputation just to get access to intubate. I'm going to talk to the firies.'

Tilly added the syringes she'd filled to an IV roll, fastened it and then pulled on a pair of gloves. 'I'll climb up and have a look. I'm a lot smaller than you and I might be able to reach further.'

Harry frowned. 'Be very careful where you're putting your own hands. If anything moves—the patient or the machinery—you could end up trapped yourself and the last thing we need is another patient.'

'I know that.'

The noise and activity around her was increasing steadily as Tilly found a foothold on a metal bar of the hay baler and started talking to their patient as she leaned in.

'Hey, Jase…you probably won't remember me but we went to school together. Tilly Dawson? My dad's been the GP in Craig's Gully for ever.'

'Tilly…yeah… I remember… What the heck are you doing here?'

'I came down to visit Dad for Christmas. And I took this call because I'm a doctor now too.' Tilly shone the torch to follow the line of the trapped arm but couldn't see past a roller with sharp-looking blades. 'I'm an emergency medicine specialist.'

'Oh, yeah… I heard something about that.' Jason's voice was getting weaker and the cry of pain he uttered was quieter but no less agonised. 'Help me…' he groaned. *'Please…'*

'I'd like to get a line into your good arm. That'll be the fastest way to deal with your pain.' Tilly could reach Jason's uninjured arm, but his elbow was sharply bent and the muscles locked. 'Can you try and let go with this hand?'

'No...' Jason sounded terrified. 'I'll fall...'

Floodlights were being set up beside Tilly and she could hear sirens getting louder as both an ambulance and a police car arrived on scene. She could hear Harry's voice sounding calm as he asked quick-fire questions about the approach being planned to try and free the trapped limb and directed people to different tasks, including finding something solid to get beneath Jason's feet. She knew the man supporting Jason would be getting tired enough to need replacing but she didn't expect it to be Harry who wrapped his arms around Jason's chest.

'I've got you, mate,' he said. 'I'm not going to let you fall.'

Tilly could actually feel the rumble of Harry's voice as much as she could hear it, because it seemed to go from her ears right down to her bones. If she was terrified or in pain, she thought, that deep, calm voice and the promise in his words would be exactly what she needed to hear. She could, in fact, imagine putting her life in Harry Doyle's hands with no hesitation at all.

'You can let go now, Jase,' Harry added. 'You're safe. And Tilly needs that arm so we can help you with that pain as fast as possible.'

Jason was sobbing but he did let go and it was reassuring to be able to assess the radial pulse she could feel in his uninjured wrist and find it was strong enough to suggest that Jason hadn't yet lost a dangerous amount of blood. Harry held him as Tilly juggled her supplies to get a tourniquet around the arm and a wide bore cannula slipped into a vein and then secured firmly with tape. And then she could finally administer drugs that were going to deal with the pain and terror that this young farmer was suffering.

Tilly could hear the sound of the rescue helicopter arriving as she felt Jason's body relaxing as his pain receded. Harry was calling for more help in supporting the weight of their patient and then he moved himself, climbing up so that he was right beside Tilly.

'I'll hold him from this side,' he said. 'Can you get on the wheel and see if you can feel what's going on with his other arm? It would be good to know how long it might be before we'll be able to get him down to ground level.'

This was a lot scarier than the challenge of gaining IV access. Tilly had to slide her hand past those sharp blades, following the line of Jason's arm into a dark space. Within seconds, she could feel the end of one of the spikes that were there to gather and move hay from the ground. It was right through Jason's arm, just below the elbow. There was more space in this part of the machinery, so Tilly stood on tiptoes and leaned in a little further. She wanted to reach his wrist, to feel for a pulse and then his hand to make sure it was still intact after having gone past those blades. Her face was very close to Jason's now.

'You had long hair.' His words were slightly muffled, as if it was an effort to speak. He didn't seem to be aware of what was happening around him. 'I tied your plaits together when I was sitting behind you...'

Harry was just as close to Jason on the other side so she could hear his chuckle. 'Sounds like you were the class clown,' he said. 'Like me.'

Tilly could feel another spike that was very close to

Jason's wrist. Or was it angled up through his palm? Was it anywhere near the artery? Could that metal tubing cause potentially fatal blood loss if it moved during an extrication attempt?

'I seem to remember him sticking a whole bunch of pencils through them once,' Tilly said aloud. 'And everybody laughed at me when I got up.'

She was gently exploring Jason's hand as she spoke. The metal prong felt like it was involving several fingers.

'Don't try moving them,' she said, 'but can you feel me touching your fingers? Here? And here?'

'Yeah...'

'How's the pain level, mate?' Harry asked. 'On a scale of zero to ten with zero being no pain and ten the worst you can imagine?'

'Dunno...' Jason sounded sleepy. 'Maybe six...?'

'And what was it when we arrived?'

Jason gave a huff of sound almost like laughter. 'Bloody twenty-six, mate...'

'Good to know. We'll keep you topped up so it won't ever get that bad again.' Harry was watching Tilly as she lifted her head. 'I'm going to get someone else to come and hold you for a bit. Maybe someone on both sides. Tilly and I need to talk to the experts and decide on the quickest and safest way to get you out of this.'

'I need to get home,' Jason mumbled. 'I've got kids, you know? And it's nearly Christmas...'

With the helicopter crew now on the ground they were able to join the discussion of how best to manage both the extrication and medical management for Jason. It was an intense exchange of expertise with factors to consider such as the danger of a respiratory arrest from the powerful analgesic drugs and the vibration that could make the injuries worse with hydraulic tools being used to cut into the metal of the farm machinery.

Of all the medics present, Tilly was the only one small enough to be able to reach Jason's impaled arm and it was her own idea to try and support the limb as they gained access. That way they would know if the vibration and manipulation of the metal could be creating additional issues and the fire officers could change to using an oxy acetylene torch, which might be slower but would cause far less vibration. Tilly's ability to reach Jason's arm would be even more important in that case, because she would need to protect his arm, with water-soaked dressings, from heat transfer that could cause severe burns.

And, of all the rescue people present, the only person Tilly wanted right beside her during this next phase, the one responsible for supporting Jason's body weight, was Harry. Because she could only do this if she could trust that she wasn't going to be suddenly jolted by the weight of Jason's body shifting. It was still surprisingly easy to trust Harry because she could still hear the echoes of his voice reassuring Jason.

'I've got you, mate... You're safe...'

Harry had never been in a situation quite like this.

He was acutely aware of everything happening around him—the noise of the pneumatic gear, every bump or shudder in the metal framework of the machinery he was leaning against, even anybody walking past who might be close enough to interfere with his task of keeping Jason's body as still as possible.

Should he have tried to talk Tilly out of putting herself at risk by having her own arm inside that machine as they tried to dismantle it? If Harry could have taken her place he would have, in a heartbeat, but all he could do now was his absolute best to keep Tilly as safe as possible. And applaud her, silently, for her courage as the rescue workers worked, slowly and carefully, to get him free.

The farmer who'd raised the alarm had a toolbox in his truck so some machinery parts could be unbolted and prised free. The 'Jaws of Life' cutter and spreader took care of other barriers to get in to where Jason's arm was impaled but each step was being taken with the utmost caution.

Harry was not only focused on keeping Tilly safe, he was doing his best to both distract and reassure Jason as well as watching for any warning of him losing consciousness or going into respiratory or cardiac arrest.

Tilly was clearly thinking along the same lines.

'I can't believe you're a dad, Jase,' she said at one point. 'Doesn't seem that long since we were at school.'

'I've got three… Oldest is nearly five…she's so excited about Christmas…'

'I'll bet she is,' Harry said. 'What's she asked Father Christmas for?'

'She won't tell me. She'll only tell Santa… Hey… isn't it your dad, Tilly, who does that?'

'Don't spread it around,' Tilly told him. 'But it's going to be Harry this time. Father Christmas with an Irish accent. We'll have to see how that goes.'

'Ireland's closer to the North Pole than New Zealand,' Harry protested. 'It'll be all good. And Jase? I promise I'll let you know what it is she's set her wee heart on. With a bit of luck you might have it already wrapped up and under the tree.'

Jason made a sound that was almost laughter. 'Hope not… We've got her a pony…'

'Oh…she's going to be so excited. I've still got my first pony, Spud. He's really old now but I still love him to bits. You're close to the pony club grounds so that'll be handy.' Tilly was doing her best to keep Jason distracted. 'How big is the pony you've got?'

'Not big. He's a Shetland.'

'What colour?'

'Sort of yellow, I guess. With a white mane and tail.'

'A palomino. My favourite colour. What's his name?'

'Pudding.'

Tilly laughed. 'That's a great name. Is he nice and quiet?'

'Bombproof, they said.'

'Sounds perfect.'

When exterior sections of the machine had been cut clear and the rake was exposed, they had to switch to the oxy acetylene torch. Wads of gauze soaked in saline were passed up to Tilly, who covered the exposed skin on Jason's arm around each of the protruding spikes so that they could be separated from the reel. She put goggles on to protect his eyes and wore a pair herself and they tucked the edges of a burn blanket into gaps for extra protection.

When Jason was finally lifted clear he went straight into the skilled care of the air rescue team. They assessed his vital signs, hooked him up to monitoring equipment and topped up his pain relief and then padded and bandaged the impaled spikes to make sure they weren't going to move en route. The team was so efficient, it felt like only minutes later that Harry and Tilly were standing in the paddock, watching the helicopter take off. Sharing a glance that was like a huge sigh of relief.

'That could have been so much worse,' Harry said. 'He needs urgent surgery to remove those spikes but I don't think there's any danger of him losing his arm.'

'He might not even lose any of its function,' Tilly agreed. 'But he could have lost his life.'

'I'd better remember that promise, hadn't I? Except…how will I recognise his daughter? I don't even know her name.'

'I'll ask Dad. He'll know.'

The ambulance from Queenstown was heading off to another job. The fire crew were packing up their tools. The helicopter was nothing more than a tiny flashing light far enough away to be one of the stars.

'What was that you were saying?' Harry asked as they packed away their own kit into the back of the ute. 'About it being so boring being a rural GP?'

Tilly made a huff of sound. 'That's not the kind of job that happens every day. But it is another reason I wouldn't want to be one. You know all your patients. You went to school with them, or you see them in the supermarket when you're getting your groceries.'

'I guess that would kind of blur the lines between your professional and personal life,' Harry agreed. 'But there's another side to that coin, isn't there?'

Tilly's glance was suspicious.

'Doesn't it make it feel more like they're real people and not just statistics in the throughput of an ED? That you're a significant person in their lives?'

'It means you can end up knowing things about their

lives or their bodies that you can't tell anybody else and…and I don't really like keeping secrets.'

'So it makes a whole community a bit like a family, huh?' Harry held the passenger door open. 'I'll drive back, shall I?'

'Thanks.' Tilly nodded. 'I'm a bit wrecked, to be honest.' She leaned back against the headrest as he began to drive them home and closed her eyes. 'I must have used way too much adrenaline in the last couple of hours.'

It was only then that Harry remembered what had happened moments before they'd responded to that emergency call. The fear he'd seen in Tilly's eyes.

Whatever had caused that reaction was none of his business, was it?

He didn't want to get involved with Tilly's life, did he?

Harry drove in silence for several minutes.

He was already involved, wasn't he?

And it was his business. Because…what if he'd caused that fear?

Their headlights made a yellow arrow-shaped signpost glow just ahead of them and Harry braked sharply enough for Tilly's eyes to snap open as she sat up straight.

'What are you doing?'

'That signpost said this is Craig's Lake.' The four-wheel drive vehicle was bouncing over potholes on a shingle road. 'I'd like to see it.'

'It's not that spectacular,' Tilly said. 'More like a big pond, really.'

It was big enough to have a grassy area to park on, picnic tables to wander past and a pebbled beach where you could stand and admire the moonlight on water that was still enough to be reflecting the dark shapes of the surrounding hills.

It was Harry who broke a silence that felt deeper than this small lake probably was.

'Was it something *I* did,' he asked Tilly quietly, 'that scared you? Did I make a mistake in thinking you wanted me to kiss you?'

He heard the way Tilly sucked in her breath. She hadn't expected this. She didn't want it.

Harry didn't break the silence this time. He simply waited. He could sense that she was struggling with whether to say anything or not and if she chose not to he would respect her boundaries. He was about to suggest they went home when she did finally speak.

'It wasn't your fault,' she whispered. 'It was mine.'

To his horror, Harry saw a fat tear escape Tilly's eye and trickle down the side of her nose.

Oh, no...what had he done now? The Ice Queen was melting.

There was something so heartbreaking in both Tilly's words and that sad single tear that there was only one thing Harry could do now.

He folded Tilly into his arms.

And simply held her.

CHAPTER SEVEN

THIS SHOULD HAVE been mortifying.

Tilly knew perfectly well that she had a reputation for being aloof at work. Uninterested in gossip, even less interested in any attention from male colleagues. She suspected nobody particularly liked her but that didn't bother her too much because she knew that everybody respected her. They knew how good she was at her job and they knew she could handle anything without falling apart or making stupid mistakes.

If it became public knowledge that she was capable of falling apart to the extent that she was sobbing in Harry's arms it would be just as embarrassing as anybody finding out she'd pretended that she was in a relationship with him. But Tilly wasn't even thinking about something like that happening. She knew it wouldn't, in fact, because she knew that she could trust Harry Doyle.

She'd pretty much been trusting him with her safety for more than the last hour or so and she'd done that with the conviction that she would be quite prepared to trust him with her life. So maybe that was why—for the first time in at least ten years—Tilly was letting herself experience an emotional release.

Because she felt *this* safe…

Turning off the tears turned out to be a bit harder than letting them escape. At some point Harry had got them both sitting on the pebbles of the lake shore but that must have been a while ago because, by the time Tilly noticed, Harry's shirt was soaked. She found herself dusting it with her hand in the forlorn hope it might dry it off.

'Sorry…'

Harry still had his arm around her and he gave her a squeeze. 'I'm not bothered,' he said. 'It's probably warm enough to go swimming, and if I did that my shirt would get a whole lot wetter than this. Unless I went skinny-dipping, of course.'

Tilly made a strangled sound, halfway between a sob and laughter and that made Harry smile.

'That's better. Now…are you ready to talk to me?' He still hadn't taken his arm away. 'I'd still like to be sure that this wasn't my fault. Because I'm already quite sure it wasn't yours.'

Tilly knew that if she moved from where she was leaning against Harry's body, with her head tucked in under his collarbone, he would lift his arm instantly. So she kept very still.

'It was,' she said quietly. 'I'm…um…different from most people.'

'I already knew that.' She could hear the smile in Harry's tone. 'That's not necessarily a bad thing, you know.'

'It is when you're… When you can't…'

The words died on Tilly's tongue as she turned her face into Harry's damp shirt. How could she possibly say it out loud? Especially to someone like Harry who was so gorgeous and had probably already lost count of how many women he'd made love to. No wonder they were lining up hopefully, like that young nurse, Charlotte. If he could *kiss* like that, imagine how it would feel to go further. All the way...

Maybe it was the fatigue of having depleted her adrenaline levels, both with her reaction to Harry's kiss and then the intensity of the rescue scene they'd both been so involved with. Maybe it was the feeling of safety Tilly had found in Harry's company. In his touch. Or maybe it was simply that she was over dealing with this entirely by herself because it was too lonely. Hopeless, even. She'd never know what it was like to be made love to by someone like Harry...

'When you can't do sex,' she heard herself whispering into the darkness. 'Because you're frigid...'

Who knew that it was possible to communicate incredulity without making a sound? It was the way Harry's muscles tensed. The way she found he was looking at her when she lifted her gaze. The huff of sound he made finally that was like an exclamation point.

'You're *serious*...'

Tilly didn't say anything. Because there was nothing more to say?

Harry blew out a breath. 'How do you know?' he asked.

'I just do.'

'Uh-uh... I'm not buying that.' Harry was watching her. 'I kissed you not so long ago, in case you've forgotten. There's a lot you can tell about someone when you kiss them.'

Every disparaging thought Tilly had ever had about

how much Harry would know about sex because he was such a player and didn't actually care about all the women he played with evaporated in that instant. He *did* care. And perhaps he *could* read what was going on in a woman's head when he was kissing her.

Oh...dear Lord...

But Harry's voice was softening. Gentle now. 'You got scared, didn't you?'

Still Tilly said nothing.

Now Harry's voice had a grim edge to it. 'Did the person who scared you happen to be the same person who suggested that you were frigid?'

This time Tilly's silence was broken by Harry's curse.

'Is it someone who lives around here? Is that why you don't like coming home? Just tell me who he is, sweetheart, and I'll go and punch his lights out.'

The sound Tilly made this time was much closer to laughter than a sob but she could feel something soft and warm blossoming deep inside.

Harry was angry about what had happened to her.

And he'd called her *sweetheart*... Like her father did. Only it didn't feel remotely like the way it did when her father said it.

'He doesn't live around here,' she said. 'But I guess it was part of the reason I stayed away. Why I didn't say anything. To anyone. I couldn't bear it if my father knew. Or anybody else, because that's what this place is like. Everybody knows everything and I'd always be the girl who went to university and was stupid enough to get herself...'

She couldn't say the word.

* * *

But Harry could. *'Raped...?'*

He swore under his breath at the way Tilly cringed, which confirmed his guess. This was worse than he'd thought. He'd been imagining that some bastard had tried it on and accused Tilly of being frigid because she'd refused to go to bed with him. But he'd bullied or *forced* her to have sex with him after she'd made it clear she didn't want to?

Harry was aware of several emotions vying for supremacy.

Anger that this had happened to her. So much anger it could tip into rage with very little additional provocation.

He was also filled with an empathy for Tilly that made him want to hold her close again and offer some kind of comfort.

But there was shame in the mix too...for ever having thought of her as being an 'Ice Queen' without even considering that there might be a story behind the way she presented herself to the world. Or, rather, hid from it? A horrible, heartbreaking story.

'Oh, my God, Tilly,' he said slowly. 'Did you report him? Did you get help to deal with it?'

That shake of Tilly's head wasn't a surprise. Harry had already guessed that she'd kept this hidden. That she'd dealt with it herself by pushing it aside. Bottling it up. Good grief...the kind of damage that could cause was appalling.

'I couldn't,' Tilly whispered. 'Because it was my fault... I'd gone out with him. I wanted it to happen but...but not like that. I wasn't ready but he said I'd led him on. That if I stopped being such a prude I'd end up liking it as much as everybody else did. He said...'

'*He* said?' Harry broke into her hesitant speech. 'He made you believe that it was somehow *your* fault? You were gaslighted, Tilly. You do realise that, don't you?'

Tilly's shrug had a tone of despair. 'He said that if I told anybody he'd make sure everybody knew that I was frigid...that I was a waste of time as a woman and no one would ever want to touch me. There were people at uni who knew people from around here. And everybody around here knew my mother, who was the most beautiful, *sensual* woman they'd ever seen. The word most people used about my mum was passionate, and they might have meant about her career but we all knew they really meant more than that. I heard men say more than once that my dad was a *very* lucky man.'

'Tilly...' Harry was shaking his head. 'When Maggie showed me that photo of your mother today, I thought it was *you*. That if you untied your hair you'd look like your mum's twin.'

'As if...' It was Tilly's turn to shake her head. 'I was the gawkiest kid. I was too skinny and kind of clumsy. I had awful hand-eye co-ordination. Riding my pony was the only sport I was ever good at.'

'Did your ears stick out?' Harry lifted his hair with his thumbs to expose his ears and made a face at the same time. He knew he was reverting to that emotional escape he'd perfected so long ago, by being the class clown, but he hadn't known that it could still work just as well—and for other people as well as himself.

Because, to his delight, Tilly actually laughed. 'You *do* look like a leprechaun,' she said.

Harry let his hair fall and straightened his face. And then he waited a beat to let any echoes of joking dissipate.

'And you look like an astonishingly beautiful woman,' he said quietly. 'I couldn't see past the wall you put up because you do a good job of not letting the world see who you really are. Maybe I couldn't see a reason to try.' His smile was gentle. 'You can be quite intimidating, you know, Dr Dawson. You keep people at more than arm's length.'

Tilly was looking down, playing with a pebble she'd picked up from the beach. 'I guess it was safer. And then it just became normal and it didn't really matter any longer because I love m1y job so much.'

Harry watched her hand close around that pebble and hold it. He knew it still mattered. Tilly was missing out on a huge part of life. Wiping out an entire future for herself. Staying away from an incredible part of the world that she clearly loved had also become normal, hadn't it? No wonder her father had been worried about her. He must have seen the changes in his daughter as she'd distanced herself but would have had no idea why.

The saddest thing was that, with the right help, it should have been possible for Tilly to have been able to move on without losing so much of her life. Maybe it was *still* possible, but Harry couldn't think of what he could say to open a conversation like that. Or what he could do to help her, other than to try and make her laugh.

'You know what?' Harry made it sound as if he was about to change the subject. Or suggest that it was time they headed home?

'What?'

'You're a great kisser.'

The stone dropped from Tilly's hand as her head jerked up, her jaw dropping. He held her gaze for a long, long moment. When he spoke again, his voice was as quiet and still as the moonlit lake in front of them.

'You can trust me, Tilly. You know that, don't you?'

She nodded slowly but he could see that trust in her eyes. He knew it had quite a lot to do with the tense rescue scene they'd just completed together where she'd had to trust him to help keep her safe, but this wasn't about any professional relationship they might have. It very clearly went a lot deeper than that or Tilly would never have told him something she'd kept secret for so long.

'And you can tell me anything at all and it won't go any further. I quite like keeping secrets, me.'

He could see something added to that trust now. Appreciation, perhaps, that not only had he heard something she'd said to him a while ago, he understood how hard it must have been to keep her own terrible secret.

'You should also know,' he added, 'that I'd never, ever do anything you didn't want me to do.'

Again, Tilly nodded. Even more slowly. As though she was thinking carefully about what he'd said. As though she was thinking there *might* be something she would want him to do?

'I wish I could show you how wrong you are to believe that you're frigid. I wish that I knew how to erase that fear you've built up over far too long.'

Oh...there was a thought.

Maybe he did know how he could help her do that. If he was gentle enough and patient enough—if Tilly would let him, he could show her at least a part of what she was missing out on. And that could change her life, which would be…

Possibly the best gift anyone could give Matilda Dawson?

Not that he could wrap it up, mind you. Or offer a voucher. He couldn't even put it into words without it sounding…what…weird? Sleazy, even?

He could let himself think about it, though. To tap into how attracted he was to Tilly and how easily that could spark desire. He could imagine kissing her again and how it could lead to something more, and maybe she would be able to see everything he couldn't say aloud as he continued to hold her gaze.

It was Christmas, after all. What better time to offer a gift?

It was an odd thing, this feeling of being so safe with someone.

As if the child she had once been, so long ago, was peeping out from a hiding place in her head—or her heart—that had been so effective Tilly had almost forgotten that little girl she had once been still existed somewhere deep inside. She could still feel that kind of safety that came from being tucked up, snuggled into bed or onto the couch beside her daddy, knowing that he would read her favourite story until she was sound asleep.

Even more oddly, it made Tilly yawn. A deep, whole-body stretching kind of yawn, filling her lungs with the cool night air and ending with an audible sigh.

Except Harry didn't seem to think it was odd.

'Come on… I'm not surprised you're exhausted.'

He got to his feet and held out his hand to help her up. 'It's been one hell of a day, so it has.'

Tilly let him take her hand and pull her up. A strong, warm grip that made her feel as safe as everything else about this man.

It seemed impossible that she'd met him at the airport only this morning as no more than an acquaintance. A work colleague who was doing her a favour because he felt that he owed her something or it just suited him to be out of town for Christmas. Now, it felt as if she'd known Harry for ever.

In fact, she'd never felt quite like this before. Ever. The scientific part of her brain suggested that it might be due to hormone depletion after the adrenaline-filled hours she'd just experienced. Simple fatigue might have been enough on its own. Or it could be a psychological effect of having talked about the incident that she knew perfectly well had left her with a degree of PTSD.

A far less scientific explanation was coming from the feeling that seemed to be centred around her heart, that feeling coming from knowing that someone cared enough to be angry on her behalf. Who had listened to her innermost fear and dismissed its likelihood as nothing other than the result of manipulation and abuse. Who'd said he didn't believe a word of it. Who'd also said she was a great kisser...

And...if the way he'd been looking at her only moments ago was anything to go by, he hadn't been put off by anything she'd told him. He looked as if he wanted to kiss her all over again.

And, heaven help her, but Tilly wanted him to.

Not just yet, though. She wanted to savour this feeling of safety and let it embed itself so it couldn't be lost again. Along with believing that what Harry had implied was correct and there wasn't anything wrong with her sexuality—because, if that was really true, it could change everything.

Possibly her whole life…

CHAPTER EIGHT

IT WAS THE sound of laughter that woke Tilly the next morning.

Male laughter.

Sunlight was streaming through the curtains in what had always been her own room in this wonderful old, rambling house. In the same moment that Tilly realised it was Christmas Eve, she also realised she'd slept in. For someone who was always awake at the crack of dawn, seven-thirty felt like half the morning had been wasted but she felt too good to beat herself up over it. She had, in fact, had a better sleep than she could remember having in…well…possibly her entire adult life.

She hadn't even had any dreams, she thought, as she pulled on a pair of cut-off jeans and a tee shirt after a quick visit to the bathroom. Old clothes, because her brain was waking up properly now and she remembered that they hadn't been able to cut down that baby pine tree her father wanted for the living room. It had been too late by the time she and Harry had got home last night and Tilly had been both physically and emotionally exhausted.

She could hear another shout of laughter as she brushed her hair. Harry's laughter. Suddenly, it was more than Tilly's brain that had woken up. Her body was coming back to the land of the living with surprising enthusiasm. She could feel an echo of that heat she'd felt with Harry's touch when he'd done that bit of play-acting about having fallen in love with her at first sight and it was merging with how she'd felt in the wake of that kiss yesterday—being so hyperaware of every one of her senses—still able to taste him on her tongue, even. But there was a new element to the mix of memories and awareness.

That feeling of safety.

Of hope, perhaps?

Definitely happiness, anyway. Tilly didn't bother taking the time to find shoes or scrape her hair back into the usual tight braid she wore. She could feel her own laughter on the tip of her tongue as she walked into the living room, despite not knowing what was going on.

'What's so funny?' she asked.

Both men looked up and the expressions on their faces made Tilly stop in her tracks. Her father's face was softening with pleasure at seeing her, the crinkles around his eyes and the tenderness of his smile made it almost look as if he was about to shed a tear. It was a look of pure love.

What made Tilly's heart skip a beat was that there was something in the expression on Harry's face that was oddly similar. Apart from a spark of something that *couldn't* have been more different—an appreciation of what was being seen that not only ignited that heat again instantly but threw a significant amount of new fuel on the blaze. She had to look away before she melted into a puddle.

'Oh…you've got a tree already.'

'Your man was up early,' Jim told her. 'He not only helped me get washed and dressed, he went and found the trees and sent me photos so I could choose the perfect one. We were just waiting for you to get up before he cooks breakfast.' He winked at Tilly. 'You've found a keeper this time, love.'

Tilly sucked in a breath. How awful would it be if her father realised that she didn't have any hold on Harry whatsoever so there was no chance of 'keeping' him? He wasn't even planning on staying in the same country as her for much longer. On the plus side, however, at least she didn't have to worry about her father discovering the truth himself, especially having witnessed that kiss last night.

'I wanted to help choose the tree.' She knew she sounded a bit grumpy. She was also staring at the tree propped up in a red bucket, as if she was trying to find fault with a task that had been completed without her involvement. There were strings of lights draped around it and a few decorations had been hung.

'You needed your sleep, sweetheart.' Harry was delving into a cardboard box. 'Oh, my…' He was laughing again. 'It's a leprechaun, so it is.'

Tilly was still staring at the tree as she recognised the decorations already on the tree. The reindeer that looked more like a corgi with very strange ears. The angel that could have been an anaemic bat. 'Oh, no… how could you, Dad? I thought I threw those dreadful things out twenty years ago.'

'I rescued the box from the rubbish bin.' Jim sounded satisfied. 'You made them and they're family treasures. And I do believe that's an elf, not a leprechaun,' he told Harry. 'Although, if it makes you feel at home, lad, there's not that much difference, is there?'

The small figure made out of baked modelling clay had long, spidery green legs and arms and an oversized red hat with a pompom. This was about as embarrassing as having her baby photos displayed. Except, as Harry got to his feet and carried the elf to the tree, he gave her one of those smiles. The kind that was probably responsible for legions of women falling in love with him without any encouragement, but this time it didn't make her feel the slightest resentment.

It made her smile straight back.

And it made her realise that, after last night, she had stepped into the same space all those other women had visited, only to leave with broken hearts. Luckily for Tilly, she knew that any visit she might be making into Harry Doyle's fan club was a very temporary thing and, even if there was something real creeping into the game they were supposed to be playing—on her side, anyway—it was only for a day or two, so it couldn't do any real harm, surely? If anything, it would only make it more convincing when she broke the news to her father that a real relationship had come to an end, with her and Harry going their separate ways.

Harry looped the elf's string around the tip of a branch. 'Brilliant idea to put the string in the middle of his back,' he said. 'Makes him look like he's flying. Wait... I know who this is... He's Super-Elf, isn't he?'

Tilly shook her head, but she was laughing along with both the men and it was suddenly easy to push any misgivings about her feelings for Harry aside. 'I'll get breakfast started,' she said. 'Bacon and eggs?'

'Sounds great,' Jim said. 'I'd kill for a cup of tea too.'

'How's that ankle feeling this morning? Have you had some painkillers?' Tilly went towards her father. 'I should check the swelling in your toes. And your capillary refill.'

'Already done,' Harry said. 'And I'm happy. As long as he's careful to keep his weight off that foot, I think he's well on the road to making a good recovery. Speaking of which—' Harry headed back to the stack of boxes '—we just got a call from the surgeon who took those spikes out of Jase's arm.'

Flashes of the dramatic rescue of the young farmer replayed themselves in Tilly's mind, but the overarching memory was that Harry had been by her side. Keeping her safe as she'd tried to keep Jason's arm safe.

'Is he okay? Has he had surgery yet?'

'He was in Theatre within an hour of the helicopter landing, after they got all the imaging they needed to see whether any major vessels or nerves were involved. He got very lucky—the worst damage was a cracked ulnar, which should heal very quickly.'

'Jase's dad drove his wife, Sandra, up to Dunedin while his mum looked after the kids,' Jim added. 'He got out of surgery about three a.m., but apparently he's well enough this morning for them to agree to discharging him into our care. I said we'd keep a close eye on him and make sure he's taking his antibiotics. He should be back in time to catch the village barbecue and carol singing this evening. Which reminds me, Harry...we need to get that Santa suit out and make sure it fits you. I think it's out in the barn somewhere. Let's hope the mice haven't got into the box. Tilly'll find it, won't you, sweetheart?'

'After breakfast,' she said. 'It was already on my

list. Along with getting that tree decorated—with some proper ornaments. And I want to check on Maggie and then get into Queenstown for a spot of power shopping or there won't be very much under the tree. Then we'll need time to get Harry into his Santa outfit before we head into the village. What time does it all start?'

'Father Christmas needs to be on his throne by five o'clock,' Jim said. 'It takes at least an hour for the photos and chats and there's the games for the kids and then the barbecue. I used to sneak into Sally's house next door to take the suit off while that was happening, and that way I could go into the church for the carol singing at seven o'clock.'

'Is there a rule that Father Christmas doesn't go to church?' Harry sounded curious.

Tilly nodded. 'Church is about the real Christmas story. There's a nativity scene, and old Mrs Baker plays the electric organ for the carols, and everybody gets to hold candles.'

'And I get to go as me,' Jim said. 'It helps keep the secret about who Santa is.' He sighed heavily. 'I look forward to this every year. I wonder if I could persuade Lizzie to take me if we can fit the wheelchair into her car.'

'Lizzie? The nurse who was looking after you yesterday?'

'That's her. She's coming out this morning to make sure I'm behaving myself. And she's on her own since her husband died a few years ago, so she might like some company on Christmas Eve.'

'Oh?' Tilly's eyebrows rose. 'Is there something I should know about going on here?'

'She's a friend,' Jim said. 'That's all.' He leaned

back against the pillows on the end of the couch. 'She'll be happy to help me do the tree if she's got the time, but I won't be short on help today. I've been getting calls from all over the district. News sure gets around here fast. Who needs social media when you've got a country town?'

'That's so true,' Tilly murmured.

It was no surprise that she found herself meeting Harry's gaze when she glanced in his direction. He knew how she felt about the lack of privacy in country towns. He was also reminding her that nobody was going to hear anything about Tilly's past from him.

'You can trust me, Tilly. You know that...'

'So you don't have to worry about me being on my own today,' Jim continued, seemingly oblivious to the silent communication going on in front of him. 'You'll be able to take your time and show your man why Queenstown is so famous all over the world.'

Her man.

He was Tilly's man.

It should have been disturbing to know that he was successfully deceiving a man as nice as Jim Dawson, but instead Harry found he was having no problem with the assumption at all.

He *was* Tilly's man. At least until the day after tomorrow, when he had his return flight booked. More importantly, he *wanted* to be Tilly's man—in every sense—even if it was only going to be for a blink of time. He wanted to give her the gift of being able to believe in herself and, if she would let him, he wanted to give her the confidence to embrace her sexuality and stop putting up barriers to a future that could include a partner and maybe even children.

And it felt as if they'd both taken the first step in the right direction last night at the lake. Tilly was wearing shorts this morning, that showed off those long, slim legs. Not only that, she hadn't scraped her hair back in that severe style. It was falling in long, loose waves right down her back and, like her mother in that old photo, she was looking impossibly gorgeous.

Even better, when he'd watched her walk into the living room this morning, he could see *and* feel the difference in the way Tilly was moving in her own skin—more freely, as if an outer shell was much less of a filter to what others could see. She looked...more relaxed. Happier, even?

Whatever. Harry had felt an unspoken but surprisingly strong bond with Jim Dawson in that moment, as they'd both watched her come into the room. For very different reasons, maybe, they both felt proud of her, didn't they? The world, for both of them, had just become a little brighter thanks to Tilly's presence. Happiness was contagious, wasn't it? And it could be given and received at exactly the same time, which only made it bigger.

Better.

They were all at ease with each other enough for banter and laughter to be only a breath away. Soft poached eggs on the toast made from yesterday's sourdough loaf, along with crisp bacon and grilled homegrown tomatoes tasted better than any breakfast Harry had ever had and he blamed Tilly's cooking, a little later, for how tight the Santa suit was when he had to squash the pillow in to do up the wide black belt.

'It's perfect,' Tilly told him. 'You've just got the wig and hat, and the beard, to go on. Oh…and the glasses, of course.' She held out the round gold-rimmed spectacles.

'I'll melt,' Harry warned. 'Have you any idea how hot this outfit is?'

Jim laughed. 'They'll find a shady spot for you. And a cold beer when no one's looking. It's all in a good cause, lad. You'll be amazed what you'll find out about Craig's Gully. Hope you're good at keeping secrets.'

Harry let himself catch Tilly's gaze again. He'd already done his best, this morning, to reassure her that he would never betray her trust, but it was good to be able to say it aloud.

'Keeping secrets is one of my superpowers,' he told Jim. 'Even the torture of being cooked alive in a Santa suit won't drag them out of me.'

He collected another secret or two after as he and Tilly enjoyed a late lunch at one of the many appealing eateries in the wharf-side area by Queenstown's Lake Wakatipu, in the heart of a crowded shopping district that offered everything from local crafts to designer fashion. Sheltered from the sun by big umbrellas, they ate crayfish salad and watched people bustling past doing their last-minute Christmas shopping.

'Do you think Maggie was being honest when she said she was feeling good today?' Harry was frowning. 'You know her a lot better than I do.'

'I think she was.' Tilly nodded. 'When you were taking the kit back out to the car she told me not to worry because she wasn't going to die this year. She said there was no way she was going to spoil the memory of Christmas Day for any of her grandies.'

'I love Maggie,' Harry said. 'I'd love to have had a grandma like her.'

'Me too.' Tilly smiled. 'But how lucky was I to have her as a surrogate mum when I needed one.'

Perhaps they were both thinking about their mothers as they ate in silence for a while. Harry felt the need to lighten the mood and a glance at the lake, where people were water-skiing in the distance and kayaking closer to shore, made it easy to change the subject.

'There's so much to do here, isn't there?' he commented. 'One of those travel shops we passed had a window full of the stuff you can do around here, and I was having a look while you were choosing that bunch of flowers. You can do four-wheel drive excursions up the Skippers Canyon, Lord of the Rings tours, jet boat adventures. And isn't this where bungee jumping got invented?'

'It really started on a Pacific Island and then got copied by some English guys who were into dangerous hobbies, but this was certainly where it became a thing.'

Harry was still scanning the lake. 'What's the big boat coming in? It looks like a steamship.'

'It is. It's our iconic *TSS Earnslaw*, which I believe is the only remaining coal-fired steamship that takes passengers in the southern hemisphere. I remember my first cruise when I was about four and I thought it was the most exciting thing ever.' Tilly bit her lip. 'Is this when I should confess I'm a total wimp and I've never done the jet boats in the rapids or gone up the Skippers and I have no desire at all to do a bungee jump?'

Harry pulled in a breath, ready to tell Tilly that the last thing in the world he would ever call her was a wimp. That he knew exactly how much courage it had taken to keep her dreadful secret and not only face life but to succeed in everything she'd chosen to do.

He wanted to tell her that, no matter what, he admired her immensely. And that, even if he didn't really have any right to be, he was enormously proud of her. But the opportunity to say anything vanished before the words had gathered coherently because Tilly jumped to her feet.

'On second thoughts, we don't have time for confessions. And I'm sure you've heard enough of mine, anyway.' Tilly wrinkled her nose as she turned away. 'Why don't you stay here and enjoy the view while I finish up getting the boring bits and pieces like wrapping paper and ribbons. I know Dad's favourite shop too, and I'll pop in to get him a new shirt. Something he might not choose for himself.'

'Like a pink one?'

'Yeah…' Tilly grinned. 'Perfect. I'll say it's from both of us.'

'He might hate it.'

'Don't worry, you'll never even know if he doesn't wear it. You'll be on the other side of the world by then.' Tilly was making it sound like a good thing that he'd be so far away. 'We'll have to head back in an hour at the latest, so we've got time to turn you into Father Christmas.'

'I'll go for a wander myself,' Harry said. 'Meet you back where we parked?'

'Good idea. Hey…find yourself some swimming

shorts. The forecast is good for tomorrow, and we'll have plenty of time to go for a swim.'

Harry did find himself some shorts he could swim in. He bought a box of craft beer and had it gift-wrapped for Jim, but then a window display in an artisan's workshop caught his eye and he knew exactly what he'd been hoping to find.

Something that would remind Tilly of this blip of time in her life.

That would remind her of him…

She'd done her best to forget about it.

She'd kept herself busy ever since she'd woken up this morning, but it didn't seem to be helping.

Matilda Dawson wanted Harry to kiss her again and the wanting had been getting stronger and stronger all day. It had kicked into action when he'd given her that look—the one that told her what she already knew—that there was no doubt at all that she could trust him.

The wanting had gone up several notches as he'd kept her laughing over breakfast and she had hoped that the privacy of the old stone-built barn when they went to find the Father Christmas costume might have been enough for the desire to become contagious, but there was no hint that Harry was even thinking about it.

Why would he? Tilly thought. He'd only kissed her last night because they were being watched by her father and it was like producing an ace from his sleeve in the game they were playing.

So maybe we should give him something more interesting to see…?

He'd held her so close last night, beside the lake, but maybe she'd imagined that he ended up looking at her as if he was thinking of kissing her again? Why would he when she'd just finished telling him about the trauma of having been forced to have sex? Maybe all that had been in that look was what she had felt in their closeness. That understanding and tenderness on his part. That feeling of safety on Tilly's part that had unlocked something deep inside that she'd thought she'd lost for ever—the ability to trust a man she didn't know, along with a physical yearning that had clearly distilled into something so much stronger for having been ignored for so many years.

She couldn't initiate something herself, though, in the barn or anywhere else for that matter. Not after the way she had involuntarily reacted to Harry's kiss last night. What if he didn't actually want to kiss her again? And, even if he did, what if she had a panic attack or something in response to anything more than simply a kiss? Even if there was only a limited time that she would be working with Harry before he went home to Ireland, the fact that he knew about something so intimate—so *humiliating*—about her would make everything so much worse.

So…it had to be Harry's choice if or when anything else was going to happen between them. If that turned out to be nothing or never, Tilly still had something that she was always going to be very thankful for. The gratitude made her invent a reason to escape from Harry during their shopping trip to Queenstown. She wanted to find a gift that was special enough to make him realise that he'd given her much more of a gift than giving her father a happy Christmas believing that his daughter had found true love.

Harry had given her the gift of being able to believe

that he was right. That there was nothing wrong with her and that she didn't deserve the horrible label of being frigid that she'd allowed herself to believe. Because nobody who had an aversion to sex could feel this level of desire. Or this need for something Tilly had believed she could never want again and…and it was making her feel alive.

Not the kind of alive that had become almost an addiction in the last ten years—with that adrenaline rush of facing an intense situation when someone's life was in danger and your heart was racing and every sense was heightened. The kind of rush that was the reason why she loved working in the emergency department so much and could never have imagined wanting the quieter working life of a rural GP.

But this kind of alive could also make your heart speed up, couldn't it? It could heighten every sense like taste and touch and make even the colours around you and the warmth of the sunshine on your skin seem more intense. Maybe the difference was the destination. The aftermath of fighting for someone's life could leave you feeling either victorious or defeated but it was also a state of being that was hard to unwind from.

The destination that *this* kind of being alive could take you to was the complete opposite.

Peace.

Contentment.

The feeling of coming home after a long day's work, where you could take a deep breath and simply *be*…

Like the way she'd felt in Harry's arms last night, when the tears had gone and her fear had been washed away with them.

The feeling of home but with the bonus of not being there alone.

With that thought humming in the back of her mind, it turned out to be very easy to choose the gift she was searching for.

It had everything. It would remind Harry of his time in New Zealand. It had a meaning that captured the essence of what he had given her with the promise of potentially a new life. It was something he could keep close so he would never forget, but he could also keep it private. As private as the secret he was keeping on her behalf.

Best of all, he would be able to see it. And touch it. And it would remind him of her.

CHAPTER NINE

IT WAS STARTING to feel a lot more like Christmas when Tilly and Harry arrived back at the old family villa after their shopping expedition.

Suddenly, there was too much to do. They needed to change clothes and head into the township for the Christmas gathering in Craig's Gully, but there were parcels and bags to be unpacked from the Jeep and hidden carefully so that surprises didn't get spoilt if they ran out of time to wrap gifts. There was Christmas music playing and the living room was a bombsite, with emptied boxes and packing materials scattered everywhere but also with a magnificently decorated tree, its lights already twinkling and parcels underneath.

Lizzie had been there helping Jim Dawson with the decorations for hours and she wasn't leaving any time soon, apparently.

'I've told him he can't go to the barbecue,' she told Tilly, 'and now I'll have to stay long enough to make sure he doesn't try to persuade anyone else to take him out gallivanting around the countryside.'

'It smells like you're already cooking dinner. Or have you been baking?'

'People have been coming by. Bringing casseroles

and mince pies and gingerbread and all sorts of other things to go under the tree. I think it's a bit of a shock that their beloved local doctor could have killed himself falling off the roof.'

Tilly didn't need to see that hint of a smile on Harry's face as he slid a quick glance in her direction to remember what he'd said about being a country GP and being significant in the lives of so many people. That a whole community could become like a family. Seeing the love and support that was coming out for her father did make it seem like a balance to the side of a close-knit community that Tilly couldn't handle—the gossip and judgement that came from everybody knowing too much about everybody else.

She was still thinking about it when she was getting changed into a summer dress, having hidden her parcels in the back of her wardrobe. She might have been an only child but the bond she had with her father was unbreakable. She knew that kind of bond was the same but with more strands to it in bigger families and she'd seen the support of family groups gathering in the emergency department over many years now.

There was a special glue in those bonds that came, at least in part, from knowing everything. You celebrated the good stuff but you still accepted people despite any not so good stuff and that was the kind of acceptance that built and strengthened those bonds. It had to be a diluted form of that glue that brought unrelated people in communities together. And a not so diluted form that created real friendships.

Like the friendship that seemed to be forming between herself and Harry? He knew about her bad stuff but he not only accepted her, he seemed to like her more. To care more.

Tilly paused for a moment after pulling sandals onto her bare feet.

It felt good, this bond that was forming with Harry.

So good that, like seeing the outpouring of concern from the community for her father, it made Tilly wonder if she'd made a mistake by allowing herself to become so distant. Why had she spent so much of her life trying to be so independent, anyway? To prove that she didn't desperately miss her mother when she wasn't around so that people wouldn't feel sorry for her? Because she adored her father and didn't want him to feel any worse when he was already stressed, trying to cover all parental duties when he was missing his beloved wife and he still had to respond to all the needs of a community that depended on him? Whatever the reason had been, Tilly had learned as a child that she could cope on her own and had believed it had stood her in good stead when it had felt as if her life was falling apart as an adult. Had it, instead, been the foundation for barriers she'd strengthened ever since?

Perhaps it was because it was Christmas that was making her so aware of the concept of family. Maybe it was because of her father's accident. Or it could be that something else was the catalyst for what was making Tilly's heart feel as if it had broken out of some kind of cage and was filling up more than it had ever been able to do before. Making her yearn for things she had believed she would never be able to have.

It seemed quite likely that that something else was Harry Doyle...

* * *

Tilly's soft cotton, floaty dress was a complete con-
trast to Harry, who was resplendent in the full Father
Christmas attire designed for a northern hemisphere
Christmas as she drove him into Craig's Gully township late that afternoon.

The grass square with a war memorial in its centre
was a hive of activity.

There were old oak trees around the edges of the
grass square, which provided some welcome shade.

'There's your throne.' Tilly pointed to an oversized
chair, covered in red velvet, under one of the trees. A
Christmas tree covered in shiny baubles was on one
side of the ornate throne and two small ponies with
reindeer antlers on their heads and strands of tinsel
tied into shaggy manes and tails were tethered on the
other side beside a large bucket of water.

'They look like the ponies Maggie's grandchildren
were riding yesterday,' Tilly said.

'Thank goodness they're in the shade. Along with
my throne.' Harry pushed the white curls of his wig
off his forehead. 'I knew it was crazy to have Christmas in the middle of summer. I've only got my togs
on underneath this outfit but I'm already cooking. The
coat is sticking to my back, and you have no idea how
itchy this beard is.'

Tilly could only offer him a sympathetic smile. One
that melted into something even softer as she noticed
that his ears were showing through the curls beneath
a hat that was a size too small.

'You're a hero for doing this, Harry,' she said. 'My
dad thinks you're the best thing since sliced bread and
that I'm the luckiest girl in the world.'

She had to look away from Harry now. Away from those adorable ears and those captivating blue eyes. She didn't want him to see anything in her face that might make him wonder if this pretence might be getting a bit out of hand. To see something that might make him feel sorry for her when they stepped back into reality the day after tomorrow? The way he'd felt about having to disappoint that young nurse, Charlotte?

Thank goodness she could make it sound as if she was simply going along with how well Harry's acting gig was going in public.

'Look...you've got more members of your fan club already.'

A small queue was forming in the shade on the Christmas tree side of the throne. A young mother with a toddler in her arms, another pushing a pram and several older children who were unaccompanied. Their parents were no doubt amongst the adults who were firing up the barbecue grills, setting food out on trestle tables in another shady spot and organising games for the children. Someone's father was setting up a camera to record the annual tradition of sitting beside Father Christmas and spilling their most secret wishes.

'I remember coming here,' she told Harry. 'And even though I knew it was my dad being Santa, I still loved it. When I got older I couldn't understand why people did this on a day when they would already be so busy, the day before Christmas, but... I think I get it now. Tomorrow is plenty of time for all the smaller families to be together. This is celebrating that big family you were talking about.'

She waved a hand at the scene around them. Someone was handing out ice creams from a half wine barrel full of ice and another barrel had cold drinks for the adults. 'You were right when you pointed out that there's a positive side to everyone knowing your business. I think I'm only just realising how much I've missed it.'

Was it because those barriers she'd probably started building way back when she was just a kid, missing her mum, and had made impenetrable after the trauma of the assault, were starting to crumble? Because she felt different since last night?

Because of Harry…?

That internal melty feeling was threatening to bring tears to her eyes. The need to give something back to Harry suddenly seemed of the utmost importance because…good grief…this felt like a whole lot more than gratitude for anything he'd done for her.

It felt a lot like love…

She caught his gaze. 'I'm beginning to think being a GP in Craig's Gully might not be such a bad thing,' she said quietly. 'And I think I get why you feel you need to go back home to Ireland. I really hope you find what you're looking for there because…you deserve to be happy, Harry.'

Tilly also wanted to tell him how special he really was. How very glad she was that he'd offered to come home and share Christmas with her. She could have even told him that she loved him in that moment—in a light-hearted kind of way that a friend could say it so it wouldn't lead to any awkwardness later—but the arrival of Father Christmas had been spotted and excited children were jumping up and down.

'Santa! Santa! Santa!'

'Good luck,' was all she had the chance to say in the end. 'I'll come and save you from heatstroke later.'

If he hadn't been quietly cooking inside the Santa suit, this would have been quite fun. Harry had never been into dressing-up so it was a novelty to be disguised so well that, even if people knew him, he couldn't be recognised. Tilly was the only person here who knew who was inside the suit and he liked that it was a secret just between them. He sat on the throne and had small children sitting on his knee, babies in his arms, older children sitting on cushions beside him and even dogs lying at his feet as photographs were taken and secrets were whispered. He heard about the toys and games and electronic devices that children were hoping would arrive overnight.

Tilly turned up with an icy cold beer in a paper cup.

'Ho-ho-ho!' Harry said. 'You're a good girl, Matilda.'

'The queue's getting shorter,' she told him. 'Hang in there. Can you see the little girl in the pink tutu?'

Harry peered over the top of the gold-rimmed spectacles. 'Yes.'

'That's Ava. Jase's daughter?'

'Ah…' Harry finished his drink and handed Tilly the empty cup. 'Do you think he remembers the promise I made to find out what she wants for Christmas?'

'I know he does. He just asked me to remind you.'

Tilly pointed to where picnic rugs and chairs were being set up near the tables and, sure enough, Jase was sitting on one of the chairs, his arm in a sling and a smile on his face.

When it was Ava's turn to whisper her secret, Harry

found himself holding his breath, but the little girl was suddenly shy.

'What is it that you'd like Father Christmas to bring you, pet?'

'I forget…'

'Have a think about it while we smile for our photo. Is that your mummy there? With your baby brother?'

'Yes. My daddy's got a sore arm.'

'I know. But it's going to get all better soon. Can you see my reindeer?'

'They're not reindeer,' Ava giggled. 'They're ponies.'

Harry lowered his voice. 'Do you like ponies, Ava?'

'I love ponies,' she whispered back.

'Is that what you'd really like for Christmas?'

Ava nodded and Harry patted her head. 'I'll see what I can do.' He raised his voice to a cheerful boom. 'Merry Christmas. Ho-ho-ho…'

Right at the end of the queue were the twins he recognised as Maggie's grandchildren. They were both wearing red headbands with Christmas decorations on them.

'Which one of you is Sammy and which one is George?' he asked.

'I'm George.' The girl had three tiny angels on her headband. 'And he's Sammy.' Sammy had a Christmas tree made of green felt on his headband. It was decorated with tiny golden balls and bows made of silver tinsel.

'How do you know our names?' Sammy sounded suspicious.

'I'm Father Christmas. I know everything.'

'You're not the real Father Christmas. He's at the North Pole and he doesn't get here till tomorrow.'

'Okay…you got me.' Harry was too hot and tired to argue. 'I'm one of his helpers.'

'Where's the real one?'

'He's busy wrapping presents. And loading up his sleigh. He comes to New Zealand first, did you know that?'

'Which way does he come?'

'From the north.'

'Which way's that?'

'Um…' Harry wasn't sure, so he waved vaguely at the hills. 'Up there. He'll come over the top of those hills later tonight so you'd better tell me what it is you're hoping for most of all so I can get a message to him.'

'We already wrote him a letter,' George told him.

'That's good.' Harry nodded. 'But you could tell me too.'

'We both want the same thing.' Sammy still sounded suspicious. 'If you know our names you should know about that too. Unless the letter didn't get there…'

George tugged on his sleeve. 'I'll tell you,' she whispered. She knelt up on her cushion and put her mouth so close to his ear that it tickled. He could hear her gulp of breath that advertised how important this was. 'We want Nana to get better.'

Oh…

Harry closed his eyes in a long blink as he pulled in a breath.

'I know what she said,' Sammy growled into the silence. 'So…?'

Harry looked down at the small boy, still lost for words.

'So...can you do that?' Sammy demanded.

'I'm so sorry that your nana's sick,' Harry said carefully. 'But I know that it's very special for her to be able to have this Christmas with you.'

'So you're not going to make her better.' Sammy glared at Harry as he slid off his cushion. 'You can't, anyway, because you're not the real Father Christmas. Come on, George.'

But George sat there for a moment longer, gazing up at Harry with tears about to spill from her eyes.

Harry bent his head and spoke softly. 'Sometimes, getting better can be about when things stop hurting,' he said.

George nodded slowly. 'Like when my foot stopped hurting,' she said, 'After Geronimo stood on it.'

'Is Geronimo your pony? I mean your reindeer?'

'No, he's Sammy's pony. My pony is called Bilbo and he's too kind to step on anybody's toes.' She was smiling as she climbed off the throne. 'I need to go and find Sammy,' she said. 'And my mum. She said we could have an ice cream next and maybe that will make Sammy feel not quite so sad.'

Harry took off his spectacles as he watched her go after her brother. He was using the sleeve of his jacket to wipe his eyes as Tilly appeared from nowhere.

Her brow furrowed as she looked up at him. 'Are you okay?'

'I don't think I've ever been this hot in my entire life,' Harry told her. 'I might actually have hyperthermia.' He let his breath out in a sigh. 'And I just had Maggie's grandchildren tell me that the only thing they want for Christmas is for their nana to get better.'

'Oh...' Tilly's eyes seemed to get bigger and darker.

She looked over her shoulder at the crowd of people sharing food and laughter as children played around them. And then she looked back at Harry and he knew that she knew being part of that group was the last thing he wanted right now.

She held out her hand.

'Come with me,' she said. 'I know exactly where you need to be.'

The lake was deserted.

Tilly knew it would be, because everybody who might have been there was at the barbecue in the town square, so this was not only private, she'd known it would provide exactly the kind of serenity that Harry badly needed.

She needed a bit of it herself, to be honest. Harry had told her, word for word, about his conversation with Sammy and George and his suggestion that Maggie being free of her pain was a form of 'getting better' had squeezed her heart enough to bring tears to her eyes.

He was going to make the best father ever, she thought as she brought the Jeep to a halt. And the woman he chose to be the mother of those six children was yet to discover how lucky she was.

The lake was as still as a mill pond. The scorching heat of the sun was softening as the long summer twilight began, but the stones of the beach had soaked up the warmth enough to make the clear, cool water of this small lake even more inviting.

Harry had removed the big black belt and unzipped the jacket of his suit, throwing the pillow into the back of the Jeep as Tilly had driven him here. He had also discarded the hat, wig, beard and spectacles and kicked off the black boots, but he still looked...almost shell-shocked.

'Why don't you get the rest of your kit off?' she suggested as soon as they were standing on the beach.

'What?'

'You've said you put your swimming shorts on underneath, didn't you?'

'Yes, but...'

'It's going to be the fastest way for you to cool off. I can pretty much guarantee we've got this place to ourselves for a while, so you could go skinny-dipping if you prefer. I won't look...'

Tilly tried to find a smile but found her lips were strangely wobbly as she remembered what Harry had said only yesterday about having to go swimming naked because he hadn't brought his togs with him. It felt a lot longer ago than yesterday. A lifetime ago, in some ways...because this wasn't stirring feelings that were going to make her unbearably nervous. Tilly couldn't feel even a hint of that kind of fear and the relief was as overwhelming as whatever emotions Sammy and George had stirred in Harry.

Standing there with his sweat-dampened curls, bare feet, the pants of his suit rolled up to his calves and the red and white jacket open so that his bare chest was visible was making Harry Doyle the sexiest Santa Claus imaginable but, also strangely, Tilly wasn't feeling any shafts of that heat that she was learning could be triggered by physical desire. She wasn't even thinking about wanting Harry to kiss her again.

This was something deeper. Emotional rather than physical. This was about things that were going to be lost, like the grief that Maggie's grandchildren were going to have to experience soon. It was about things that had already been lost, like both their own mothers. Like Tilly's ability to trust. Or take risks. And about whatever it was that had been keeping Harry from finding what he was searching for. There was love in that mix too. The love that Harry had to give. Her gratitude—and love—for what he'd already given her.

This was about life, Tilly realised. As huge and complicated and wonderful and sad as it all was and how much it mattered to find a connection with another human who could be there when it was all a bit too much.

Harry hadn't moved. He was staring at Tilly as though he was seeing her for the first time, but she couldn't blame him. Just a day or so ago he wouldn't have believed that the 'Ice Queen' would be suggesting a skinny-dip. She wouldn't have believed it herself.

Not that she was going to go quite that far. Tilly was wearing a perfectly respectable bra and panties under her dress.

'Last one in's a rotten egg,' she announced, reaching for the hem of her dress so she could pull it off over her head.

The stones hurt her feet and the water was cold enough to make her squeak, so Tilly had to keep going until it was deep enough to dive and then swam as hard as she could. By the time she surfaced her body was adjusting to the temperature of the water. She used her legs and arms to keep her head above water, waiting for that delicious moment when it would start to feel like cool silk rippling around her body, and she scanned the lake around her to see where Harry was.

There was no sign of him.

She could see the heap of red and white fabric on the beach, so he'd stripped off, but if he'd followed her into the lake he hadn't left so much as a ripple. A beat of alarm made Tilly's breath catch in her throat. Had Harry been even more overheated than she'd realised? Had the sudden immersion in cold water given him cramps or a cardiac arrhythmia? Had he sunk without a trace and was drowning?

The squeak Tilly had made on entering the water was nothing to the squeal as she felt her ankle being gripped and tugged. Her head went underwater but she was released instantly and she came up spluttering—with laughter. The best she could manage in return was to scoop water in her hand and aim it for Harry's face. The water fight that ensued lasted for a good ten minutes and left them both exhausted and breathless, from treading water and laughing so hard. By tacit agreement, when they found themselves in water at neck level when their feet could touch the stone bed of the lake, a truce was called and they stayed still as the ripples subsided and the echoes of their laughter vanished into the fading light.

It was Tilly who broke the silence. 'Feeling better?'

Harry grinned at her. 'So much better.'

'Want to get out?'

Harry shook his head. 'I think I might want to stay here for ever.'

Tilly smiled. 'For ever is quite a long time, you know.'

'I might change my mind in a minute or two. It *is* getting colder.'

'I think I'm getting goosebumps.'

She felt Harry's finger brush her arm under the water. 'You are. Okay…it's time to get out.'

Except neither of them made any movement other than the gentle rocking that meant they could keep their balance in the water and, although the water was crystal clear, the ripples were enough to blur the image of their bodies so the only part of Harry that Tilly was aware of was his face. He had wet hair plastered to his head and she could even see droplets of water in the tangle of his eyelashes, but it was those astonishing blue eyes that captured her. No. It was the way he was looking at her.

There was no one watching them. No one to appreciate any performance intended to convince them that Harry was head over heels in love with her, but that was how this gaze was making Tilly feel. She had no idea whether her foot slipped on the pebbles beneath them, or whether there was some mysterious current in the lake that made it happen, but it felt as if she simply floated even closer to Harry and it was instinctive to catch her balance by reaching out to touch the bare skin of his shoulders. The warmth of his arms coming around her should have counteracted the goosebumps caused by the cold water but, in fact, she could feel them become more pronounced when she lifted her face and felt the touch of Harry's lips against hers.

It was when she felt the soft, silky touch of his tongue against hers that she was aware of a warmth through her entire body that no chilly lake water could possibly compete with. A warmth that made it impossible for Tilly to freeze, in any sense, and there was only one thing she wanted to do.

Kiss Harry back.

And to stay here for ever.

* * *

They'd been in the water for too long.

As welcome as the cooling effect had been after hours of sweltering in that Santa suit, when he felt Tilly beginning to shiver in his arms Harry knew it was time to get out.

Which meant it was time to stop kissing her as well. But maybe that was a good thing because he couldn't quite remember whose idea it had been to do it in the first place and he had to be very, very sure that it was something that Tilly wanted as much as he did.

The stones on the beach still held the heat of the sun but Harry draped the jacket of the Santa suit around Tilly's shoulders.

'Have you got a towel in the car?'

'No. Just the bag with your change of clothes. I wasn't planning on swimming.'

'Of course you weren't. You should still be at the barbecue. Do you want to head back?'

'It'll be all over by now. The carol service will be just about finished. Everybody will be heading home so they can get the kids to bed as early as possible.' Tilly smiled. 'They'll probably be up again at about five a.m. when it starts getting light. Another disadvantage of having Christmas in the middle of summer, I guess.'

'I think I'm starting to like it,' Harry said. 'There's something about this place. Something that feels like Christmas even when it shouldn't. It's breaking all the rules.'

'Like roaring fires and mulled wine and lots of snow?'

'Exactly.'

'Did you always get a white Christmas in Dublin?'

'Not at all. It only happens once every few years.

I've got a photo of one when I was about eight. I think it was 1995. My mam and I built the best snowman ever, with lumps of coal for his eyes and buttons and proper forked branches so that his arms had hands with fingers.'

'No… I don't believe it. Fingers?'

'I've got a photo. I'll prove it to you. I gave him my hat and scarf to wear.'

'I'd like to see that.'

He could hear the smile in Tilly's voice but didn't turn his head to see it.

'Everyone said the most spectacular white Christmas ever in Dublin was in 2010,' he told her. 'There was so much snow and it made everything so much prettier. Even the tenement block Mam was still living in didn't look so bad with all the edges softened and the lights shining.' Harry stared out at the still lake, as if he could see the reflections of his own life in its surface. 'She was already sick with the cancer, but she never told me about it. And that was the last Christmas we ever had together…'

It had to be trickles of water still escaping from his hair that were rolling down his face like tears. Harry didn't cry. He'd learned not to when he'd been about Sammy's age, because it only made the bullying worse. It was time to make someone laugh. Himself as well as Tilly with any luck, if he could think of a good joke.

But then he heard the tiniest sound of a sniff and, when he turned his head, he saw Tilly rubbing her nose. He could see the tears making those dark eyes of hers shimmer in this soft light and the knowledge that she had absorbed his own pain made something shift in his chest. Something that moved enough to give his heart room to expand. Yeah...this felt like Christmas.

Because it felt like family. It felt like love. And wasn't that what Christmas was all about?

Harry reached out to use the pad of his thumb to brush away a tear that escaped, curling his fingers around her jawbone at the same time. Because he wanted to kiss this woman again. And again.

He wanted, very much, to make love to her, if Tilly wanted him to. And if it happened to be on a deserted lake beach as daylight faded, using a Santa suit to cushion the stones, it could well become the most favourite Christmas memory ever.

Tilly knew what he was thinking. He could see his own thoughts reflected in her eyes. He could feel the warmth of her skin as he leaned towards her. And he heard the sharp intake of her breath. Not because of his touch, though. There was another sound they could both hear—the demanding ring of a phone coming from the front seat of the Jeep.

'I'd better get that,' Tilly said, pulling the jacket around her as she scrambled to her feet. 'Nobody would call at this time of night on Christmas Eve if it wasn't something important.'

CHAPTER TEN

THE TENSION IN Tilly's voice cut through the serenity of their surroundings like a knife.

'How long ago? Where's George? Is someone with Maggie?'

Harry was on his feet and pulling clothes from the bag on the back seat well before she finished the call. He knew the people that were being discussed. He knew that, somehow, he was involved.

And Tilly's expression confirmed it.

'Remember what you said to Sammy?' she asked. 'About where the real Father Christmas is?'

'That he was in the North Pole?'

'That he would be coming over the hills later tonight. That was Dad on the phone. He got a call from Doug Grimshaw, who wanted to talk to you about what you'd said. Apparently, George told him that Sammy's gone to find Father Christmas. He wanted George to go with him, but she was scared so he said he'd go by himself, and she wasn't allowed to tell anybody because it was a secret.'

Harry's heart sank like a stone. 'He thinks the "real" Father Christmas can make his wish come true. That I couldn't do it because I was only his helper.'

'And now he's disappeared,' Tilly said. 'They didn't stay for the carol service because they had arranged for someone to video call from the church and the family were going to join in from around Maggie's bed. The twins said they wanted to put the ponies back in the paddock by themselves and take all the tinsel off. That was a while ago now and nobody knows where Sammy is and he took his pony so he could have gone quite a long way already. People are heading up to the Grimshaws' farm to help look for him. If they can't find him before it starts getting dark they'll have to call in Search and Rescue, but there's no guarantee there'll be a full team available on Christmas Eve.'

'This is partly my fault.' Harry said quietly. 'I need to be there. I have to help.'

When Tilly and Harry went home to get some warmer clothes and suitable footwear for trekking up hills on a high-country sheep station, it was clear that Jim Dawson felt just as strong a need to be there.

'I delivered those twins,' he said gruffly. 'And Maggie was your mum's best friend, Tilly. I'm part of that family. Harry, go and find some woollen jumpers in the chest of drawers in my room and bring one for me as well. Grab some socks while you're at it. I reckon my gumboots will be a perfect fit for you.'

'I'll stay with him,' Lizzie said. 'Have you got some camping chairs? That way, I can at least make sure he's not standing around too much on his crutches.'

'We need torches. And spare batteries. I'll find them,' Tilly said.

'Should we fill some Thermoses with hot water?'

Lizzie asked. 'And take some of that baking that's been arriving all day?'

'With any luck they will have found Sammy by the time we get up there,' Tilly said, 'but yeah… I'm sure a cup of tea and a mince pie would still be welcome.'

They were far from the only people to have thought of what might be needed if a missing child wasn't found in a hurry. A paddock near the gate to the homestead gardens was filling up with utes and four-wheel drive farm vehicles. Even the local fire engine and a police car were parked on the grass. A trestle table that had probably just been packed up recently from the barbe- cue in the town square was already laden with plates of food people had brought and there was a small platoon of Thermoses to one side. Jim Dawson, propped up on his crutches, took over organising mugs and bottles of milk. Tilly saw him wave a hand at Lizzie, probably dismissing her suggestion that it was time he sat down somewhere and put his foot up.

The paddock could be seen from the homestead fur- ther up the hill and Tilly could imagine that Maggie was sitting in her bed, watching what was happening. Feeling sick with worry about her grandson. It felt as if everyone was worried sick as she walked with Harry towards the group of people gathering at another gate that led onto a bare hill beside the driveway. There were people on horseback coming very slowly down the slope and one of them was leading a pony.

'It's Geronimo,' someone said. 'Look, he's still got a bit of that tinsel tied to his tail.'

'But where's Sammy? I can't see him.'

'That pony's limping. He's hurt himself.'

'Probably put his foot in a rabbit hole. They're everywhere up there.'

'Better than a mine shaft.' A man's quiet voice was grim. 'There's plenty of those around in these hills too.'

One of the men on horseback was Doug, and Tilly assumed the man beside him was his older brother, John, the twins' father. They had farm dogs with them and someone following on a quad bike. It was Doug who spoke to the group waiting for them.

'We found Geronimo up past the ridge where there's a patch of beech forest. It's too rocky for the quad bikes past there and dangerous for the horses now that it's getting dark.' He cleared his throat. 'There's no sign of Sam, and if he could hear us calling he's not answering.'

Tilly caught Harry's gaze. That his uncle was using his formal name made this all sound so much more serious. That Sammy wasn't responding to calls when he had to be frightened after falling off his pony was even more worrying. Was he hurt? Unconscious? Harry was wearing a large backpack that was filled with first aid gear from her father's vehicle. Tilly was wearing a smaller one that contained a drug kit and a small oxygen cylinder. They would be ready to deal with whatever they found—if they could find Sammy in time.

'We've been in touch with the police and available mountain search and rescue personnel are being contacted and will be on their way from Queenstown asap. In the meantime, some of us can fan out and start a search on foot. Bruce is over there near the table, and he'll take your details if you want to join the line and he'll make sure you've got a torch and a means of communication. We've got a few two-way radios available, but he'll take your phone numbers and make sure you've got his. Tilly—we're going to put you in charge of anything medical that's needed, is that okay?'

'Of course.'

'Go and see Bruce and he'll make sure you've got a radio.'

'Bruce was our local cop when I was growing up,' Tilly told Harry as they turned away. 'I thought he would have retired long ago.'

And maybe he had but he was here tonight, along with so many other concerned friends and neighbours, even if they couldn't do anything to help other than being here—like her father. They were here to offer support. To be part of the caring. Tilly had that feeling of her heart filling to overflowing again, but this time she couldn't attribute it to the bond she could feel with Harry or because it was Christmas. This was definitely about family and, more specifically, the kind of family that Harry had reminded her existed in a form large enough to contain an entire community.

It was in that moment that Tilly recognised the deep yearning she had to come home. To live and work in this rugged country, amongst people that she already cared about. That she could trust would care about her.

Doug was off his horse now and loosening the girth of his saddle. Someone was leading Geronimo away.

'At least we know he's in this paddock,' Doug called as people began moving towards where Bruce was stationed. 'But it's a big one. At least ten acres and it gets pretty gnarly further up past the native bush. Don't join the line unless you're a confident tramper. Stay in pairs and please...be careful. We don't want anyone else hurt up there.'

Anyone *else*...

Without thinking, Tilly found herself reaching for Harry's hand as they followed the group. Feeling the squeeze of his fingers curl around hers and, even better, that he didn't let it go added enough extra to whatever was filling her heart to make it ache—as if this addition had jagged edges.

Because, when she came home to this place and these people she loved, she was going to be a world away from Harry and she would never feel his hand holding hers again and Tilly had the disturbing feeling that the ache she could feel in her heart right now might be only the tip of an iceberg she could never have dreamed was even on the horizon. She pulled in a deep breath to steady herself and Harry must have heard it because he turned his head to catch her gaze.

'We'll find him,' he said. 'Because we won't stop until we do.'

Tilly could feel the level of Harry's involvement in this disappearance of a small boy. She could hear his determination to succeed and how imperative it was that they *did* succeed and...and she loved him for caring that much.

She loved him for who he was.

She had fallen in love with Harry Doyle, it was as simple as that.

The consequences of her heart being stolen so unexpectedly would have to wait. For now, Tilly welcomed the rush of warmth that came with acknowledging that love because it brought with it a wash of hope.

They were going to find Sammy.

This would be okay.

It *had* to be okay. Because anything else was unthinkable on the eve of Christmas Day.

The temperature dropped as daylight faded and the shadows of the uneven, rocky ground became a minefield of accidents, like a sprained ankle or a broken wrist, waiting to happen.

That was why Harry was keeping a firm hold of Tilly's hand in one of his, using his other hand to hold the torch and shine light into crevasses between big rocks that could easily hide a small boy who didn't want to be found until *he'd* found Father Christmas.

'Sammy,' he called. '*Sam*-my…'

It sounded like an echo of his own voice coming from the right, above the level that he and Tilly were searching, but it was someone else calling amidst the beams of other torches that flickered amongst the rocks and trees like giant fireflies.

They'd been here for what felt like hours now and Harry could swear they'd been over this exact patch of ground already. Admittedly, the initial search was hit and miss as everybody wanted to be out here searching far and wide as quickly as possible, but it had become more coordinated after the experienced members of a local search and rescue team took command. Quad bikes and a tractor had ferried people and supplies as far as they could so that a base was established for mapping the area into a grid and beginning a methodical search that would cover every square metre. And someone was on their way to the farm with a specialised search dog that had raised everyone's hopes.

'He can't have got far,' the searchers said, when they'd gathered to be reassigned sections of the huge paddock.

'Yeah…it's too steep for anyone to go further up.'

'And don't forget the headband. He's got to be here somewhere.'

The news that the red headband with the Christmas tree attached had been found, thanks to the glitter of the silver tinsel catching a beam of torchlight, had been relayed to the camp at the bottom paddock by the driveway and the searchers had all heard the cheer go up.

Maggie had probably heard that cheer from the house and must have thought that Sammy had been found but that was at least an hour ago now and nothing more had been discovered. Harry's heart felt more and more heavy at the thought of what it must be like in that big, overdecorated room where Maggie's bed was. Did she have George cuddled up beside her and any members of the family who weren't out searching sitting close enough to be able to reach out and touch them both? He hoped so. He liked Maggie. He liked everyone he'd met so far in Craig's Gully and right now he'd give anything to have a chance to talk to Sammy again.

He'd like to tell him that he knew how hard this was but that it would be okay. That, as long as Sammy had the people he loved and who loved him close by, he would be able to get through this. That he was needed. By Maggie. And his twin sister. And his mum and dad and everybody else in that big, loving Grimshaw family.

It could get you through anything, that kind of love.

'I can hear dogs barking,' Tilly said. 'It could be that the farm dogs have spotted a stranger arriving. Maybe that search dog will be able to sniff the headband and take us straight to where Sammy is.'

'It would have been better if the person who found it hadn't picked it up and taken it down the hill. It'll take longer for the dog to pick up the trail.'

Or maybe it wouldn't. The dark shape that appeared from behind them made Harry utter an oath and pull Tilly close, but the German Shepherd took no notice of either of them. He had his nose down and a long rope trailing behind him as he went past. The man on the other end of the rope sounded out of breath as he caught up.

'It's steeper…than it looks…eh?'

His dog was out of sight around a jagged tumble of rock, but the volley of barking was loud enough to make Tilly jump.

'He's found something,' the dog's handler called back. 'Follow me… No…wait…'

Harry pulled Tilly to a stop. He could see the dog, still barking, but it was facing them and there was nothing but grass and tussock to be seen in the space between them as he played his torchlight over the ground.

'Stay there,' the man ordered. 'Something's not quite right.' He had his own torch and he moved forward slowly. 'Good boy… Kobe. What have you found, mate?'

There was a long moment's silence, broken only by an exclamation of disbelief. And then both the dog and man lay down on the ground and they heard him call, 'Sammy? You down there, buddy? Can you hear me?'

The sound of a child's cry in return made Tilly gasp and brought a lump the size of a golf ball into Harry's throat.

'I'm in here… I can't get out…'

'That's what we're here for, buddy. You're going to hear me blowing a whistle now. I'm calling in the troops.'

Tilly met Harry's gaze as he reached for the two-way radio he was carrying. 'And I'm calling Maggie...'

There had to be dozens of people on the Grimshaws' land. Thousands and thousands of sheep scattered over these hills and all sorts of wild animals like rabbits and deer, goats and possums and owls, but it felt as if every living creature was holding its breath.

As if the whole world was focused on this small hole in the ground—an old, abandoned mineshaft that had been dug well over a century ago and had been partly filled in and narrowed by erosion over the decades. It had been just big enough for a small boy to slip inside, dislodging stones and dry earth in his attempts to get out, which only made him fall further but, thankfully, seemed to have prevented any significant injuries.

'My knee's a bit sore,' Sammy told Harry as he questioned him thoroughly to try and do a remote assessment. 'But that might have been from when I fell off Geronimo. I was riding him without his saddle and it made him a bit slippery.'

'It was a very brave thing to do.' Harry was lying on his stomach, shining a torch down into the hole, being careful not to make the edges crumble and rain dirt on the small, hunched figure he could see. Tilly was lying on the other side of the hole.

Sammy's voice wobbled. 'Am I in big trouble?'

'No, darling.' It was Tilly who reassured him. 'I reckon everybody's going to be too happy to get you home to be cross.'

'Can I come out now?'

'Just as soon as we get sorted,' Harry said. 'We've got the people who know how to do stuff like this, so we need to let them make a plan. It could take a wee while. Is it cold down there?'

'Yes...and... I'm a bit scared.'

Harry pulled off the woollen jersey he was wearing. 'I'm going to drop this jumper,' he told Sammy. 'Don't worry—it's soft and cuddly. If you put it on, it'll help keep you warm.'

'What's a jumper?'

'It's a jersey,' Tilly told him. 'Harry comes from Ireland, and they have different names for some things.'

'He sounds like Santa's helper.'

'You know what? They have little people called leprechauns in Ireland and they look a bit like the elves that are Santa's helpers. And do you want to know a secret?'

The big sniff from the bottom of the hole was a sign that Sammy was fighting tears. 'Y-yes...'

Tilly leaned further into the hole. 'Don't tell anybody, but Harry's got ears just like a leprechaun.'

Harry wriggled back and got to his feet as Tilly coached Sammy into putting on the woollen jersey he'd dropped. The group of men who had coils of rope over their shoulders and harnesses dangling from their hands were waiting for his report.

'I don't think he's injured. He might have grazed or bumped his knee but he can move all his limbs, he's not bleeding and he's oriented and alert. But he's cold and tired and scared so I'm not sure how well he'd manage trying to get himself safely into a harness so we could pull him up.'

'He hasn't managed to get his arms into the sleeves

of that jersey.' Tilly had joined the group. 'I wouldn't trust his ability to deal with the buckles on a harness.'

'And the shaft is too tight for any of us to get down. We'd just make it collapse further by trying.'

'It's only about five metres at the most.'

'We could dig in from the side,' someone suggested. 'Just a few metres of a channel would be enough. Then someone could lean in and catch his wrists and haul the poor wee blighter out. If he stood up maybe it wouldn't even need to be that deep.'

'It would take hours. Might not even be possible. Some of that ground has to be solid rock.'

'I'm not big,' Tilly said. 'I could lean in with someone hanging on to my ankles.'

'And fall in on top of him and break your neck?' Harry shook his head. 'I'm not going to let that happen.'

'That's why I'd trust you to hang on to my ankles,' Tilly said. She was watching Harry intently and he found he couldn't look away from that gaze. From the trust he could see in her eyes. More than trust…?

The search and rescue team were talking behind them.

'It's not such a stupid idea. She's the only one here who's small enough to not get stuck in the shaft. If she was in a harness and roped in, we've got more than enough manpower to pull her out.

'I could get a harness on Sammy.' Tilly nodded.

'You'd be hanging upside down. It's not that easy to do anything.'

'But it's worth a try, isn't it?' Harry could see Tilly straightening her spine as she reached towards the harness one of the men was holding. 'Please? If there's any way we can get Sammy back to his nana quickly, we've got to try.'

Harry sensed the change around him. Because there were enough local people here who knew exactly why time was precious for the Grimshaw family. People who were prepared to break rules or protocols and do whatever they could to help. So he couldn't try and talk Tilly out of the idea. He could only watch her being buckled into a harness and ropes being attached with carabiners and instructions being given about how to attach another harness to Sammy.

And then he could only watch her being lowered into the hole, far enough for her feet to vanish from sight. He had to stand well back because nobody knew if there were ancient tunnels that could cause sink-holes if there was too much weight at ground level. Nobody knew how easily Tilly would be able to fit through the length of that shaft either, or what the effects might be on her body. Hanging upside down for more than a few minutes could lead to an increase in blood pressure and a decrease in heart rate. It could put pressure on the eyes and lead to blood pooling inside the head. It was possible that Tilly could pass out. It was also possible that her heart could stop when blood flow to her lower body was suddenly restored to a normal level.

She could die.

And it was that thought that made the breath catch in Harry's chest and made him close his eyes in pain as he realised just how much he didn't want that to happen. Not to this astonishingly courageous, beautiful, loving, *warm* woman he'd discovered Matilda Dawson to be.

He didn't want it to happen to someone he cared about *this* much…

He'd never been so relieved as he was in the moment, only minutes later, when Tilly was pulled back to safety. And, when it looked as if she might be about to faint when she tried to get up, he was the one who reached her first and held her steady in his arms.

'Don't move,' he told her. 'It's okay. I've got you…'

The pounding in Tilly's head was finally receding as little Sammy was carefully pulled out of the mineshaft and Harry was able to check him out physically and confirm that he was, miraculously, uninjured.

It was his father, John, who carried him off the hill and up to the homestead as the overjoyed volunteers began to pack up and go home to their own families—not before they'd shared a cup of tea and some Christmas baking, mind you.

Tilly found her father still behind the trestle table, pouring hot water into a large teapot.

'It's time you went home,' she told him.

'I'll wait a bit. You're going up to the house?'

'Yes. Just for a minute. Harry and I want to check on Maggie. She will have been through the wringer in the last few hours.'

Jim nodded. 'It's been a Christmas Eve to remember, that's for sure. Thank goodness we've had a happy ending.'

Tilly could see past the smile on her father's face. 'You're in a lot more pain, aren't you?'

'He's been on his feet too long,' Lizzie told her. 'I'm going to check that foot in a minute and, if necessary, I'll cart him off to hospital, don't you worry.'

Tilly smiled. 'Thanks, Lizzie. Might see you at home again a bit later?'

'Not likely, lovie.' Lizzie grinned back. 'It's almost midnight and at my age we all turn into pumpkins after that.'

By the time Tilly and Harry reached the homestead and were welcomed inside, Sammy was cuddled up beside Maggie on her bed and nobody seemed at all bothered by the amount of dirt that had been spread on her sheets. George was snuggled under her nana's other arm. Tilly knelt by the head of the bed and Harry perched on the end. The rest of the family drifted further away, as if wanting to give Maggie privacy with her medical team. Sammy's mother called to her son.

'You hungry, Sammy? We've got cheese rolls that have just come out of the oven. They're your favourite.'

'Ooh, they sound good,' Harry said. 'What's a cheese roll?'

'South Island specialty,' Maggie told him. 'You'd better check that Tilly knows how to make them, Harry. It's at the top of the list for something a good southern wife should know how to make.'

Tilly jumped in to try and skate over the awkward moment. 'How are you feeling, Maggie? Can we do anything to help? How's that pain level?'

Tilly could see the way George snuggled even closer in beneath her grandmother's arm.

'It'll get better, Nana. That's what Santa said. It'll stop being sore.'

'It will, my darling girl,' Maggie said quietly. 'It will…'

Sammy also leaned closer. 'I'm sorry, Nana. I couldn't find Father Christmas to make our wish come true.'

'Some wishes aren't meant to come true, my love.' Maggie closed her eyes, her hand stroking Sammy's hair. 'But you know that part of me is never going to die, don't you?'

Sammy raised his head. 'What part, Nana?'

'The part that lives in here.' Maggie touched his chest. 'In your heart. It'll be there for ever. Even when I'm not here, you can talk to me whenever you want and, if you stay still and listen very carefully, you might even hear me say something back.'

Both George and Sammy were wide-eyed. They stared at their nana and then looked at each other. And smiled.

Tilly looked from the older woman and these beautiful children to the man sitting on the end of the bed. Not that she could see Harry very well because her eyes were filled with tears. But she could feel the tenderness of that smile and was quite sure that he was blinking back his own tears.

She could also feel her heart fill to bursting point again. Overflowing, in fact, as they all became aware of the faint sound drifting in through the open door of the house. A glance through the windows showed them that most of the horde of volunteers who had shown up to search for Sammy hadn't gone home just yet. Someone must have had the supply of candles that had been used for the carol service in the back of their ute and everybody was holding a tiny flame.

And they were all singing.

Silent night, holy night...

Tilly blinked away her tears and now she could see Harry's face with absolute clarity. And he was still smiling as he stood up and held out his hand.

'It's time we let Maggie rest,' he said. 'Let's go home, Tilly.'

CHAPTER ELEVEN

THE LYRICS OF the favourite carol were still in Tilly's head when they arrived home to a house that was completely dark apart from the twinkling coloured lights they could see through the big bay window of the living room.

'It's officially Christmas Day, Tilly.' Harry came around the car and opened the passenger door. 'Merry Christmas.'

Tilly had her phone in her hand. 'I've got a message from Lizzie. They've put Dad on complete bed rest in the ward and have his leg elevated to try and get the new swelling down. She'll give us an update when there's more news but says not to expect him home for Christmas dinner.'

'Oh, no… This wasn't part of the plan.'

Tilly tipped her head back against the seat and closed her eyes. 'No.'

None of it had been part of the plan, had it? She hadn't planned on her father hurting himself or Jason falling into a hay baler. She hadn't planned on Harry finding out her secret or discovering that maybe she'd really like to be a rural GP after all. Or having to go head-first down an abandoned mineshaft.

And she most definitely hadn't planned on falling in love with Harry Doyle.

It was officially Christmas Day. Which meant that tomorrow Harry would be flying back to the north island. Getting a step closer to tying up loose ends and heading back to his home in Ireland.

'Hey…' Harry's voice was soft and much closer to her ear than she might have expected. 'You still awake, Bat Woman?'

A smile curled the corners of Tilly's mouth. Harry hadn't wanted her to do that upside-down bat thing down the mineshaft, had he? But how proud of her had he looked when she came back up from the shaft having successfully attached the harness to Sammy? And, as for that smile when they'd been privileged enough to be part of that precious conversation between Maggie and her grandchildren…well…

Tilly didn't have time to finish that dreamy thought because she felt one of Harry's arms slide behind her back and the other beneath her knees.

'I'm not surprised you're exhausted,' he said. 'Come on… I'm taking you to bed.'

Oh…there was a thought…

Tilly *was* exhausted. Emotionally as well as physically, so it wasn't that hard to quell any urge to restore her independence and walk inside by herself. Or to try and find any remnants of those protective barriers she'd relied on for so long and push Harry away. She didn't need to, anyway, because that unfinished thought had been about just how lucky you could be to have someone like Harry care about you. How much you could trust someone like him.

So Tilly simply wrapped her arms around Harry's

neck and let him carry her into her bedroom. And when it felt as if he was about to put her down, she instinctively tightened that hold a little and lifted her face so that it became an invitation to be kissed. One that Harry seemed only too happy to accept.

And that kiss was so gentle. So tender that Tilly would have been only too happy to drown in it. She could feel herself sinking, in fact, but it turned out that Harry was just putting her down on her bed, without breaking the kiss. She could also feel the feather topping of her mattress creating the soft feeling of the interior of a nest and her pillow denting as it cradled her head. She could also feel the tension of Harry's muscles changing. He was really going to put her down this time, wasn't he?

'Don't go,' she whispered. 'Please...?'

'I wanted to find something. I have a Christmas gift for you, Tilly.'

The windows of Tilly's bedroom only looked out at her father's extensive vegetable garden but there was enough moonlight coming through them to be able to see Harry's face clearly. She couldn't see the blue of his eyes, but she could feel the intensity of his gaze and that it was just as tender as that kiss had been. She held on to it as she gathered possibly the most courage she'd ever needed in her life.

'You don't need to go anywhere to give me what my wish is for this Christmas.'

He knew.

He knew that Tilly felt safe enough to ask him for something she could never ask of anyone else. A chance to find out if she could get past the damage that had been done to both her mind and body. It could only ever be Harry who could give her that gift because he was the one who'd given her the confidence to see the real truth and she knew, deep in her soul, that he had the kindness and patience to make it safe. Even if this time together, away from the only reality they'd previously known, would be over in no more than a matter of hours, he had the power to change her whole life.

To help her become a person she could be proud of being...

The touch of Harry's fingers as they traced the outline of her face was as gentle as everything else about this man.

'You're so tired, sweetheart... Are you sure?'

Was she sure? Even though it was highly likely that this would increase the heartbreak that was rushing towards her like an emotional freight train?

Yes, she was sure. Maybe partly because of that impending heartbreak, even. Because it meant she could feel this kind of desire. This level of love. This fierce need to be this close to Harry that was a heat that melted every other thought as his lips claimed hers again.

Perhaps the exhaustion actually helped to make this the perfect time, allowing Tilly's body to go with the gentle flow of Harry's lovemaking and avoid any subconscious urge to back away into any familiar, safe space. It was Tilly who begged for more in the end, welcoming the most intimate touch of all with her arms wrapped so tightly around this man she loved that she couldn't quite tell where her body ended and his began. And that only made it even more perfect.

It was the heat that finally woke Harry.

In that first heartbeat of consciousness he was aware

of several things. The softness of Tilly's body curled against his, with her breath a puff of extra warmth on his skin. The tingle of his own body that wanted to remind him of everything that had happened right up until the birds were announcing the imminent arrival of dawn—not that he was likely to forget a single moment of the most astonishingly memorable sex he'd ever experienced.

He was also aware that it was Christmas Day. That there was blazing sunshine outside already and it would probably be even hotter than yesterday. And he was realising that the sunshine and heat didn't feel so wrong now. It didn't make it feel any less like Christmas.

Real Christmas had very little to do with places or weather. It was about people and the connections between them, wasn't it? The kind of joy a baby's birth had brought centuries ago. The peace that someone could bestow on her beloved grandchildren as a final gift. The community spirit that could bring so many people together, not only to find a lost little boy, but to celebrate by staying together and using a Christmas song to share that connection. And, okay, it might be about showing how much you cared by giving things to others, but some things couldn't be wrapped—couldn't be seen, even—but they could potentially be the most precious gifts ever bestowed.

Like the gift that he and Tilly had shared during the earliest hours of this Christmas Day. The gift of trust. Of passion. Of a love that would be there for ever, even if they ended up a world apart.

Harry bent his head and pressed a kiss onto Tilly's hair. Just a soft touch but it was enough to make her eyelashes flutter and then lift to reveal her eyes. Harry was so glad he'd woken first because that meant he could see the moment that Tilly became aware of a whole lot of things, just like he had, and he could see that she was as happy as he was. That this had to be the best Christmas morning ever.

'Hey...' Harry whispered. 'Merry Christmas, Bat Woman.'

'Merry Christmas, Leprechaun Man.'

'Shall I get up and make us some coffee?'

'Not just yet.' Tilly brushed her lips against his skin, closing her eyes. 'I want to make sure I remember the dream I had about you.'

Harry could feel the rumble of his soft laughter as he pulled Tilly closer. 'It was no dream. I was there too, remember?'

Tilly's eyes opened. 'I've got a gift for you.'

'I think you already gave it to me.'

The flush of colour in her cheeks was a delight. 'No...this is something you can take back to Ireland with you. Oh...' Her eyes widened. 'What time is it? I should probably have put the turkey in the oven hours ago. And I have to look up a recipe for bread sauce and pick a whole bucket of peas from the garden.'

But Harry shook his head. 'The food is like snow,' he said. 'It's not the thing that makes it really Christmas.'

There was a question in Tilly's eyes.

'This is,' he added. 'Family. Friends. Feeling like you're home...' Then he smiled. 'There is one thing that I'd really like for Christmas dinner, mind. And I don't think it'll take too long.'

'What's that?'

'That potato thing. The one my mammy used to make for me.'

'Potato gratin.' Tilly was smiling back at him. 'I think I can manage that.'

Harry leaned down to kiss her. 'Let's do it together.'

It was easy enough to find a recipe online and, as luck would have it, they had all the ingredients they needed and plenty of time before they were planning to go and visit Jim in the hospital and take him his Christmas gifts.

They sliced potatoes very thinly and layered them with the butter and cream and garlic they'd melted, sprinkling in salt and pepper, thyme and Gruyère cheese. They baked it until it was golden and bubbly on top and crispy and brown around the edges and, when it had cooled just enough, they ate it, sitting outside in the shady courtyard—in the space where Harry had kissed Tilly for the very first time.

'This is the best Christmas dinner I've ever had,' Harry announced.

Tilly thought so too, but that wasn't only because of the food. Like Harry had said, this was about the company she had and the connection she was never going to lose with the man who had given her the gift of a new life.

'Are you going to open your present now?'

'Are you going to open yours?'

The two small boxes were sitting on the table, looking remarkably similar apart from their colour.

'Wouldn't it be funny if we've given each other exactly the same thing?' Tilly reached for the silver box.

'It would.' Harry picked up the green box.

They opened them together and Tilly stared at the intricate silver design of the necklace nestled on rumpled silk. Harry was blinking at a greenstone pendant with a rustic string cord.

'It's a koru,' Tilly told him. 'It's a Maori design based on the unfurling bit of a new fern frond. It represents creation. A new life but also coming back to a beginning—a point of origin. It made me think of you going home to Ireland and finding the new life where you belong, at home.'

She could see the movement of Harry's throat as he swallowed. 'And yours is a Celtic symbol. A Dara Knot, which symbolises strength and courage. The kind you've got. The kind that you can use to find the new life that you deserve.'

Tilly could feel the tears gathering in her eyes as she picked up the beautiful piece of jewellery. 'We *have* given each other the same thing.'

'Except I'm not sure I want to find my new life in Ireland.' Harry was holding the smooth greenstone carving in his hand. 'I'm not sure it's going to feel enough like home any longer.'

'Why not?'

'Because you won't be there.'

'I could be,' Tilly whispered. 'If you wanted me to be?'

But Harry shook his head. 'You belong here,' he said. 'I've only been here for two days but I can see that this is your home. You have family here. A whole community that you belong to.'

'But maybe this won't feel completely like home for me now, either.'

Oh...the blue of Harry's eyes had never been so intense. 'Is that because I wouldn't be here?'

'I think it might be.'

'I like it here,' Harry said slowly. 'I'd like to visit Ireland again, of course, but I think I could live here. Possibly for ever.'

Tilly drew in a shaky breath. In real terms, she and Harry had only just met. There was no way they could know what the future held or whether how they felt about each other could grow into something permanent and precious. But even for ever had to start somewhere, didn't it?

With a moment, just like this...?

Her smile wobbled. 'For ever is quite a long time, you know.'

Harry's smile didn't wobble at all. 'I know...'

EPILOGUE

Five years later...

'MUMMA?'

'Yes, darling?'

'There's *boots*. Like Dadda's.' Three-year-old Maggie was very excited, leaning forward so that it was impossible for her father to do up the buckle of her car seat harness. *'Look...'*

Tilly looked. She didn't need her daughter to be pointing at the roof of the old villa to know that Harry had done what he'd sworn he'd never do. He'd climbed up onto the roof and put Santa's legs into the chimney with his feet sticking out. And wee Maggie thought it was as hilarious as Tilly had when she'd been a small child. She was beside herself with mirth as Harry finally did up the buckle.

'He's up-down, Dadda. He's stuck...'

'Your Mammy's good at being upside down too, sweetheart. But she didn't get stuck, thank goodness...' He winked at Tilly, reaching out to take the plastic container full of cheese rolls—their contribution to the Craig's Gully Christmas Eve community barbecue—from her hands.

'I'd get stuck now,' she said. 'I might get stuck even if I'm not up-down.'

Harry eyed the impressive bump of her belly and his smile widened. 'You might, to be fair… I know I said I wanted six kids, but they don't have to all come at once.'

'It's only twins.'

Harry held the door open so that Tilly could climb into the truck. Then he leaned in to kiss her. 'I'm just going to check on…you know…'

'I know…'

'Where's Dadda gone?'

'He'll be back in a minute, darling. Shall we listen to a song while we wait?' Tilly opened her Christmas folder and put the music through the car's speakers. A New Zealand version of a carol that was a family favourite, that had one of the three Kings of the Orient in a tractor and another in a car.

She watched Harry disappear into the barn. He'd be checking that her father had finished getting into the Father Christmas suit and that Lizzie was all set to drive him down to the town square. Tilly smiled. Her father had grown a beard himself in the last couple of years, so he was beginning to look rather like Father Christmas even without the costume.

A perfect grandfather.

And an amazing father, as always. His wedding gift to Harry and Tilly, only six months after he'd first met his potential son-in-law that Christmas, had been to sign over the old family homestead to them. He needed a smaller place in town, he'd said. A place that Lizzie could help him choose because it looked like they were set to keep each other company for the rest of their lives.

That first year had been so busy for all of them with a wedding to plan and living and work arrangements to update. It had only got busier since then but none of them were complaining. Tilly hadn't ended up taking over the family practice from her father, but who would have guessed that a job in the emergency department of their local hospital would have opened up? Or that Harry would embrace getting the qualifications to become a GP and to join a bigger practice that gave him time to be a popular local doctor, a very hands-on father and even a member of the mountain search and rescue team?

With the support team, including Jim and Lizzie and offers of local help streaming in ever since the news of the twins' arrival had spread like wildfire, Tilly knew exactly how lucky she was to have the career she loved so much and now the joy of a family she'd never dreamed of having.

The chorus of the song was coming on again and Maggie was singing along about the king on his scooter...tooting his hooter...with far more enthusiasm than tunefulness. A glance in the rear-view mirror showed Tilly that her father, in the Santa suit, was climbing into Lizzie's car and Harry was carefully closing the door of the barn behind them. Maggie might realise that it was her grandpa who was hearing her secret wish for Christmas this year, but she would have no idea that the magic had already happened.

Pudding was being hidden in the barn until tomorrow morning. How lucky was it that Jason's children had outgrown the bombproof little palomino pony just as Maggie was ready for more than simply sitting on Spud, who was still enjoying life but really only wanted to stand in the shade of the nearest tree.

Tilly could do with the shade of a tree to sit under right now. It was going to be another hot Christmas Day tomorrow and maybe they could take Maggie to the lake in the afternoon for a swim. After they'd done the whole traditional Christmas dinner thing, of course. Lizzie was coming early to help with all the cooking, but Tilly and Harry had already prepared their favourite part of the feast and the baking dish filled with potato gratin was in the fridge, all ready for the oven.

She could see Harry striding back towards the car now. He was close enough for Tilly to see the way he looked up at the roof of the house and she could see the grin that advertised how pleased he was with reinstating another Christmas tradition. Her love for the man she had married was a huge squeeze around her heart that never failed to take her breath away.

He'd be sneaking off to climb the roof and put the Santa legs in the chimney every year from now on, wouldn't he?

For ever.

Tilly was smiling at Harry as he climbed into the driving seat. A misty kind of smile that came from a place of pure joy.

How lucky was she that for ever was such a long time?

* * * * *

SNOWBOUND WITH HER OFF-LIMITS GP

ANNIE CLAYDON

MILLS & BOON

CHAPTER ONE

'ALL RIGHT. Out with it. What's bugging you?'

Aunt Celeste had never been slow to ask that question. Over the years, Dr Sam Douglas had replied giving details of superhero action figures that had failed to materialise when Father Christmas came to call, school exams, girlfriends and then increasingly complex medical questions. Aunt Celeste had given sage advice on them all.

'Nothing.'

'Come on, Sam. Spill.'

Sam pressed his lips together, leaning forward in the driver's seat of his car to look up at the sky. When they'd started out from London it had been a crisp and fine morning, but now that they'd reached Norfolk there were deep banks of cloud on every side of them. Now flakes of snow were beginning to drift lazily down, melting as they hit the windscreen.

'What does the weather forecast say?'

'Oh, Sam! Stop worrying about the weather, will you? If I didn't know better I'd think you were starting to sound very middle-aged…' Aunt Celeste rummaged in her handbag and Sam handed her his phone.

'It's group dynamics. You become a starry-eyed teenager and it brings out the responsible adult in me.'

Aunt Celeste laughed, tapping on the small screen in front of her. 'It says…possible snow showers tonight and tomorrow—that's all right, Paul's house looks gorgeous in the snow. Very picturesque. It snowed just before Christmas and we snuggled up together, it was wonderful.'

Perhaps Aunt Celeste hadn't yet thought of the possibility that the two dozen people who were due to arrive tomorrow evening for the weekend, to celebrate the engagement of Dr Celeste Douglas and Dr Paul Grant, might be put off by snow. Sam decided to keep his fears to himself.

'You have unread texts, darling.' Aunt Celeste's ceaseless curiosity had diverted her from any grim thoughts about the weather. 'Don't you want to stop and see who it is?'

'Not particularly. Why don't you take a look?'

Aunt Celeste gave a mock sigh. 'Since you're giving me the choice, then you clearly haven't been making very good use of your time since I saw you last. So no, you can look for yourself when we get there.'

Sam chuckled. Aunt Celeste made no secret of wanting to see him as happy as she and Paul were, but her solution was rather less open-minded than usual. Happiness consisted of finding a girlfriend who might send you the kind of texts that you didn't want your aunt to read.

He couldn't agree with her there. Happiness was being free of the way that his father had treated his mother after she'd tried to leave him. Not having to constantly examine whether his own behaviour was following the pattern of stalking and coercion that his father had established.

Alice had been the final straw, the one who had brought him to the point where being single was the only way he could find some peace. Sam had worked hard to make her as happy as he was, but Alice wanted something more. Or maybe something different. He had no way of knowing because when Alice had left she'd refused to explain why. Confusion had given way to something much darker and Sam had made the mistake of showing his anger...

Never a good idea. Particularly when he'd seen his own father so angry with his mother on so many occasions, trying to impose his will on her. Sam had come to his senses, and not tried to contact Alice again, which was clearly exactly what she wanted because she hadn't tried to contact him.

'I think the snow's getting a little heavier.' Aunt Celeste had propped his phone back on the dashboard and was peering out of the window now.

'We'll make it. Even if I have to carry you through a blizzard.'

Aunt Celeste reacted just as he'd wanted to the hyperbole and let out an amused *Ha!* 'I appreciate the thought, but that's not going to be necessary—we'll be there in less than half an hour. Anyway, Paul and I have waited long enough for this and I'll have you know that if there's any carrying to be done you'll be stepping aside and allowing him to do it.'

Paul Grant was the spryest seventy-year-old that Sam had ever met, in addition to being a very eminent paediatrician. And he and Aunt Celeste were good together.

Sam smiled. 'Nothing can come between you, eh?'

'As it happens, no. Despite our advanced age.' Aunt Celeste shot him a defiant look.

'Hey, you don't need to convince me, you know that. What didn't you understand about my saying I was thrilled for you both?'

'Thank you, darling. There have been a few whispers.'

About a Douglas marrying a Grant? Sam had shrugged that one off as being ridiculous. And so what if Celeste Douglas was sixty-five and Paul Grant was seventy? Love was hard to find, and even harder to keep, Alice had shown him that. Paul and Aunt Celeste had managed to beat all of the odds and take a fragile and elusive thing and turn it into gold. That should never be dismissed.

'Whispering because they didn't dare make such a ridiculous suggestion out loud?'

Aunt Celeste chuckled. 'Point taken. And if the snow gets worse and no one turns up we're not going to let it cramp our style, are we?'

Sam was happy with that. A few days spent with two of his favourite people, without being faced with questions about how his mother was doing, as if she'd been frozen in time and after twenty years was still a victim. None of the polite avoidance of any mention of his father, or the way he'd died either.

Aunt Celeste frowned suddenly, as if she'd just thought of something. 'Although Paul mentioned last night that he'd asked his granddaughter to come down early and help with all the preparations…'

'Then I won't be playing gooseberry, will I? Is this the granddaughter that's a doctor?' Sam grinned at his aunt. Just as most of the Douglas family were doctors, so were most of the Grants.

'That's a very safe guess, on the basis that three out of four of them are and the one who isn't is in Australia at the moment.'

'Then we'll have something to talk about, while you and Paul exercise your ingenuity over finding quiet corners to canoodle in.'

That brought a smile to Aunt Celeste's lips. 'Ingenuity is always worth the effort, I find. And Eloise is a very nice girl, whatever anyone says.'

Eloise Grant. Sam had heard Aunt Celeste mention the name before, but he couldn't place her.

'You know I don't have much truck with gossip.'

'If the Grants don't turn up you won't be bothered with it. But if they do manage to brave the weather...' Aunt Celeste pressed her lips together. 'I can't tell you the exact truth of it, because I don't know either. Eloise told Paul, but he hasn't told me. I respect that in him, that he can keep a confidence.'

Sam chuckled. 'That's got to be driving you crazy.' Aunt Celeste's curiosity and her belief that talking about things was always a positive step were no great secret.

'I understand completely. She needs to talk about it in her own time, and I don't see why anyone thinks that she has to justify her actions to them. It's a matter of principle.' Aunt Celeste grimaced. 'Yes, it's driving me crazy.'

That was that, then. Sam was more than happy to just follow instructions and close his ears to anything that resembled gossip, but it was no surprise that Aunt Celeste wasn't content to leave the matter there.

'Eloise was involved in a scandal a year ago. We all turned up to her wedding and her fiancé was left standing at the altar. He seemed quite heartbroken. His mother said that they'd all had an inkling that something was wrong, but that this had come as a complete surprise. Although quite what he was doing standing in the church looking surprised if he *did* know that something was wrong...'

People didn't always act logically. Breaking off a relationship was never easy, and Sam had made it harder for Alice by believing that they could work things out and becoming increasingly angry when she refused to give him any chance of doing so. It was possible that Eloise Grant understood why a woman might refuse point-blank to explain, the way that Alice had done, but the trickle of alarm that was currently working its way down Sam's spine told him that he was better off not knowing.

'She just disappeared, for two weeks. Then she *had* to come back because of her job, but she's only ever spoken to Paul about why she did it. I've always rather felt that she was misjudged over that.'

Sam tried to shake off the conflicting feelings of *having* to know why but not wanting to. He'd told everyone that he and Alice had parted amicably and it had been a joint decision. Aunt Celeste wasn't tactless, and she probably wouldn't be saying all of this now if she knew that Sam was still quietly agonising over reasons that Alice shouldn't have had to give but his raging heart had demanded of her.

'Misjudged, how?' He didn't want to ask, but not asking was unbearable.

'Since Eloise wasn't there to give her side of things, the Grants all immediately believed the fiancé and thought that Eloise had acted very badly. I didn't like him all that much. He was much too charming...'

'You don't like charming?' Sam was running on automatic now, keeping his eyes fixed on the road.

Aunt Celeste gave the same *Don't-you-know-anything?* sigh that had punctuated his teens. 'I like thoughtfulness and sincerity in a man. I'd describe that as charming. I don't have much time for charming as a means to an end.'

It was just like Aunt Celeste to pick a different side from the one everyone expected her to. She was his father's sister, but even at the height of the battle between his parents she'd kept an open mind. She'd supported his mother, along with Sam and his brother and sister, at the same time making it clear that she was able to still love his father even if she didn't approve of his actions. When the restraining order had finally persuaded his father that the marriage was over, and he'd started to drink heavily, it had been Aunt Celeste who had moved heaven and earth, trying to get him some help.

'And what's your means to an end in telling me all this?'

'Am I really *that* transparent?'

Sam flashed her a smile. 'Always. It's one of the things I like about you.'

'You're a kind man, Sam. Paul was worried that Eloise would find some excuse not to make this weekend, because of all the gossip. She's been... I would say hurt, but I get the feeling it's more a case of having been damaged. After everything you went through in your teens, with your father, you know how that feels, don't you?'

He did, but that didn't mean he knew what to do about it. Aunt Celeste could be a little too confident in people sometimes, and the idea of following Eloise if she ran from a crowd of disapproving relatives, and making everything right for her, seemed impossible. Even if he had the heart for it, and right now he wasn't sure whether simply passing the time of day might not be too challenging.

And then, unexpected as always, Aunt Celeste saved him from the awkwardness of a conversation that he'd really rather not be having.

'Sam! You missed the turning!'

'Uh? Oh… Yeah.' In his determination to focus on the road ahead and not Eloise Grant, he'd driven straight past the wrought iron gates that accessed the tree-lined drive that led to Paul's house. Sam slowed the car, turning around.

When he drew up outside the magnificent Tudor manor house he stayed in his seat for a moment, wondering what the next few days might bring. Aunt Celeste turned her astute blue-eyed gaze onto him.

'Are you all right, darling?'

'Why wouldn't I be?' Sam decided to forget about everything else and concentrate on the next few moments. 'I thought you might want me to stay out of the way while you raced to the front door and melted into your fiancé's arms.'

Aunt Celeste rolled her eyes. 'Practicality before romance, Sam. Slipping on a patch of ice and falling flat on your face isn't a good look, at any age. I thought we'd decided that *you* were going to be the adult of the two of us…'

* * *

Eloise's grandfather was standing at the window of the large sitting room, made cosy by a roaring fire. His hands were in his pockets and he was looking silently out at the flurries of snow.

Eloise knew why she was here, earlier than all the rest of the guests, and in possession of one of the sprawling old manor house's seven bedrooms, instead of staying at a nearby hotel like most of the other guests. It was Gramps' way of telling the rest of the family that he supported her and that anyone who didn't shouldn't bother to attend the party. It crossed Eloise's mind that Gramps' gesture had backfired pretty spectacularly and that her mere presence was about to jinx the whole weekend.

'I'm sorry, Gramps.' Eloise joined him at the window.

'What have you done now? Broken all the best china?' Gramps smiled mischievously down at her.

'I'm sorry that it's snowing.'

'Ah. Someone's put you in charge of the weather?'

It was difficult to resist Gramps. Eloise nudged his elbow with hers. 'Perhaps I should rephrase. I'm sorry to see that it's snowing.'

'Better.'

Gramps had been a tower of strength. He was the closest family member she had left, and when she'd returned from the hotel she'd been hiding out in after her wedding was cancelled, Eloise had come here. He'd asked no questions, simply hugging her and being there for her when the whole story had come spilling out.

The stream of condemnation from her family had been partly her fault, because she could have managed things a great deal better. The day before the wedding had been a nightmare of discovery and confrontation, and she'd suddenly seen Michael in a completely different light. When Eloise had asked him if it was true that he'd fathered a child with his previous partner, and had rejected every opportunity to see the boy, he hadn't denied it.

The promise of spending her life with the man she loved, and who she could trust to do the right thing, had been ripped in two, but she'd tried to salvage it and told Michael she'd support him in forming a relationship with his son. He'd been angry, raging at her that if she was going to spoil all of his plans for their future together by dwelling on a minor inconvenience from his past then the wedding was off. They'd managed to stay civil with each other long enough to compose an email to send to all of the guests, and then Michael's face had hardened again and he'd told her to leave everything to him and get out of his sight.

She'd trusted Michael one last time and left, running away from the dream that had come crashing down. It was only when she'd returned that she'd realised that the email had never been sent, and that Michael had diverted any awkward questions about his own part in the sudden separation by pretending she'd unexpectedly left him at the altar. In her absence there had been ample time for the gossip to turn her into a monster.

Her extended family might have trusted her enough to wait and listen to her side of the story, but they hadn't. Eloise had been met by minds that were already made up, and everyone had expected her to apologise for leaving Michael. When she'd refused there was little more to be said. So it had become increasingly easy to apologise for everything else, snow included.

Gramps was craning forward, trying to see as far along the drive as possible.

Eloise nudged him again. 'Celeste is on her way. She'll be here soon.'

Gramps chuckled. 'I know. Give me the pleasure of waiting impatiently for her, eh? Even if you're not quite sure I'm doing the right thing.'

'She makes you happy. What's not to like about that?' Eloise *wasn't* sure. She liked and respected Celeste, but still couldn't quite chase away the feeling that any relationship carried with it the risk of heartbreak. Gramps was semi-retired now, and he deserved to look forward with some guarantee of peace.

'I'm curious. Do you honestly think that Celeste has it in her to keep secrets from me? Even if she really set her mind to it...' Gramps smirked down at her. 'I couldn't keep anything from her either.'

'Apart from *my* secrets.' Eloise wondered if she hadn't asked a bit too much of Gramps, but he'd volunteered the suggestion that he'd say nothing to anyone.

'That's different, and Celeste understands that. She believes in talking about things, but she also believes that you should do it in your own time, and not give in to other people pressuring you. As do I.'

Eloise gave Gramps a hug. 'What would I do without you both?'

Gramps smiled. 'Not everyone's like Michael, you know. One day you'll get around to trusting in that belief.'

One day. Not today, though.

'Let's just concentrate on you and Celeste until that happens, shall we?'

Eloise couldn't spoil this moment for him. As a dark blue SUV drove slowly into the courtyard in front of the house she saw Gramps smile with excitement.

The occupants of the car seemed to be talking for a moment. Then a man got out of the driver's seat, pulling on a thick fur-collared parka that made his shoulders seem even broader and making his way round to the passenger door to offer Celeste his arm as she emerged from the car. Gramps only had eyes for her as she took a few steps and then seemed to change her mind, letting go of the man's arm and waving him away, before heading for the door at a faster pace.

Gramps hurried to open the door for her. Something made Eloise stay at the window. Maybe the notion that Gramps and Celeste would want a few moments alone to greet each other. Maybe she just couldn't take her eyes off the man as he watched Celeste, an amused look on his face, and then made his way back to the car to fetch the suitcases.

This must be Celeste's nephew. Gramps had told her about Dr Sam Douglas, and how close he and Celeste were, but the first thing about him that Eloise noticed was that he had the most gorgeous smile. A shiver ran down her spine as she watched him heave the suitcases effortlessly from the boot of the car.

She was out of the habit of appreciating a stranger's smile. That wasn't altogether a bad thing, since the charm and the smile of the man she'd once loved had made it so very difficult for her to see the truth about him.

'Darling…!' Celeste appeared in the doorway. 'We

made it! Although it looks as if the weather's taking a turn for the worse.'

'I'm sure it'll clear up soon.' Eloise glanced back at the window in the hope of seeing some evidence of that, but the snow showed no signs of stopping. But Celeste looked so excited and Gramps was smiling so broadly that now wasn't the time to wonder whether the guests who were expected tomorrow would be able to make it.

Celeste flapped her hand cheerfully. 'It doesn't matter. The four most important people are already here, and we won't be able to help having a wonderful time, will we Paul?'

'I can't see how we can manage to avoid it.' Gramps was smiling and Eloise couldn't resist following suit. It was nice to be called an important person in an engagement celebration, instead of being consigned to a corner as if she'd put a hex on the marriage just by being there.

'Sam…' Celeste called out into the corridor as the front door slammed shut. 'Come and meet Eloise…'

She was holding her breath. Quite why, Eloise wasn't sure. She felt herself pull her shoulders a little straighter and then heat rose to her cheeks as Celeste's nephew walked into the room.

He was blue-eyed, like Celeste. Sandy-haired, with the same face shape as his aunt, only the line of his jaw was harder and more masculine. When he smiled, there was a trace of Celeste's ebullient warmth.

'It's a pleasure to meet you, Eloise.' He sounded as if he actually meant it as well. Sam Douglas advanced on her, holding out his hand.

'You too, Sam. Welcome.' Her words sounded jarringly enthusiastic. Sam was as delicious close-up as he was at a distance, perhaps even more so. That was one very good reason to keep her distance, but right now it seemed there was no option but to shake his hand.

The sudden shock of his icy fingers made her jump. Or maybe it was just his touch. Sam grinned suddenly, making Eloise feel even more awkward.

'Sorry. Cold hands.' He took a step back, holding his hands out to the roaring fire in the grate.

'Quite unforgivable in a GP,' Celeste teased him. 'Eloise works in Accident and Emergency.'

Sam turned, giving Eloise another spine-tingling smile. 'Only in this family, eh? We've barely been introduced, and we already know what kind of doctors we are.'

Actually that was something of a relief. Eloise would far rather be judged as a doctor than anything else, because in that sphere at least it was considered that she had something to give. She was actually beginning to wish that the snow would get a little heavier because, even if Celeste didn't know all the details, she'd always dismissed the gossip as hurtful rubbish. And the look in Sam's eyes gave no hint that he knew anything about it. Eloise felt a sudden swell of warmth towards them both.

'You must be famished. I have soup and sandwiches waiting for you in the kitchen.'

Concentrating on food, in the cool air of the kitchen, might dispel some of the heat that seemed to be radiating from her, quell the irrepressible thought that Sam could warm his hands against her skin any time he liked.

Celeste took off her coat, displaying a thick purple sweater with an iridescent scarf. 'Wonderful! I'll come and help.'

'No you don't. Stay here and warm up by the fire.' She hadn't been able to help noticing Sam's scent, and she needed some time alone to talk some sense into herself. Eloise didn't wait for anyone to protest, leaving Gramps to sort out the coats and hurrying to the kitchen.

CHAPTER TWO

THE WOMAN WHO had left a relationship without feeling the need to explain why. As soon as Sam had laid eyes on her, he forgot all about how much he'd been hurt when Alice had done the same to him.

It was tempting to feel that someone so luminously beautiful couldn't be all bad. Sam knew that looks were never a measure of character. But someone that vulnerable? He might not be able to put his finger on any one thing that she did which made him come to that conclusion, but vulnerability was one of those things that people wore. Like happiness or grief, or any of the other feelings that seemed to soak through a person and shape them.

And he couldn't deny that she *was* beautiful. Her thick sweater and jeans couldn't disguise a light grace of movement. Dark hair, piled up on the back of her head so that it revealed the fine curve of her neck. Dark eyes, whose depths seemed to contain every thought, every possibility, that the world around her could offer.

Aunt Celeste and Paul were sitting on the sofa together, talking happily, and Sam chose one of the armchairs by the fire. Eloise returned with a tray, refusing to let anyone get up and help her with the rest of the lunch things. And when she finally did sink into an armchair she seemed on the alert still, relaxing only when Aunt Celeste pronounced that everything was quite delicious and absolutely perfect.

A people pleaser, then. Sam seemed to be turning into an amateur detective, assessing the lines of tension on her brow and the way her gaze darted from one person to another, checking that everyone was in agreement with Aunt Celeste's opinion. The dark shadows under her eyes might give some clue to a sleepless night, over something that was worrying her…

And on the other hand they might be the result of something completely different. Amateur psychologist took over from amateur detective and started making a similar list of unqualified pronouncements. Maybe his fascination with her was something to do with a yearning to repeat past experiences, in the hope that they might work out better than they had with Alice…

Paul's phone rang, and Celeste fell silent suddenly. A quick conversation, that everyone got the gist of, and then he ended the call.

'That was my sister…' Paul turned his lips down as he addressed Celeste. 'She wants to know what the weather's going to be like tomorrow.'

'Oh, really…' Aunt Celeste laughed. 'As if any of us knows that. I'm glad you told her to go with the flow. I'm sure everything will work out one way or another.'

Eloise frowned, picking up her phone. Pretty much a perfect frown, indicating that something was amiss but she was about to correct it. Sam wondered whether she considered herself responsible for the weather, and toyed with a vision of her banishing the clouds and summoning sunshine.

'They say that we can expect more tomorrow...' Her frown deepened, as if she was working on that.

'There's your chance, darling!' Paul flashed a mock-serious look at Aunt Celeste. 'If marrying someone who lives in the path of a cold northerly airstream is going to be a problem you'd better say so now, before it's too late.'

'I'm thinking about it.' Aunt Celeste was smiling up at him, clearly not thinking about it at all.

It didn't take a detective or a psychologist to work out that they were joking, but the look of sudden uncertainty on Eloise's face betrayed a flash of doubt. Sam laughed quietly, wondering if that might prompt Aunt Celeste to make the inevitable choice a bit more quickly.

It didn't. Aunt Celeste and Paul were still teasing each other, each of them playing hard to get. But suddenly Sam found himself drowning, lost in Eloise's gaze, and the way that she suddenly smiled in response to his prompt. Breathless, he was pulled inexorably down by the feeling that making her smile was the one and only thing he wanted to do. Feeling his fingertips tingle as his heart pumped out the message that her smile was so easily won, and then wondering what on earth had happened to make her so fearful for Paul and Aunt Celeste.

She gave a little shake of her head and then a shrug, as if to acknowledge her mistake. For a moment there was more, as if she saw everything about him even though they'd only just met. And then suddenly she got to her feet, catching up a folded piece of paper from behind a glass ornament on the deep stone hearth.

'Do you think we should call everyone? Let them

know to keep an eye on the weather forecast for Norfolk?'

She held the sheet out to Paul, clearly hesitant to do it herself, and he nodded, taking it. 'Yes, I think that's a good idea, Eloise.'

Paul had started to make the calls, Aunt Celeste sitting beside him, adding her good wishes to his when he finished each one. Eloise had made coffee and then returned to sit on the other side of him and check the list of guests as he worked through it. Sam drank his coffee, then took the suitcases upstairs, finding that each bedroom had a name card affixed to the door. Paul's had pink hearts drawn around his and Aunt Celeste's names, and when he opened the door to put her case inside he smelled flowers and saw a bright arrangement on a sturdy chest of drawers by the window, along with a glass bowl which, if he wasn't much mistaken, contained Aunt Celeste's favourite chocolates.

Sam walked to the end of the hallway, past the bedrooms labelled *Grant*, and found *Sam Douglas*, unable to stop himself from pausing for a moment to look at the careful penmanship. Inside, the room was warm and inviting. The grand old fireplace, the wood panelling and the windows that stretched around two sides of the room were fixtures, but the arrangement of red-berried holly on the mantelpiece and the towels carefully folded on the bed were finishing touches that didn't seem much like Paul and Aunt Celeste's jolly *make-yourself-at-home* attitude. The last time he'd been here he'd been told where his bed was, given permission to take whatever he wanted from the fridge and left to his own devices.

Maybe Eloise felt she had something to prove. When he opened the door of the bulky old armoire the smell of sandalwood drifted out and he saw fresh lining paper on the shelves. It seemed that Eloise felt she had more than just something to prove…

Sam unpacked his case, reckoning that the phone calls might take a while. It was still snowing outside, making the warmth of the room seem even more cosy, and he resisted the temptation to stay here and read the book he'd brought with him. He should brave the terrors of the sitting room, and the ultimate discomfort of finding that the woman who he'd rashly assumed might be someone he wanted to avoid had caught his attention and wasn't letting go.

When he returned to the sitting room, Aunt Celeste informed him that everyone had been contacted and some had already expressed doubts about whether they'd make it tomorrow. They were, however, going to make the best of things. Paul laughingly agreed and that was that.

'I have to go down to the village.' Eloise smiled, tapping the side of her nose when Paul shot her an enquiring look. 'Just errands.'

'Can it wait?' Paul asked.

'I may as well go now; it doesn't look as if it's going to stop snowing.'

'I'll come with you, then….' Paul stood and Aunt Celeste got from her seat as well. Eloise was shaking her head, telling them to stay by the fireside together, and they were protesting that they wouldn't let her go alone, and then Sam heard his own voice, coming from a place that seemed unfamiliar to him.

'I'll go with Eloise. You two stay here.'

Everyone looked at him. It made perfect sense. Paul and Aunt Celeste could stay here, whispering a few sweet nothings to each other, and instead of uneasily playing gooseberry Sam would go with Eloise. The other voice in his head, warning him to stay away from Eloise, was quiet for a moment, as if it knew that a ten-minute walk down to the village couldn't possibly do any harm, and it was the obvious thing to do in the circumstances.

'I can pick up anything you need.' Eloise was looking at him uncertainly, although Paul and Aunt Celeste seemed happy with the arrangement.

Then Sam's instinct kicked in. She was vulnerable, eager to please, and the thought that he needed to stay away from her seemed suddenly ridiculous. He summoned up his easiest smile.

'I could do with stretching my legs...'

Suddenly, she was the only person in the room. And when she smiled, that was the only thing that mattered to him.

'Okay. I'll get my coat.'

Eloise was wearing a dark blue parka and a bright red knitted hat pulled down over her ears, which made her delicate features seem even more charming and elf-like. Large flakes of snow were drifting lazily down now, and enough had settled to leave two sets of footprints behind them on the drive, Eloise's smaller ones next to his.

They'd been walking silently, and Sam turned to look back at the house. The redbrick arches above the doors and windows were lined with snow, and the roof was almost covered.

'It looks very picturesque in the snow, doesn't it?' He heard Eloise's voice beside him. 'If things just stay like this it'll be perfect. Enough snow to make the place look magical, and not enough to stop people from getting here.'

That was a big ask. In Sam's experience the weather was usually too much of something or not enough of it, but Eloise seemed so determined that this weekend should be just right.

'Paul and Aunt Celeste appear to think that everything already is perfect...' Love—true love—was almost impossibly hard to find, but if you did it was resilient and couldn't be ruined by everyday difficulties.

From her expression, Eloise clearly didn't quite agree with that. But she said nothing, turning to make her way around the curve of the driveway to the high wall that surrounded the property.

Outside, there seemed to be more people walking than driving, just a few sets of tyre marks on the road and many footprints on the path that ran alongside it. Sensible, since conditions weren't great for driving and ice was forming in the indentations of tyre tracks. Someone had obviously already skidded to one side...

Just as Sam realised that there were no tracks that indicated the mystery car had corrected its course, he saw Eloise quicken her pace. Up ahead, there was a gap in the sparse hedge that lined the other side of the road.

She was running now and he followed, struggling to keep up with her on the slippery surface. When he got to the hedge he saw a small SUV, nose down at the bottom of a shallow embankment on the other side, and Eloise slithering down towards it.

Sam followed, and by the time he reached the car,

Eloise had already carefully opened the driver's door. He could see a woman in the back seat, a boy of around five in her lap, and a baby carrier that was covered with a blanket next to her.

'Bess…' Eloise clearly knew her. 'Are you hurt?'

The woman seemed uninjured and had started to cry with relief. 'No, we're okay. We weren't going at any speed, and the car just slid off the road. Thank goodness you're here, Eloise…' Bess shifted the boy from her lap, starting to clamber forward between the seats.

'Sit tight for a minute. I'm going to get in and just check on you and the kids…' Eloise reached in, laying her hand on Bess's shoulder in a reassuring gesture.

'No! Eloise, you don't understand. It's Gran. She's fallen and she's out in the cold…'

Eloise's face set in an expression of determination. 'Where is she? At home?'

Bess nodded miserably. 'In the back garden. She's got one of those alarm buttons where you can talk to the operator, and they called me. They've called an ambulance as well, but I thought I could get to her more quickly.'

'Okay. One minute.' She turned to Sam. 'If I go back and get my car, can you stay with Bess?'

Not a trace of *If-that's-okay-with-you?* or *If-you-don't-mind?* in her expression. She'd already made her decision about the best way to do this and Sam nodded in agreement.

'Take mine if you want—the key's on the hall table.' His four-wheel drive would probably handle the conditions better than the blue run-around he'd parked next to this morning.

Eloise gave him a smiling nod, turning quickly back

to Bess. 'Give me the keys, Bess, and I'll go over there now. Sam's a doctor, he'll stay with you.'

Bess seemed about to protest, and then thought better of it. Eloise's tone brooked no argument, and as soon as Bess had handed over a keyring with two keys on it from her handbag she started to scramble back up the embankment. Something told Sam that there was no need to turn and watch her go, because Eloise wouldn't look back for the reassurance she'd seemed to crave earlier on.

He took her place at the door of the vehicle, leaning in. Bess had dissolved into tears now, but he needed her to keep her cool for a little while longer.

'Bess… I'm Sam. Look at me. How long have you been here?'

'Not long… Ten minutes maybe… I called Tom, my husband, but he's at work and it'll take him another half an hour to get here. I didn't dare leave the car, because I wasn't sure I could get up the embankment with both of the kids…' Bess was getting more and more agitated.

'That's okay, Bess. You've done really well, and I want you to take a couple of slow breaths for me.' Sam waited while she did so. 'You're sure that neither you or the children are hurt?'

'No, we're okay. They were both strapped into their seats, and Aaron's been talking to me.' Bess drew the little boy back onto her lap.

Sam reached forward, moving the blanket that covered the baby carrier so that he could see inside. The baby seemed warm and responsive and when Sam turned his attention to Aaron the little boy stuck his tongue out cheekily.

'Please, Sam. I'm so worried about my grandmother...'

Sam didn't envy Bess's situation—torn between keeping her children safe and the knowledge that her grandmother urgently needed help.

His priorities were clear though; Eloise's decision had made that possible. His first concern was Bess and the children, while hers was Bess's grandmother.

'Eloise is on her way to your grandmother, Bess. I'm here for you. We're going to take the children up to Paul Grant's house.'

Bess nodded, opening the back door of the car so that Sam could unclip the baby carrier. She and Aaron climbed forward and got out of the car, and Sam motioned to her to start walking with the boy, the few hundred yards to where the embankment was less steep.

He'd caught up with her by the time they reached the hedge. Sam pushed through, holding the baby carrier out of reach of the bare frozen twigs, catching little Aaron when he evaded his mother's grasp and scrambled through on his own. He could see part way along the drive that led to the manor house now and Paul and Aunt Celeste were hurrying towards them, zipping up their coats as they came.

Bess pushed through the hedge and as he shepherded the family across the road he saw his own car, the windscreen hastily cleared, nosing its way towards them. Sam gave the baby carrier to Aunt Celeste and set Aaron back onto his feet so that Paul could take his hand. His car drew up beside them, and the passenger door was pushed open.

'Get in...'

Sam hesitated for a brief moment, wondering whether

Eloise was going to slide out of the driver's seat. Apparently not.

'I know the way. And I'm a very good driver.'

He couldn't help a smile as he got into his car. He'd just met a different Eloise, decisive and suddenly confident, and he already liked this side of her much better than the one he'd been introduced to.

The thought of Granny June outside in the snow had pushed Eloise forward, across the slippery ground and back to the house. Calling to Gramps and Celeste while she found the keys to Sam's car, she'd left them to hurry down to meet Bess, while she quickly grabbed the medical kit that Gramps kept ready in the cupboard under the stairs. She'd hurriedly cleared the windscreen of the worst of the snow and ice and started the car, going as fast as she dared on the driveway.

At the back of her mind, she was wondering if Sam had got Bess and the children out of the car yet. She might need some help when she got to Granny June's, particularly if the ambulance hadn't arrived. The relief when she saw him crossing the road wasn't entirely in response to that.

Tall and broad, holding the baby carrier in one hand, his other arm supporting Aaron against his chest. The little boy's arms were flung around his neck and Bess was walking beside him, her smaller frame shivering in the icy wind.

It was a brief snapshot, but it embodied all you would want in a man. Strong and yet caring. Good with kids—Michael's behaviour had made that one particularly important. Brave and resourceful couldn't really be applied to pushing your way through a hedge that wasn't thick enough to put up much resistance, but Eloise's imagination was on a roll…

The windscreen was starting to mist, and when Sam got into the car he pressed the controls to open the windows of both the driver's and front passenger's doors. Her view of the road ahead cleared suddenly and the blast of cold air had the added advantage of bringing her to her senses. She'd accepted Michael as her own personal hero far too readily, and making that mistake again would be reckless.

'How far is it?' Sam had been sitting quietly in the passenger seat, but clearly he was as eager to get to Granny June as she was.

'It's not far, she lives in Mazingford.' Eloise turned off the road into the minor road that was signposted to Mazingford, feeling the car begin to slip slightly on the icy road. He must feel it too and she wondered if he was beginning to regret letting her drive.

'I've got it…' She changed gear and felt the tyres grip again.

'I know.'

She didn't have time to debate whether this was wishful thinking on Sam's part, or he really was that confident in her. Mazingford High Street was up ahead, and Granny June's cottage was in one of the small roads on the left. She drew up outside Granny June's yellow front door, turning to reach for Gramps' medical bag on the back seat.

Sam turned too, smiling when he saw the bag. 'I'll bring this. Go and get the front door open…'

Eloise jogged to the door, her hands shaking as she put the key into the lock. She had to forget everything else now. All the times she and Bess had played at

Granny June's when she was little, and spent her summers here with Gramps. Everything that had happened since, and the feeling that she had somehow to prove to Sam that the gossips were wrong about her. None of that mattered right now. What mattered was that she had a patient who was in need of her professionalism.

She ran through the house, opening the back door. At the end of the path, next to the bird table, she could see Granny June, lying motionless in the snow. As Eloise started forward, her heart thumping with trepidation, Granny June moved. She stumbled towards her, kneeling down in the snow.

'Eloise…' Granny June trembled out her name.

'Hey there, Granny June. Bess sent me.'

Granny June was well wrapped up, in a long waterproof parka and fur-lined boots, and it seemed that they had done their job in keeping her relatively dry. Curling her hand carefully behind Granny June's head, to protect it from the cold ground, Eloise started to tick off the points on her mental checklist.

Then the crunch of footsteps behind her and the sound of the heavy medical kit being put down onto the ground told her that Sam was there.

'I don't see any blood. She's breathing without difficulty and…' Her fingers found Granny June's pulse. 'Sixty BPM…'

'Not bad, eh?' Granny June's voice was weak but she was alert and coherent.

'I'd put it at very good.' She heard Sam's voice behind her. 'You'll be inside in the warm very soon, but bear with me while I do a few very quick checks to make sure you didn't hurt yourself when you fell.'

Eloise turned, giving him a quick nod. There was

a reason why you didn't assess and treat friends and family for traumatic injury unless it was unavoidable. Sam could take that step back and make cool-headed decisions about Granny June's medical condition. The risk of moving her had to be weighed carefully against the obvious need to get her inside and out of the cold, and now wasn't the time for Eloise to be showing him how well she could handle a situation.

A woman's voice crackled through the alarm that Granny June had around her neck.

'Are you still there, my love? What's happening?'

'I'm here…' Granny June's voice seemed a little stronger now.

'I'm here too, I'm a doctor. My colleague is examining June and we'll have her inside in the warm as quickly as we can.' Eloise bent over, speaking into the small intercom.

'Thank goodness. Is there anything I can do for you? Call someone?'

Eloise thought quickly. Bess was waiting for news, and Gramps could be trusted to give that news to her reassuringly, without making any rash promises. She gave his phone number to the woman, who read it back carefully.

'You'll be speaking with Dr Paul Grant, he's with June's granddaughter now. Please tell him that we're here, and checking June over for injuries, but she seems okay…'

'I'm fine!' Granny June interrupted. 'I just wish I could get up!'

Eloise heard the woman laugh, and then her voice became businesslike again. 'Got it. I'll call him right now. And you are?'

'Dr Eloise Grant. Tell him we'll be moving June into the warm as soon as possible.'

'I could really do with a cup of tea!' Granny June shot Eloise a reproachful look.

'I'll bet you could,' the woman replied. 'I'm going to leave you now that you're safe. Good luck...'

'Thank you, dear.'

Before Eloise could add her own thanks, there was a click as the operator closed the connection to the intercom. Eloise made a silent promise to herself to find the woman and thank her for everything she'd done, and set about checking Granny June's hands for injury. They were so cold, and all she wanted to do was hug her.

'Any pain?' She heard Sam's voice behind her.

'I don't think so. Granny June, do you feel any pain? Don't be brave now, you must tell me.'

'No pain.'

'Did you hit your head when you fell?'

'No, darling. I just...slid. But I couldn't get up again.'

Sam would be checking for a broken hip, to see if that had caused the fall. It would be obvious and something they needed to take heed of when moving her. He was working quickly, covering all of the bases, but Granny June's face registered no pain.

'No blood or bumps at the back of her head?' Sam murmured the question quietly.

'No...not as far as I can tell.'

'Right then. Time to get you inside for that cup of tea.' Sam gave Granny June the most reassuring smile that Eloise had ever seen.

Granny June smiled back, trusting him. Eloise

might have a better appreciation than she did of all the things that might go wrong, but somehow that smile seemed to work into her soul, demanding that she should be confident.

Sam waited for her to position herself so that they could lift Granny June together, one on each side of her. Then, on his word, they carefully guided her to her feet.

'Try just one step for me, June.' He was smiling still, watching carefully as Granny June slowly took a step, wincing as she did so.

'My ankle hurts a bit.'

'Okay, don't put any weight on it. Eloise and I will support you. Anything else? Your back or your hips?'

Granny June shook her head. Carefully, slowly they made their way to the back door, and Sam reached forward to open it. The kitchen/diner was warm and cosy after the chill of the garden, and Granny June was led to the banquette that stood at the far end of the dining table, giving a deep sigh as she was carefully lowered onto it.

'Better now?' Sam asked and Granny June nodded. 'We'll just get your coat and boots off, shall we? That'll help you warm up a bit.'

Eloise fetched a footstool from the front parlour and Sam lifted Granny June's feet onto it, taking off her boots and carefully inspecting her ankle. He pronounced it a little swollen and said that it should be checked over at the hospital, and left Eloise with Granny June while he put the kettle on for a cup of tea.

'My fingers hurt.' June looked at her bright red hands with dismay.

'That's because they're warming up. We'd be more worried if you couldn't feel them.'

June regarded her thoughtfully. 'Is Sam your friend, dear?'

Granny June was clearly feeling much better now, and the question wasn't as innocent as it sounded. She was always on the lookout for good boyfriend material for Eloise, and Sam was admittedly *very* good boyfriend material. Good lover material as well, if she wasn't very much mistaken.

'No, he's Celeste's nephew.'

'Ah. Nice.' Granny June was looking at Sam speculatively as he made the tea, clearly not ready to give up on his potential just yet.

'Bess got stuck on the way here. She's with Gramps and Celeste.' Probably best to leave the part where Bess's car had rolled down an embankment for later.

'Really?' The observation had the required effect, and Granny June's attention switched from Sam. 'The snow's not that deep, is it? Although the weather forecast says we'll be getting more.'

'Engine trouble, probably. Shall we give her a call so you can speak to her? She'll be worrying about you.'

CHAPTER THREE

JUST AS SAM was finishing a more thorough examination of Granny June, the ambulance arrived, the crews clearly busy from injuries caused by the worsening weather conditions. It was agreed that they would take Granny June to the hospital, for X-rays on her ankle and to check a minor swelling that had appeared on her elbow, and Bess and her husband Tom appeared as Eloise was getting ready to go with Granny June.

'We got here as soon as we could.' Bess was reassured now, by the quiet preparations and Sam's easy manner. 'Your grandfather and Celeste are at our place, babysitting.'

Eloise smiled at the thought. 'No doubt Gramps is having a whale of a time playing with all of Aaron's toys.'

'He and Celeste were lining up for a fight with his superheroes when we left. Thank you so much, Eloise. I dread to think what could have happened if she'd been out there any longer...'

Eloise hugged her friend. 'Then don't. Granny June's okay, and that's all that matters. You're going with her in the ambulance?'

'Yes, Tom will follow in his car, and we'll bring Gran back to our place afterwards.'

'That's good. Time for you to go, now...' Sam was helping the ambulance crew carry Granny June out of the house, and Eloise pressed the door keys into Bess's hand.

'Thank you.' There was time for one last hug and then Bess hurried out to the ambulance.

Tom closed up the cottage, shaking their hands and thanking them, before climbing into his car. It was snowing more heavily now, large flakes dancing in the pools of light along the road. Eloise heaved a sigh, stopping to look.

'It's like a chocolate box, isn't it?' Sam came to stand beside her, gesturing an acknowledgement of Tom's wave.

Somewhere along the way she'd lost that. The idea that, on a picture-perfect snowy evening, doors and windows could conceal just warmth and peace. Ever since betrayal and deceit had become a part of her life, it had seemed that it must be everywhere.

'Yes. It's a very pretty part of the world.' Maybe she should trust Sam's assessment of *this* situation as well, even if it did seem much harder than trusting his medical judgement.

'Where will they take June? Is it far?'

'No, they'll be taking her to the Community Hospital, it's only a few miles away. They have X-ray facilities, and can keep her in overnight if there's any cause for concern.'

Sam nodded. 'Might be the best thing. She had a shock, and she was very cold by the time we got to her.'

It was Eloise's turn not to think about what *might*

have happened. If she hadn't seen Bess's car, or if Sam hadn't decided to come with her to the village...

'Thank you. For being there.'

He smiled, brushing a snowflake from her hair in a sudden gesture that could mean anything. Maybe he hadn't quite switched off yet, from the tender care that he'd shown for Granny June.

'I'm glad I was. You're close to June and Bess?'

Why did that feel like an opportunity to apologise to him, when it was just a question? She'd acted professionally, despite all of her fears for Granny June. Gramps had been right, she did apologise too often, and turning over a new leaf might just as well start with Sam as anyone.

'Yes. My mother died shortly after I was born, and I used to come up and stay with Gramps and my grandmother during the school holidays. Bess and I used to come here and play a lot.'

He nodded. 'I'm sorry to hear about your mother.'

It was more of a yearning than anything else. For someone who would belong to her and would support her come what may.

'Gran filled in for her really well. You know, teenage advice and what to do about boys...' Maybe Sam didn't want to hear about that. He was Celeste's nephew, after all.

'You must miss her.'

Eloise puffed out a breath, which hung in the air between them until the wind caught it and blew it away.

'I miss her. Gramps was devastated when she died, but the one thing that the two of them always used to say is that life goes on.' She turned to Sam. 'I'm really happy to see him with Celeste. They're good together.'

Sam nodded. 'How does your father feel about it? If you don't mind my asking.'

'My father remarried and went to Indonesia eight years ago. He and his wife have two young children and they take up most of their attention.'

'He's not expressed an opinion, then?'

'Not that I've heard.' Eloise had tried to keep in contact with her father, but there had always been some excuse about why he couldn't come to the phone or make a video call, and slowly they'd drifted apart. She'd felt angry and neglected, and then she'd come to terms with the loss, because moving on was one of those things that wasn't always a choice.

Maybe the cold shiver that ran down her spine was because they were standing outside in the snow. Maybe because Sam's questions reminded her that she was alone in life, with only Gramps to protect her. Or maybe it was because the warmth in his eyes seemed to hold the kind of understanding that she craved.

'It's cold out here. We should get home...' She grabbed at the first, most obvious, explanation rather than contemplate the other two.

He nodded, pulling his keys from his pocket. 'Want to drive?'

It was an obvious tease, and she didn't need to feel grateful that he'd even considered the possibility of giving his car keys back to her. Eloise shot him a smile and headed for the passenger door.

It had occurred to Sam that there was still time to run.

The more time he spent with Eloise, the more he was fascinated by her. Her vulnerability, and how she seemed so alone and hurt. Her warmth and the way she'd cared for her friends. And the way her strength had suddenly shown itself, when it was needed. That had been the biggest turn-on of all, and in allowing himself to even think that way Sam was stepping into the same dangerous territory he'd inhabited with Alice.

It wouldn't be so difficult to manufacture an excuse about being needed at his practice in London, Paul and Aunt Celeste would insist that he went. It was looking increasingly as if the party wasn't going to happen, and by tomorrow he might find that it wasn't so easy to go anywhere.

Instead, he took off his coat. Eloise was drawing the curtains, stopping to look out of the sitting room window.

'Do you have to be back at work on Monday morning?'

Sam shook his head. 'No, I'm not due back at the surgery until next Wednesday.'

She nodded, smiling. 'That's good. If this keeps up the roads might be blocked over the weekend, but they're usually cleared within a couple of days. It would be awkward to be stranded up here if you had to work.'

Not quite as awkward as things were now, trying to navigate his way through all of the uncertainties. All of the things that challenged his peace of mind and made him feel that he wanted things that he'd already decided he couldn't have. But Eloise's smile, and her apparent pleasure that he wasn't going to be driving back to London this evening outweighed all of that.

They were both hungry, and there was enough food in the kitchen to feed an army. Eloise went for quick and easy, and half an hour later they sat down at the kitchen table to sausages and mash. One bite was enough to indicate that Eloise hadn't sacrificed taste for speed.

'These sausages are great. And the onion gravy's *got* to be a secret recipe…' He couldn't help grinning at her. Eloise's response to praise was always a glowing smile, as if she hadn't expected anyone to notice all of the effort she put into things.

'The sausages are from one of the farms in the area. And yes, the onion gravy's a secret recipe so don't ask me for it.'

'You've put a lot of work into this weekend.'

This time she blushed a little. 'I wanted everything to be perfect for Gramps and Celeste.'

'Things haven't quite gone to plan so far, but it's not been so bad, has it? When I called Aunt Celeste just now to see how they were doing, she said they were having a wonderful time and that she couldn't stop and talk because your grandfather was putting Aaron's train set together. Apparently her supervision is an all-important part of the process.'

Eloise chuckled. 'They have a lot of fun together. I just hope that everything's going to be all right tomorrow…'

That doubt again. As if disaster was always waiting, just around the corner.

'Whatever happens, it'll be fine. We'll make it so, eh?'

She hesitated and then smiled. 'Yes. Thanks.'

They ate in silence, too hungry for much conversation, and then Eloise leaned back in her seat, toying with the last sausage on her plate. 'You and Celeste are very close, aren't you?'

Sam nodded, as he swallowed his last mouthful of food. 'Yes. She did a lot for me and my brother and sister when our parents' marriage broke up. Provided us with a safe place away from all the conflict. It was a very messy break-up.'

'I didn't realise. I shouldn't have mentioned it...' Eloise had secrets and she should respect that Sam might well not want to talk about this.

'It's okay, it's all ancient history. I was thirteen when my parents split up, and it had been coming for as long as I can remember. My father wouldn't accept that my mother wanted to leave him, and he started stalking and harassing her. He'd turn up at the house at all hours of the day and night, and in the end she had to take out a restraining order. Aunt Celeste did the one thing that no one else did and kept speaking to both sides.' He stretched his arms, rubbing the back of his head. 'She spoke her mind, of course. Didn't pull any punches.'

'Pulling punches doesn't seem much like Celeste's style.'

That made him laugh, only there was a trace of bitterness there. Eloise wondered if the sudden haunted look in his eyes mirrored that of her own. It wasn't pleasant to watch.

'It's not her style at all. She loved my father, he was her brother. But she had no hesitation in telling him that he had to stay away from my mother, or in supporting Mum in a practical sense. Or trying to get my father to take some help when he started drinking. I was nineteen when he died, and Aunt Celeste was devastated.'

'I'm so sorry. That must have been a very difficult loss for both of you.'

'There were a lot of missed opportunities, but you

can't force someone to take help when they don't want it. His liver began to fail but he wouldn't give up drinking. Aunt Celeste helped me come to terms with that too.'

The hurt in his face belied his assertion that this was all in the past. Those wounds still remained, and maybe they always would. Sam was living with something as well, and that made it even more necessary for her to keep some kind of emotional distance while they were trapped in such close proximity to each other. His peace of mind seemed as fragile as hers was.

But she couldn't help it. She wanted to acknowledge the chaos and pain of his childhood, and her feelings must be showing in her face. Sam's gaze caught hers, and she saw the lines of tension in his brow soften. He gave a little nod, as if he'd seen her thoughts.

'Thank you. It's all a long time ago now.'

It was an effort to break that sweet connection, but Sam clearly didn't want to say any more. Eloise got to her feet, leaning towards him to pick up his plate.

'Would you like some dessert?'

He shook his head. 'Thanks…but shall we wait until Paul and Aunt Celeste are home?'

Gramps had called, saying that Granny June had been released from hospital with a badly sprained ankle, and that she'd be staying with Bess and Tom while she recovered. They'd be home in half an hour.

While Eloise set to work making dinner for them, Sam was making his own preparations. He disappeared into the scullery and she heard him opening and closing drawers and cupboards, obviously looking for something. Before she could go and see what he was doing he reappeared, holding candles, napkins and silver cutlery.

'I thought we'd eat in here, it's warmer than the dining room...'

He nodded, starting to arrange the candles at the centre of one end of the long table. 'Yeah, that's what I thought too. No reason not to make it nice, eh?'

Eloise smiled. He'd said that he'd help to make the weekend a success, whatever happened, and that clearly wasn't an empty promise. 'Shall we break out the champagne, then?'

He thought for a moment and then nodded. 'Champagne with bangers and mash. I like your style.'

By the time she heard Gramps and Celeste at the front door, the champagne was chilling in an ice bucket. Crystal glasses shone in the candlelight and the bangers and mash was ready to be served on the best plates.

'It looks great.' She took a moment to survey the table. 'You said you'd make things nice for Gramps and Celeste...'

Something flickered in his eyes, the warmth greater than even candlelight could achieve. 'What makes you think it's for them? This is for you.'

She caught her breath, but Sam was already gone, out into the hallway to hang up the coats and shepherd Gramps and Celeste through to the kitchen. Hugging the thought that he'd done this for her against her chest like a warm, comforting blanket, she turned back to the range to start serving the food.

There were exclamations of delight from Celeste, along with Gramps' quiet chuckle of approval. Eloise and Sam sat with them at the table, sipping champagne and eating nibbles while Gramps and Celeste tucked into their meal. It was impossible not to feel that Sam was watching her, and when Eloise turned and mouthed *Thank you* he smiled.

There was ice-cream for dessert, and then they repaired to the sitting room, taking their glasses with them while Eloise prepared coffee. When she brought the tray in, Gramps smilingly got to his feet.

'I think this is the right time for my speech, don't you, Celeste?'

'Absolutely, Paul.' Celeste beamed at him in anticipation, although she must already know what he intended to say. 'Let's hear it.'

'Don't you want to wait until everyone's here?' Gramps' speech had been scheduled for the dinner on Friday evening, which had been planned to welcome everyone.

'We're here, Eloise,' Gramps chided her gently. 'I think *this* is the time for it.'

Sam had topped up everyone's glasses and Aunt Celeste had once again pronounced herself *all ears*. Paul took two folded sheets of paper from the mantelpiece, and then stood to one side of the hearth.

Sam had been in the audience for more than one of Dr Paul Grant's lectures, and he normally spoke fluently and entertainingly, without even glancing at his notes. But this time he seemed almost nervous, studying the paper in his hand.

'Come along, darling. Out with it...' Aunt Celeste came to the rescue as usual, flashing Paul with an expectant smile. He laughed, putting the paper into his pocket.

'A toast first. To Celeste, whose questionable judgement has led her to agree to marry me. I'm looking forward to many more years of bad decisions together, darling.'

'Absolutely!' Aunt Celeste laughed and took a sip of her champagne. 'And to Paul, who always knows how to lead a woman astray.'

Bad decisions and leading each other astray suited them both very well. So well, in fact, that it was tempting to make a bad decision all of his own.

Another bad decision. The one to make this meal a little special hadn't been so bad, that was fun for everyone. Telling Eloise that it had been all for her hadn't been such a smart move, but it was the truth. She seemed to take every disruption of the plans for the coming weekend so much to heart, and her sudden smile had been so delicious that it was hard to bring himself to regret anything.

The champagne was making his head swim. Or maybe that was just watching her, as she took a sip from her glass. Or being caught watching her, as her gaze found his and a smile sprang to her lips before she looked quickly away again.

Sam turned his attention to Paul, who was already getting on with the first part of his speech.

'The year is now 1802, and two young men are fresh-faced students at medical school. Aloysius Grant and Henry Douglas became firm friends. The opportunity to quarrel over women never presented itself, in fact it's said that Aloysius went to some lengths to engineer Henry's introduction to his future wife. They were young, had all of the advantages that money could provide, and in learning together how to be of service to others a deep affection had been born. What could go wrong…?'

Every member of the Grant and Douglas families knew what *had* gone wrong. Paul launched into the story of how Aloysius Grant had written a medical paper, which Henry Douglas had debunked. The subsequent quarrel in the medical press had soured their relationship.

'They'd been inseparable friends, and maybe that was why they argued so bitterly, and never reconciled…' Paul gave a regretful smile at the ways of the world, and Sam felt his heart jump, as if this story really was something that was new and shocking. Maybe he should take it as a cautionary tale. If you didn't get too close to someone, then you couldn't do so much damage to each other. Sam suspected that his history and Eloise's were an explosive mix, and that they could do a great deal of damage together.

'Thirty years later when their old alma mater, here in Norfolk, was looking to grow, alumni were invited to contribute to new residences for students. Both Aloysius and Henry responded to the call, but only because each wanted to shame the other. Grant College and Douglas College were built and they still stand today, their sporting and academic rivalry a memorial to two foolish men, who each wanted to outdo the other.'

Eloise was smiling as she turned to Sam. 'You were at Douglas College?'

Sam hadn't felt much like following in his father's footsteps when he'd gone to medical school, and he hadn't changed his mind about that since. He shook his head.

'No, I broke with tradition and studied down in

London. But there was that one rugby match I rather wished I hadn't been involved in...' He turned the corners of his mouth down.

Aunt Celeste chuckled. 'I thought I did rather a good job on your nose, Sam. Are you telling me you don't like it?'

'You did a fine job. It's far better than it was before, but I didn't much like being punched in the face by the Grant team's scrum half.'

Paul was chuckling. 'I seem to remember there was some concern over there having been a ringer on the team.'

Aunt Celeste's eyebrows shot up. 'Vitriol, more like! Sam's a Grant, isn't he? So he can play for the team even if he's not a member of Grant College. I'd like to know what happened to the lad who was supposed to be playing...'

Paul and Aunt Celeste were teasing each other amicably and Sam turned to Eloise, his smile suddenly dying on his lips. Her cheeks were pink with embarrassment and she looked as if she wanted the cushions of the armchair she was sitting in to swallow her up.

There was no opportunity to ask her to explain, not now at least, because Paul had launched into an account of his and Celeste's progression from rivals to complete and loving accord. Another toast was proposed, to a new era of harmony between the Grants and the Douglases, and all four of them drained their glasses.

Then Eloise seemed to see an opportunity for escape and, before Sam could think of anything to say that might stop her, she was on her feet, collecting the empty cups and glasses and heading for the kitchen.

CHAPTER FOUR

A LITTLE TRICKLE of discomfort had run down Eloise's spine when Sam had mentioned the rugby match. It had turned into a gush of agonised embarrassment when she realised it had been *that* rugby match. And he had been *that* player.

She could come clean to him later, when Gramps and Celeste weren't around. In the meantime, the kitchen seemed like a good hiding place.

Eloise stiffened as she heard someone enter the kitchen. The old flagstones were an early warning system, and it was possible to know who was there from the sound of their footsteps. By the time she'd turned from the sink she'd managed to compose herself.

He'd made no pretence of carrying something through from the sitting room, and was looking at her silently. Eloise swallowed down the impulse to apologise, because that wasn't going to deflect him.

'I...didn't realise that you were there at that rugby match.'

'I didn't realise *you* were.'

Eloise studied the flagstones at her feet. 'Actually, I wasn't. I was...somewhere else.'

That wasn't going to deflect him either. Sam was

clearly one of those people who only became more curious in the face of things he didn't understand.

'Where?' He asked the inevitable question and she couldn't help meeting his gaze. Fair enough, maybe it was better that she came clean.

'In the boathouse. With the missing members of the Douglas College rugby team.'

His grin broadened. 'You…what? Charmed them away from the match?'

'No! That wouldn't have worked anyway. Rag week had just finished and Douglas College had been playing some pretty mean tricks on us. You really don't want to know what they did to the plumbing in the girls' bathrooms.' Eloise decided that elaborating any further sounded as if she was trying to justify herself.

'Aunt Celeste told me about that. Sounds pretty vile.' He was *still* grinning.

'Well, anyway. Feelings were running high, and we decided to pay them back. Two of their best players used to go running together and… I pretended I'd fallen on the path through the woods and broken my leg.'

He chuckled. 'Okay, I've got it. No doubt you were pretty convincing since you would have known exactly what a broken leg looked like, and when the rugby players stopped to help, a gang from Grant College jumped out at them. Probably tied them up, put them in the back of a van.'

'Car. We were gentle with them. And we didn't have to tie them up, they were outnumbered so they just came with us.' He was making this sound a lot worse than it had actually been.

'I'm disappointed.' His grin didn't look disappointed

at all. 'I have a picture of you executing a precise military operation.'

'It was nothing of the kind. We took them to the boathouse and gave them coffee and sandwiches.'

'So it was the most benign kidnapping ever. And I was the only casualty, after getting in the way when one of the Grant College team threw a punch in response to my being brought into the team when I wasn't strictly speaking anything to do with Douglas College and shouldn't have been playing for them.'

'Yes. I'm really sorry.' Eloise reckoned that an apology probably was in order for that.

He shrugged. 'You weren't the one who punched me. And Aunt Celeste fixed it.'

'It looks…great.' Maybe she shouldn't comment on that it was far too tempting to widen the parameters and tell him that everything about him was wonderful. 'I knew that those rugby matches were pretty hard fought, and I should have thought of the consequences of my actions a bit more carefully.'

Sam laughed. 'Hindsight's always twenty-twenty, I guess. I tell myself that when I browse through my own extensive catalogue of mistakes.'

He was trying to make her feel better. That was nice of him, but there was a downward quirk of his lips that made her wonder if Sam too was haunted by his mistakes.

'Would you like something else to drink? We have everything from hot chocolate to four different kinds of fruit juice.'

'Thanks, but no. I'm going to get an early night.'

That should have come as a relief. No more fighting with herself to ignore the warmth of his gaze. No more agonising over finding a way to tell him that it would be better for them both if they ignored whatever it was that was going on between them.

That was probably the best reason of all why sitting down at the kitchen table and having a heart-to-heart over mugs of hot chocolate really shouldn't happen. By tomorrow, sleep would have given her a better perspective on all of this.

Eloise smiled at him, filling the sink to rinse the glasses. 'Sleep well, then.'

Sam hadn't slept very well. A strange bed, and a house that seemed to creak around him every time there was the slightest movement. And Eloise. Determined and resourceful and yet so vulnerable. Somehow, he couldn't just let it go...

Maybe it would defuse the attraction that sparked between them if he was a bit more candid. Told her that he knew she'd been through a bad break-up and that he had too. Then they'd both know where they stood, and they could enjoy each other's company in the knowledge that there would be nothing more between them. But, on the other hand...a conversation like that might be construed as a prelude to intimacy.

In the early hours of the morning his brain must have suddenly switched off, overwhelmed by so many conflicting thoughts. When he drowsily awoke the next morning it was late.

Eloise was sitting with Paul and Aunt Celeste in the kitchen, and he made for the coffee machine.

'The weekend's off,' Aunt Celeste announced with a smile.

'You're not disappointed?' There it was again. That

wish to defend Eloise and acknowledge everything she'd done to make the weekend a success.

'Of course I am. If you'd been up a bit earlier you would have known that, Eloise has put in so much work. But there's nothing anyone can do about it. Paul's been on the phone to everyone and they've all decided against travelling up here. The weather forecast says more snow this afternoon.'

Sam looked out of the window. The snow still wasn't too deep, but any more and things would be grinding to a halt.

'Seems sensible. So what *are* you happy about?'

'It appears that we've got something else to be getting our teeth into. Paul's had a call from the local Community Hospital, who were wondering if we were available to help out if needed. We're going over there this morning to talk to their head of services. Are you in?'

Aunt Celeste knew she didn't need to ask. 'I'm in. Just let me grab some breakfast first...'

He only had time to gulp down half a cup of coffee. Paul and Aunt Celeste had already put on their coats and were outside clearing his car of snow, having decided that it would be the best to take in these conditions. Eloise smilingly went to the range cooker, opening up the warming compartment and withdrawing a bacon sandwich on a plate.

'I made this when I heard you moving around upstairs. I can either fight Gramps and Celeste off while you take a minute to eat it, or I'll wrap it up and you can take it with you.'

'You'll drive?'

She smiled. 'Yes, I'll drive.'

Clearly she was in determined mode this morning, and none of Sam's good intentions from last night could resist that. He went to fetch their coats and his car keys and when he returned to the kitchen Eloise had a foil-wrapped package for him, and a full travel cup of coffee.

'Thanks.'

Eloise pulled on her coat, taking a purple knitted hat out of the pocket and pulling it down over her ears. It looked just as charming as the red one she'd worn yesterday. 'Let's go then, before Gramps and Celeste explode from impatience...'

The Community Hospital was a large one-storey building with a pitched slate roof, which blended into the countryside around it. A couple of ambulances were parked on one side of the building, and as they entered the welcoming reception area a man in a sweater stepped forward, shaking Paul's hand.

'Thanks for coming, Paul.' He turned to Celeste. 'You're Ms Douglas?'

'Celeste, please. Plastic surgeon, although I can turn my hand to most things.'

'And this is my granddaughter, Eloise Grant. She works in an Accident and Emergency department in London. And Sam Douglas is a GP.'

'Thanks, that's marvellous. I'm Joe Parrish and I'm co-ordinating the volunteers. We're managing right now, but with more snow on the way we may be cut off from the main hospital, that's been an issue for us before. In that eventuality we'll have to deal with all the cases from this area that would normally go there, and so we'll need all the help we can get.'

'You deal with ambulance cases already, don't you?' Sam remembered that June had been brought here yesterday.

'Yes, we do, we have X-ray and scanning capabilities and we can deal with a wide range of minor injuries. We also have a couple of ambulances based here, which will take more serious cases over to the A&E department in the main hospital. We've already experienced an uptick in the number of people coming in, due to the weather conditions, but, as I say, we're managing well at the moment. But we're preparing to take in more if needs be. I'd appreciate any input you have on the planning side, Paul.'

Paul nodded. 'Of course. Maybe I can show the others around a bit first? Just so they know what they're letting themselves in for…'

There was a sizeable waiting area that was busy but nowhere near full at the moment, with several treatment rooms along one side. Paul led them along a short corridor and punched an entry code into a door, which opened onto another large space which looked as if it was currently being repurposed, examination beds lined up along one side and curtains being hung to make semi-private treatment areas.

'This is usually used for various different clinics, but it doubles up nicely as an overflow area for emergencies.'

Eloise was looking around, checking on the equipment available. 'Defibrillators?'

Paul nodded. 'You'll have everything you need. That's what I'm going to be discussing with Joe.'

She grinned suddenly. 'So I don't need to make a list, eh, Gramps?'

Paul chuckled. 'Not unless there's something you've discovered for yourself, since I taught you everything I know.'

Eloise snorted with laughter. 'No, I'm still waiting for a chance to put some of the things you taught me into practice. Give me another ten years…'

The trust between them was clear. Sam had seen yesterday that she was confident and effective when it came to her work, and yet she was so very vulnerable in her private life. Whatever the circumstances of the cancelled marriage that Aunt Celeste had described to him, they must have hurt Eloise very badly.

Eloise and Paul were still talking together and Sam's attention was drawn back to the conversation by the mention of his name.

'What do you think, Sam? We'll go back to the house and Gramps and Celeste will stay here to help Joe?'

'Uh…if there's nothing for us to do here. Just give me a call and I'll come back and collect you both, but don't leave it too late. You don't want to be stuck here.'

'Best place for us in the circumstances,' Aunt Celeste retorted. 'And anyway there's always Ted.'

Eloise smiled. 'Yes, there's always Ted. Don't forget to be back before six, because I'm cooking.'

As they walked out to the car together, Sam asked the obvious question. 'Who's Ted?'

'He's one of the local farmers. He has a motor sled that he uses on the farm when it snows—not one of those sporty one-person models, this one's ex-army and a real workhorse of a machine, it'll take four passengers easily. He phoned this morning before you were up, and said that if we needed to go into the hospital to help out we should just call him.'

'Sounds like a very handy person to know in the circumstances.'

'Yes, he is. The sled's great, I think that Celeste's rather hoping they'll be staying long enough to need it.'

'And meanwhile…what are we going to be doing?' Sam was pretty sure that Eloise had a plan.

'Well, the welcome dinner was supposed to be this evening. We haven't got any people but we do have plenty of food. And, of course, the happy couple to contend with.'

'Ah. So we're making the best of things. For them and for us?' He wondered whether Eloise would take the step of claiming some enjoyment for herself.

Her fingers brushed his as she handed him his car keys, and he saw her cheeks flush. 'If I cook then maybe you'll take care of the table?'

And maybe, like last night, she'd accept that some of that was for her and not just Paul and Aunt Celeste.

'Okay. That sounds fair. Are we going to dress for dinner?'

'Yes, I thought so.'

Sam nodded, trying not to wonder what Eloise would be wearing. This was *really* sounding like a plan.

Eloise was almost glad that no one was going to be turning up for the weekend. Given the choice, she'd rather be at the hospital, helping out, than having to contend with her whole family, together in one room. And Sam had a way of making everything special.

He followed her into the kitchen, hanging his coat on the back of one of the chairs. Sam's smile seemed so much more potent when they were alone together and Eloise tried to ignore it.

'We were going to have Beef Wellington, so that's easy enough. I can put all of the extras into the freezer and just cook one of them for tonight. I can freeze the extra vegetables as well, and just cook enough for four.'

'There'll be enough room in the freezer?' Sam regarded the fridge-freezer in the corner of the kitchen.

'There are two big chest freezers in the pantry; there's plenty of room there. We'll be having green beans with garlic, thyme and white wine, Brussels sprouts with chestnuts and bacon and roasted asparagus. Along with mashed potatoes and a hollandaise sauce.'

He nodded. 'Sounds delicious. You obviously have everything well in hand.'

In the kitchen...yes. Everywhere else...not even close.

'There is one other problem. You've seen the Great Hall?'

'Aunt Celeste showed me around the house when I first came up here for the weekend, to meet your grandfather.' He shot her a querying look. 'We're eating there?'

'That was the original plan, the Great Hall's always been Gramps' favourite place in the house. But I think that we should probably move to the dining room.'

'You like the Great Hall?'

He always asked the most difficult questions. 'Yes, I like it. It has a real sense of occasion about it.'

'Then we'll do it there.'

No amount of moving furniture was going to make the Great Hall into an intimate space for four people.

'What do you have in mind?'

Sam started to walk out into the hallway and Eloise

called him back, motioning to the door at the other end of the kitchen. All of the rooms in the house had more than one door, which made things confusing at times, but followed the Tudor practice of having rooms leading from one to the other.

There was a chill in the air in the Great Hall, which made her shiver. That was another problem. It needed to be full of people to warm up to a comfortable temperature for sitting and eating. Sam was looking around, inspecting the windows that ran along the length of the hall on one side, the massive inglenook that contained a glass-fronted stove on the other and the long oak table that was placed in the centre of the room.

'This can go over there. And we can use that smaller table.' He pointed towards the far end of the hall, where a smaller serving table stood against the wall.

'Yes.' Eloise wasn't sure how that was going to work, it would just make the empty space look even more cavernous. But she supposed that since she'd asked Sam to help she should at least sound a little positive. 'The big table comes apart, I can help you move it.'

'That's okay, I'll manage. And if we sit by the fireplace it'll be warm enough there?'

'Yes, I suppose so. But isn't it going to feel as if we're huddled around the fire with this massive space around us?'

Sam smiled suddenly. 'Will you leave it with me?'

Trust him. She could do that, if all he had in mind was moving furniture around.

'Okay. I'll prepare myself for a surprise.'

'I'm aiming for delight, actually.'

Okay, so delight was a lot more confronting. But…

She couldn't say no, the thought was far too tempting. And suddenly, delight was something she missed very much.

'I'll look forward to seeing what you come up with.'

CHAPTER FIVE

ELOISE HAD KEPT herself to the kitchen, which wasn't difficult because there was plenty to do, wrapping all of the extra food for the freezer and then preparing the food for tonight. Everything was ready to go into the oven, and when it did she would have time to dress for dinner and then serve everything without too much rushing around.

At three the sky began to darken with cloud, and Sam appeared in the kitchen doorway again. 'Paul's just called and I'm going to pick them up. I won't be long.'

'Shall I come too? Just in case they need us.'

'Paul says that they've reworked the rotas and they have enough staff coming in early to cover tonight, so we'll only be in the way. It's tomorrow when they'll most likely be calling us in.'

'Okay. So what do you think about getting a bottle of wine up from the cellar to warm up to room temperature?'

He pressed his lips together, weighing up the idea. 'I suppose…it might be better to stick to soft drinks. You never know what's going to happen. Maybe we can work on creating an intoxicating atmosphere.'

An evening spent just for the sheer pleasure of the company you were in. Eloise had forgotten how long it had been since she'd done that and right now it seemed an act of stupid self-denial to reject it.

'I'll look forward to it.'

He returned an hour later, and Eloise heard Gramps and Celeste chatting together animatedly as they climbed the stairs. Then Sam reappeared in the doorway, taking off his coat.

'Seems we just made it in time. It's starting to snow heavily now. I've sent Paul and Aunt Celeste upstairs and told them they're not to come back down again until we're ready. Apparently they've plenty to do, they're halfway through a chess game.'

'Ah, the chess game. Did you know that when Celeste's down in London they play by text?'

He chuckled. 'No, I didn't know that.'

'Gramps sends roses every time Celeste wins a game. I think he loses on purpose sometimes.' Eloise had never thought about it much before, but now it seemed an incurably romantic gesture.

'They're starting to make me feel very old and staid.'

'Me too.' Perhaps a little of the happiness was rubbing off. Eloise could almost feel the sparkle in the air. But that sparkle and the accompanying warmth seemed to revolve entirely around Sam.

'I'd better get on. Give me a call when you want me to watch dinner so you can go and dress.'

'Thanks. That won't be for another hour...'

When she heard Sam climbing the stairs and reckoned that he'd gone to dress for dinner, the temptation to sneak into the Great Hall and take a look was almost irresistible. But Eloise had promised not to, and she had enough to do to occupy her time. And then Sam appeared, wearing an evening suit. The dark waist-coat and tie emphasised his broad frame and hand-some features, bringing a whole new meaning to the word *temptation*.

'You scrub up pretty well, Dr Douglas.' Acknowl-edge it. Get it out in the open. Then it couldn't hurt her.

'Thanks.' The surprise in his tone only added to the temptation. Most gorgeous men knew it, but if Sam did then he had no time for the idea. Eloise shouldn't have any time for it either. She was already walking a tightrope, allowing herself to take more pleasure in his company than she should. But somehow that dan-ger only added to the excitement of allowing herself to feel attracted to him.

'Are you going to show me what you've done in the Great Hall now?'

He nodded, holding out his arm in a signal that she should take it. Eloise wiped her hands and took her apron off, rather sheepishly taking his arm.

And then, suddenly, she felt like a million dollars. As if her hair wasn't tied back in a scrunchie, and she hadn't been working all afternoon in the kitchen. He smiled down at her as if she were Cinderella, after her fairy godmother was through with her. He was defi-nitely the handsome prince.

It was impossible not to hang a little more tightly onto his arm, because she could smell the scent of soap, which immediately conjured up visions of Sam showering.

When he opened the door to the Great Hall, escort-ing her inside, the fairy tale started to become real.

Almost too real—reminding her that the romance of it all was beyond her aspirations now.

The subtle electric lighting, that was used to supplement the flickering candlelight from the chandeliers, had been turned off. Sam had lit the stove, and a warm glow spread across the smaller dining table that he'd placed in front of the inglenook. Two large candelabra stood on the table, each surrounded by flowers, and the surplus blooms spilled over the stone mantelpiece above the inglenook.

A pure white cloth. Sparkling silver and crystal glassware. It was simple, elegant and, since the rest of the hall was in shadow, it was intimate as well, as if they were gathered around a campfire in the darkness. To add a touch of magic, Sam had obviously found the solar lights in the storeroom and planted them outside the windows, and they illuminated the flakes of snow that were falling now.

'Sam, it's beautiful! Gramps and Celeste are going to love it.'

'What matters to me is whether you like it.' The flickering candlelight seemed to caress his face. Why wouldn't it? Light could go anywhere it pleased.

Eloise felt her breath catch in her throat, tears pricking at the sides of her eyes, at all that she'd lost. Turning away from him, she pretended to examine the flowers at each side of the hearth, putting one that had been dislodged back into place.

Somehow, she managed to face him again. To smile and pretend that she was just very impressed, and not completely overwhelmed that he'd done all of this for her.

'It's really beautiful, Sam. I love it.'

She had to go now, before she made a fool of herself. Eloise made a hurried excuse about having to go and get dressed for dinner now and then, like Cinderella, she ran from the Prince Charming that she could never have.

Sam sat at the kitchen table, fiddling with his phone. He'd restlessly checked the contents of the oven and reviewed Eloise's list and, just as she'd informed him, there was nothing he needed to do.

Which was a shame, because it left his mind entirely free to wander. Celeste and Paul didn't really need any more romance in their lives; they had it already. He'd started out trying to make a special evening for Eloise, and ended up making it for himself as well. Wondering how she might look in soft, flickering candlelight. How she might smile when she saw the result of his efforts, knowing that it would make his own heart beat faster. A heart that seemed to have slowed to monotonous regularity since Alice had left him.

He'd tried. Tried to leave the doubts and the fears behind, tried to be nothing like his father, who had asked only for what he'd wanted and disregarded everyone else's wishes. Sam had thought he'd succeeded, learning how to take a breath—sometimes more than one—and suppress his anger when it threatened to blind him to other people's wants and needs. He'd approached his relationships carefully and thoughtfully, the break-ups with particular care. Alice had been the exception to that. When she'd refused to tell him why she was leaving he couldn't dismiss his anger and when he'd felt it seep through into his reactions, heard its edge in his own voice… It had shocked him how much like his father he'd sounded.

So he'd let Alice go. Sam had moved on, the way his father should have done, never acknowledging any pain. In the year between then and now, he'd hardly even noticed how grey his life had become.

And then Eloise had reminded him all about colour and excitement and uncertainty. About the thrill of not being able to get someone out of your head. Even the sound of her footsteps, outside in the hall, made all of his senses switch to high alert. And when she appeared in the doorway his heart jumped.

'You look great.'

Eloise was wearing a bottle-green velvet dress. Plain, with three-quarter length sleeves and a hem that fell almost to her ankles, with high strappy silver sandals. The colour suited her dark hair, which was piled up on top of her head, and the dress showed off her figure. Great didn't really cover it—she looked breathtaking.

'Thank you.' Maybe his expression had indicated breathtaking, because Sam thought he saw a blush steal across her cheeks. Then she turned away, bending to peer into the oven.

He couldn't keep his eyes off her. The way she moved, and how she seemed to take the light with her everywhere she went. He couldn't keep his mind off wanting her to be happy, which was already morphing into a wish to be the one who made her happy.

'I think everything's ready…'

'I'll serve up, shall I? You can go and fetch Paul and Aunt Celeste.' Their reaction when they saw the table laden with food would be a few more grains of happiness to scatter at her feet.

She hesitated and then smiled. 'Okay, thanks.'

Sam saw her straighten, smoothing her hands across her dress as she walked out of the kitchen, as if she'd been chosen to escort royal guests into the Great Hall. Paul and Aunt Celeste were more important to her than a king and his queen, and he smiled.

Silence, as he made the first journey to the table and back. As Sam was picking up the serving dishes, ready to make the second, he heard a little scream echoing in from the Great Hall. Aunt Celeste was adding her seal of approval to the evening. When he walked back to the table, she was hugging Eloise tight.

'This looks great, Sam, thank you.' Paul shot him a broad grin. 'I don't use the Hall unless there are a lot of guests, but I see I've been missing something.'

'Sam's good at that kind of thing.' Aunt Celeste shot him a look that made it clear she approved of his efforts. 'And Eloise... The food smells absolutely marvellous. Thank you so much...'

The glasses were filled, and they sat down to eat. Sam had put Celeste and Paul at either end of the table and, to avoid anyone having their back to the heat of the fire, he and Eloise were sitting next to each other, facing the hearth. That had been a mistake. Sam would have borne the discomfort of the fire at his back for the chance to look up at Eloise.

She was glowing. The rich fabric of her dress failed to draw his attention away from the way her face shone in the firelight. And he could steal glances to his left, bask in the pleasure that she was clearly taking in the meal.

It was a feast fit for a king. When the first course was

finished, Paul leaned back in his seat, smiling. 'What do you say we take a little break before dessert?'

That seemed to be a signal for Celeste to reach for her evening bag. 'Good idea.' She withdrew a gold-wrapped package. 'Eloise, this is for you. I wish there had been more people here, to applaud everything you've done to make this weekend such a joy for us, but we'll have to do.'

Eloise looked genuinely taken aback. When she didn't take the package, Celeste got to her feet, pressing it into her hand.

'I didn't...' She turned towards Sam, her cheeks burning. 'Sam did everything in here.'

'And you've been working hard everywhere else for days, darling,' Celeste reprimanded her. 'Anyway, this really isn't going to suit Sam.'

Sam chuckled, picking up his glass. 'To Eloise. Thank you for making this evening wonderful.'

Paul and Celeste followed suit, making the toast. But Sam could see nothing but Eloise, as she turned to him, her lips a little moist, her gaze warm in the firelight. She was the most beautiful woman he'd ever seen.

Were these just fantasies of a different life? One where he could meet someone and fall in love, without all of the hesitation and insecurity that he'd felt in the past? Sam doubted whether he was capable of constructing a fantasy like this. The way that Eloise carefully peeled the tape from the wrapping paper, flashing a mischievous smile at her grandfather, who was leaning forward, anxious to see whether she'd like her present. The curve of her cheek, flushed with the caress of the fire burning in the inglenook.

It was both delightful and challenging, but this was something real. Something he could no longer dismiss as a mere reminder of what seemed missing in his life. Eloise had not just made him notice the void, she was beginning to fill it as well.

'Oh! It's beautiful, thank you!' She withdrew a gold filigree heart on a chain from its box.

Paul and Celeste were talking, but all that Sam could hear and see was Eloise. She fumbled behind her neck with the chain and suddenly he found himself on his feet, carefully fixing the clasp. Inhaling her scent as if it might save his life.

She turned a little, her hand on the pendant, smiling a *thank you* to Celeste and Paul. And then her gaze met his. Suddenly it felt as if they were the only two people in the room.

Sam was beginning to feel that he'd lost too much. Avoiding a nasty break-up meant avoiding having something that you wanted to keep. But he wanted to keep the longing that he felt, as Eloise's lips curved into a smile that seemed private and all for him, the wish to know her, to be able to talk about anything and share everything. He felt like a thief, stealing every last drop of romance from an evening that had never been designed to be for him and Eloise. But still, he couldn't help wanting more…

Sam had thought of everything. The fireworks that had been planned for the evening weren't going to work in the heavy snow that was falling outside, but when he fetched the dessert from the refrigerator he arranged table fireworks around it, so that when he entered the

Great Hall there was a sparkling blaze of light to accompany him.

He quietly steered the evening to its close, via surprise presents from Gramps and Celeste, who had told each other that they wouldn't exchange engagement gifts but had both secretly broken the rule. Celeste had given Gramps a new watch, engraved with a loving message, which replaced the old and rather battered timepiece on his wrist. And they'd all trooped upstairs to see the room that Gramps had had decorated as Celeste's new study.

'It's so pretty, isn't it?' Eloise stopped at the large window at the top of the stairs, looking out on the falling snow. 'And such a shame that it brings so many challenges.'

Sam chuckled. 'Isn't that always the way? Maybe we shouldn't think about the challenges—they'll always be there. Just take the pleasures.'

Perhaps Sam wasn't talking just about the snow. Maybe Eloise wasn't either. Tonight did seem like one of those times when she could take the pleasures and forget about the challenges. Sam proffered his arm and she took it.

'Oh!' As she turned towards the stairs, she missed her footing on the uneven floorboards and the high heels did the rest. Suddenly she found herself in Sam's arms.

Gramps and Celeste were already downstairs and at this moment they might as well be a hundred miles away. And using this moment to feel the strong lines of his body against hers seemed like a strangely good idea.

'Did you twist your ankle?' No one had ever enquired after her health with such a delicious smile.

'No. This house really isn't made for wearing high heels.'

For a moment, he didn't seem to realise that meant he could let her go now. She felt the pressure of his arm around her waist pull her a little closer. Sam's breath caught suddenly and her own heartbeat began to race frenetically. Any moment now, it was all going to prove too much to bear.

'We should go and see what they're up to down there.' The slight quirk of his mouth, and the way he kept hold of her for just a few seconds longer, betrayed his reluctance.

'Give them a moment more together.' Give *us* a moment more... The words tripped off Eloise's tongue before she could stop them and Sam nodded.

She felt his fingers brush the back of her hand, then encircle it loosely, raising it to his mouth. She barely felt the brush of his lips. It was a slightly old-fashioned recognition that might have been given any number of times at tonight's formal party, if more people had turned up. But the look in his eyes made it seem both intimate and exciting.

'Eloise... Sam... What are you two doing up there?' Celeste's voice broke the spell, and she came to her senses. Michael had been the one person she should have been able to trust, but he'd betrayed her. She hardly knew Sam, and kissing him now would be a bad idea. She couldn't see how that might possibly change in the foreseeable future.

'Nothing...' she called back, wondering whether Sam's thoughts were the same as hers. It wasn't nothing at all, but that was what it had to be.

* * *

Precious, precious moments. They'd seemed to Sam to last for years. As if caught in Eloise's gaze, he'd been sucked into a vortex where time stood still. As if they'd said all of the things that needed to be said, got to know and trust each other, and found themselves in a place where just this one look was enough to hold everything that a man might feel for a woman. To receive everything that he couldn't help wanting in return.

And, of course, it had to end. They'd been called back and Eloise had clung to his arm on the stairs, in a sweet echo of what had gone before. By the time they reached the Great Hall, where Paul and Aunt Celeste were rearranging chairs so that they could sit in front of the inglenook for coffee, there were two feet of empty air between them.

It seemed that Grant family traditions were much the same as those of the Douglas family and the after-dinner talk drifted to medical matters. Paul had been approached to write a book based on a series of lectures he'd given, and Aunt Celeste had been proofreading the first few chapters for him.

'It would really interest you, Sam. It's about doctor-patient relationships in primary care. Some of the conclusions are applicable to many different kinds of structures where knowledge and trust are involved and it's very readable, even if you're not working in a medical setting,' Aunt Celeste remarked.

'I'll be very keen to get my hands on it.'

Paul smiled an acknowledgement. 'I'll send you the first few chapters if you're interested. I'd very much like to hear your comments.'

'I'll just mention that Sam's story from last Christmas, about a lady he visited on Christmas Eve, is very applicable to Chapter Two.' Aunt Celeste was trying to make the remark sound casual and failing dismally. Everyone forgave her for her rather obvious networking style, because behind it all she had good intentions and a very clear understanding of medical issues.

'I'll bear that in mind…' Sam smiled at Paul.

'Why not tell us?' Eloise had been silently following the conversation and spoke up suddenly.

Right now, everything seemed to hang on her words, her reactions. They could have been having a conversation about garden spades, and Sam would have assessed it by Eloise's response. Sam gave in to the inevitable and started to recount how he'd responded to an urgent call from an elderly woman patient on Christmas Eve. It had turned out that she needed someone to fix the fairy to the top of her tree because she couldn't reach.

'What did you do?' Eloise's eyes were bright with interest.

Sam shrugged. 'I put the fairy on the tree for her, made some cocoa and we sat down and watched a carol service on TV. I was still on call, but no one needed me, and I'd just be sitting at home otherwise.'

'My nephew the softie,' Aunt Celeste teased him.

'What was I going to do? She was all on her own. And we had a great time. We sat up until midnight and she broke out the chocolate liqueurs and we wished each other Happy Christmas.'

'And did you? Have a happy Christmas?' Eloise asked.

The warmth in her face was driving him crazy with longing. Sam decided not to mention that he'd gone back the next day with mince pies and a present for

Mrs Cornelius. It wasn't strictly relevant and he wasn't sure he could take too much more of Eloise's approval.

'The other doctors from the practice are all married with families, so I generally volunteer to cover Christmas Day. In the New Year I arranged for someone from a charity that organises companionship for the elderly to visit her.'

Paul nodded. 'Which was no doubt the best thing you could have done to improve her general health.'

'We'll have to wait and see. But yes, she seemed much happier the last time I saw her.'

The evening was winding down, and Aunt Celeste began to yawn behind her hand. When she and Paul excused themselves, Eloise got to her feet and did the same. Sam decided that he'd better turn in as well, and followed them up the stairs, wishing Eloise a good night as he passed her door, forcing himself to walk to his own room without looking back.

He should get a good night's sleep, but Sam was still wide awake. He took off his jacket and tie, then remembered he'd left the book he'd brought with him downstairs. Feeling the chill of the air in the hallway, he walked as quietly as he could along the creaking floorboards, and down to the sitting room. His attention was drawn to the window and he drew the curtains back, looking at the snow outside with the eyes of a practising doctor, rather than a man who had been foolish enough to see the world as a sparkling place for the last few hours.

The snow must have been a couple of feet deep in places, and if this kept up there would be injuries to deal with tomorrow. Blocked roads, which meant that ambulances and paramedics would be struggling to get to their patients. The hospital would be contending with potential staff shortages and increased demand for its services, and that was very bad news.

Bad news that provided him with a challenge. One that was easier to face than this evening's challenges had been. Sam turned from the window, making for the light switch, but before he reached it something caught his eye and he froze.

She was walking along the gallery, which ran at head height along the far wall of the sitting room and was generally used as a short cut from the main staircase to the back of the house. Eloise had folded a thick, pale-coloured blanket like a shawl and draped it around her shoulders. Underneath, a thin white nightdress foamed around her ankles. Somehow she was managing to avoid every creak in the floorboards as she walked and her footsteps were silent. She seemed almost ghostly in the darkness, unaware that he was below her, staring up at her.

She disappeared, and he broke free of the spell. Sam picked up his book from the coffee table listening for anything that might tell him where she'd gone.

Nothing. He couldn't hear her outside and wondered if she'd gone to the kitchen for a glass of water. He should go back upstairs, but something led him in search of Eloise.

By the time he found her in the Great Hall, led by the light that was coming from the fireplace, the chill in the air was making him shiver. She was sitting inside the inglenook, a candle propped in one of the alcoves, her bare feet stretched out towards the stove.

'Can't sleep?' She looked up at him.

'I came downstairs to fetch my book.' Luckily Sam

still had the book in his hand as evidence, and Eloise nodded. 'What are you doing in there?'

'It used to be my thinking place, when I was a kid. Come and give it a try.'

Sam couldn't resist. He ducked into the inglenook, finding that when he was inside there was enough space to stand straight and it was surprisingly roomy. The bricks, once stained by smoke, had been cleaned and there were two polished wooden benches let into the wall, one on either side of the stove. Even though the fire had been banked up for the night, the inglenook was beautifully cosy.

'I can see why you like it. It's really warm in here.'

'Yes, it's like this all winter, even when the fire isn't alight. The bricks take in the heat and you're sheltered from the draughts. That was the original idea of an inglenook, a place for the family to keep warm in winter.'

Sam sat down on the bench opposite Eloise. 'Penny for them?'

CHAPTER SIX

SHE JUST HAD to tell him, didn't she? If this was her thinking place, then it stood to reason that Eloise had some thinking to do, and Sam had asked the obvious question. The answer—that she'd been thinking about him—was a place that she wasn't sure she trusted herself, or Sam, enough to go.

'I'll go first, shall I?' He smiled.

Thank you. Thank you *so* much. Eloise nodded, wondering if his thoughts were the same as hers.

'I've got a confession to make. I know that you probably weren't looking forward much to this weekend. Aunt Celeste told me that there was a lot of unfair gossip and bad feeling when your wedding was cancelled at the last minute.'

For a moment she was powerless to speak. Swallowing the lump in her throat didn't make things any better, because Eloise didn't know what to say.

'You don't pull your punches, do you?'

He nodded, something like warmth in his eyes. Eloise couldn't bring herself to trust it any more.

'To be honest, I've been feeling a bit uncomfortable about it. Knowing and not saying anything.'

Okay. That was...it seemed reasonable. These

seemed like the actions of a man who cared about the people around him. Who maybe cared a little bit about her.

'And Celeste warned you…' That was a sentence she really didn't want to finish. Celeste had warned her beloved nephew against having too much to do with her. That was probably fair, but it was something of a disappointment.

He raised his eyebrows in surprise. 'Aunt Celeste gave up warning me about things years ago. She was concerned that someone might say the wrong thing, and wanted me to step in and whisk you away if I saw that anyone was giving you a hard time.'

Eloise hadn't realised how much that might mean to her. She'd told herself that she didn't care what anyone else thought, because Gramps knew what had happened, and he supported her all the way. That the comments, mostly behind her back but some to her face, weren't sticks and stones and they couldn't hurt her. But she saw her hand shake as she wiped tears from her face.

'That's so nice of Celeste. I should thank her.'

'Not right now. Probably not ever. I think her intention was that this was going to be a covert operation. I'd move in and divert your attention while she and Paul executed a pincer movement and took care of the guilty party…'

He was trying to make her smile. When she did, she saw warmth blossom in his eyes. Anyone who thought blue was at the cooler end of the colour spectrum should meet Sam.

'What happens in the inglenook stays in the inglenook, then.'

He nodded, stretching his legs out in front of him towards the remaining heat of the stove. Shadows played around his face from the candle, emphasising the strong line of his jaw.

'The wedding...' They both spoke together and Sam smiled.

'You should go first.'

Eloise took a deep breath, trying to order her thoughts. 'After my wedding fell apart, I went away for two weeks, thinking that by the time I got back everything would have quietened down a bit. I hadn't been answering my phone or looking at my email while I was away, and when I read all of the messages, and realised that everyone was really angry with me, I came up here to see Gramps.'

'Who, no doubt, had something constructive to say.'

'He said that I should talk about it in my own time, and not let anyone else push me into doing so before I was ready...' It had been the first loving thing that anyone had said to her. Gramps had trusted her and believed in her. Eloise felt a tear prick at the side of her eye and brushed it away.

Sam was silent for a moment, his brow furrowed in thought. 'And you're not ready now?'

Eloise shrugged. 'I don't know...' Was this Sam's way of asking what had happened? Was she going to give in to the impulse to gain his approval and tell him, when she'd refused to tell anyone else apart from Gramps?

'My guess is that when you are sure you'll know. I can see why you really needed to hear Paul tell you that other people wanting to know wasn't a good reason for you to talk about it.'

A little shiver of alarm ran down Eloise's spine. Sam was right, but she couldn't see how he'd come to that conclusion. Maybe she'd been foolish in trusting him, even this far, when she really had no idea what his reaction would be.

'Why would you think that?'

'Because…forgive me if I have this wrong…'

'Forgiven.' She just needed to hear what he thought, whatever that was.

'You've already experienced loss.' Sam was clearly treading carefully, watching for her response. 'Your mother and grandmother, and then your father.'

That was fair. 'Yes. Dad couldn't make it for the wedding, and he stayed out of things afterwards. He said it was all too complicated.'

'Maybe you just needed someone to make it very simple. To put you first, without really needing to know exactly what had happened. That's what families are for, isn't it?'

She hadn't thought about it like that. She'd just been so grateful that Gramps *had* supported her, and Eloise hadn't questioned it. Sometimes another point of view came with twenty-twenty vision.

'You have a point. I've always felt that this is the place I really belong, and I needed to know that I still did.'

Talking to Sam made sense of it, even if it brought no answers. It was still hard to trust him, even if he hadn't done anything to deserve her misgivings. Perhaps trust was one of those things that never quite mended, and Michael's betrayal had broken hers irrevocably.

'Can I ask you something?'

He gave a short, barking laugh, as if he knew that whatever she was about to ask might be confronting. 'I can hardly say *no*, can I?'

'Everyone can always say no.' She waited for his answer and, when it didn't come, Eloise asked her question. 'You seem to understand what a bad break-up is like. How much it hurts.'

He shrugged. 'Yes and no. When my parents broke up it was devastating for the whole family. But that's not really what you were asking, is it. There's a difference between being involved in your parents' break-up and being blamed for your own.'

He was very perceptive. Very honest. He seemed to see straight through her and yet somehow he was still here. Still talking.

'I guess so. It's hurtful, either way.'

'It's always been very important to me to respect my partner's right to do whatever she wants. To let her leave, without standing in her way.' He gave a wry smile. 'I don't want to be like my father.'

'That's a good thing, isn't it?'

'I think so. Sometimes it's hard to find closure when someone ends a relationship without telling you why.'

Eloise caught her breath. Did he think that was what she'd done? They seemed suddenly to be staring at each other from opposite sides of the same bad situation.

'I...my fiancé...ex-fiancé... Michael. He was part of the decision and knew exactly why I left.'

Sam looked up suddenly. Something about the way that he couldn't quite meet her gaze told Eloise that she'd just answered the question he hadn't dared ask. He might be a careful and tactful man, but that wasn't the real reason for his restraint. Sam had been hurt too, and he was as cautious as she was.

'I didn't mean to draw any parallels. That's quite different.'

And yet suddenly she felt that he'd broken their connection. She couldn't find Sam's warmth, or his honesty, any more and whatever he was thinking seemed to be reserved for him alone.

'I just meant...' Eloise shrugged. 'I suppose that *is* what I meant. I want you to know.'

He nodded. 'It matters that he knows. No one else needs to.'

'It sounds as if there's something you don't know.' Maybe she was pushing Sam a little too far, asking him to talk about things he didn't want to talk about. But he seemed to be carrying a burden, and maybe he just wanted to put it down for a while.

'My last break-up was the un-messiest in human history. Even Aunt Celeste missed it and she's got unerring radar for those kinds of things. My ex, Alice, said she wanted to take a break and wouldn't tell me why. That was painful in a lot of ways...'

'I hate to tell you this, but that sounds pretty messy to me. Like an explosion in an enclosed space.'

Sam grinned suddenly. 'Yeah. It felt a bit like that too.'

There was nothing more to say. They had answers but there were no conclusions to be drawn, other than that they both needed to tread very carefully. But this was a place from which she could start to know Sam better, without constantly questioning herself about whether she'd said or done the right thing.

'It's been a good talk. I've appreciated it.'

'Me too. But I think that the wondrous effect of the inglenook has to be taken in small doses at first. This is my first time, remember…'

He stretched his arms, and Eloise felt the same thrill that she always did when she watched Sam move. There was a controlled power in his body that always made her shiver.

'I'll see you in the morning, then.' Eloise didn't move. She'd wait until he was safely upstairs and in his own bedroom, so that there was no opportunity to say *yes* to him if he suggested they spend a little more time together tonight. Now that they'd talked, it seemed less essential to grab at every moment with him, fearing that it might never happen again.

'Yes. Don't stay down here too long. I think tomorrow's going to be a busy day.' He got to his feet, ducking out of the inglenook.

'You still want to work with me tomorrow, then?'

He turned, bending down to give her a spine-tingling smile.

'More than ever.'

The expected call came in early the next morning. Aunt Celeste and Paul were sitting at the kitchen table while Sam made a second round of toast for them all. He'd lain awake just long enough to hear Eloise's quiet footsteps in the corridor as she'd gone back to her room and had then fallen into a deep sleep, which he blamed entirely on the benign power of the inglenook. He'd dreamt of Eloise, but those dreams had been free of the nagging doubts and questions that had been bothering him ever since they'd met.

The instant chemistry between them was still challenging, in the face of all their differences. But he understood those differences a little better now, and Eloise had seemed to understand them too. There was a measure of relief in that, and maybe it would allow them to both concentrate on today's work at the Community Hospital.

'Should I go and wake Eloise?' Aunt Celeste asked, and Paul shook his head.

'She's coming. Just had a shower.'

'You know by the creaks in the floorboards, don't you?' Aunt Celeste smiled at him. 'Goodness only knows how these Tudor people managed anything in the way of intrigue. The floorboards must have given them away every time.'

Sam took note of the information, hiding his smile. No intrigue allowed, even if Eloise did seem to know her way around the creaks.

'They probably didn't creak quite so much when the house was built.' Paul leaned back in his seat. 'You don't like it?'

'I adore it, darling. Advanced warning of when you try to sneak up behind me...'

Sam's attention was distracted as Eloise walked into the kitchen, carrying an emerald-green hat that matched her sweater. When he smiled, she smiled back.

'How many hats do you have?' This was the third he'd counted in as many days.

'A woman can't have hats?' She shot him a look of good-natured defiance, which sent tingles down his spine. There was something about Eloise's defiance that really turned him on.

'I didn't say that.' He took the hat from her hand, putting it onto her head.

Eloise chuckled, pulling it down over her ears. 'Are we up for the hospital today?'

'Yes, and Paul's called Ted already. He's going to meet us with the motor sled, down by the road.' He handed the plate of toast he'd made for himself to Eloise and she picked a slice up, taking a bite.

'You're really going to wish you had a hat when we get to the sledding part of things…'

Last night's snowfall had been heavy, and even if the roads had been passable they would have had to dig their way to Sam's car. They set out along the driveway, struggling in the deep drifts.

Even that short journey was taxing, and by the time they neared the road Aunt Celeste was doubled over, tired out from lifting her feet in the deep snow. Paul was with her, trying to get her to walk just a few more steps, and she was shaking her head.

'You and Eloise go on ahead… I'll catch up, I just need a few moments.' She straightened a little when Sam came to help.

Eloise slid past him, taking Aunt Celeste's arm. 'We're not going anywhere without you.'

'Darling, that's very kind but…' Aunt Celeste protested, but Eloise was clearly not taking any arguments this morning. Sam wondered if she'd found a way to thank his aunt, for having stood by her.

'Look, it's not so deep up ahead.' Eloise pointed to the tree-lined entrance to the drive. 'Sam and I can move the worst of the snow away while you get your breath back.'

Aunt Celeste was a tough cookie, but she knew another strong woman when she saw her. And she knew that families didn't leave each other behind. She nodded, standing with Paul while Sam and Eloise scooped out a narrow path for her.

Eloise had been so eager to do anything she could to please when Sam had first met her. But her fierce protectiveness in taking Aunt Celeste's arm and walking with her to the end of the drive was different from that. Paul had noticed too, but he said nothing, watching the two of them with a smile.

When they reached the road, Sam could see a bulky motor sled at the bottom of the slope on the other side, and a dark-haired middle-aged man leaning against the side of it. He waved, and Eloise helped Aunt Celeste down the slope, bundling her into the front seat next to Ted.

It was a noisy, and very windy and cold, way to travel, but Ted's route across the undisturbed snow in the fields made short work of the journey. The motor sled drew up outside the hospital, next to the sweep of drive that had been cleared of snow to allow ambulances and cars to enter and leave. Eloise had been holding onto her hat, and now pulled it back down over her ears in a show of determination that was all hers, and made her look like a beguiling elf on a mission. Ted turned in his seat.

'I can wait. It doesn't look as if they've made much of a start on clearing the roads yet, and I might be able to get to places that the ambos can't.'

'What about the farm?' Paul asked.

'It'll be okay. All of the animals are fed and Claire's keeping an eye on things. She'll call if she needs me.'

'In that case, why don't you come inside, and we'll see what's happening?'

Ted produced a chain and padlock from under his

seat, and the motor sled was secured to a nearby tree. As they entered the hospital a blast of warm air greeted them, and Paul asked the receptionist to call Joe Parrish and tell them they were here.

It was all well organised. Joe handed Sam and Eloise a pair of scrubs each, and told them they'd be working together in the minor injuries department, which could expect to receive any severity of injury while the routes to the main hospital were blocked. Paul and Aunt Celeste were helping organise and lending their expertise where it was needed. Ted would be found a warm place to sit and some coffee, until the motor sled was needed. From the look of things he wouldn't be waiting long.

'Don't look at the queue...' Eloise joined him in the doorway to the waiting room, which was now crammed with people. He couldn't see who was a patient and who wasn't, and everyone seemed equally impatient to see a doctor.

'Yeah, I was just thinking that.' Sam turned away, following her to the overflow treatment area, which had now been readied for patients. There were triage nurses who would work out who needed to see someone most urgently; he didn't have to make those decisions. His time in A&E when he'd been training told him that he was part of a larger machine now.

They worked alongside each other, just a thin curtain separating them. Sam called to Eloise for help with a patient who had been in a car accident, and had multiple bruises and lacerations, and Eloise asked him to take over when a woman turned up with a young baby, saying that she couldn't get to her own doctor. After four hours of concentrated effort, they had fifteen minutes off to go and get a sandwich and something to drink from the canteen.

'What do you say we look now?' Sam stopped by the door to the waiting room as they walked back together. The flow of patients in the last hour had seemed to ease a little.

'Give me a minute to go hide in a corner.' She grinned at him. 'You can tell me lies if you think I can't take the truth.'

Eloise could take any amount of truth, and even though she hadn't told him everything last night, Sam understood why that was. Now, he was pinning all of his hopes for a friendship on the idea that they could turn their backs on the past, and start again. That felt risky, because new starts involved a great deal of trust. But right now, it seemed to be part of a process of looking forward, and not recklessly disregarding the lessons they'd learned.

He opened the door, looking into the waiting room, while Eloise leaned against the wall, her arms folded as if to emphasise the fact that she really *wasn't* looking.

'Not so bad. About a quarter full, and there's a man in one corner who's actually smiling.'

'Really?'

'Look for yourself…'

Eloise grinned. 'I'll take your word for it.' She looked round as Aunt Celeste hurried across the reception area towards them.

'Things seem to be under control here, so would you both be able to go out with Ted? We've had a call from a pub in Terringford. Someone's broken their leg and the village is completely cut off at the moment. Ted's not sure exactly how close he can get, but he thinks he can make it most of the way.'

Sam looked at Eloise and she nodded. 'Yeah, we'll go.'

'Great, thanks. Paul's sorting out splints and a stretcher, along with basic medical supplies, and Ted will be ready to go in five minutes. You can get a couple of hi-vis vests from the receptionist.' Aunt Celeste obviously had everything under control. 'Wrap up warm…'

CHAPTER SEVEN

THEY WALKED OUT to the motor sled, zipping up their jackets as they went. Sam could see Ted, stowing the medical equipment away under the seats, and soon they were skimming across the fields again, the wind biting at their faces. He'd completely lost any sense of where they were, or what direction they were going in, before they drew up at the side of a small stream, which was almost completely frozen over.

'I reckon this is as far as we can go.' Ted was surveying a small footbridge to their left. 'I can't get the sled up onto that bridge.'

'Where are we headed?' Sam asked, and Ted pointed to a cluster of buildings, about half a mile away. 'Right there. But the land dips in between here and there, and it looks as if the snow's drifted. Might be two or three feet deep in places. I can try going around by the road, but it's a fair way and it's generally easier keeping to the fields because there are fewer obstructions.'

'Seems as if it's going to be quicker to walk. What do you think, Sam?' Eloise asked.

'I'll take your word for it. You know the area better than I do. What's that, over there?' There seemed to be a caterpillar trail of people, heading through the snow towards them.

Eloise looked across at them, shading her eyes from the glare of the low sun. 'I think they're digging. If the guy we're going to see needs to go to the hospital, and the sled can't get to him, then we're going to have to get him to the sled.'

Ted nodded. 'When you get there, let them know I'll be on the other side of the footbridge. If they know of a way to get closer, give me a call, but I don't want to risk getting stuck somewhere.'

'Okay, will do. Shall we leave the stretcher here, or do you want to take it with us, Sam?'

'Let's leave it here and just take the medical bag. No point in carrying too much through the snow now if we can send someone back to get the stretcher when there's a path dug.'

They walked across the footbridge, sliding down the icy sheet that covered it on the far side. Once they were on solid ground, the first few hundred yards weren't too bad, but suddenly Eloise took a step and sunk down into the loose, powdery snow.

'Oh! Stay over that side, Sam, it's deep here.' The snow was already up to her knees, and she was still sinking gently. A shout echoed across from the men who were digging, and Sam saw two of them gesturing to keep to the left, where he'd been walking.

'Great. Telling us that a bit sooner might have been useful.' She raised her voice, yelling back to the men. 'Doctors!'

'Go that way!' one of the men yelled back, gesturing again to their left.

'Right then. We'll go left, shall we?' Eloise rolled her eyes, and Sam couldn't help smiling.

She pulled her hat down over her ears in a now familiar gesture. She'd sunk a bit further now, and was struggling to get out of the snow. Sam took a step towards her, and she waved him back.

'You're heavier than me so you'll sink faster.' She looked around, her gaze coming to rest on the bag he was carrying. 'How about detaching the strap and just sliding it over to me? I think I just need something to hang on to. I'm not stuck but I can't get any leverage.'

Sam bent down, unclipping the strap. Winding one end around his arm, he spun the other end across the surface of the snow towards her. Eloise reached out, catching hold of it.

'Got it? I'm going to try and pull you out. Tell me if you want me to stop.'

'Okay. Now's really good. I'm still sinking.'

As Sam pulled, Eloise dropped onto her stomach. Her legs slid out of the snow easily and she scrambled towards him. He hoped that she wasn't too wet, but she got to her feet seeming ready to press on.

'Thanks.' She was brushing snow off her jacket and waterproof trousers. 'I'm not going to do that again. It was no fun at all.'

It was hard going, and Sam could feel moisture seeping over the tops of his boots, but they made it. Eloise stopped for a moment to ask the men who were digging if there was a better way around for the Skidoo, and one of them shook his head.

'No, the road's pretty narrow, and it's partly blocked by a couple of abandoned cars. A one-seater sled could make it, but Ted's is too wide.'

'You're going to keep digging then? We're going to need to get our patient over to the sled.'

'Yeah, we've got more people coming. We'll get there.'

'Great. Thanks.'

Eloise's practicality and easy manner seemed to allow her an entrée into this rural community where everyone knew everyone else. It was easy to trust her professionally, and Sam was working less and less hard to trust her personally now. The group of men stood back to let them through and they hurried along the pathway that had already been dug from the back door of the pub. When they entered the main bar, it was empty.

'Hello! Doctors!' Eloise called out and a voice sounded from the other bar.

'Through here…'

The man was lying on one of the long upholstered benches, in a smaller snug bar. His shoe and sock had already been removed, and his trouser leg cut. From the look of his leg it was probably broken. A man and woman were with him and the man stepped forward to greet them.

'This is my pub. Kevin's taken a fall, and we brought him in here.'

'Where did he fall—outside in the snow?'

'No, he fell down the steps to the basement. I got the lads to carry him back up here and we made him as comfortable as we could.'

Understandable, but maybe not the best thing to do in the circumstances. Sam guessed she would have preferred to have seen the leg kept immobile as long as there were no immediate dangers in keeping Kevin where he was, but Eloise didn't press the point. Her disciplined use of her time was obvious—she gave no impression of rushing, but her questions were all to the point and about things that they needed to know.

'All right. One of our priorities is to find a way of getting him safely to the motor sled, so if you can find a few more volunteers to help the men who are already digging that would be great.'

She turned to Kevin, kneeling down beside him. 'Hi Kevin, I'm Eloise and this is Sam, we're both doctors. Just for the avoidance of any doubt, I can see that your leg must be hurting, but is there anywhere else that you feel pain?'

'No.'

'Good. Bump your head? What about your back— did you land on the base of your spine?'

She was calm and assured, getting as much information as she could in the shortest possible time. It was a little different from Sam's work—he might not always have as much time as he wanted to spend with his patients, but he had access to their records and could assess them in that context. Eloise was starting from scratch, and she was clearly very good at setting people at ease and inspiring confidence. Sam was confident enough in her to take a back seat role.

'All right, here's the one you've been waiting for. How much pain do you feel on a score of one to ten? One, you're feeling pretty good, and ten's the most pain you've ever felt.'

'Um… Don't know. Seven? And a half, probably.'

'Seven and a half. Ever broken a bone before?'

Kevin shook his head. 'I had appendicitis when I was a kid. I think that might have been a ten.'

'Ever had an allergic reaction before?'

'Feathers. They make me sneeze.'

'Oh. Okay. Hear that, Sam? No feathers.'

'Gotcha.'

Eloise left Sam to administer the analgesic and carry on with some basic checks, while she took a pad from her pocket, writing down the time and the details that Sam was calling out as he went. She was rubbing her leg and suddenly put the pad down, stripping off her waterproof trousers. Underneath there was a wet patch on one side of her jeans, which must be so cold by now that it hurt. Sam reached for the pad and Eloise went to stand by the radiator, rubbing her leg.

'Resting heart rate sixty beats a minute.' She was back and smiling as if nothing had happened. 'That's perfect, Kevin.'

Kevin grinned. 'I like to keep myself in shape. I do gym work twice a week.'

'Great. I'm afraid you might have to give that a rest for a while, but make sure you get back to it when you can. How old are you?'

'Twenty-two.'

'Got a girlfriend?' That meant that the next part of this was going to hurt.

'Nah.'

'Waiting for the right one to come along, eh?'

Kevin grinned suddenly. 'Yeah. There's someone I like, a girl at the gym. We go for coffee.'

Eloise nodded. 'Just getting to know her, then. It's nice to have someone who shares your interests, isn't it. This next part's going to hurt a bit, but we'll be as quick as we can. Just hang on in there, eh?'

She'd planted the idea of the girl that Kevin liked

in his head. Maybe he'd be a little braver for her, and maybe for Eloise. At this moment, Sam would have walked across hot coals for her.

Eloise examined the leg, stopping when Kevin cried out. 'Sorry about that. We're all good, nearly done.'

She was quick but careful. Kevin began to shift a little and Sam urged him to stay still, while Eloise kept going.

'All done.' She gave the lad a dazzling smile. 'You did great, and you can rest a bit now. Take a few deep breaths. Your leg's broken, as we thought, and we'll be putting a temporary splint on it, which will make you much more comfortable. Then we'll take you to the hospital. That's going to be a ride on a motor sled, I'm afraid, but we'll have you well strapped in and it won't take very long.'

'Ted's motor sled?' Kevin asked. 'I asked him if I could go for a ride on it once and he told me to sling my hook.'

'Well, he won't be doing that today. This one's all about getting you where you need to go.'

'Cool. Don't suppose I can drive it, can I…?'

'No, Kevin. I don't suppose you can. Particularly after the injection that Sam's just given you. How's it feeling now?'

'Better. More comfortable.'

She sorted through the bag, finding the splint that she wanted. Then she turned to Sam, murmuring quietly, 'It's definitely broken, I felt it move. Thankfully, carrying him up here doesn't seem to have made it any worse and I don't think it's misaligned. We'll have to be very careful when we put the leg into the splint, though. I'll lift it and you slip the splint underneath?'

'Yep. That's good.'

She turned to Kevin again. 'Nearly there now...'

When Sam walked out of the pub, he found that the village had been busy. Men, women, and even a few children were digging, and the path through the snow almost reached the Skidoo. He called Ted, asking him to get someone to bring the stretcher down and turned just as a snowball whizzed through the air, hitting him on the shoulder.

'Gotcha!' Eloise was almost doubled up with laughter, and Sam couldn't help but smile. Working seemed to bring out a sense of fun in her, an assurance, which made her even more difficult to resist.

'Not fair. Where's my warning?' He bent down, gathering up a handful of snow, but he was too slow. Eloise had ducked back into the doorway before he could pack the loose snow together. But as he drop-kicked the snowball into a shower of small pieces she popped back out again.

'Grants don't play fair, Sam. Didn't you know?'

Eloise was exhausted and aching by the time they got home. She'd spend half the afternoon in wet jeans, which had only dried out after they'd reached the warmth of the hospital, and she'd taken Kevin into the temporary A&E department to arrange for X-rays on his leg, before going back to work alongside Sam for another couple of hours.

Ted had already taken Gramps and Celeste home, and he returned just as it started to snow again, taking them back over fields that shone in the moonlight. As soon as the front door had closed behind them, Celeste hurried out of the kitchen, stripping them of their coats and shooing them into the sitting room. They flopped down at opposite ends of the long sofa, too tired to even speak.

'How do you think the party's going so far?' Sam was leaning back, staring at the ceiling, his feet stretched out towards the fire.

'Good. Perhaps we should do next Christmas in A&E.' Actually, Eloise had done last Christmas in A&E. Not with Sam, though.

'Too much. We should save this kind of celebration for the really big events.'

'You've got a point. We'll see if we can book the kid who tried to bite me. He really made my evening.'

Sam turned his head towards her. 'Somebody tried to bite you? Did he break the skin?'

'No, but he had fantastic muscle tone in his jaw. Didn't you hear me yowling on the other side of the curtain?'

'Come to think of it, yes, I do recall it. I thought you were torturing Kevin again.'

'No, Kevin and I are cool. He asked me if I wanted to go for coffee with him.'

Sam's grin surfaced suddenly and he put his hand to his heart in a gesture of mock dismay. 'You were going to go for coffee without me? I'm devastated.'

Eloise laughed. 'Don't be jealous. I told Kevin that coffee assignations are special and that he should keep them for the young lady he likes at the gym.'

As soon as the words had left her lips, Eloise knew she'd said the wrong thing. The humour died in his eyes, and he wiped his hand across his face.

'I'm not jealous. I'm sorry if it came across that way. You can go for coffee with whoever you like.'

Actually, she couldn't and Sam knew that just as well as she did. A twenty-two-year-old patient, with enough analgesics in his system to be legally intoxicated, was way off-limits. But that wasn't really the point. Sam had spent much of his childhood watching his father trying to coerce his mother back into a relationship. He'd seen controlling behaviour and probably jealousy and he'd rejected that in his own life, to the point that he felt he had to apologise if a little harmless flirting went in the wrong direction.

And Sam was the last person who should feel that way. He was a kind man, who'd shown her nothing but respect. She'd made a mistake and this was one that she could own.

'Sam, I guess you might know what real jealousy looks like, and I shouldn't have joked about it. I didn't think and it's you that deserves an apology, not me. I'm really sorry.'

'Don't...' He stopped himself, starting again. 'Actually, I really appreciate you saying that. My father was a very jealous man, and it's a bit of a sore point.'

There was more to say. But no need to say it right now, because Sam had reached out, propping his arm on the cushions at the back of the sofa. When Eloise did the same their fingertips barely touched, but the contact meant everything. They'd broken through one piece of the barrier that separated them.

'Eloise... Sam...' Celeste's voice drifted through from the kitchen. 'Dinner's ready!'

Sam smiled, shaking his head at his aunt's timing. He leaned forward and when he brushed a kiss against her cheek Eloise felt exhilaration run through her veins like fire. She'd made no mistake—Sam felt just the same as she did. But whatever they decided to do about it was going to have to wait.

CHAPTER EIGHT

IT HAD BEEN a good evening, not a great evening, and Sam had been left with an inevitable feeling of unfinished business. After a leisurely meal, followed by an hour around the kitchen table talking, Paul had gone up to Eloise's bedroom with her to investigate why the radiator wasn't giving out any heat. Aunt Celeste had gathered up her book and her glasses and made for her bedroom, and Sam had had little option but to go to his.

That was okay. It was hard to leave the smouldering glances that had passed between him and Eloise behind for the night, but they had an understanding now. Their relationship might turn into any one of a thousand different things but, whatever came next, they could be honest with each other.

The following morning, Ted met them by the main road again and dropped them off at the hospital, leaving them to join other farmers in helping to clear the roads that led to villages that had been cut off. The local council was clearing the major roads, and by tomorrow they should be able to make the journey by car. But the Community Hospital was still under pressure, struggling to reach everyone who was already under their care and to deal with the flood of injuries that had been caused by the icy weather conditions.

They'd worked for three hours and the crowd in the waiting room was beginning to thin out a little. Just as Sam was wondering whether they might be able to take ten minutes for coffee, Aunt Celeste came hurrying into the treatment area.

'Eloise, Sam… We have a patient coming in, from one of the houses that's just a little way along the road. There's an ambulance team there now, and he's had a myocardial infarction. Can you get ready to receive him?'

'There's no way of getting him across to the main hospital?' Eloise frowned. The treatment room was well equipped, but Sam knew that it wasn't the best place for emergency cases like this.

'It'll take far too long by road, even if they can make it. We've put a call in for the air ambulance, but they're very busy and it may be anything up to an hour before they can get to us.'

Eloise nodded. 'What facilities do we have here? I know there's a defibrillator, and an ECG. Do we have an echocardiogram?'

'Yes, and the sonographer is on her way down. Blood tests can obviously be taken here, but they're sent over to the lab in the main hospital.'

Eloise puffed out a breath. 'Okay, so no results for any blood tests we do. We'll take the patient's history, diagnose and medicate, and…hope that what we have here is enough.'

It wasn't an ideal situation by any stretch of the imagination. Eloise was used to having the resources of a large hospital at her disposal, and she was obviously frustrated. But when the ambulance crew arrived, she turned to their patient with a bright smile on her face. Sam was relieved to see that he was conscious and even managed to return her smile.

'Hello there. My name's Eloise and I'm a doctor. You're Terry... Sixty-two years old... Do you have anyone with you, Terry?'

'No, I called my brother and his wife when I first started to feel ill but they can't get here.'

'Yeah, this snow's making getting around difficult isn't it.' Eloise was flipping through the notes that the ambulance crew had left. 'Don't you worry, we'll be taking good care of you and if you give me your brother's number I'll make sure he knows what's going on. You're having pain in your chest and upper arm, and you feel sick and breathless.'

'Yes, Doctor. Am I going to the main hospital?'

'We're getting some transport arranged for you right now, just in case you need it. But we'll be treating you here for the time being.' Eloise gave Terry another bright smile, as if nothing was bothering her about the arrangement. It was important to keep heart patients as calm as possible, and Sam reckoned her smile was better than any sedative.

'Okay, I need...' Eloise turned and found that there was no nurse standing behind her waiting for instructions. 'I'll go and get some medication to make you feel more comfortable and my colleague will be taking good care of you in the meantime.'

She turned to Sam, the smile falling from her face to leave an intent look. 'Could you see what you can get in the way of history, do another ECG, and get the echocardiogram started whenever it arrives?'

Sam nodded. Turning to Terry, he introduced himself and started to go through the list of questions that needed to be asked.

Half an hour later, Terry had been given blood thinners and analgesics to alleviate the pain in his chest, and Eloise had co-opted one of the nurses to sit with him and administer oxygen when it was needed. There were ECGs from the ambulance crew, and after he'd arrived here, tucked into his notes, and Sam had managed to get hold of his GP to get a full history. The sonographer was carrying out an echocardiogram when Paul arrived, wanting an update.

'From the look of the ECG, it's an NSTEMI.' Eloise and Sam had stepped away from Terry's bedside and Eloise handed the ECG printout to Paul. 'See, there's a T wave inversion with no progression to the Q wave.'

That was relatively good news. An NSTEMI was a partial blockage of the coronary artery, and less serious than a full blockage, although it was still considered a medical emergency.

Paul nodded. 'Okay, I've been on to the air ambulance and they'll be another half an hour. Can you keep him stable?'

'We're going to have to. His medical history isn't very encouraging, hypertension and high cholesterol, and there's a family history of heart disease. He doesn't take much exercise and he's a little overweight.'

'Has his GP addressed any of this?' Paul looked at Sam.

'She said that she's been trying.' Sam hadn't been much impressed with the GP's monitoring of Terry's health, but knew from experience that any doctor relied on patients turning up for appointments and doing as they were asked. 'I've made a note, and hopefully the hospital can get to the root of the problem and make sure that the situation's resolved.'

'I'll speak to one of my contacts over there and see what she can do.'

'Is there anyone in the medical profession you *don't* know, Gramps? If so I'll hunt them down and introduce them to you.'

Paul shot her an amused look. 'It gets things done, Eloise. I'm sure that Sam would agree with me.'

Sam held up his hands in a gesture of surrender. 'Don't involve me in this. Particularly since I'm not sure whether this is a professional or family disagreement.'

'Bit of both probably.' Eloise shrugged. 'And it would be great if you *could* get someone to find out what's happening and address the issue, Gramps.'

'My pleasure—' Paul smiled at her '—Dr Grant.'

Eloise was trying not to show it, but she was worried. She'd done every test that she could, and had written a very full set of notes. Terry was responding to medication and when the air ambulance arrived he was in a stable condition. But as Sam was seeing his next patient off she popped her head around the curtain that separated them, suddenly all smiles. The consultant she'd been speaking to at the main hospital had called to say that Terry had arrived, and thanked her for her thorough work in a difficult situation.

'It's made me realise how lucky I am to work in a large hospital where everything's on site. How on earth do you coordinate everything, Sam?'

'I have contacts…' Sam chuckled as she shot him a

look that could have sliced through concrete. 'Are you ready for lunch?'

'Ten minutes. I've just got to finish up with a dislocated finger...'

The small cafeteria was bursting with people, and Eloise made a beeline for a table that had just become empty, leaving Sam in the queue still with their sandwiches and drinks. When he squeezed past busy tables, avoiding coats that had slipped onto the floor, she was sitting staring at a local paper that someone had left behind on the table.

'What's that?' Whatever it was, it appeared that it was far more interesting than the sandwich and coffee that Eloise had raced here to get.

She lowered the paper. When Sam tried to take it from her she held onto it and he had to give it a little tug before she'd let go.

It was actually a very nice picture—Eloise and him, outside the Grand Elk pub yesterday, her arm curved still from throwing a snowball, and his raised to shield himself. Sam assumed that it was the headline that had prompted the annoyed look on Eloise's face.

Doctors in snowball fight outside Grand Elk pub, where man lies injured!

His first thought was to shrug it off, the way he always did with anything that angered him. Sam's second thought was to get in touch with the paper and ask for a copy of the photograph, because it had caught Eloise's smile and the joyous way that she'd moved when she'd taken one moment to break the pressure of the afternoon. Neither of those were going to help.

'That's not the whole story, is it?'

'No, but it's what everyone's going to think.'

And what everyone thought had already hurt her. Sam considered what Eloise's next course of action might be, and somehow the anger and hurt didn't seem quite so inappropriate when he felt it on her behalf.

'We're not going to apologise for this.'

'We? I'm the one throwing the snowball.'

'I'm sure that's a smile on my face, isn't it?' Sam squinted at the picture. The resolution of the image didn't make it easy to see, but he remembered smiling.

He scanned the short article. It briefly alluded to a man having been taken to hospital, and then added insult to injury by asking readers to send in their own pictures of people taking time off to enjoy the snow.

'It's just annoying. There are people here working really hard, staying overnight away from their families so that they can keep the place running. And they don't even mention that. They pick a picture of me horsing around in the snow.'

'That's not your fault. The paper's misrepresented things.' A thought occurred to him. 'Do you suppose that Joe Parrish has seen this? He might issue a statement.'

'And say what? He wasn't there, and the camera doesn't lie.'

In this instance it had. 'Can you do something for me? Let me sort this out.'

Eloise shook her head, taking the paper from him and folding it in half, then throwing it onto the seat beside her. 'Let it go, Sam. It's irritating, but it doesn't really matter. Let's just rise above it.'

All the things he'd risen above, over the years. His father's behaviour, the way that Alice had left him. He'd be giddy from altitude sickness before too long...

'Okay. We'll rise above it. Will you give me your permission to say what I think, though?'

He saw the look in her eyes soften as she smiled. 'Always say what you think, Sam.'

A shiver ran down his spine. That sounded a lot like trust.

'You're sure?'

'Eat first.' She pointed to his sandwich. 'And drink. We're back on duty in half an hour.'

Part one of his plan was to call Aunt Celeste, and get her to mention the article to Joe. Sam had no doubt that her talent for convincing everyone of her own point of view would ensure that Eloise wasn't questioned about the article.

Part two had been slightly more difficult. But the application of a little judicious outrage while chatting to one of the nurses did the trick. By mid-afternoon, pretty much everyone that they were working with was talking about the 'nonsense' in the paper, and he even heard one of Eloise's patients telling her how unfair it all was, particularly since she was a volunteer.

'What are you doing, Sam?' She popped her head around the curtain as soon as she'd dealt with the man. 'This isn't a propaganda war, you know.'

'I just mentioned it in passing.' He gave her an innocent look.

Suddenly she smiled. It was like the sun breaking

through clouds on a rainy day, and Sam couldn't help smiling back.

'What am I going to do with you, Sam?'

Anything she liked. He resisted the temptation to tell her so. 'Doesn't the Grant family stick up for their team?'

'Not all of them. It appears the Douglas family is currently running rings around us on that score.' She gave him a wry smile, disappearing back behind the curtain.

Eloise felt it, even if she chose to dismiss it. And if Sam was going a little over the top about defending her on this, then maybe it was because he could do nothing about the other issues she'd faced with her extended family.

He couldn't do anything about the issues he'd faced with his father either. Or the way he felt he had to measure every one of his actions against that, striving to be different. But this he could do something about. And now he'd made his mind up, he wouldn't let Eloise down.

Sam turned to the woman who was being shown to his cubicle by one of the volunteers. She was cradling her arm and he could see bruises and swelling around her wrist. Another fall, if he wasn't much mistaken.

'Hello, I'm Sam and I'm a doctor. Sorry you've had to wait so long…'

'Where did Sam go?' Eloise met up with Gramps and Celeste a couple of hours after her shift was supposed to have finished. They'd worked through the backlog of patients, and the night staff seemed to have everything under control. Sam had been right there with her, and then suddenly he hadn't. She'd looked for him but couldn't find him anywhere.

'He'll be along later.' Gramps propelled her out of the hospital, waving to Ted, who had just drawn up in the motor sled.

'How's he going to be along later, if we leave him behind?' Eloise had an idea that Sam was off somewhere, trying to correct a newspaper article that was annoying but in the scheme of things really didn't matter so much. She felt a little guilty about that, because he really should be on his way home for something to eat.

'He'll manage.' Celeste seemed to have some inkling of what was going on and put her arm around Eloise's shoulders, perhaps for comfort and maybe just to make sure she didn't escape and go to find Sam. 'And there's no point in trying to stop him. Sam gets it into his head to do something, and he does it.'

Eloise wondered how Celeste would take it if she mentioned that Sam had said much the same about his aunt. Probably not badly—they seemed close enough to have made that clear already.

'I heard you mentioned that newspaper article to Joe Parrish. I really appreciate it…' There was no need, but it meant a lot that Celeste had stood up for her like that.

'I told him the truth, that's all.' Even so, Celeste looked pleased that Eloise mentioned it. 'I don't like it when people are given a hard time for something they didn't do.'

'Well, strictly speaking, I did do it…'

'Oh, you Grants, you're so literal about things!' Celeste shot her a grimace. 'I saw the article and the clear implication was that you and Sam were messing around all day and ignoring people who needed you. That's not fair, is it, Paul?'

Gramps chuckled. 'No, darling.'

'Don't you *no darling* me, as if you're just agreeing in order to keep the peace, Paul.' Celeste smiled up at Gramps.

'No, my sweet. I've already told you what I think about it. Weren't you listening…?'

The two of them walked to the motor sled, teasing each other amiably. They made Eloise feel around a thousand years old sometimes, seemingly free of the burdens that life brought and madly in love with each other. There was no way that Eloise could ever see herself doing that again, however much she wanted to when she felt the warmth of Sam's gaze.

But Sam and his gaze were nowhere in evidence. Eloise sat in the kitchen, playing with her food for a while, and when Celeste decided to have an early night and finish her book off in bed, Gramps said he'd join her. Eloise hovered by the window, watching as it began to snow again outside.

Then she saw him, a dark figure trudging along the drive, his hat pulled down around his ears and his hands in his pockets. She resisted the impulse to run to the door for a full thirty seconds, and then walked out into the hallway, opening the front door to find Sam kicking the snow off his boots in the porch.

'You must be freezing!' Not the way she really wanted to greet him. A kiss to welcome him home would have been better.

He grinned at her. 'It's chilly out there. Just started snowing again.'

'How far have you walked?' That wasn't the way she wanted to greet him either.

'I got a lift most of the way.' He took off his gloves and coat, rubbing his hands together to warm them.

'Come and warm up. I'll heat some soup for you and there's half a shepherd's pie in the fridge.' Eloise chivvied him into the kitchen, moving him out of the way of the cast iron range cooker so she could heat the soup. He was standing close, leaning against the oven as if gravitating towards the heat.

'Any other questions?'

'No. But whatever you've done, you didn't really need to...'

She'd said the wrong thing. Eloise had meant it as a thank-you for going that extra mile for her, doing more than was necessary in defending her. But Sam suddenly stiffened, walking over to the other side of the kitchen to stare out of the window. Suddenly the room felt very cold.

It was impossible to let this go, and just leave things as they were. If explaining made everything worse, then so be it. Eloise followed him, nudging him gently to get his attention, which seemed to be focused on the falling snow outside.

'I meant that you didn't need to do whatever it is you've done, but I really appreciate that you walked that extra mile for me. Particularly since you were walking it in the snow...'

The ghost of a smile flickered on his face. 'Even if I was fuming all the way?'

Sam had an issue with anger. Through all of the

ups and downs of the weekend, this was the first time she'd heard him express even the slightest exasperation with anything, and she could understand why. His father must have been an angry man.

'Being indignant on my behalf makes me like it even better. Just as long as you weren't *too* indignant with the newspaper people.'

His eyebrows shot up, and the look on his face was almost one of guilt. 'Did Aunt Celeste tell you?'

'No, your secret was safe with her. But it's not much of a leap. You weren't at the hospital when we left and the newspaper's office isn't too far from there.'

She heard the soup begin to bubble ferociously. Eloise grabbed his hand, not willing to end this conversation just yet, and Sam followed her across the room. She pulled the pot off the hotplate, turning her attention back on him.

'So did you pound on their door, demanding to be let in?'

He was smiling now. 'No, I gave them a call and asked if anyone was in the office, because I wanted to drop in and correct an error. I had coffee with a young man whose job description seems to be dealing with whatever happens after six o'clock.'

'And you didn't put snow down the back of his neck?' She could tease him a little now.

'No, I didn't. I may have felt like doing so when I arrived…'

'That's okay. As long as you didn't actually do it. And I really do appreciate you having gone to such lengths for me.'

'Even if you don't need it?'

'It's the thought that counts and I reckon I needed

that. I *was* considering apologising but… I think I may be done with saying sorry. Unless I actually am sorry, that is.'

He gave a smiling nod. 'That's not a bad idea. You don't have anything to be sorry for.'

'Not for the snowball. For the other thing.'

'You mean calling a halt to your marriage? Can I ask you something?'

'Go ahead.' Eloise almost wished that he would insist on knowing what had happened. It would be an end to all of her conflicting feelings about telling him. But Sam had told her she didn't need to explain, and that had been the end of it.

'Did you love him?'

'When I said I'd marry him I did. When I left I wasn't sure, but what I did know was that I had no respect for him.'

'And now?'

'No. Not even a little bit.' How could she? Michael had taken his revenge on her, letting everyone turn up at the church when he knew full well that she wasn't going to be there. When *he'd* told her to go.

'That's all that matters then. If you don't love him then you don't need another reason.'

'How do you leave these things behind? Do you know, Sam?' He'd been hurt too.

'If I did, I'd tell you. I don't.'

'Too bad.' She turned her mouth down. 'I was hoping there might be a magic formula.'

Maybe her magic formula was standing right here, and she just didn't see. She didn't need someone to forgive her, because the only forgiveness that really mattered was the one that she could find for herself.

She needed someone that she could trust, and Eloise could see herself trusting Sam. In a sudden impulse she shifted against him, winding her arms around his neck.

That burning gaze of his. She could get lost in it, feeling its warmth sear her. At this moment, there was nothing she wouldn't do to have him close.

She felt Sam's arms tighten around her, and the hard strength of his body against hers. His lips touched hers, holding back to make the moment last, in an exquisite blend of longing and temptation.

And then tenderness gave way to passion and he kissed her. Eloise felt Sam's body move against her, saw the way his eyes darkened suddenly, and she knew that he was all hers.

'We can't do this, Sam. Not even if we really want to.' There might be a time when she could trust him, even one where she could trust herself. But the future wasn't here yet. Maybe it wouldn't ever be.

'Yeah, I know. But you make me believe it's possible, Eloise.'

'You make me believe it too.'

'Then…could we try it one more time? Just one more kiss?'

'Because staying in this beautiful house, being snowed in together is so romantic?' Eloise wasn't entirely sure that she wanted Sam to sweep her off her feet like this. It was what Michael had done, using the charm that he'd later used against her.

'No, I want you to know exactly what you're doing. Kissing me in a cold kitchen, when we're both tired from a day's work.'

What Sam wanted seemed far more romantic than

anything that Michael could have dreamed up. Two cool heads and the commonplace, turned into magic by being together.

'Another kiss would be my pleasure, Sam…'

CHAPTER NINE

IT HAD BEEN hard to go to his room alone. Not having any condoms to hand wouldn't have been a deal-breaker, because Sam was sure that they could still find things to do together. But he wasn't going to think about that. Wanting Eloise was terrifying, because he'd never wanted a woman as much, and certainly never after having known her for such a short time. It was the kind of sure knowledge that nothing would be right until they were together that he'd seen in his father's actions.

Sam had woken before dawn, looking out of the window to find that another couple of inches of snow had fallen. That wouldn't be enough to block the roads that were already open, but the conditions would be icy. He got dressed, hoping that the creak of the stairs wouldn't wake everyone up, and slipped out of the house.

He'd roughly cleared almost half of the driveway when Eloise appeared, her arms wrapped around her as she ran towards him, the thick sweater she was wearing obviously doing nothing to keep her warm.

'Brr… It's cold this morning. Come inside. I've made you some breakfast.'

Sam didn't need to be asked twice. A little exercise, to work off the nerves about whether his conversation at the newspaper office was going to come to anything, had seemed like a good idea, but now he was getting cold and tired. He followed Eloise inside, knocking the snow from his boots before seeking the warmth of the kitchen.

Paul and Aunt Celeste were already up, and there was a place set for him at the table. Eloise set a plate down in front of him, containing bacon, eggs and tomatoes with a pile of hash browns.

'That's just what I need. Thank you.' Sam noticed that Eloise's tablet was lying on the table.

'It's there. I've seen it.' Eloise was grinning at him, and he realised that she was one step ahead of him.

'I didn't tell Eloise to look.' Aunt Celeste was keen to protest her innocence. 'But you can't stop an intelligent woman from working things out. It goes against the grain.'

He nodded, starting to tuck into his breakfast. 'All right. So what did it say?'

'It's a lovely piece.' She sat down opposite him, beaming. 'Right at the top of their news pages on the web.'

'It's called *"We'd like to set the record straight"*,' Aunt Celeste added approvingly. 'It'll be published in next week's paper as well.'

'Good. I'm going to finish my breakfast and read it through. Just to make sure they put in everything I asked them to.'

Eloise winced. 'You had a list?'

'Aide memoire.'

No one looked particularly convinced of that. But

Sam didn't want to share any more. If he couldn't go back and put the past right, then maybe he had some say over the future. Last night, when he'd held Eloise close and kissed her and she'd kissed him back, he'd seen a tantalising possibility of what that future might be.

But right now he had to stop thinking about that. When breakfast was finished, they left Aunt Celeste and Paul to clear away and he and Eloise went out to finish clearing the drive. That, and working alongside her at the Community Hospital, was the kind of sharing that was real and able to provide solid foundations of trust that they could build on.

At lunchtime the stream of patients began to dry up, and they had a whole hour's break. Sam was looking forward to spending the time sitting with Eloise and drinking coffee when one of the other volunteers, a nurse who had left her two small children with her husband to go back and help at the hospital, came up with a better idea. Lottie's mischievous sense of humour had kept them all going when it seemed that they'd never cope. And her announcements in the waiting room had become legendary, making patients feel that they were part of a group effort with their doctors, and that they would all be seen in order, even if there was a long wait.

'Snowball fight!'

Eloise clapped her hand across her mouth, almost dancing with glee. 'That's so wrong…!'

'Yes, isn't it. Whatever would the papers say?'

'I could call them and let them know…' Sam took his phone from his pocket.

'No! They have to track the story down for themselves, Sam.' Eloise was laughing. 'There's no fun in it if they don't.'

Paul and Aunt Celeste had caught wind of the enterprise and trooped out with them onto the open land behind the hospital.

'Douglas versus Grant, eh?' Aunt Eloise took Sam's arm. 'I'm claiming the best throwing arm.'

'Oh, really?' Eloise pulled a face of mock outrage. 'Watch out for your nose, Sam...'

He chuckled, covering his nose with his hand, and Aunt Eloise gave Paul a very sportsmanlike hug before he was sent off to join Eloise and the other three people on their team.

'Right now, Sam, I can't throw as well as you, particularly since I had that frozen shoulder. So I'll keep you going with snowballs, and you just keep throwing.'

Sam raised his eyebrows. 'Don't you think that you should exercise the shoulder a bit?'

'Well, of course, and I do.' Aunt Celeste rolled her eyes. 'But we're talking about family honour.'

'You should have thought about that when you went and got engaged to a Grant.' Sam grinned at her.

'Nonsense. Paul and I fight all the time, we both rather like it. *You* might think about it, Sam...'

Had Aunt Celeste's knowing eye seen what was happening between him and Eloise? It was just as well that she hadn't asked outright, because Sam had no way of explaining it, or how he felt about it. But right now that didn't matter, because Eloise and Paul were lobbing snowballs in their direction, and Aunt Celeste had already dodged a particularly well aimed one. After the stress and hard work of the last couple of days, this was fun.

* * *

At two o'clock the doctors in the temporary A&E department started to compete for patients. Then at three the announcement came. The hospital was enormously grateful for everything that the volunteers had done in helping to keep things going. Now that the roads were open again, and the main hospital was accessible to ambulances and patients, they should go home, secure in the knowledge that they'd done a fantastic job.

Paul seemed restless, energised by the early mornings and the gruelling workload. Sam could identify with that, they'd been doctors with a mission that had suddenly been whipped out from under them. He couldn't regret that there were no patients left to treat, but adrenaline was still buzzing in his veins.

'What about the pictures?' Paul nudged Aunt Celeste. 'That film we wanted to see is still on.'

'Is it? That's a good idea, we really shouldn't miss it. How do you both feel about subtitles?' Aunt Celeste turned to Sam and Eloise.

'Um....' Eloise looked up at Sam. She clearly felt the same as he did, that Paul and Aunt Celeste's taste in films was great, but that she wanted something that didn't require sitting still for two hours.

'Perhaps we'll give that one a miss. Catch it later in London.' Sam ignored the knowing look that passed between Aunt Celeste and Paul. Whatever they thought they knew was probably far less complicated than the facts and it was best to leave the explanations until he and Eloise knew what to explain.

'You could give Sam the tour,' Paul suggested, smiling at Eloise.

'The tour?' Sam had already been shown around the house.

'Yes, Gramps and I worked out a tour, as a fun thing to do for the house party. It takes in all of the hidden things that no one ever sees about the house.'

'Sounds interesting.'

'It is, very...' Aunt Celeste seemed to approve of the idea. 'The house has been around for so long that it's gathered up a lot of fascinating little foibles. There's a priest's hole...'

'I didn't know there was a priest's hole. Where?' The tour was beginning to sound more interesting by the minute, particularly since his tour guide was so remarkably beautiful when she was brimming with excitement.

'Ah!' Eloise tapped the side of her nose. 'Come with me and I'll show you.'

It was the perfect excuse. Paul and Aunt Celeste had decided to go and check out the new Indian restaurant in town after an early showing of the film they wanted to see, and said that they wouldn't be home until nine o'clock. That gave Sam five hours alone with Eloise, in a house that had more spare bedrooms to explore than they could ever possibly need.

The house was chilly, which seemed to be its normal state during cold weather, but Eloise led him to the kitchen, which was always an island of warmth. She heated up some soup, from a seemingly inexhaustible supply in the freezer, and showed him the back of the pantry door.

'How old is some of this graffiti?' He ran his finger across the clear acrylic sheet that protected the door.

'We don't know about most of it. Some of it's pretty ageless.' Eloise pointed out a heart, scratched deeply into the wood, with two initials. 'Whoever *"EW"* and *"JP"* were, I hope they had a nice life together.'

So did Sam. Both he and Eloise knew that things didn't always work out the way you'd planned, but it suddenly seemed important that they had for these two anonymous lovers.

'But look—this one.' She pointed to a fainter inscription and Sam narrowed his eyes, trying to make it out.

'*"I left my leg..."* What's that...?'

'*"At Waterloo."* And his heart is here.'

'Ah, yes.' Sam could see now that this was what the wobbly script was saying. 'So that must be almost two hundred years old.'

Eloise nodded. 'This one's a bit more recent. It was written by Gramps' mother, at the end of the war. My great-grandmother.'

'*"VE Day, 8th May 1945. May God bless the peace."*' Sam grinned. 'It's all here, isn't it? Love, injury and loss...hope for the future.'

'Yes, that's what makes it so fascinating. We're not so very different from the people who wrote these. I'm here too. I remember Gramps taking the cover off and telling us that it was important we were there.'

A little lower down on the door, Paul's initials were there, along with those of his first wife. Underneath, three more groups of linked initials.

'That's my parents, John and Elizabeth Grant. Gramps helped me do my initials underneath, when I was eight years old. And look, there's Gramps again, with Celeste.'

Sam nodded. 'I remember Aunt Celeste telling me

about that, when Paul first asked her to marry him. She said that she was very touched that he wanted to include her on the list of family names, but I didn't realise that it was on the back of a door.'

Eloise laughed. 'That's the thing about this house. It can be very grand, but it's the little things that mean the most. Come and see the priest's hole.'

She led him into the sitting room, and challenged him to find it. After taking the most obvious route, and rapping his knuckles on the wood panelling, Sam looked for secret levers in the fireplace and peered behind the bookcases.

'Okay, I give up.'

'You're sure? You haven't been near it yet…'

Sam looked around the room. The steps that led up to the first-floor gallery were a possibility, but the space beneath them was concealed by wood panelling and Sam couldn't find any openings that a man might slip through.

'You're getting warmer…' Eloise teased him, and Sam walked up the steps, knocking the stair risers as he went.

'I can't work it out.'

Eloise chuckled. 'You had the right idea. Here, let me show you.'

She joined him on the stairs, and ran her fingers along the edge of one of the wooden stair treads. A click sounded, as if a lever had been released, and Eloise swung the two top steps upwards to reveal a small cavity. Sam looked inside.

'That's no more than a couple of square feet. No-one could fit in there.'

Eloise laughed. 'Which is exactly what you're supposed to think. It's a hiding place for valuables, but at the back…

She pushed at the wooden beams at the back of the compartment and they swung to one side. Reaching in she flipped a switch and a light came on revealing a brick lined hidey-hole, extending downwards under the stairs.

'If anyone did work out how to lift the stairs they'd find the smaller cavity and most likely stop there. Even if they did investigate further, the beams can be secured from the inside so they won't move.'

Sam bent down to look. 'Clever. And if you removed the wood panelling under the stairs, you'd just see a brick wall behind it.'

'Yes, that's right.'

'And this is the only one?'

'We've looked and we can't find any others—but then they're very cleverly concealed. Celeste had an idea of doing some kind of sonar survey, and Gramps is looking into how that might work, so maybe they'll find a few more.'

Sam took another look inside, wondering what it would be like to have to hide away in here. As he reached in to switch off the light he felt his hand snag painfully on something.

'Ow.' When he looked he saw blood. 'I think I found a nail.'

Eloise took his hand, inspecting the wound. 'Probably rusty if I know this place. Are you up to date on your tetanus jabs? I should have warned you that you need to be if you go exploring here.'

'I'll be fine. Although if you've got a plaster… Before I pass out from loss of blood.' Eloise had been squeezing the small cut and it had started to bleed more freely.

'Just making sure there's nothing in it.' She let go of his hand, and Sam followed her to the kitchen.

'Hold it under the tap.'

'That's what I'm about to do.' Two doctors fighting over one small cut had the potential to get ugly. Sam rinsed his finger, watching as Eloise reached up to one of the high cupboards, punching the combination lock before flipping open the door.

The cupboard was large and very full. Eloise was stretching to get a good view of the upper shelf and Sam turned the tap off, walking over to see if he could make out its contents any better.

'That's one of the things I like about Paul. He doesn't stint on medical supplies.'

'No, but I wish he'd organise them a bit better. *He* knows where everything is, but no one else can find anything.'

Sam reached up, moving some of the contents of the shelf to one side to get a better view. As he did so, two boxes became dislodged and fell out of the cupboard, and Eloise caught them.

'Ah, here we are. This one's plasters…' She fell silent and Sam was suddenly aware that he'd been standing very close to her. The other box contained condoms.

She dropped it suddenly, as if it would burn her, turning round quickly to face him. 'We don't need to worry about those, do we.' She opened the box of plasters, taking out the largest one.

No, they didn't. Sam held out his hand, and she somehow managed to apply the plaster without touching his skin. But her scent still caressed his senses, calling to him that any decision could be made at any time.

'Thanks. That's great.' It was one thing to know that the roads were clear now, and that Sam could get into his car and drive to find a chemist's shop that was open. It was quite another to have a box of condoms fall out of the cupboard. Sam had never felt that the fates had any sway over his life, but even he had to admit it was an awkward coincidence.

This was crazy. He didn't need to hide behind practicalities to control his own actions and desires.

Eloise picked up the box, turning it in her hand. When she came to the side that displayed a use-by date she was still again, and Sam couldn't help but notice that it was over a year away.

'I don't know what these are doing here anyway.' She stuffed the box back into the cupboard, slamming it shut, and Sam heard the lock engage. As if that made any difference. Eloise could open the cupboard back up any time she wanted...

He tried to tear his mind away from all of the possibilities that seemed to be leaving no room for anything else. 'So what's next on the tour?'

She was silent for a moment. 'The desk that Gramps put in Celeste's study has three secret compartments.'

'Three?'

'Yes. And the wall at the back of the property is part Roman. Gramps has extended it but he used contrasting stonework that complemented the Roman part, but also made it obvious that it was different.'

'Fascinating.' Eloise was fascinating. Her hair, her eyes. Her skin, and the way that her cheeks were flushed in the warmth of the kitchen. He could take or leave both the Roman wall and Paul's extension of it.

'It's cold outside, though. And if you wanted to stay here…?' Eloise took a step towards him. 'This place feels like home to me, Sam, and decisions I make here can't be left behind or thrown away. If you feel differently, then I won't mention it again.'

Right now, Eloise was the only truth that he could rely on. The only thing that seemed constant in a world that had thrown this challenge at him when he'd least expected it. Eloise wanted him and the sheer joy of that dissolved all of his fears. Sam didn't know how he would come to terms with wanting her as much as he did, but that seemed like an obstacle that could be surmounted now.

'Paul and Celeste won't be back for another four hours.' He knew that, almost to the minute, because he'd been counting the moments he had to spend alone in her company and valuing each one. 'There's nothing I'd like more than to spend that time in getting to know you better.'

Still, he couldn't make the first move. Consent wasn't a concept that Sam had ever struggled with. It was perfectly simple. There were no smudged lines, no difficulties in knowing whether a woman had made the decision that she wanted him. But his father's continual disregard of his mother's wishes had made Sam even more careful, wanting even more for it to be spoken in a way that gave no room for doubt.

Eloise was motionless for a moment. Maybe she'd give up on him and turn away, and he'd have to deal with that.

'Sam, I want you to take me upstairs and make love to me. Is that clear enough for you?'

She'd put two and two together and she understood. And he knew now too. In one swift movement he lifted her off her feet, perching her on the kitchen worktop. 'Give me the combination...'

Eloise was smiling now. 'Make me.'

He kissed her, feeling her body mould against his. Exquisite. Sam wondered how long it would take before she gave him the number, and hoped that she might hold out a little longer. He slid one hand around her back, covering her breast with the other. Even though she was wearing a thick sweater, and no doubt a couple more layers of clothes underneath, he heard her cry out.

'More, Sam.'

'You want to play this game?' He could do that. Pulling her hard against his body, so that she could feel just how much he wanted her, he slipped his hand under her sweater.

'Oh! You'll have to do better than that, though...'

He whispered exactly how much more he could do, and she wriggled against him. The feeling stoked the fire in his veins, and he described another scenario in slightly more detail.

'Sam! Three-seven-four-eight.'

'You're sure, now?' He held her close, planting kisses on her neck, finally managing to free his hand from the layers of clothes under her sweater, so that he could touch her skin. He let his fingers trail to the clasp on her bra, and then forward, to skim the softest skin of all.

'Three-seven-four-eight, Sam!' Her arms were clasped around his neck, and suddenly she let him go, pushing him away from her a little. He felt her hands

move to the front of his jeans and almost choked with
the intensity of his reaction to her touch.

'Do it!' She knew that she had the better of him, and
her voice took on a commanding tone. Sam reached
above her head, punching the combination into the lock
and hooking the box of condoms out of the cupboard.
Eloise took them from him, pushing him away as she
slid forwards, planting her feet back on the floor.

'Come upstairs. Right now.'

CHAPTER TEN

SAM WASN'T INDECISIVE. It just seemed that her decisions, the things that she wanted, were more important to him. Eloise could see why. He'd grown up in a house where his father had consistently ignored his mother's wishes. This waiting, the hesitation were just proof that Sam was an honest man who she could respect, and she wanted him all the more for it.

She led him along the gallery to her own bedroom, wondering what he'd make of the high four-poster bed and hoping that it might give his imagination something to work with. As she opened the door, she felt chilly air on her face.

'Uh. The radiator's not working again. I thought that Gramps had fixed it. Perhaps we should go to yours…'

He sat down on the bed. 'It's okay. I'll keep you warm.'

This was a big step for both of them. They were pulled together by powerful chemistry, despite all their caution over having been hurt. But, right now, it seemed that all they really needed to know was that they'd keep each other safe and warm. She walked over to him and he wrapped his arms around her.

That slow pace of his. The way he stretched out

every moment into something delightful. Eloise had been with men who liked to start slow before, but Sam was so exquisitely good at it.

'I love to play a little first...' she whispered in his ear. 'Just so you know.'

He chuckled. 'I love the way you tell me exactly what you want. And I like to play too.'

It was a smooth, slow ascent to fever pitch. When Sam undressed her, he didn't rush, letting her feel the chill air on her skin, along with the heat of his body. If sex was all about different kinds of sensation, and Eloise reckoned that it was, then Sam was the man who could make the most of every one of the thrills running through her body.

Under the thick, heavy bedcovers he did things to her that made her blood begin to boil. Finally she called time on it.

'Sam... Sam, are you ready?'

She felt his breath, warm against her skin as he sighed. If he had any clue about how she was feeling, and she hadn't held back in telling him, it would be satisfaction at a job well done.

'I'm ready. You?' He rolled her over onto her back.

'More than you can ever imagine...'

He reached for the condoms. After the sharp longing and lazy pleasures of the last couple of hours, the delicious languor was broken. She felt his weight on her, and a sudden, warm feeling blooming through her as her body reacted to his and took him inside.

Sam was no longer hesitant, no longer needing any of her words to guide him. He'd found out exactly what she liked, and he seemed intent on hearing only incoherent sounds of pleasure. No one could resist this for very long, and she felt tears prick at the sides of her eyes as the long-awaited release began to build.

And then it happened. There were no words, because that would have been impossible. But Eloise could feel his every reaction, and Sam had suddenly broken free of that thoughtful, exquisite rhythm of his and surrendered to the moment. She heard him catch his breath, and knew that they were finally alone together, cut free from the past.

Just a little longer...

But it was too much to be able to control or to keep. Eloise felt Sam's body begin to stiffen and he held her tight as her orgasm drove everything else away, dragging him over the edge with her.

The intensity of it almost dazed her. Sharp aftershocks ran through her body, and Sam shifted, curling his arms around her. Words really didn't cover this. Nothing did. There had been no thought, just sheer emotion.

Had he felt it too? Eloise had no doubt that he had. Would he admit to it, though?

'Are you okay?'

That was a start. Whether he knew it or not, he'd just acknowledged that they'd gone beyond the bounds of what either of them had expected.

'Much better than okay. What did you do to me, Sam?'

'I was just wondering what you'd done to me...'

'I didn't...'

The truth started to seep in. Sam was a wonderful lover, he watched and listened, and did everything to please her. But they'd both glimpsed something more than that, something un-thought and instinctive. She hadn't done anything to make it happen, and neither had he.

'This is what happens between us, then. You and me together?' She wanted more. Now that she'd seen the place where nothing existed but Sam, she wanted it back.

'I suppose...' Sam's brow creased in thought. 'Maybe not every time.'

He didn't sound very convinced of that, and neither was Eloise. But this was their first time together, and they were only just getting to know each other. If she wanted to concentrate on something, then she should concentrate on the knowledge that Sam was the best lover she'd ever had. They probably weren't ready yet, for the brief moments of complete freedom they'd experienced. That would come in time.

'I really want to find out.'

Sam kissed her. 'Yes. Me too.'

He hadn't noticed that Eloise had set an alarm, but Sam was glad she had. They were dozing comfortably in her bed, warm as toast under the thick, heavy quilt, and Sam had forgotten all about Paul and Aunt Celeste coming home at nine. So, apparently, had Eloise, because she jumped to attention, sitting upright in the bed.

'Uh.' She rubbed her eyes. 'It's okay, we have half an hour...'

'Unless they're early,' Sam teased.

'They won't be. The film ends when it ends, and Gramps doesn't believe in rushing good food.' She frowned. 'Although the restaurant could turn out to be terrible, which might speed up their timetable.'

'Relax. What's the worst that could happen? They come home right now and find us in bed together. You refuse to apologise, and your grandfather locks you in your room and then takes me down to his study and shoots me.'

Eloise chuckled. 'He wouldn't do that. He really likes you.'

'He's really going to like the things you just did to me?' Sam raised an eyebrow and received a play punch in response.

'You did some things to me as well. I'm going to go and take a shower and wash off the evidence.' She got out of bed, and Sam watched as she skittered across the room, towards the oak door that led to the en-suite bathroom.

She was gorgeous. Mesmerising. They had a meeting of minds that had made the meeting of their bodies beyond anything that Sam could have imagined. If he *had* been able to imagine this, then he would have baulked at the loss of control. The raw intimacy that had lasted for only a moment, but had been far stronger than his resolve to always think about his actions and how they might affect his partner.

But there was no going back on something that had rocked his world so thoroughly. He had to own it, and have the courage to find out where it was going to go. Because the one thing that he'd been trying to avoid had happened, and Sam was committed.

They'd tidied up downstairs, closing the priest's hole and washing up the pan and mugs of half-drunk soup. The box of condoms was safely back in the medicine cabinet, and Aunt Celeste and Paul were fifteen minutes late.

And they'd come to a decision. An impromptu afternoon spent together was one thing, but creeping to Eloise's room tonight, when they were both guests in the house, was quite another. This might be a leap of faith that Sam wasn't entirely ready to make, but he had to think of Eloise now too. She wanted to tell Paul, needed to be honest with him, and so that was what Sam wanted as well.

'Hello you two.' Aunt Celeste stopped short at the kitchen door, sensing that something was up. 'What are you doing, sitting in here?'

'Nothing!' Eloise blurted out the word. That was essentially true. Sam had taken his hand from her shoulder, and was no longer leaning towards her to catch her gaze.

'Oh. Well, fair enough. The film was wonderful, wasn't it, Paul?'

'Yes, you must try and catch it down in London. I think we'll be going back to the restaurant again as well, eh, Celeste.'

'Definitely. The food was very tasty.' Celeste hung her coat on the back of one of the kitchen chairs. 'I could do with some hot chocolate now.'

'I'll make it.' Eloise seemed to have lost her nerve completely and went to stand, but Sam reached out, brushing her arm. She gave him a little nod, and sat back down again.

Aunt Celeste gave them a querying look and headed for the range, grabbing one of the saucepans from the shelf on her way. Paul sat down at the table opposite them, folding his hands together, and Eloise looked up at him.

'What's up, Eloise?'

'There is something I want to tell you…'

Paul had clearly worked that out. He nodded, and Sam decided that since Eloise had already committed to this conversation, he should step in and help.

'Eloise and I have decided we'd like to see a little more of each other, when we go back to London.' Everyone ignored the clatter of the saucepan as Aunt Celeste dropped it onto the flagstones.

'See a little more of each other? You mean professionally?' Paul asked, his gaze on Eloise, obviously trying to gauge her reaction. Sam reached out, resting his hand on the back of Eloise's chair in an attempt to suggest an alternative, and Eloise straightened suddenly.

'No, darling! Professionally, my foot! They're going to be seeing a little more of each other *personally*,' Aunt Celeste interjected. 'I dare say they've been spending the afternoon seeing each other personally.'

Sam closed his eyes. Aunt Celeste's no-nonsense approach to life was usually a joy. Sometimes it wasn't. He jumped when Eloise suddenly spoke up for herself.

'Yes. We have.'

'Ah!' Paul scratched his head, seeming perplexed. 'And you're happy about that?'

'Yes, Gramps.'

That was good to hear. If he'd thought for one moment that Eloise had any regrets about this afternoon he would have had to order himself out of the house in deep disgrace, before Paul got the chance to do it for him.

'Well, that's a piece of nice news, isn't it, Paul?' Aunt

Celeste picked up the saucepan, inspecting it for dents. 'There's something about the Douglases and the Grants, isn't there? When we're not at each other's throats, we get on very well indeed.'

Paul chuckled amiably. 'It seems so. Hurry up with the hot chocolate, darling, and we'll drink a toast to that.'

The radiator in Eloise's room seemed to be mysteriously working again, and was warming the place up now. Sam sat in the armchair by the window, looking at the bed, the covers pulled straight now to give no clue as to what had happened there.

Paul had beckoned Eloise into the sitting room, and she'd whispered to him to wait for her here before going to talk to her grandfather. Sam had little doubt that the conversation had something to do with his and Eloise's relationship and, even though Paul had seemed quite happy with the news, there was still that slight unease that came with knowing that people were talking about him.

He heard Aunt Celeste's footsteps on the stairs and then those of Eloise and Paul, still talking quietly. Then the door opened and she walked over to him.

'Hey you.' She smiled, sitting down on his knee.

'You're looking thoughtful. Are you okay?' Sam curled his arms around her shoulders and suddenly the world seemed right again.

'Yes, I am. Gramps wanted to ask me if I was happy.'

'I don't blame him. I was wondering the same thing.'

Eloise leaned up, kissing his cheek. 'You make me happy, Sam. If I seem to be fighting it a little, it's because I can't believe my luck in having met you.'

Yeah. He was fighting it too. But when they were together like this, it didn't seem so much of a battle.

'You told Paul that?'

'I told him that this last year hasn't been easy, but that I really want to leave it behind. And he's really pleased for us.'

The question that had been bothering Sam just had to be asked. It *could* be asked when he was holding her, because Eloise gave him the strength to try to believe in the future.

'What would you have done if he hadn't approved? If Aunt Celeste hadn't.'

She pursed her lips. 'I would have told you that you couldn't come to my room tonight. It's Gramps' house, after all, and we're guests. I would have told *him* that I was leaving with you and that I'd stay with you, because that's my choice to make.'

'Good answer.' That was exactly what Sam had wanted to hear. That Eloise was able to break free from the past and give him some of the security that he craved, in a relationship that was already fraught with uncertainty.

'You were thinking I might give you up, just because someone told me to? Where's your faith in me, Sam?'

'I have faith. I can see how hard it might be to lose practically everyone over one relationship, and then see the one person who's stood by you disapprove of another.'

'Gramps trusts me and I should have trusted him a bit more in return.' Her eyes danced mischievously and she shifted in his arms, feeling under her sweater to pull something from the pocket of her skirt.

'He gave you those?' Sam chuckled when he saw the packet of condoms.

'Just in case we hadn't been able to get to the shops. I told him that if he looked inside he'd see that there were already some missing.'

Fair enough. At least Eloise had thought to mention that they were being sensible. Sam wondered whether it would be appropriate to have a man-to-man chat with Paul and tell him that he'd throw himself out of the nearest window rather than harm her.

'And what did he say?'

'He said he was glad that we were being responsible. Sometimes he thinks I'm still seventeen, it's really rather sweet of him.' She snuggled against Sam's chest. 'Are you going to be sweet to me now?'

'Would you like me to be?'

'Yes, I would. And I'd like to return the favour as well. Find out all of the things that you like.'

That was a little more challenging. Sam wasn't altogether comfortable about asking for what he wanted, because his father had done that so vociferously, and expected his mother to just give in to his every whim.

'I like your pleasure. Very much.' He kissed her and thoughts of his dysfunctional family dissolved suddenly. 'Let me make tonight all about you.'

Sam was amazing. Finding a man who could make a night all about her—who wouldn't want that? And he'd clearly enjoyed it, generous in his own lovemaking and finding his passion in the way that he carefully attended to hers.

There was more, and they both knew it now. Eloise could wait, until Sam felt confident enough to tell her what *he* wanted.

Waking up wasn't an orderly process any more.

Tasting the dregs of a dream, and realising that it *was* only a dream and the real world was still there. Dozing a little and then deciding it was time to get out of bed.

With Sam, it was more a matter of sitting bolt upright in bed and realising that they'd stayed too long in each other's embrace and should be somewhere else. Or just deciding that they could face the music later, because the only urgency seemed to be the one that she felt in his arms.

Eloise had checked out the upstairs hallway, and Sam had gone back to his room to shower and dress. He'd be leaving for London today, and she was already missing him. Already wondering what would happen when she followed him, tomorrow. When she went downstairs, she found a note on the kitchen table in Celeste's handwriting.

The hospital doesn't need us and it's a beautiful morning, so we've gone out for a walk. xx

Short and to the point. Eloise smiled. Celeste had probably decided that she and Sam might like to have breakfast alone—Gramps wouldn't have thought of that on his own—but she wasn't going to make a thing of it. She and Gramps were probably out somewhere making snowmen. Eloise called up to Sam, and he appeared at the top of the stairs.

'We've got the place to ourselves. Gramps and Celeste have gone out for a walk, so we can canoodle over breakfast.'

'That's nice of them.' He joined her at the bottom of the stairs. 'Have they called the hospital?'

'They must have done. Celeste says we're not needed

there. We could have some toast and coffee and go out and find them if you like. They won't have gone far.'

'Nah.' He bent to kiss her. 'This winter we can concentrate on sitting around the fire and sweet nothings. Next year's soon enough for building snowmen.'

'You think so?' Firelight and sweet nothings *did* sound a lot more attractive at the moment. But the mention of even a tomorrow seemed huge at the moment. 'There's going to be a next year?'

He looked down at her thoughtfully. 'I honestly can't say, but I hope so. We'll have to wait and see.'

This was all so new. It all felt so delicious and yet so very precarious. Trusting in anything felt as if it was a dangerous game, but the sweet chemistry between them, the way that Sam seemed to understand her made hope agonisingly easy.

She didn't get the chance to tell him how much she wanted next year because there was the sound of voices at the front door, and when Sam went to open it Gramps and Celeste were kicking snow from their boots in the porch.

'Ah, you're up.' Celeste's face was pink and cheery. 'Do you want to come and build a snowman? I can't believe we don't have one yet.'

'No...' Sam swung round, grinning at her as they both spoke together and then turned to Celeste.

'Thanks for the offer, but we'll stay in the warm. I think it's my turn to make breakfast, isn't it...?'

CHAPTER ELEVEN

SAM HAD PACKED his case and gone out to put it into the car. He'd kissed Celeste and shaken Gramps' hand, thanking them again and congratulating them on a weekend that hadn't quite turned out as planned, but was all the better for it. Then Gramps and Celeste disappeared into the kitchen, leaving Eloise to put on her coat and walk with him to his car, past the four new snowmen that stood at the front of the house. Gramps and Celeste had insisted they come outside and Sam had made an impressive snowman with broad shoulders and pieces of coal for its eyes. Eloise had made a smaller one, donating her second favourite hat for it to wear.

Sam leant back against the door of the car, putting his arm around her.

'I won't be kissing any snowmen while you're gone. Not even the handsome ones.' Eloise bit her tongue. She knew that Sam didn't like even the smallest insinuation that he might be jealous, but on this occasion he didn't seem to mind.

'Especially not handsome ones.' He even made a joke of it, pulling her close and resting his cheek against the top of her head. 'I'm working tomorrow. You're driving back to London in the afternoon?'

'Yes, that's the plan.'

'Well…if you feel like dropping round to my place in the evening… Or if it's too soon…'

Sam's diffidence again. He always gave her a choice, and sometimes that sounded as if he didn't really care. Eloise was learning that he was just doing what the past had taught him.

'I'd love to. Only… I don't know your address.'

He laughed suddenly. 'Come to think of it, I don't know yours either. I'll text you when I get home, and you can text me back with yours.'

'Do that.' A text from Sam, letting her know that he was home safe, was something else to look forward to. She stretched up, kissing him, and watched as he got into his car and drove away.

When she walked back to the house, Celeste was in the kitchen making tea. A banging from upstairs told Eloise that Gramps was probably using a mallet on one of the radiators to restore it to working order.

'We're going to have to do something about those old radiators. Paul insists he knows what he's doing, but I've told him that a heating system is nothing like the human body and we should call a plumber. Maybe summertime's best though.'

Eloise sat down at the table. 'Yes, you don't want people taking your heating system apart in this weather. I expect they're just full of air, or sludge or something, and Gramps is just moving it around with all that banging.'

'Yes, probably.' Celeste put a cup of tea down in

front of her and sat down. 'There's something I want
to say to you, Eloise.'

Sam. A shiver of unease crawled up Eloise's spine.
She tried to hold onto the warmth, hold onto all the
optimism, but it seemed that Sam had taken that with
him, along with the rest of his luggage.

'What is it?' She hardly dared ask. It would be easy
enough to duck the conversation. A muffled curse had
sounded from upstairs and she could always pretend
to go and see whether Gramps was all right. He obviously was, because the banging had started up again.

But if Sam had left nothing else, he'd left a measure of courage behind him, and she could at least do
him the honour of listening to what Celeste had to say.

'It wasn't my place, but I told Sam about the business with Michael, when we were driving down here. I
didn't mean to interfere, and personally I think you're
better off without him and did the right thing...' Celeste puffed out a breath.

'Sam told me that you were planning a pincer movement, to save me from anyone who decided to give me
a hard time.'

'Did he? Well, it's kind of him to assume that I had
something that sophisticated up my sleeve. But Sam's
a good man and he means a very great deal to me. I
know he'd be furious if he thought that someone was
being bullied and I'd kept quiet about it.'

'I appreciate it, Celeste, thank you. It was a kind
gesture, and...some of the decisions I've made haven't
been exactly good ones.'

'It's absolutely up to you who you marry, and what
you choose to say about it. Paul tells me that he said
much the same to you.'

'Yes, he did. Maybe I shouldn't have sworn Gramps to silence. I appreciate the way you've stood up for me...'

Celeste shot her a quizzical look. 'You think Paul told me what to think? He did, of course, but I'd already come to my own conclusions. I don't know if you remember, but your wedding was the first time that I was his official plus one. I was keeping my mouth shut and my eyes skinned in case any of the Grants decided to come at me with a hatchet.'

Eloise laughed. Celeste just loved to play the old rivalry up a bit. 'I remember. We were all dying to catch a glimpse of you and I told one of the ushers to seat you and Gramps by the aisle, so I could see you from there.'

'Well, sometimes you can see things a little more clearly from the outside of a group of people, and it seemed to me that this Michael character was far too keen on telling a long story and getting everyone's sympathy. Most people aren't that charming when they're as heartbroken and innocent as he purported to be. When you came home, and you were clearly very upset about everything, and completely at a loss, I reckoned I knew who was in the right.'

Eloise reached for Celeste's hands. 'I don't know what Gramps has done to deserve you but, whatever it was, I'm really glad it worked. Thank you.'

Celeste chuckled. 'I'm glad that whatever I did to deserve Paul worked too. Even if he has lured me away to creaks in the night and heating that only works sometimes.'

'There's one place in the house that's always warm. It's my secret thinking place, and I don't think Gramps even knows I go there. Would you like to see it?'

The look in Celeste's eyes told Eloise that she knew exactly how this was meant. 'Thank you, darling. I'd love to.'

Eloise got to her feet, leading Celeste to the Great Hall.

One long night, and a very busy day, hadn't taken the edge off Sam's longing. He wanted to see Eloise more than he could say, and also rather more than he ought to. He trusted her, but it was still hard trying to be the man that she deserved. Someone who would love her and never hurt her.

He would find a way. Eloise had told him that she wanted their lovemaking to be about him as well as her, and in the brief moments that thought deserted him he'd found something precious. Something that had transcended anything he'd ever done before. He had to do what he thought was right, though.

But he could text her, and they'd spent an hour talking to each other last night. And Eloise would be arriving back in London this evening and driving straight to his place.

His phone rang and one look at the display made him turn the corners of his mouth down. This was the one night that he didn't want the evening receptionist at the surgery to contact him.

'Hey there, Maria. What's up?'

'I'm *really* sorry, Sam. Mrs Cornelius has called, and she was crying... I expect it's just a repeat of the Christmas Tree Incident...'

Mrs Cornelius hadn't called since then, apart from ringing to thank Sam for sending such a nice woman round, and telling him that she was going to try out a community centre that she'd recommended. Sam wasn't so sure that this was nothing.

'That's okay. She wants to see me?'

'She asked for you. I can speak to Dr Chowdhary instead.'

'He's got more than enough on his plate already with the evening surgery.' The snow was never as deep in London as in other parts of the country, but the heat of the city meant that snow melted and then froze as ice. There were still plenty of patients with weather-related injuries to deal with. 'I'll go.'

Sam made for the front door, grabbing his coat and putting everything that was set out on the kitchen counter back in the fridge on the way. He texted Eloise to tell her that he'd been called away to a patient and would be back as soon as he could. She would understand.

She *would* understand, wouldn't she? He twisted the spare door key from his keyring, ready to slip it into its hiding place for Eloise to let herself in. And then he heard the lift doors open and saw Eloise, staring at her phone.

'No…! Tonight of all nights…' She turned the corners of her mouth down in disappointment.

'I'm so sorry.' Sam was upset too, and trying not to show it.

'Can't be helped.' She smiled suddenly, the cocktail of every kind of emotion leaving Sam unsure of how to respond. 'Where are you going? I can come with you if you like.'

'Mrs Cornelius—the Christmas Tree lady. But don't you want to wait in the flat? You can check things out while I'm gone.'

Eloise rolled her eyes. 'The only thing I want to check out is *you*, Sam.'

The lift doors began to close and she waved her hand impatiently across the sensor to open them again. Then she reached forward, grabbing the front of his jacket and pulling him into the lift.

'Come along. Don't keep her waiting...'

No, he shouldn't keep Mrs Cornelius waiting, but the time it took the lift to creak down the five floors to the basement car park was all his. When she pulled him close, his conflicting emotions lent a demanding edge to his kiss and he drew back.

'Don't keep *me* waiting, Sam.' She murmured the words. He kissed her again, feeling the thrill of his own demands couple with the urgency of hers.

The lift jolted to a halt too soon. Taking hold of her hand, he hurried to his car, wondering what had just happened. Why Eloise was the only woman he'd ever met who spurred such desire in him, and how she seemed to take pleasure in that.

'I'... I'm disappointed too. A little cross, even...' He ventured the suggestion as he flipped the remote to unlock the car.

'I know.' She gave him a luminous smile that made Sam's heart lurch in his chest and got into the passenger seat.

There were three sets of traffic lights between his flat and Mrs Cornelius's. Sam knew that because the lights had been against them on two occasions and, instead of drumming his fingers on the steering wheel, he'd turned for a glimpse of that smiling connection between them before he put the car back into gear, ready to drive.

Mrs Cornelius lived on the top floor of a small block of flats and was a long time answering the door. Eloise turned, resting her ear against it.

'I can't hear anyone moving around.' She pressed the bell again.

'Maybe a neighbour has the key. Or, if the worst comes to the worst, I have a crowbar in the boot of the car...'

'Wait.' Eloise bobbed down, looking through the letterbox. 'I can see her feet. She's on her way...'

Slowly. It was another minute before Mrs Cornelius opened the door, which was longer than it took Sam to make a diagnosis. When he glanced at Eloise, she nodded her agreement.

'Hello, Mrs Cornelius. It's Sam, remember me?' He stepped inside, taking Mrs Cornelius's arm, in case she was unsteady on her feet. 'And this is Eloise, she's a doctor too.'

'Two of you. Am I that ill?' Mrs Cornelius's speech was slurred, but she could still speak. That was good, because all of the other signs, her drooping lip and one hand hanging uselessly at her side, indicated that she'd had a stroke.

Eloise gave her a scintillating smile. 'No, you're not that ill. Just that important.'

She stood back, watching, as Sam helped Mrs Cornelius into the sitting room. Everything she did, the way she moved. Eloise was storing everything away in her head, getting a complete picture of which parts of Mrs Cornelius's brain had been affected.

And Mrs Cornelius was watching too, her bright

blue eyes fixed on Eloise's red coat and hat as Sam sat her carefully down on the sofa.

'I'll call an ambulance. You see if you can find out a bit more...'

Eloise nodded. Bending down in front of Mrs Cornelius, she took her hand. 'This is a bit scary, isn't it. But we're going to make sure that you're okay. Is it all right if I take you through a couple of things, to check out how you're feeling?'

Mrs Cornelius nodded. 'I like your hat...'

'Thank you.' Eloise chuckled, taking off the hat and putting it in Mrs Cornelius's lap. 'I sewed a white fur bobble onto it, because I made it for Christmas. It's really soft...'

Mrs Cornelius's hand moved to the hat, probably just as Eloise had intended. Sam turned away, dialling the number for the emergency services. By the time he'd got through, Eloise already had some of the information he needed.

'She says she's been feeling like this for about an hour and a half. She made dinner for herself and sat down and ate it. Then her next-door neighbour popped in...what time was that, Joy? About five o'clock?' She glanced at Mrs Cornelius, who nodded.

'Okay, I'll go and check.' It was important to know what time the stroke had started to take hold, because clot busters might be a treatment option when Mrs Cornelius got to the hospital. Sam relayed the information to the emergency operator, and went to knock next door to see if he could find the neighbour who had seen her.

He struck lucky on the first door. The young woman who answered had been in to see whether Mrs Cornelius wanted a lift to the shops at the weekend, and she confirmed that she'd seemed fine and was showing none of the symptoms that Sam asked about.

'She'll have to go to the hospital?'

'Yes, we've called an ambulance and it's on its way.'

'I'll go with her.' The woman called over her shoulder, 'Odette, it's Mrs Cornelius. From what the doctor says she's had a stroke and needs to go to the hospital. I'm going to go with her...'

Sam hadn't actually said anything about a stroke, but most people knew the symptoms and he guessed that his line of questioning made it pretty obvious. He went back to Mrs Cornelius's flat, telling the neighbour to knock when she was ready.

Eloise got to her feet, her gaze still on Mrs Cornelius as she spoke to Sam. 'She has obvious facial weakness, and she can't raise her right arm at all. Her speech is a little slurred but she's able to form the words, and I gave her a pen and paper and she wrote her name and address down.'

'Good. I've spoken to the neighbour and she says that she was fine at five, no symptoms then. She says she'll go to the hospital with her. The ambulance is on its way, they reckon fifteen minutes.'

'Great. What's the neighbour's name?'

'No idea.'

Eloise gave him a grin. 'Okay, I'll manage.'

She squatted back down in front of Mrs Cornelius, who was stroking the bobble on her hat, the other hand lying useless in her lap.

'Joy, Sam's been next door to talk to your neighbour. He didn't get her name...'

'Odette and Frankie.' Mrs Cornelius supplied the

information, which no doubt went into Eloise's mental notes straight away.

'Frankie, then. She called to Odette,' Sam added.

'All right, so we're pretty sure you're going to need to go to the hospital, to get some treatment. Frankie says she'd like to go with you—would you like that?'

'Yes… Yes, I'd like Frankie to come with me. Does Sam know what's wrong with me?'

Since Eloise had done most of the diagnostic work, Sam reckoned that she would be allowed to feel a little indignant. But her smile never wavered.

'Yes, he does. And you know that Sam's a great doctor, right? He doesn't miss anything, so you called the right person to come and see you.'

Mrs Cornelius nodded, tears welling in her eyes and falling down her cheeks. She tried to wipe them away with her hand, and Eloise produced a clean tissue from her handbag.

'All right, my love. It's all right.' She gently wiped Mrs Cornelius's face and then hugged her, in a gesture that was completely non-standard in any rule book he'd ever seen, but nonetheless immensely effective.

By the time the ambulance arrived, Sam had called the surgery and had a set of notes and Mrs Cornelius's medical history to pass on to the paramedic. Frankie was sitting next to her on the sofa, holding her hand. He saw Eloise put her hat onto Mrs Cornelius's head as the ambulance crew got ready to go, telling her that she couldn't go out without something to keep her head warm.

They watched as the ambulance drew away and then Eloise took his arm. 'I think she's going to be okay, Sam. She has a good chance. I've seen people come into A&E who are a lot worse than this, and who recover well.'

He narrowed his eyes. 'And how would you know that? I thought that A&E was a matter of doing your best for people and moving on.'

She shot him an innocent look. 'Following up, to gauge the effectiveness of our treatment, is an integral part of the process, I'll have you know.'

'Of course.' Sam smiled down at her. 'Along with the giving of hats.'

Eloise aimed a play punch at his arm. 'I like to maintain patients' spirits when they're in an emergency situation, whenever I can. And I've got loads of hats. I can always knit another one.'

'You knit?' Sam knew exactly how to give Eloise pleasure, but he had to admit that he knew very little else about her.

'Yes, it's a great way to relax in the evening. Sitting down with my needles in front of the fire.'

'Don't let me stop you, then. If you want to go home and get started on a replacement...'

'And let you eat alone?' She plucked a supermarket sticker from the sleeve of his coat, that must have transferred when he was putting everything back into the fridge and gone unnoticed. 'Free range steak. Very nice.'

'It's about the only thing I can cook.' He grinned down at her.

'Since Celeste tells me you can't cook *anything* that doesn't either go in the oven or the microwave, then that's a lot better than I was expecting.'

'Oh, so you've been interrogating Aunt Celeste, have you?'

'Yep. Twenty-seventh of July.'

'Correct. Anything else?'

'No, that's it. I know your birthday and that you can't cook. I actually don't even know how old you are.'

'Thirty-five. You?'

'Thirty-two. See, this getting-to-know-you process is really quite painless.'

Sam hoped so. They'd shared so much, but so little, before tumbling headlong into an affair. They couldn't go back now. They just had to trust in the connection that had sparked between them, right from the start.

'So...' He unlocked the car, opening the passenger door for her. 'I'm offering you the chance to come home with me and find out a bit more about me. And warm your ears, of course.'

'I accept. Particularly the ear warming part...'

CHAPTER TWELVE

SAM'S TRANSFORMATION OF the Great Hall hadn't been a chance stroke of luck. He had an eye for interiors, and his flat was gorgeous. Part of a block built in the nineteen-twenties, he'd echoed the theme of the curved windows and Art Deco fireplaces with light fittings and other accessories of the same style. But he hadn't stuck slavishly to the theme, he'd just added furniture that complemented the space, and in breaking all of the rules he'd made something that was both stylish and all his own. His solid oak bedroom suite would have been at home in any modern setting, but the clean lines complemented the ornate fireguard that stood in front of a cast iron fireplace.

'This is beautiful, Sam.' She sat down on the bed, finding that it was very comfortable too. 'My decorating style is more whatever fits in the car.'

He chuckled. 'That works. Feel free to try out the bed any time you like.'

'I was wondering if you'd like me to try out your cooker first.'

'Do you mind?'

'No, I love cooking and I don't do enough of it, living on my own. You can watch and learn. I also like

eating, so I reckon this is an investment in my future.'
Eloise took his hand, pulling him to sit down next to
her on the bed.

He held her hand between his, staring down at it.
'Is this going too fast, Eloise?'

It *did* all seem to have happened at the speed of
light. They'd been stuck in the snow, with nothing of
their real lives to hold on to, but still they'd connected,
both physically and emotionally. They'd laughed at
each other's jokes, and seen things through each other's eyes. Sam understood her, and she felt that she
understood him.

'Maybe. But I'm going to stick with it, because I've
never had anything like this happen to me before. I
can't let go of you now, Sam, just because it's happened so quickly.'

He smiled suddenly. 'I can't let go of you either.'

'And tomorrow evening you can come to my place,
and move the furniture around a bit if you like, I'll
learn something from you. It would be really boring
if we found that we were just the same, wouldn't it?'

He lifted her hand to his lips, kissing it. 'I won't
move a thing, Eloise. It'll be perfect, just as you are.'

The last three weeks had been amazing. During the
week, there wasn't much time for anything other than
a couple of hours' relaxation and then tumbling into
bed together, but they'd made the most of it. They'd
talked, picked books to read from each other's shelves,
listened to each other's music. She'd seen photographs
of when Sam was little, although the expected ones of
a young child with his father seemed to be missing,
and Eloise had shown him hers.

The weekends were different. Two days to explore all of the things they loved about London. Sam took her to the National Gallery, and his knowledge about art and paintings made everything seem to come alive in a way that paint on canvas never had before. Eloise took him to her favourite markets, knitting him a hat to keep him warm as they browsed the stalls. They went to the cinema and tried different restaurants. Eloise gritted her teeth and climbed to the top of Tower Bridge with him, but couldn't hide her dizziness when she looked down through the glass-floored walkways. Sam had to admit that he never ate fish, after going to a sushi bar to meet with a group of Eloise's friends. It was as if life was once more beginning to circle them with the protective shield of everyday checks and balances.

He'd given her so much, and now she was going to ask for the one thing that he'd held back from giving her. It was Friday evening, and they had the weekend ahead of them. Now was the time to take another step in their relationship.

'Sam, I want to talk to you. About sex.'

'That's a great subject to start the weekend off with. Shall we take this into the bedroom?' He took a couple of glasses from the kitchen cupboard and reached for the bottle of wine he'd just taken out of the refrigerator.

'No. Let's talk here.' Eloise sat down at the kitchen table. She'd thought carefully about this, and decided that a serious conversation about sex was best had out of the bedroom. And probably not in the sitting room either, where comfortable chairs and the sofa had already provided them with temptation that hadn't been resisted.

'Okay.' Sam frowned, putting the bottle and glasses aside and sitting down. 'Do we have a problem?'

'No, I love every moment of the time we spend together. In and out of bed.'

'I love it too. There's no reason why we can't love it a little more.' He seemed tense now, choosing his words carefully. Eloise had hoped that the conversation might be a little easier than this was shaping up to be.

'Yes, and it's nothing bad, Sam.' She reached for his hand and held it tight. 'You're the lover I've always wanted, someone who cares about what I'm feeling and what I want…'

'I'm sensing there's a *but* coming.' That tenderness that she loved so much showed in his face. 'Just tell me. We can put this right.'

Sam meant that *he* would put it right. He'd do whatever it took to make her happy, he'd already made that clear in his words and his actions. Eloise took a breath. Sometimes there was nothing for it but to come out and say exactly what you meant.

'I want to make *you* happy, Sam. You hear my fantasies then you make them real, and it's amazing. I want to do the same for you.'

A pulse beat at the side of his brow now. Eloise had known that getting through to him about this wouldn't be easy, but she hadn't realised it would be so hard. How much Sam had invested in the belief that he had to work every day to be nothing like his father.

'Let me be the one who hears you sometimes, Sam. That's what I really want.'

She just had to trust that he would understand, because Michael hadn't when she'd challenged his view of how their relationship ought to be. That there should be no secrets and that there was room for his son in their lives. Sam was the better man, and Eloise had to trust in that.

She could almost hear him thinking. In the silence, the quiet tick of the clock and the distant noise of traffic suddenly became very loud.

'You're not talking about just the bedroom, are you?'

He was very astute. Conversations with Sam had a tendency to turn into more than she'd bargained for.

'What happens there is a reflection of everything else. The balance of our relationship…'

Sam nodded. 'I'm not sure that I know how to change that.'

'It's up to us both, not just you. I know you listen to what I want and how I feel, and I have to trust that. Trust myself to be able to say what's really on my mind.'

Eloise had done that once and her heart had been broken. That was over now. Michael was gone and she was glad that she hadn't made the mistake of marrying him. But since then she'd learned the habit of keeping her thoughts to herself.

He reached out suddenly, holding his hands open on the table. 'Hold on to me. I promise I'll hold on to you.'

That was what she really needed right now. She took his hands, and his fingers curled around hers. Warm and secure, the way he always made her feel.

'Telling me what you want doesn't make you like your father, Sam.'

She felt his grip tighten. Holding on to her still. Sam shrugged, puffing out a breath.

'All we ever used to hear when we were kids was what my father wanted, and he put Mum through a very hard time when the marriage broke up. Afterwards she told me that one of her reasons for staying strong was that she wanted to show us kids that the way he acted wasn't how a man should act.'

'She sounds like a strong woman, who defended her children. Hard act to follow.'

Surprise showed in his eyes. Then he nodded. 'Yeah, maybe... You think I try too hard?'

'I think you don't need to try, Sam. You've seen all of the things that happen when a man tries to take control of his family, and all of the heartbreak that causes. You've rejected that and you're not like your father.'

'I may need a moment to think about that...'

'That's okay. This isn't an ultimatum. I want you to think about it.' That was another challenge for both of them to consider. They couldn't just turn their backs on this, however much she was afraid of losing what they had. Sam had to know that she wasn't just going to disappear and leave him not knowing what had happened between them.

'Eloise...' There was such warmth in his eyes. Such feeling. 'I think I'm falling in love with you. Actually... I'm pretty certain that I am.'

'I'm pretty certain I'm falling in love with you too, Sam. So let's make sure we get this right.'

There was no lack of warmth about the evening. Touching, kissing. Laughing together. The intimacy between them was about as close as Eloise had ever been to sex with her clothes on, and it was very close. Giving him time to think, removing the expectation that they'd be going to the bedroom at any moment, had somehow made *not* going to the bedroom very special.

Sam went as far as asking her whether she minded

if he just held her tonight. It was what he wanted, what felt right to him at the moment, and Eloise wanted that more than anything. She propped herself up on the pillows in the bedroom wearing a T-shirt and pair of shorts that she kept here for lazy Sunday mornings, fiddling with the remote on the TV as a way of not noticing that he too was getting changed.

'Do you fancy a film?' She handed the remote to him.

'Yeah…' He flipped through the programme list. 'This?'

'No, not in the mood for gritty realism. I've been doing that all week.'

He chuckled. 'Good point. This…?' He found a feature length cartoon animation.

'Yes. Perfect.'

He paused for a moment, before he started the film.

'You know. There's always consent…'

Eloise chuckled. 'You mean that thing we've just been doing?'

Sam frowned. 'It's a bit more important than just deciding what film we want to watch, isn't it?'

'Yes, of course it is. You know the difference between yes and no?'

'Yes, I do.'

'I know how to say either of them, Sam. At any time.'

He nodded, putting his arm around her shoulders and pressing the remote to start the film.

This was the most unexpected thing that anyone had ever done. Sam had grown up knowing what he didn't want to be, and not thinking too much about what he *did* want. He'd told himself that he would always respect a woman's wishes, and that he must listen well to achieve that. And then Eloise had turned all of that on its head. She'd told him he was good enough already, and that she wanted to listen and fulfil some of his wishes.

But that was why he loved her. He knew their conversation had been hard for her, but he'd seen a new determination in Eloise. She didn't want to settle for what was comfortable, or even something that was amazingly good. She wanted the things he hadn't known how to give, and made them feel possible.

She'd started to yawn, and Sam had turned the TV off. Then he'd asked the question that he hadn't known he could risk asking, because it allowed for everything he'd been dreading. Stepping back for a moment and reconsidering gave her the opportunity to slip away from him.

'Will you give me some time...?'

'As much as you want, Sam. I'm not going anywhere.'

They slept, curled up in the bed together. Warm, comfortable and secure. And out of that security came the feeling that if he loved her well enough, then he could learn to combine his own desires with hers. It had happened once before, on their first night together, and he'd been trying not to think about it ever since.

Sam woke as the first feeble light of morning began to disturb the darkness. Quiet sounds of movement from the bathroom made him wonder momentarily what day it was, and then he remembered it was Saturday.

And Eloise was already up? Then he remembered last night. She was just giving him the space that he'd asked for. She knew as well as he did what usually happened when they woke up together on their days off.

By the time she tiptoed back into the bedroom, bare-footed and wrapped in a towel, her hair wound loosely at the back of her head, he was fully awake. Eloise glanced in his direction, turning the corners of her mouth down.

'Did I wake you?'

'No, I've been waiting for you to come back.' Maybe Eloise would take the hint, drop the towel and get back into bed.

She gave him an amused look, obviously not in the mood for hints this morning. Walking over to the wardrobe, she flipped the door open to reveal the full-length mirror fixed inside, pulling her hair down.

It was difficult to know whether she meant this as a come-on, because everything she did fascinated Sam. But suddenly he knew exactly what he wanted. It wasn't so outrageous, and nothing they hadn't done before. The really shocking thing about it was the idea that he wasn't going to just wait and hope she might ask.

He got out of bed, standing behind her and winding his arms around her waist. As he dropped a kiss on her neck, he felt her fingers close around his wrists, holding them in place. She must be able to feel how aroused he was, because she moved against him, her gaze meeting his in the mirror.

'That's nice…' She seemed to melt into his arms as he kissed her shoulder. Everything…everything told him that this was exactly what she wanted, but still he had to ask.

'You want to make love?'

'Yes. What do you want, Sam?'

The question emboldened him. Sam pulled the towel away, letting it drop to the floor. His hands skimmed her body and she leaned back against him, closing her eyes.

'I'd like it if you watched...'

Her eyes snapped open, meeting his gaze in the mirror. 'I'd like it if you lost the T-shirt...'

Sam pulled his T-shirt off. He wound his arms around her, one hand on her breast and the other travelling slowly downwards.

'Sam!' Her gaze was still fixed on his reflection in the mirror, and he felt her begin to tremble. His desire, along with hers, tangling together to make something that they'd only glimpsed before now.

Slowly, gently, because he wanted to see her face as passion took hold of her, he started to move his fingers. Locked in this embrace, in this moment, he suddenly understood just what surrender was. There were no fears, no doubts, just the certain knowledge that what he wanted was as much of a turn-on for Eloise as it was for him.

'This may take a while.' He whispered the words and felt her shudder of delight.

'Yes. Sam, please... I really want you to take your time...'

It had been amazing. Eloise had never felt such longing for anyone, never felt such complete surrender. Sex with Sam had always been the best she'd ever had, but this was so far off the scale that there wasn't even a way of comparing.

He'd loved it too. Sam's newfound confidence had

allowed her own to blossom. When he'd lain back, telling her that the next time she came he wanted her to take him with her, she'd felt a new kind of freedom, a new pleasure in her own assertiveness because it was now a part of his.

She snuggled against him, holding him tight. 'I think we're getting better as we go, Sam.'

Eloise felt him kiss the top of her head. 'Maybe we should just agree on stopping here, eh?'

Really? 'You don't want to do this again?'

'No, I mean stopping to explore this idea. Explore each other a little more and who we really are. Really getting to know all of the possibilities.' He was laughing at her consternation.

'Ah. Yes, I think we could find lots of possibilities. Not right now, you understand.'

Sam chuckled. 'No, I think I'm temporarily out of possibilities. We do have the whole weekend, though.'

'My thoughts exactly...'

Sam had never been happier. In the two weeks since that marvellous, explosive weekend, when they'd not moved from his flat, they'd been finding their place together. Somewhere that it was safe for him to express his own wants and needs, and where Eloise could trust that her own past was where it should be—not forgotten but in the past. And since the laws of physics didn't seem to apply to the way that he loved her, having more room for his own desires and feelings left more room for Eloise's.

It bothered him sometimes, generally during the couple of nights a week that they spent alone, that he was becoming so dependent on her for his happiness.

That he couldn't imagine himself without Eloise. But since it was what she wanted too, he couldn't bring himself to voice his doubts about whether or not that was a bad thing.

She arrived at his flat late, after a Friday evening emergency at the hospital. Waiting for her smile made it all the more special, and she pulled a bundle of photographs from her handbag.

'I found yet another pile of photos. I really should organise them all and put them into albums. Or at least in the same place…'

Sam chuckled. Eloise printed her photographs out, and had a habit of using them as bookmarks and scattering them around in odd places, so that she came across them every now and then. His own photographs were carefully ordered and sorted, excluding those that provoked any kind of reaction, and he loved the way that she didn't feel the need to censor her childhood.

'I quite like seeing them in instalments. Particularly the ones you'd forgotten were even there.' Eloise had covered her face in embarrassment at a few of them.

'Ha! In that case, welcome to another episode of my horrible teenage fashion sense and mortifying attempts to seem sophisticated whenever someone whipped out a camera.'

'I love your teenage fashion sense. Would you like a glass of wine?' Sam had just poured himself one.

'A couple of sips of yours would be fine, if you don't mind. I'm too tired for anything more.' She went into the sitting room, throwing herself down onto the sofa.

Sam joined her, pushing his glass across the coffee table towards her, and picking up the photographs. He knew most of the people in them now, her grandmother and her father, and older ones of her mother, which Eloise always paused over with a hint of regret.

'Is that Bess? And June?'

Eloise moved closer, looking over his shoulder. 'Yes, and the boy is Tom. She was going out with him for years, ever since they were sixteen.'

Another piece of her past that was as valuable to Sam as it was to Eloise. He flipped through the photographs, smiling at the ones of Paul engaged in renovating the old wall of the manor house.

And then... Eloise with a man he didn't know. She seemed different somehow, in a way that Sam couldn't quite put his finger on. Less animated, her smile less ebullient.

Eloise whipped the photograph from his hand. '*That* shouldn't be there...'

'Michael?' Sam asked before he could stop himself. If the photograph gave no hint of what Eloise might be thinking, her reaction now said it all.

She nodded, her cheeks reddening. The man was very handsome, and he and Eloise looked like the perfect couple. Jealousy stabbed at Sam, all the more virulent for being so unexpected.

'Hey! Don't do that.' He reached out, stopping her from tearing the photograph in two. He couldn't unsee the image now.

'It shouldn't be there, Sam. Michael's not a part of my life.'

Sam got her meaning, but she was making things worse. If Michael didn't mean something to her still, then she wouldn't need to pretend that he'd never existed. He took a breath, trying to steady the pounding of his heart. He should let this go, but he couldn't.

'Like it or not, he *was* a very big part of it. You can't just pretend that didn't happen, Eloise.'

Sam was trying to be calm. Trying to speak rationally, even though the fears and uncertainties that he'd dismissed as being part of his past were tearing at him. What if this relationship with Eloise really was too good to be true? If the process of finding their own space together meant that they were existing in a vacuum that couldn't withstand intrusions from the real world?

She was staring at the photograph, her thoughts unreadable. The space between them seemed to be increasing with every moment that passed and, rather than let it just inexorably rip them apart, Sam got to his feet and walked over to the window.

'If you want me to tell you what happened with Michael, you should just say.' Eloise sounded hurt and Sam turned. There was still time to make this right.

'That's not what I mean, Eloise. Even if you never tell me…' He stopped to think for a moment. 'If you never tell me then it'll hurt, because I'll feel that there's still something that's wounded you and you can't trust me with it. But I can deal with that.'

She frowned. 'What *do* you want then?'

Good question. Sam didn't know. All he knew was that everything seemed to be suddenly out of control. He wanted to hold her and comfort her and calm all of her fears. But jealousy and anger were taunting him, telling him that he'd made a mistake in feeling that this could last, and all of his worst fears were justified.

'I want you to be free, Eloise. I don't know how you're going to do that. I don't have any suggestions.

You'll have to work that out for yourself, because you won't tell me what happened.'

That came out much more angrily than he'd meant it to. Eloise heard it too, because she jutted her chin in a look of defiance.

So...what? What you said about my not needing to tell anyone because it was no one else's business... that was all just words, was it? What you thought you *should* say because it was what I wanted to hear?'

'That was then, Eloise. Are you telling me that nothing's happened between us since? That you still don't trust me?'

'No! Sam, I'm not going to do this with you. I'm not going to let you tell me how I should feel about something you know nothing about.'

'Tell me *why* I know nothing about it, why don't you?'

Raised voices. Angry words. Things said in the heat of the moment, that were the worst version of the truth. Sam didn't want this, and the only thing that he could do was turn his back on her, looking out of the window. For some reason, the world outside was just as it always had been, and hadn't burst into a fiery inferno.

They hadn't argued before. They'd disagreed, struggled to find common ground at times, and Sam had found that hard. But there had never been this unreasoning anger, which was distorting the balance of their relationship. He hadn't let that happen because he was afraid of it.

And now Sam knew why. He'd felt the force of his father's anger at times when he was a child, and seen what it had done to his mother. He'd made his own decision about the kind of man that he wanted to be and he didn't want to feel this senseless rage. Other people had arguments, got everything out of their system and then patched things up again. Not him. For Sam, every argument hacked away at his identity, casting him slowly adrift from the person that he wanted to be.

It was one of life's excruciating ironies that in encouraging him to express his own wants and needs Eloise had made him happy but also begun the process of splitting them apart. Sam could no longer pretend that he was able to function in a normal, healthy relationship.

'I should go.'

Had Eloise been reading his thoughts? Sam instantly began to regret them.

'What?'

He almost crumbled. Almost begged her to stay. And then he realised that Eloise understood exactly the same thing that he did. That neither of them could stop their past from interfering in their present, their future.

'I just want to go. Please.' Her voice trembled, but she knew what she was doing. And she was right to do it, even if it did hurt. Even if she knew that if she went now there was no coming back.

He turned, just in time to see her pressing her lips together, getting to her feet and storming out of the sitting room. He heard her pulling her coat out of the hall cupboard and the sound of her weekend bag being kicked across the floor. Then the front door slammed so hard that the glass skylight over the top of it rattled, and there was the sound of keys hitting the floor as she posted the copies he'd had made for her back through the letterbox.

Sudden nausea made him move, hurrying to the

bathroom. He hadn't lost Eloise. He'd deliberately forced this separation. And, however much he wanted to, he knew that it would be wrong to ask her to stay.

And now...? As the shaking and the cold sweat began to subside, Sam made himself a promise. He could never let Eloise see him like this again. Angry. However much this hurt, he would let Eloise go.

CHAPTER THIRTEEN

SIX O'CLOCK IN the morning, and Eloise was on the train. Today was going to be a round trip of eleven hours—if she was lucky—and she wouldn't be home again until midnight. But it was necessary.

It had been a hard decision to leave Sam, but it was the right one. He'd been angry, but he'd been right—she wasn't done with the past any more than he was. After three weeks, she was still missing him as much as she had the moment she'd walked out on him. She'd cried and tried to sleep. Called a friend to get the name and number of a good counsellor, who'd listened to what she had to say and booked in another two-hour session later in the week. It was becoming increasingly obvious that there was still a lot to talk about.

She hadn't called Sam, and he hadn't called her. Eloise wondered whether he'd picked up the phone to do so as many times as she had. But it wouldn't do any good. They both had too much baggage, too many unresolved issues. She'd left it a few days and then emailed Gramps to tell him that she and Sam were no longer together, in case he should be embarrassed by not knowing. Then she'd received an odd email from Celeste.

Eloise had written back, questioning it. Surely talking to Sam's mother wasn't really appropriate in the circumstances. She'd received an immediate reply, which read like the written equivalent of Celeste stamping her foot in exasperation.

Trust me. It's not mine to talk about, but I promise you that Elsa will welcome it.

Eloise had wondered whether there was anything that anyone could say that would make this right. But, even if it seemed hopeless, she couldn't let Sam go without taking this chance. Celeste and his mother would take care of him, the way that she couldn't any more, and maybe Sam's wounds would begin to heal. That would make all of this worthwhile.

Eloise had written a carefully worded email, and it had become obvious that Elsa's wish to speak to her was genuine and that there was something she wanted to say. This was far too important to do by email, or even a video call. France was a long way to go, but nowhere was too far if there was any hope of it helping Sam. So Eloise got onto a train, changing at Calais for the high-speed TGV service that went south, into the heart of France.

Elsa and her partner were standing together at the station, and Eloise recognised them from the photo they'd sent. It was left to Hugo, Elsa's partner, to keep the conversation going in the car. Elsa looked as nervous as Eloise was.

Elsa and Hugo's apartment was bright and beautifully decorated, with more than a trace of Sam's talent for interiors, only with a more feminine touch. Elsa led her into the sitting room, inviting her to sit down on a high-backed antique sofa.

'How long do you have, Eloise?'

'Three hours. We have plenty of time.' Maybe a few pleasantries first, to break the ice.

'Wonderful. Then you have time for lunch. I'll get busy...' Hugo smiled and left the two women alone.

Eloise fidgeted and smiled, and Elsa smiled back. 'How is Celeste?'

'Well, she and my grandfather seem extraordinarily happy together.'

'So I hear. Celeste saved my life, even though my ex-husband was her own brother. Her capacity for rolling up her sleeves and getting involved is...' Elsa's eyes glimmered with quiet humour '...wonderful. If a little startling at times.'

Eloise laughed, feeling instinctively drawn to Elsa's good-humoured kindness. 'Celeste's been very good to me too. And you're right, very surprising.'

'I owe her a great deal. I'll be going over to England in a week's time for a visit, and I'll be staying with Paul and Celeste for a few days. But I wanted to speak privately with you first.'

'I'm so pleased you've asked me. It's not something I'd expect, but I'm very grateful.'

'I think we've all seen the futility of taking sides. That silly business with the Douglases and the Grants has taught us all that. And there's something I want you to know about Sam.'

'You should know... I don't think there's any possibility that Sam and I will be getting back together again. There's just too much that we both have to get through.'

'I understand that. It may help you to know how much Sam's had to face, and in truth it'll help me as well.'

'Then I'd like to thank you for wanting to share it with me.' The long train journey, and Elsa's wish to talk, already had Eloise on edge, but the atmosphere in the room was so full of things that were unsaid. It was enough to frighten the stoutest of hearts, and make the bravest of souls feel that retreat might be an option.

Stand your ground. If Sam never knows that you're brave enough to do this for him, then at least you will.

'You know that my divorce from Sam's father wasn't easy. He wouldn't accept it.' Elsa was looking at her steadily.

'Yes, Sam told me. He said that his father was... persistent.'

'Your word?' Elsa smiled. 'You don't need to be tactful with me, Eloise. I lived it, I know exactly what happened.'

'Sam said that his father was very angry. He came calling at all hours of the day and night, and wouldn't listen to you when you asked him to leave you alone.'

'That's true. One of the reasons I left Sam's father was that I didn't want my children to be affected by his anger. Sam was old enough to understand that, but maybe he saw that as a burden, rather than my wish to let him know that I'd always defend him.'

Elsa got to her feet, opening a drawer in the elegant sideboard and taking out a framed picture. Wordlessly, she handed it to Eloise.

For a moment she thought it was Sam. And then the style of the jeans and the woman sitting beside him told her that it wasn't. There was something different about the face too.

'This is...you? And Sam's father?'

Elsa nodded, clearly waiting for Eloise to come to her own conclusions. That wasn't so difficult and it was happening with stomach-turning speed.

'They're so alike. Apart from...'

'The nose.' Elsa smiled. 'That was Celeste's doing. Sam broke his nose at a rugby match and when Celeste set it for him she made him a little more handsome.'

Maybe Eloise should confess her own part in it all. That didn't matter right now. There were more important things to say. 'I've never seen a photograph of Sam's father. Although I suppose that his resemblance to Celeste should have made me realise he took after the Grants. I didn't think about it too much...'

But this was everything. The answer. When Sam looked in the mirror every day, he saw the man that he didn't want to be.

'Sam never really saw that his anger is so much more like Celeste's than his father's.'

Eloise thought for a moment. 'You mean...that impulse that Celeste has to go and do something about it, if she sees that something's wrong?'

'Yes, exactly. Sam has that same kind of passion, to make things better. Speaking as his mother, I believe that Sam could do anything he sets his mind to if he'd only allow himself to.'

'I think he could too. But he keeps that bottled up, because he doesn't want to be like his father.'

Elsa nodded. 'He needs someone like you, Eloise. Someone who cares about him enough to see that.'

'I need someone like him...' Eloise felt her eyes fill with tears.

'I won't make any suggestions about what you should do next. I just felt you should know.'

'Thank you. I really appreciate your talking with me. I know it can't have been easy.'

'A great deal easier than doing nothing.' Elsa took the photograph from Eloise's hands, as if it pained her to look at it too much, and put it back in the drawer. 'I'll go and see whether Hugo has a cup of tea for us. I have more photographs, of Sam when he was little. Would you like to see them?'

That was going to hurt. But Eloise had learned that sometimes hurt was necessary if you wanted to heal. 'I'd *love* to. Thank you.'

Sam had been driving himself hard. Running until he almost dropped from exhaustion, so that he'd get a night's sleep. Walking two extra miles for his patients, because the only way that he could squeeze any satisfaction out of his own life was to make a difference to theirs.

It wasn't working. In his dreams, he still heard the door slam, and then Eloise's keys falling to the floor as she posted them back through the letterbox. Still saw her face, and woke with a start to find she wasn't there.

He'd spent the weekend in Norfolk, after Aunt Celeste had called to invite him, obviously having caught wind of the fact that he and Eloise were no longer together. Aunt Celeste had made it clear that if he wanted to talk she would be pleased to listen, and he'd politely declined the offer, saying that it was over and he was pretty cut up about it, but there was nothing anyone could do.

He visited Joy Cornelius, who had just come out

of rehab after her stroke, taking French pastries and a packet of her favourite tea. Joy's quick arrival in hospital after her stroke had meant that she could be scanned, and that clot-busting drugs could be given, which had ameliorated the effects of the stroke considerably. Apart from a slight slur in her speech and a weakness in her hand, both of which were improving, Joy was her old self.

'It's so nice to see you, Sam. I never got to thank you properly for putting me in touch with the people at the Community Centre. They have some wonderful clubs and activities, and it's so nice to think that I can go there any time I get a little lonely.'

'All part of the service, Joy.'

'No, it's not. Eloise is lucky to have you, you're a kind man. I have her hat, by the way. I washed it for her to give it back. It was a lovely thought and very warm.'

Sam chuckled. 'I think she wanted you to have it.'

Joy beamed at him. 'Such a nice girl. You're lucky too.'

'Eloise and I are…' He didn't want to go into details about that. 'We're just friends.'

'Ah. So I've put my foot in my mouth, have I?'

'No, that's okay.' The thought that Joy's clear blue eyes had seen something between him and Eloise was making him feel oddly happy. Stripping away all of the complications and pain, and for one moment leaving him with just the connection that had brought the two of them together.

'We were together, but we decided to call it a day.' The words just slipped out, propelled by longing. As if the more people who knew, the more real it was.

'You let her get away?'

Sam picked up the rehab putty that he'd brought with him, moulding it into a ball. This was a little more firm than the one that Joy had been using, and she was ready for that now.

'Complicated.' He handed her the putty. 'Give this a try.'

Joy started to mould it with her fingers, nodding as she did so. 'It's a bit more difficult.'

'Yes, that's the idea.'

'Did you put up a fight?'

He supposed he deserved that. He'd just been giving Joy a friendly lecture about how she needed to push herself to regain full use of her hand.

'It's not my place to fight a woman.' He laughed as Joy raised her eyebrows. 'Only you, Joy, when you don't do your exercises.'

'That's not what I meant…' Joy gave him a knowing look, and tried again with the putty.

She didn't seem about to elaborate, and Sam should just leave it. Eloise wasn't coming back, and if she did he'd send her away again. But the one, small chance that Joy might have something to say, that could show Sam a way back to her, was nonetheless a chance. Which made it far too valuable to miss.

'What do you mean, then?'

Joy sighed. 'You're a clever man, Sam, but you don't know everything. You don't fight a woman to get her back. You fight *for* her.'

Sam nodded. 'I see. Thanks…' Suddenly the world had opened up. Sam had no clue what fighting *for* Eloise meant in practical terms, but this was one of those times when one little word made all the difference.

He smiled at Joy, picking up the booklet that lay

beside her on the coffee table. 'Shall we have a look at the exercises your physiotherapist left you? Just go through them again and make sure that you're doing them correctly...'

CHAPTER FOURTEEN

TRY AS HE MIGHT, Sam couldn't get the words out of his head. Fighting Eloise, imposing his own will on her, was a shameful thing to do, and he'd avoid that at all costs. Fighting *for* her seemed a lot more honourable.

Of course there was a practical side to it all. What he wanted was to have Eloise back. That was obvious. How to fight for her? That was a little less clear.

He wondered whether he should call Alice. Apologise and ask her out for coffee, to see if she'd give him any insights about why she'd left. And what could have stopped her. And then Sam realised. He didn't need closure, not any more. He didn't need anyone else to tell him who he was, because all he needed to be was the man who loved Eloise. Now, his only decision was *when* to do what he knew he must.

Even that was taken from him when he found himself getting up early on Saturday morning, deciding not to give shaving a miss and selecting a sweater that matched his shirt instead of just grabbing whatever was clean. By the time he got to his car it was as if there had never been any choice in the matter.

All the same, he faltered before walking up Eloise's front path. The curtains in the sitting room were closed, and he wondered whether he'd come too early. Then he saw her at the window, drawing the curtains back. His heart almost stopped as she darted backwards and then the front door swung open.

'Sam… Sam, please don't go.' She looked so beautiful. Hair wet from the shower still, and a loose yellow sweater with jeans. Like all of the Saturday mornings he could ever want, rolled into one.

'I'm not coming in.' He walked up the front path, stopping in the porch.

'Why not?' Eloise frowned at him.

'I want to ask you…if you'll come to my place some time… To talk. I could cook dinner.'

'What's going on? Why can't you come in and talk now, since you're here?'

That was an alteration to the plan that he hadn't anticipated. 'I've made my mind up and I don't want to give up on what we had together. I thought that an invitation would give you time to think about how you felt about that.'

'Sam.' She gave him the smile that had always let him know that things were all right. 'If you think I'm going to endure your cooking, just for the convenience of having time to think, then I don't need it. I have something I have to say to you and I was going to give you a call today and ask you over.'

She led the way into the sitting room. He noticed that the easy chairs were still where he'd suggested she place them, pushed back a little into the bay window to give the room a little more space. The large coffee table in front of the sofa still had the shimmering glass bowl that he'd found in the kitchen at its centre. Eloise had great taste, but she thought she didn't and tended not think too much about making the most of her rooms by arranging them nicely.

None of that mattered. It was just easier to think about that than what he'd come here to do. Because now that he *was* here, it was difficult to imagine what he could possibly say that would persuade Eloise to take him back.

All Eloise wanted to do was fling herself into Sam's arms. That would be the easy way to go, because they could rely on the connection between them to smooth over everything else. The harder, stonier path was through all of the things that were keeping them apart, and that was the one that they had to take if they were going to work anything out between them.

She sat down on the sofa. Sam retreated to the other side of the room, sitting in one of the easy chairs in the window.

'Sam, your mother contacted me.' That wasn't quite right, and she had to choose her words better than this. 'Actually, Celeste did and said that your mother wanted to talk to me, and I contacted her...'

He smiled. 'I get the picture. Mum and Celeste executed a pincer movement. They do that kind of thing.'

At least he didn't seem too upset by it. That had been the first of Eloise's concerns. 'So I went to France...'

His eyebrows shot up. 'You went all that way? For a chat?'

'I thought it was important, and it turned out that it was. I would have gone a lot further than that, because she was very kind to me and...she helped me see some things more clearly.'

'I'm grateful to you for making the journey.' Sam

looked at her thoughtfully. 'I think you'd better tell me what she had to say.'

'She showed me something. A picture of your father.' She saw the shock in Sam's eyes, but he said nothing. 'It must have been so hard for you, knowing how much you looked like him and wanting to be different.'

Sam nodded, rubbing his nose thoughtfully. 'You really did do me a favour when you kidnapped the Douglas team's star rugby player.'

It was so like Sam to try to turn the conversation to a lighter note. But Eloise wasn't going to allow him to distract her.

'Celeste made a good job of it, so I won't disagree with you there. That's not the point. What I want to say to you is that we all inherit a few things from our parents. The way they bring us up puts a few more things into the mix. But, ultimately, I believe we have free will. You are the man you've chosen to be.'

'It's a nice thought…'

'No, it's not just a nice thought. I can see why you would think differently. Your mother told me that one of the reasons she left your father was that she wanted a better life for you and your brother and sister—'

'That's a nice way of saying that she saw his anger in me, isn't it?' Sam turned the corners of his mouth down.

'No, it isn't. She told me that if you were like any of the Douglases you were like Celeste. I agreed with her. Celeste doesn't take any nonsense from anyone, but she uses her passion to make things better.'

Eloise was beginning to feel breathless, fear tearing at her. Sam's reaction seemed resigned, as if this was something that couldn't be changed and would always haunt him. She was fighting for them, and she needed him to as well.

He was here, though. Eloise had spent five days thinking about this and still hadn't managed to work up the courage to get into her car and go and ring his doorbell.

'The reason I didn't get married was...'

Sam held his hand up. 'I don't need to know.'

'I need to tell you. You were right. I haven't let go of Michael properly, and that's not fair on you. You deserve to be trusted.' Eloise took a breath, trying to steady herself. 'The day before we were due to get married, I was sorting through some papers, trying to find Michael's passport, and I found some other papers, pertaining to unpaid maintenance for a child. I asked him what they were, and he told me that he'd been in a relationship before he met me.'

Sam nodded. 'That happens.'

'Yes, but what doesn't happen is that you leave someone when they're pregnant, and then pretend they don't exist when you make a new relationship. He hadn't even seen his child, and even though there was a maintenance order in place he'd stopped paying. It wasn't just the lies. How could I marry a man who was willing to turn his back on his own child?'

'And you didn't tell anyone? Why not?'

'I thought everyone knew that we'd cancelled the wedding. We wrote an email together, and he started to get really angry. *"Get out of my sight"* were his exact words. Then the next day he turned up at the church, with everyone there, and pretended he'd been stood up at the altar. I didn't know that he hadn't sent the email until I got back, and by that time... Michael could be very charming and he'd persuaded everyone that I'd just run out on him.'

She could feel tears running down her cheeks. 'That was why I left you. Because I wasn't ready to tell you the truth. I was afraid to tell you what really happened, that you wouldn't be on my side. I couldn't bear to hear you telling me to get out of your sight.' She couldn't even look at Sam, let alone meet his gaze.

'It hurt. But that's on me, because I wouldn't take the risk of trying to stop you. I've thought about this, and I'm not afraid of telling you that I want to be with you.'

He got to his feet, coming to sit down on the sofa next to her. Sam took her hands in his and Eloise clung on tight.

'But what do we do now, Sam? Can we even get over all of the things that have happened to us?' Eloise's courage failed her for a moment.

But he was there for her. Sam tipped her chin up, catching her gaze. 'We stop fighting each other, and we fight *for* each other. When I falter you hold me up. And when you falter I'll take you in my arms and carry you.'

'Sam… Don't say that unless you really mean it…' She didn't dare believe him, because she wanted to so much.

'I mean it. If you kiss me now, I'll never run from you again, and I won't let you run either, however hard it gets. Don't imagine that's necessarily a good thing, because we have a lot to work through and it may get very hard.'

'Bring it on, Sam.'

He kissed her. Not the tenderness of a reconciliation, but the raw possessiveness of a man who knew what he wanted and was going to fight for it.

'I want you to marry me. You can say yes or you can say no. It won't make any difference...'

Eloise grinned at him. No one but Sam could make a proposal quite like that and make it sound as if he was offering her everything that she'd ever wanted.

'You mean you don't mind which? No is as good as yes?'

He shot her a reproachful look. 'I mean that I'll love you whatever you say. I'll want to be with you and fight for our relationship. You might feel it's a little too hard...' He was teasing her back now.

'The harder the better. Yes.'

He laughed out loud, an expression of relieved joy. 'Yes. Really?'

'Yes, Sam. Are you worried I won't turn up?'

'No, because I'm not going to let you go.'

She could hear his heartbeat as he held her close. Honest and true, the heart that she would always cherish.

'We'll be busy for the next couple of days, then.' He smiled, kissing her cheek.

'Busy? Why, what are we going to do?'

'My mother and Hugo are up in Norfolk at the moment, with Paul and Aunt Celeste. They'll all be down in London on Wednesday, and by then I'll have to have bought you an engagement ring, and taken you to a romantic proposal dinner.'

'But you've just proposed. If you think this was just a trial run you can forget it, Sam, because I've said yes now, and I'm holding you to it.'

'Good. I'm holding you to it as well. Only Mum and Aunt Celeste are going to want to see the ring and hear all about my efforts in making the perfect romantic evening to propose to you. And Paul's definitely going to want to know that I'm a suitable husband-to-be, who'll treat you as you deserve to be treated. So I figured we might do it all over again before Wednesday. If you don't mind, that is.'

She hugged him tight. Sam knew how important family was to her, and sharing this with them was perfect. 'I think it's a beautiful idea. Aren't you forgetting something, though?'

'I'm not forgetting anything. This afternoon will be quite soon enough to go and choose a ring, because I'm rather hoping that this morning you'll be otherwise occupied.' The come-to-bed look in his eyes told her just what he had in mind.

'I was rather hoping I might be too…'

CHAPTER FIFTEEN

Six months later

THE MAN SHE'D met had been paralysed by self-doubt. And the man Eloise had married today was free to love her with his whole heart.

Sam had freed her as well. There had been arguments, silences and fears that had to be spoken about before they could be dismissed. But through it all they'd loved one another. Eloise had never felt such happiness, and she knew that Sam felt the same way.

Their wedding had been held in the tiny church near to Gramps and Celeste's Norfolk home. Eloise had set her heart on a winter wedding, after they'd settled in to their new house, but their plans had suddenly changed. When she'd walked downstairs five weeks ago, clutching the pregnancy test, Sam had hugged her tightly then fallen to his knees, begging her to marry him now, because he couldn't wait another moment.

Five weeks wasn't long to plan a wedding, but it had been done with such joy that everything had just fallen into place. The reception was held in the garden of the manor house, and as darkness fell the guests had begun to leave and the caterers started to clear up. Gramps had fetched lanterns from the house, hanging them in the pagoda on the lawn, and Sam and Eloise joined him and Celeste there, together with Elsa and Hugo.

'This is so pretty. Do you think we can get something like it for our wedding, Paul?' Celeste asked.

'I could build one.' Gramps liked nothing better than a construction project. 'Style it in keeping with the house, with maybe a fire pit and some kind of removable glazing for the winter.'

Celeste caught her breath. 'That would be lovely! With roses around the perimeter...'

'We've done it now.' Sam leaned over to kiss Eloise. 'There's no stopping them, is there?'

'There's no stopping us either.'

She'd loved every moment of the last six months. Sam had loved her so well, so faithfully, that even the arguments, the moments when one or the other of them had faltered momentarily, had been an expression of how they were moving forward together.

All she had to do was touch his hand, to see him smile and feel the warmth of his gaze. Sam was sure of her love as well, and they could look forward to the future.

'When Celeste caught Eloise's bouquet by mistake...' Gramps was recounting the highlights of the day now '...and shouted, *"Eloise, you missed!"* and threw it again.'

Elsa was laughing too. 'I caught sight of it coming straight at me and ducked. Hugo had to catch it for me.'

'Taking aim with a bunch of flowers isn't as easy as it looks. But it got to the right place in the end.' Eloise grinned at Elsa. 'So have you and Hugo decided where you're going to get married yet?'

'We thought London. We'll be moving back when Hugo's current work contract expires, and our families are here. Perhaps I can come and stay with you, in your lovely new house, to scout out a few locations?'

Sam chuckled. 'Whenever you want, Mum. Although it's a lovely undecorated house at the moment.'

'That's why we need Elsa.' Eloise nudged him. 'She'll be able to give me some ideas for the nursery.'

Sam smiled, leaning forward to kiss her. 'You *know* I can't wait to get started with that. Another six months is a long time to wait.'

'It'll go so fast.' Elsa laughed. 'Before you know it, they'll be packing their bags and going to medical school.'

'Or…anywhere else they want to go,' Sam added.

'That sounds like a fine idea to me. Far too many doctors in the family already. We need a few…' Celeste paused, obviously trying to think of another job that might appeal, and everyone laughed.

'I'm going to propose a toast.' Paul rose, catching up the last champagne bottle from the ice bucket and adding a drop to everyone's glasses, while Sam fetched sparkling water for Eloise.

'Aloysius Grant and Henry Douglas had no idea what their falling-out might lead to. Celeste and I fell in love while in vigorous confrontation over some minor detail concerning Grant College and Douglas College.'

Celeste laughed. 'Until someone reported us for holding hands in the quad, and we were each thrown off our respective committees for conflict of interest.'

'Then Sam and Eloise had the great good luck, although no one quite knew it at the time, to be the only guests at our engagement party. And now we're looking forward to Baby Grant-Douglas, who will be a much-loved addition to our new blended family of Douglas and Grant.'

Eloise felt Sam squeeze her hand. He was so excited about becoming a father. Their baby would grow up at the heart of a close and loving family.

'And now, on the very day that Eloise and Sam are married, our beloved Elsa accepted Hugo's proposal.'

'Elsa turned me down six times, but seven is my lucky number.' Hugo laughed, kissing Elsa's hand.

'So, ladies and gentlemen, please raise your glasses to Henry Douglas and Aloysius Grant. Misguided they may have been, but they have brought us all much happiness, laughter and love.'

'Now and for ever.' Sam whispered the words as he and Eloise joined in with the toast.

'Douglas and Grant!'

* * * * *

COMING SOON!

We really hope you enjoyed reading this book.
If you're looking for more romance, be sure to
head to the shops when new books are
available on

Thursday 24th November

To see which titles are coming soon, please visit
millsandboon.co.uk/nextmonth

MILLS & BOON®

Coming next month

RESISTING THE SINGLE DAD NEXT DOOR
Louisa George

'Carly.'

She turned to face him, her belly dancing with lightness. 'Yes?'

'Thanks again.' He leaned in and pressed a friendly kiss to her cheek.

She closed her eyes as the touch of his skin sent thrills of desire rippling through her. She pulled back, looked at him and caught the heat in his gaze, the need.

She should have turned then and climbed into her truck. She should have driven away into the darkness. But she was transfixed by the way he was looking at her, as if she was…everything.

His previous words about not being distracted seemed to melt from her brain and all she could focus on was his face, his heated eyes, his delicious mouth. So tantalisingly close.

Later, when she thought back to this moment—and she thought back to this moment a lot—she wasn't sure how it had happened. One minute they were looking at each other, the next moment they were kissing. Hot, hard and greedy. Desperate. Frantic. Out of control.

The heat of his mouth made her moan and stoked the burning in her belly. She spiked her fingers into his hair and pressed her lips against his, her body hard against his. The outline of his muscled chest pressed against her and, lower, she could feel just how much he was enjoying this. How much he wanted her.

'God, Carly...' His hands cupped her face and held her in place as he captured her bottom lip in his teeth, then took her mouth fully again and kissed her, kissed her and kissed her.

He tasted of hot chocolate and a warm, delicious spice that she couldn't get enough of. He smelt of the smoky fire. He tasted of coming home and of somewhere new, exotic and enticing. Exciting.

It was too much and not enough all at the same time. She didn't want it to end, this night, this kiss lasting for...

Someone committed to staying around.

His words came back to her in a hard jolt of reality. She had an interested buyer visiting tomorrow. A plan to be gone as soon as feasibly possible. So kissing Owen was an impossible and ridiculous idea and a sure-fire way of ruining the fledgling friendship they'd grown.

What on earth was she doing?

'Sorry. I've got to...' She took two shaky steps away from him, jumped into her car and got the hell away.

Continue reading
RESISTING THE SINGLE DAD NEXT DOOR
Louisa George

Available next month
www.millsandboon.co.uk

MILLS & BOON

THE HEART OF ROMANCE

A ROMANCE FOR EVERY READER

MODERN

Prepare to be swept off your feet by sophisticated, sexy and seductive heroes, in some of the world's most glamourous and romantic locations, where power and passion collide.

HISTORICAL

Escape with historical heroes from time gone by. Whether your passion is for wicked Regency Rakes, muscled Vikings or rugged Highlanders, awa the romance of the past.

MEDICAL

Set your pulse racing with dedicated, delectable doctors in the high-pressure world of medicine, where emotions run high and passion, comfort love are the best medicine.

True Love

Celebrate true love with tender stories of heartfelt romance, from the rush of falling in love to the joy a new baby can bring, and a focus on the emotional heart of a relationship.

Desire

Indulge in secrets and scandal, intense drama and plenty of sizzling hot action with powerful and passionate heroes who have it all: wealth, statu good looks…everything but the right woman.

HEROES

Experience all the excitement of a gripping thriller, with an intense romance at its heart. Resourceful, true-to-life women and strong, fearless face danger and desire - a killer combination!

To see which titles are coming soon, please visit

millsandboon.co.uk/nextmonth

JOIN US ON SOCIAL MEDIA!

Stay up to date with our latest releases, author news and gossip, special offers and discounts, and all the behind-the-scenes action from Mills & Boon...

 @millsandboon

 @millsandboonuk

 facebook.com/millsandboon

 @millsandboonuk

It might just be true love...

GET YOUR ROMANCE FIX!

Get the latest romance news, exclusive author interviews, story extracts and much more!

blog.millsandboon.co.uk